LOVE IN THE RAIN

He drew Julie more closely beneath the shelter of the big umbrella. It made a sanctuary for them, and her face was like a rose, flushed and rain-wet.

"May I kiss you, Julie?"

In answer she lifted her face and gave him her lips, closing her eyes as she felt his mouth come down on hers, nervously and uncertainly at first, but then so firm and compelling that unconsciously she began to struggle against him—and yet not against him, but against that strange wildly sweet thing born of his kiss within her own self. . . .

Later, as they walked in the rain and Jeremy talked about his ambitions, Julie felt a cold hand on her heart. He wanted the world at his feet, and all she wanted was her love in her arms.

THE
SHADOW
MARKET

Netta Muskett

PYRAMID BOOKS NEW YORK

THE SHADOW MARKET

A PYRAMID BOOK

Copyright © Netta Muskett 1938

Pyramid edition published May 1975

ISBN 0-515-03758-3

Printed in the United States of America

Pyramid Books are published by Pyramid Communications, Inc. Its trademarks, consisting of the word "Pyramid" and the portrayal of a pyramid, are registered in the United States Patent Office.

Pyramid Communications, Inc.,
919 Third Avenue, New York, N.Y. 10022

"Hurry up, Julie. You'll be late. It's gone eight o'clock!"

"All right, Mum. Shan't be a jiffy. Just laddered a stocking."

There was a wail from the dining-room.

"Oh, Jul-*lie*, what about my sums? You *promised*!"

And a cajoling entreaty from the hall, "Julie, let me have a lend of your lavender-water, just this once."

Mrs. Cave appeared in the open door way of the kitchen. All the doors at 26 Hemming Road stood open as a rule. It enabled the Caves to carry on their conversations, severally and collectively, without let or hindrance.

"Children," said the voice of authority, "you're not to stop Julie. She'll be late, and then that Madam'll carry on like anything."

"Oh, Mum, she promised she'd go over my sums," wailed Dick, aged ten, from the sitting-room, in which the family did almost everything but sit.

"I only want the lend of her scent," said Biddy.

"Well, she's not going to be bothered with either of you this morning so . . ."

But there was a quick step on the stairs, the flourish of a shabby bag, mended gloves, the family umbrella, and Julie herself was amongst them.

She was a trim little person, Julie Cave. She was small and rounded, with a face which nearly always wore a smile and which, just now, was flushed with her haste. She had warm, steady brown eyes, crinkly brown hair that simply refused to be sleek, a nose that was faintly tip-tilted, a mouth that was sweet and generous.

Her brown suit had seen long service, her sturdy little shoes had paid many visits to the repair shops, her stockings were so neatly mended that they scarcely looked mended at all, while on her head was perched a Robin Hood cap with a gay green quill. It defied anyone to discover that it was last year's pancake cut up and turned back to front!

The children fell on her.

"Julie, gimme a lend of your lavender-water!"

"Julie, my sums!"

"Take your sandwiches and go, Julie, and never mind their bother"—this from her mother.

Julie glanced at the grandfather clock in the narrow strip they called the "hall."

"All right, Mum. I did promise Dickie, and if I take the bus at the corner for once, I can make it. Come on, you reptile. Where's the book?"—flinging down her bag and umbrella and stuffing her gloves into her pocket.

"Oh, Julie, gimme a lend . . ."

"Oh, all right, Biddy, get your lend for Heaven's sake and be quiet—only don't take the lot and fill up the bottle with water, like the last time!"

Julie finished on a warning note as her sister's skinny legs vanished up the stairs.

"O.K., baby," replied Biddy, happy now that she had, as usual, got her own way, and Julie smiled and turned her attention to the grubby, blotted exercise-book offered her anxiously by Dick.

"What a horrible mess!" said his sister with a friendly groan. "What are they?"

"Weights and measures, and I don't know how the blots get there. They just come."

"Oh, Dickie, and I never could remember how many pounds to a ton!" bemoaned Julie. "Got a table-book?"

Dickie produced a much-thumbed copy while Mrs. Cave hovered anxiously about. It was too bad the way Julie let those two put on her, and she was with her long day's work to do; but what was the good of talking? Julie always had been too good-natured and always would be, bless her! She could never bear to say "no" to anybody.

Well, at least she could go upstairs and prevent that little monkey from taking every drop of Julie's scent and drenching herself with it before she went to school. This was obviously the day they had their art class. Art, indeed. Biddy couldn't draw the tail of a cow, but that did not prevent her from being the most devout pupil since the class had been taken over by that Bert Arnley. Art indeed! When Mrs. Cave was young they had another name for it!

Five minutes disposed of the worst of Dickie's troubles, and Julie, remembering in time that she must no longer kiss a man of ten, squeezed his inky hand, sniffed with an inquiring grin at Biddy as she came down the stairs, flung her lovely, infectious smile at all of them, came back for a moment to kiss her mother again, and was gone.

6

Somehow, to all of them the house looked darker and felt quieter, though Julie was undoubtedly the quieter member of the family.

She popped her head round the door again.

"Oh, Mum, don't you take any more of that work from Tyler's if they won't pay you the rate. I'll get Madam to let me bring something home for you. We've got a big trousseau order in.

"All right, darling. I'll ask to see Mr. Tyler himself when I take this parcel back. Now hurry, Julie."

Mrs. Cave stood at the door for a moment to watch her girl run down the street, saw that she had managed to catch the bus, and then turned to hustle the other two off to school.

"It's a shame the way you two make Julie hang about just when I've managed to give her an extra half-hour in bed," she said. "You ought to be ashamed of yourselves."

She only grumbled half-heartedly, though. She was too happy in her children and there was too much genuine affection in that family for real fault-finding.

"Julie doesn't mind. She's a sport," said Dick, cramming his books into his satchel and wondering if his jar of tadpoles would go in as well, and whether they would travel safely as far as the school.

On second thoughts, he would leave the tadpoles at home. He might meet Jimmy Elson, and he owed Jimmy one for splitting on him yesterday, and if he had to remember the jar of tadpoles he wouldn't be able to pay his debt with interest.

He unloaded the jar on the kitchen table.

"Mum, give them their raw meat, will you? I've got it in my pencil-box"—digging out the unsavoury scrap from amongst the pencils and other less legitimate contents of the box. "And see that Spencer Tracy doesn't eat the lot, will you? He's such a greedy little beggar that Boris Karloff never gets any unless you watch."

"Darling, I don't know the difference," said Mrs. Cave, eyeing the two inhabitants of the jar doubtfully. She lived in terror of their developing the legs which might bring them out of their jar to roam the house at will.

"You'll soon see when you feed them. Spencer just wolfs the lot if you don't fend him off. I must bunk. G'-bye, Mum," and he pecked at his mother's ear and ran off.

Biddy wrinkled a small and perfect nose at the jar.

7

"Filthy little beasts, boys are," she said. "Bye-bye Mother darling. See you at lunch," said that young madam with an "air." She had recently decided to become refined—whenever she remembered it.

Mrs. Cave looked at the pert but undeniably pretty face of her younger daughter.

"Biddy, have you been at Julie's powder?" she asked sternly.

"Oh, only just a flick of the puff," said Biddy airily.

"It is quite an unnecessary attention to a face that's only fifteen," said her mother. "Besides, Julie never has a thing of her own."

Biddy smiled serenely and kissed her.

"Don't worry about that. She'll be welcome to all I have later on, and it'll be a lot more than a box of Woolworth's powder and a bottle of lavender-water, you'll see!" and she took her departure with a funny little mincing walk she had lately developed as an adjunct to the "refinement."

Mrs. Cave could not resist a smile, though there were times when she wished her younger daughter had a little more of the elder's sound common sense. Biddy was going to a handful, where Julie, bless her, had been only an armful.

Left alone in the quiet house, Mrs. Cave set about her day's work, her thoughts centered, as they so often were, on Julie. It was all very well to tell the other two children they were not to hang on their elder sister. She hung on her herself. She always had done since that day when her young, beloved husband had been knocked down in the street and killed, leaving Dickie a mere baby, Biddy a toddler, and Julie a little girl at school.

And now Julie was twenty and earning a living and as much of the living for the others as her mother would allow. She had always been clever with her needle, and a scholarship to a trade school had equipped her for her present hard work at Monique's in Bond Street.

Dear Julie!

Her mother's eyes were very tender as she thought of her. What would any of them have done without her cheerful courage, her refusal to be downcast, her capacity for mothering them all, even Mrs. Cave herself? Sometimes the thought of Julie's leaving them caught at her mother's heart; leaving them for a home of her own, as she surely must some day. She was so well suited to home life. She would make a wonderful wife and mother.

Mrs. Cave was determined that, when the time came, she would be no selfish mother to stand in the way of Julie's happiness, but her loving mind could conceive of no man to whom she would trust her girl without a qualm.

So far as she knew there was no man remotely in Julie's life, and there was such perfect trust and confidence between her and her mother that Mrs. Cave felt sure she knew all there was to be known.

There was dear, stolid old Ben, of course—Ben Elson, brother of Dick's *bete noire*, Jimmy—but he was more like a brother than anything else. Sometimes she wondered . . .

Meantime, Julie was pursuing her well-known course to Bond Street, hanging on to a strap in the jolting bus, pushing her way out again at Leigham Court Road, dashing across the road when for a few moments the traffic lights held up the cars, glancing hurriedly at the clock at Streatham Hill Station to see if she were in time for the 8:16, which would land her in the work room just on the stroke of nine.

The train was at the platform. Dash it, of course the man *would* want to see her season ticket just that morning, though he knew perfectly well she had one! Down the steps—on to the platform—heavens, she wouldn't do it! Yes—no—she caught at the handle of a door just as the train started to move.

"Stand back, there!" shouted a warning voice, but just in the nick of time a hand opened the door from the inside, an arm shot out, collected Julie, hauled her in—and the thing was done!

She was in.

The tall young man who had done all these obliging things for her was still standing, indicating with a gesture his vacated seat.

Julie, breathless still and with the green feather sticking up at an absurd angle, shook her head and smiled.

"That's all right," she said. "I don't mind standing."

The young man insisted. Julie insisted. Eventually, with rising color and a little sound of annoyance, the young man sat down in the seat. At that very moment the train lurched, and Julie sat down on it too—but after it was occupied. She sat herself plump down on the knees of the young man!

"Oh!" she cried, astonished and confused, struggling to

get her feet to the floor so that she could stand on them again, but only succeeding in standing on his brown, polished shoes.

He slid deftly from under her, leaving her in possession of the seat.

"You might just as well have taken it in the first place," he murmured crossly, for all the other people in the carriage had been interested and amused spectators of the episode, and no young man likes to feel he has been made to look foolish, especially by a strange woman.

He tried to look aloof and dignified. He felt aloof and dignified—had every right so to feel.

Then he caught the eyes of the strange young woman. Brown eyes, they were, deep and soft and warm, but just then they were laughing; and, after a moment's uncertain pause, Jeremy's eyes laughed too. They were blue and twinkly. They were rather like Dickie's eyes when he had been caught in some mischief, thought Julie. His hair was something like Dickie's, too, though it was not quite as fair and it was better-groomed and cut shorter. Dickie always put off going to the barber's until his hair was curling over his collar at the back. If it were any shorter, he felt he was not getting his money's worth when he went to have it cut.

But at hair and eyes the likeness to Dickie ended, Julie discovered on further surreptitious investigation. Jeremy's face (she did not know, of course, that he *was* Jeremy) was long and rather thin, and beneath the blue eyes were faint shadows that told of—what? Julie had no idea, but somehow she found those shadows rather pathetic, and many strange things entered Julie's heart by the gateway of pity; though so far they had been limited to stray dogs and cats, a bird with a broken wing, a shy and very dirty child or two. They had not, up to the moment, included strange young men.

Now that he was standing at his full height, she saw that he was tall and broad-shouldered even though so thin. She glanced at his hand, lying near her against the rather shabby navy blue of his suit. It was a large square hand with the nails beautifully shaped—a hand which could not decide whether it belonged to a dreamer or a man of action.

Her eyes stole upwards towards his face, and she flushed to discover that, at that very moment, he had been looking

10

down at her. They looked away at once, but that brief contact, broken almost before it was established, had succeeded in tying their thoughts together.

Jeremy, keeping his feet by various acrobatic devices, read his newspaper. Julie took out her knitting—one of Dickie's endless supply of socks. The woman on her left glared as Julie's elbow touched her in working. By an odd coincidence Jeremy trod on the woman's toe a split second later. He could not have noticed that he did so, thought Julie, for he did not even take his eyes off the printed page to apologize.

At Victoria the scramble started again. If she managed to get on the first No. 25 bus, she would be in good time. If she got crowded out and had to take the second one she would have to ride right to Bond Street instead of getting off at the corner of Piccadilly, and that would cost her an extra penny.

She struggled in the crowd round the step of the bus, put up her foot in readiness, and then was somehow propelled from the rear so that she took a flying leap on to the platform of the bus before she realized she was going to move. She glanced round, startled. The young man from the train was just behind her, but he was not looking at her—did not appear even to know she was there. It was unthinkable that he had been the means of that violent propulsion!

She sat down with dignity. He sat down beside her and began to read his paper again. She observed that it was the same page that he had been reading all the way up in the train, and it was odd that he should find it such rich reading, for she could see that more than half the page was taken up by an advertisement for weight-and-measure production! A brawny individual with a huge chest, clad in bathing-shorts obviously too tight for him, was striking a bench with a clenched fist, his arm muscles standing out like enormous oranges. He was a revolting sight, and the caption beneath the picture read "Wouldn't YOU *like to be like* ME?"

Jeremy, glancing sideways at her, saw her eyes on the page, and he became aware for the first time of the advertisement. Then Julie's eyes glanced up at his, full of fun, full of that question which the brawny man was so fiercely asking.

He disdained an answer, disdained even to move the of-

11

fending page, and Julie rose as the bus neared her stopping-place.

Then Jeremy spoke.

"No, I wouldn't," he said in a fierce whisper and folded up his paper roughly.

Julie stared at him for a moment, startled. Then she laughed right into his face and stepped off the bus. She was longing to look up when, a moment later, the bus passed her—just to see if by any chance he happened to be looking. She resisted the temptation. She was not the sort to "pick up" anyone, she told herself severely.

So she never knew whether he really had looked.

He had, of course.

Julie found the workroom filled with even more than the usual bustle. Miss Pryke the forewoman, was giving out a dozen orders at once and listening at the same time to a long and detailed explanation by Mrs. Tanner, one of the designers, and as Julie hung up her hat and coat and pulled on her green regulation overall, Madam herself could be heard in the outer room where the cutters worked.

"What's up?" asked Julie in a whisper to the "improver" who worked with her.

Sally Basset looked up with a grin.

"That trousseau. They want it by the eighteenth."

"What a hope!"

"*She*'ll see we do it," said Sally with conviction. "We shall all be working overtime till then, and I've got a date with my boy for Friday night. He won't half be wild!"

"I'll try to get you off for Friday," Julie comforted her.

The improver was directly responsible to her for her work.

"You're a dream, Julie! Say, don't you ever go out with a boy yourself? You never seem to have a date."

Julie smiled, and took from its tissue-paper wrappings the work they had put away the night before. They were making nightdresses for the bride, lovely, filmy things like cobwebs and very little more durable. Julie loved work like this. Sometimes she dreamed of herself as the bride, able to wear such things in the fairy-tale she had been telling herself all her life, embroidering it with fancies that changed with her changing years, a secret, hidden fairy-tale which not even her mother knew.

Then she would go across the work room for something,

catch sight of her small round figure in the long mirror, and come back to her seat in self-derision. These gossamer trifles (no one could call them coverings) were for the marvellously willowy Society girls who came into the showroom, not for little round work-girls who sat in the room upstairs all day long.

She answered Sally's question idly, not as if it were a serious one at all.

"No, I never seem to have a date, do I? Boys don't come my way—much," the last word added as a tribute to Jeremy's blue eyes.

Not, of course, that Jeremy had actually come her way at all!

Sally laughed self-consciously. She was a colorful young person and never faced the world without her two essential articles of equipment—lipstick and a roving eye. Together they rarely failed to achieve something.

"If they don't come your way, you have to go theirs," she giggled. "You never get a boy by sitting and waiting for one. You've got to go out and look about you!"

"I don't think that would appeal to me much," said Julie. "I guess if I ever do get a boy, he's got to be the one to do the finding. I'm not even sure I'd know what to do with one if I got one, either!"

"Oh, he'd know what to do O.K.," laughed Sally. "Say, why don't you try to get off as well on Friday and come with Alfred and me? We're going to the Pally, and you'd soon get fixed up with a nice boy there. I could get to know any amount of 'em if it wasn't for Alfred"—with a self-conscious smirk.

"What's the Pally?" asked Julie, matching her silks carefully.

"Pally di Dance. We have no end of a time there on Friday nights, and Alfred doesn't half look a lad in evening dress. It's evening dress Friday nights. Makes me feel all over alike to look at him in his!"

"Well, I can't dance anyway, even if I had a boy to go with, so that settles it," said Julie.

She was beginning to realize that, for some reason or other, she was feeling restless, as if she wanted something to happen, though it was most unlikely that anything would.

"Can't *dance*!" echoed Sally, amazed. "Why, what on earth do you do with yourself of an evening?"

13

"Oh, I don't know. Nothing very much. I go home, and we have a jaw, all of us, and the kids do their homework, and then when they've gone to bed Mum and I clear up and have our supper. That's nice, all to ourselves. Then we sit and knit, or do bits of sewing or mending or odd jobs. There's always a lot to do with two kids like ours."

"But don't you *ever* go out?" asked Sally incredulously.

Julie did not often talk about herself. She never felt she had anything to say which would be interesting to these girls, with their completely different lives and interests. It sometimes made her feel a little wistful at the good times they seemed to be having, at their various "boys" and all the excitement such implied. Then, back at home with Mum and the children, knowing herself so beloved there, so welcomed, so greatly needed and desired, she would tell herself with a deep satisfaction that she had something which far outweighed all these passing excitements, all the restless seeking for pleasure, for change, for something new. She felt sure that she had pure gold where they rummaged in a heap of tinsel and gilt.

Only sometimes, just now and then, she felt this restless urge of life, as if she wanted to grasp, if only for a brief moment, something of all this that seemed to be passing her by.

Deep within her quiet, steadfast mind she knew that what she wanted was something different from the tinsel and gold, the playthings of an hour. She wanted to take hold of something which would not turn to dust in her hands, would not amuse her for an hour and then cease to matter. She wanted something which would strengthen beneath her grasp, not weaken.

So when Sally asked her with wide and wondering eyes if she never had any fun, she smiled but would not give herself away.

Soon came Miss Pryke with long lists, with work-sheets, with complicated and fussy calculations of numbers and hours and wages.

"You'll all have to put in as many extra hours as you possibly can for the next six weeks, girls," she said. "Morning *and* night."

She was an acid-faced spinster with a heart that had withered within her. Sometimes Julie, in a moment of most unusual misgiving, pictured herself as growing like Miss Pryke for want of what these girls called "fun." Then, like

14

a sensible girl, she got on with her work and let the future take care of itself.

The girls groaned at the dictum.

"Snakes! Fancy having to be in before nine in the morning!" grumbled Sally. "Might as well not go to bed at all, and a fat lot of extra money *we'll* see, though I bet the old cat'll make 'em stump up good and heavy!"

Poor old Dickie and his sums! was Julie's rueful thought.

They did so want Dickie to get a scholarship. It might make all the difference to his future, and she and her mother felt it was so much more important for the boy to get a good education than the girls. Julie was all right, anyway, and Biddy—well, Biddy never did a stroke more work than she was forced to do, but she was devastatingly pretty—or would be when she had got over her present gawky stage—that both Mrs. Cave and Julie thought guiltily it couldn't really make any difference whether she learned things at school or not. She would be certain to marry young, and since she was a cool and calculating young person whose head would always rule her heart, to marry well. Julie could never imagine where Biddy proposed to find the wealthy husband she confidently intended to find, but none of them seriously doubted her ability to find him. Biddy was like that. She always knew what she wanted and kept on at it till she got it. She would get her wealthy husband, beyond shadow of doubt.

But Dick was a different proposition. If only he could be goaded, pushed, pulled, into getting that scholarship, there would be a chance for him in the future. Otherwise the two who mothered him and worried over him could see nothing for him but to leave school at fourteen and go into one of the blind-alley occupations waiting for boys, occupations from which they would be thrust at sixteen or eighteen with neither training nor knowledge, to join the rest of that tragic army of workless, hopeless youth.

Well . . .

Julie pulled up her thoughts with a jerk. It would only mean that Dickie must get up earlier so that she could go through his work with him in time for her to catch the earlier train. It wouldn't hurt him, the lazy little sprat, if only she could manage to get him out of bed without having to get her mother up too.

So that was how it happened that, for six whole weeks,

15

though Jeremy never missed the train that had once landed a brown-eyed girl on his knees, the two never saw each other.

Julie, indeed, had almost forgotten him.

2

Julie shot down the steps at Streatham Hill Station almost too late for the 8:16 again, though this was the first time she had been later than the 7:23 for six weeks!

Jeremy saw her coming, though he had almost given up hope of ever seeing her again. Perhaps it was the intense look in his eyes which drew her own, for she passed by an almost empty compartment to make a dive for the handle at which he was already fumbling.

It came open and she shot forwards and landed in his arms.

"Well stopped, sir," he remarked to himself before he realized he was going to say it aloud, and Julie laughed and pulled the Robin Hood hat to its customary angle over one brown eye.

"You can't give me your seat today," she whispered, glancing at the two rows of seated travellers and the third standing row of which she and Jeremy formed a part.

She had no more intention of speaking to him than he to her, but the thing was done and she leaned nearer to him to catch his reply.

"Either first- or second-hand," he said with a grin.

"I felt such an idiot," said Julia, her color rising at the recollection.

"And I bet I looked one," said Jeremy. "Look out, some idiot's going to open the door," and he grabbed her arm to keep her from falling out as the train lurched to a standstill at the next station.

Julie was very conscious of his hand on her arm and wanted, for no very apparent reason, to take it away. He looked so entirely unconcerned, however, that she felt she had better not call his attention to the fact that he still held her, for he was obviously unaware of it.

Outside Victoria Station he ran with her to the bus and helped her on so unhesitatingly that she knew, with a queer little feeling of excitement, that it must have been he who had propelled her from the rear that other time.

She gave him her shy smile when they were seated.

"I'd never have caught it without you," she told him. "I'm hopeless about buses."

The look he gave her made her experience her first feeling of "belonging."

"You're not much of a fighter, are you?" he asked her almost tenderly.

"I jolly well have to be! Nobody gets anywhere nowadays without a fight," said Julie laughing.

"What I mean is that you're not by nature a fighter, are you? You're not of the sort who—well, who ought to have things done for them."

Julie laughed again. Oddly, now that they were actually talking, it was she who was the more at ease. Jeremy was hesitating, bungling his words unaccountably.

He liked to hear her laugh. It was a lovely sound, fresh and young and glad, not just a smirk or a self-conscious giggle.

"It's a good thing I don't think so too," said Julia.

"Why? Don't you like having things done for you?" asked Jeremy.

"I'm one of the doers, not the done-fors," said Julie. "A two-penny, please"—to the conductor.

Jeremy took a twopenny as well and got off with her at the corner of Bond Street. It was a heavenly morning, a June morning of newly washed skies and pale, clear sunshine. The shops were full of glory, and Jeremy thought Julie looked like a flower herself as she lifted up her face and wrinkled her small button nose in ecstatic appreciation of the morning.

"Do you work here?" he asked her, preferring that she should give her attention to himself.

She nodded.

"Farther along, at Monique's. Do you work in Bond Street too?"

"Yes, curse it. I'm at Butcher's, the travel agency."

She sighed.

"What a fascinating job that must be! Don't you feel as if you were in the middle of things there? With everybody coming and going to and from the ends of the earth?"

He made a grimace.

"Good lord, no! They may go to and from the ends of

17

the earth and I have to tell 'em about it and answer their silly questions, but I'm the fixed point about which they revolve. I stay put."

His discontent was manifest, and Julie looked sorry. She would have liked to feel that he was as contented with life as, in the ordinary way, she was herself.

"You'd like to be doing the travelling?" she suggested.

"You bet I would—and you bet I'm going to, one of these days."

She caught sight of a clock.

"Do you mind if I hurry now?" she asked, for they had been strolling along as if civilization were as young as they were. "Miss Pryke's a holy terror if we're late."

"We'll both hurry," said Jeremy, stepping out so that Julie had to take little skips and runs every so often to keep up with his long strides.

They reached Monique's; not the lordly entrance in the front but a small, shabby door at the side.

"This is where I go in," said Julie.

"I'm farther along, on the other side," said Jeremy.

She nodded.

"I know. I've often looked at the windows at the colored posters of Madeira and Italy and Norway and imagined myself there," said Julie.

"And I've had a peep into Monique's once or twice, at the one dress or one hat in the window, wondering what it would be like to be able to buy them for—well, for somebody I liked very much," said Jeremy.

They smiled at each other. They seemed suddenly to have been friends for a long time.

"Do you—go out to lunch?" asked Jeremy.

"I bring sandwiches and have them in the workroom. Most of us do. I go out for a walk afterwards—on fine days," she added.

"It's a very fine day today, isn't it?" suggested Jeremy.

She looked up into the sky quite unnecessarily before she nodded.

"I have sandwiches too," said Jeremy, deciding to bolt a roll and a drink at the milk bar round the corner. "What time do you go out?"

"About quarter past one, with any luck," said Julie.

"Do you think you'll have any luck today? I do hope so," said Jeremy. "That's just about the time I go out."

They still hesitated. All about them was the lovely day,

sunshine, clear air, streets swept and garnished, window glass like crystal, brass and chromium plate winking gaily from shop-fronts—and in their hearts a song of which only youth knows both the words and the tune. Some people are so blest that they remember the song all their lives—some of the words, part of the tune, pitched perhaps in a minor key. To others it is only a faint memory of symphony of jazz. But youth knows it all, and the heart of Julie and the heart of Jeremy were singing it that morning in Bond Street on the worn step of a little door that needed repainting.

Then a clock struck nine. Even to hear that lovely song of youth, time will not stay for a second its hurrying feet.

"I'll have to go," said Julie, breathless all of a sudden and without cause—or perhaps because of that breath-taking song.

He lifted his hat. She gave him her enchanting smile. Then the shabby door closed on her and somehow Bond Street became just Bond Street again, with the marble halls and wideflung doors of Butcher's awaiting him a little farther on.

He whistled, however, as he made his way to his particular section of the counter above which hung, in huge, opulent-looking letters on a brown board, "ITALIA TOURS."

He knew them all so well, the lakes, the mountains, the seaboard, all the best hotels, the motor tours, the Grand Personally Conducted Tour beloved of Americans who liked to see all Italy in a fortnight (see vividly colored brochures). It was part of Jeremy's job to arrange such tours, and, gosh how sick of it he was! He told himself countless times that he loathed the very sound of Italy and that it was the one place on earth to which he would never want to go.

And yet this morning he let himself dally over a new pamphlet thrown on the heap on his desk, the reading-matter as highly coloured as the incredibly blue lakes, the impossibly green trees, the glorious women in native costume, black eyes and white teeth flashing against a background of purple grapes, vivid oranges, and lemons like grapefruit.

What did it really look like there on a morning like this? If London looked pale blue and yellow, he could almost believe in Italy's cobalt and gold. How would he feel if he, like those lucky others, could stroll out of the Bond Street office to find himself en route for the shores of Como, or one of those mountain glades where the sky was a blue vault above him and the ground beneath his feet a carpet of flowers?

Not going alone, of course, but with some congenial companion, with—well, with the little girl with the brown eyes that laughed, for instance. Yes, Italy had its points. . . .

A sharp rapping on the counter brought back his thoughts with a jerk from Italy to the determined-looking woman who faced him.

"Young man, I want to book a fortnight's tour of the Italian Lakes for fifteen school-mistresses in August," she said severely. "They want to go as far as they can."

"Well," thought Jerry reaching down under the counter for the appropriate literature, "if they're all like you, old dear, they won't get far even with the Italians!"

But aloud he said: "Certainly, Madam. These are the tours we specially recommend."

His client ran her eye rapidly down the list, transfixed one of them with a gloved finger.

"This one. Kindly make the arrangements for the eighth of August and send the necessary papers to me at this address," and she put down a card and stalked out.

Jeremy made a hieroglyphic in his note-book which meant "Italy out of bounds to two weeks from 8th August" for some of his special clients who would probably be coming in for his advice and suggestions soon. He would not turn them loose unwarned with fifteen school-mistresses.

Meantime Julie had run up the stairs two at a time. She felt as if there were springs in her heels that made her dance instead of walk.

Everybody seemed especially happy this morning. Madam was pleased because the trousseau had been finished in time and had met the sort of approval that meant further orders when the bride returned from her honeymoon. The girls were given a bonus all round and told they might slack off for a week or two, so they were pleased. Sally arrived wearing a large sparkling ring on her engagement finger, so she was even more pleased than the rest of them.

And Julie, for no reason she could possibly explain, was the happiest of them all.

She listened with sympathetic interest to what Sally had to say about the gift of the ring.

"Of course I always reckoned Alfred would come to the point in the end, though he's kept me dancing on a string almost long enough to lose me. I let him see there were others not so long-winded, and—well, there you are!" turning her hand about to catch the sunlight. "When I did nobble him though, I stuck out for diamonds, and got 'em while the going was good. What I say is, you've always *got* something then, no matter what happens, though I bet old Alf's still remembering what he paid for it! Still, begin as you mean to go on is what I say, and if you're soft enough to let a chap be mean with you *before* he's married you, you've only got yourself to thank for what happens after," and Sally returned to the contemplation of Alfred's ring.

Julie looked at her thoughtfully. What an odd way to think of love and marriage! Did Sally really feel she had done a smart thing by inducing her fiance to buy her a more valuable ring than he had intended, and did she get satisfaction out of such knowledge? How queer of her! As if the really important thing were the ring!

When she had eaten her sandwiches, so delicately cut and daintily packed for her by her mother, she ran down the stairs to the side door. Jeremy was waiting there for her. Their eyes met and they smiled, and somehow the day at once became brighter.

"Shall we go as far as the Park?" he asked. "Have you time enough?"

"Yes. Madam has given us all extra time," said Julie happily.

What did it matter where they went? They would be walking in the Garden of Eden anyway.

She was glad he had chosen the Park, however, rather than the street of shops. They were one with the grass and the trees and the flowers as she felt they could never be with silks and laces, with jewels and the splendors in which they throbbed no heart.

They talked; at least, Jeremy talked and Julie listened. He told her first of his morning's work, of the fifteen school-marms who would descend on unsuspecting Como in August, of the couple who did not mind what they spent so long as they could "do" Italy in the fortnight sandwiched in between the last of the Courts and the marriage of their daughter to Hiram P. Schleswiger.

"They explained that he's a scion of an old Scottish family," said Jeremy, and they laughed. It was so easy to laugh that morning.

"Do you realize that we don't know each other's names yet?" he asked presently. "Mine's Jeremy Denton."

"Mine's Julie—Julie Cave."

He stopped in their walk and held out his hand.

"Shake, Julie."

"Pleased to meet you, Jeremy," she laughed, mischievously using the phrase commonly employed by the workroom girls.

He slipped an arm within her own with a little proprietary air.

"Good. Now we know each other. Isn't it stupid what a lot of time people waste getting acquainted? And there isn't a lot of time for anybody, especially when you're young. I don't want to waste a moment of my youth, do you? I want to live every minute of it, cram it with things to remember when I'm old. Oh, hell, shall we ever be old? Will you, Julie? Shall I? How old are you now?"

"Twenty. Nearly twenty-one."

"And I'm twenty-five. That's just about right, isn't it?"

She agreed. Wasn't everything just about right on such a day?

"What were you doing when you were twenty-one?" she asked.

"At Butcher's. I went there when I was nineteen. Before then I was an office-boy in Hart Street. I thought I was going to Butcher's as a sort of stepping-off place, but I seem to have taken root instead. The only place for me to step off on to is the street, as far as I can see."

There was such longing and resentment in his voice, and he threw up his head with a gesture that was already becoming familiar to her. It was such an eager gesture. It held hope and defiance and gladness of heart.

"What would you do if you could step off?" asked Julie, for that look certainly gave no suggestion that he had accepted his rooted position at Butcher's.

He gave her an uncertain, speculative glance.

"You'll laugh if I tell you. People always do," he said.

She shook her head.

"I won't. Try me."

"Well, I want to write, to make up things —plots—stories—plays. They're buzzing through my head all the time, heaps of them, and they're good stories. I know they're good"—with that eager note in his voice, a note to match the lift in his head and the light in his eyes.

Julie's heart embraced him. She loved the shining look he wore. She was glad to be walking beside him. Her face was uplifted, her eyes wide with delighted wonder. She never doubted that he could do these things. He bore the look of a conqueror.

"Write? You mean books and things?" she asked, awed. "You'd like to be an author?"

She had a confused vision of people with flowing ties and long hair.

"Books or plays—plays for choice. I'm on one now. I've just finished the second act. I think it's good. I've got the climax there, everybody confused, everybody afraid to take a step in case things crash about them, and then the maid walks in and makes a calm announcement that sets them all by the ears and entirely alters everybody's ideas. That's good. It's dramatic. It leaves the audience on tenterhooks. They can't conceive of a way out without ruining the heroine, and none of them wants to see her ruined."

He had forgotten that he had ever felt awkward with Julie. His voice was eager, crisp, darting from word to word. There was color in his pale cheeks, and his eyes, when he flashed them her way, were like points of fire. Her own excitement rose. She grasped her shabby little bag between her two hands until the fastening, never very secure, snapped. She did not even notice that at the time.

"And she isn't ruined?" she asked anxiously.

"No. I've one or two alternatives I'm working out for the last act. It's got to be clever. It's got to be so natural that the audience will wonder they didn't think of it themselves, but subtle—intriguing—unusual. There mustn't be anti-climax. That's bad in a book but fatal in a play. It's like having fried onions for the last course of a dinner at the Ritz! It makes you forget everything else you've had until you begin to believe that the only food they serve you at the Ritz is fried onions!"

Julie laughed.

"Have you ever had dinner at the Ritz?" she asked.

He grinned.

"Never in my life. Have you?"

"Me? Heavens, no! I'd be scared stiff," said Julie.

"Scared stiff? Whatever for? They're only people there

just the same as you and me. The only difference is that they've got money and we haveⁿt—not yet, anyway. I'm going to have it, though. You watch me!"

He swaggered a little in his young arrogance that would brook no thwarting of his purpose, and Julie, watching him, seeing the set of his chin, the light in his eyes, the thrust of his thin young body as he strode along almost too fast for her, had a queer sensation. It was as if, in that moment, Fate had made a sudden twist of the shuttles she held in her hand, working the two threads together, knotting them into an intricate design—the Julie thread that so far had run so smoothly and evenly, the Jeremy thread which was so gleaming and gay.

It was time for them to go back, and Jeremy realized all at once that he had done all the talking and that, except for her name and the place where she worked, he knew no more about Julie than on the day when he had first pulled her into the moving train.

"Same train tomorrow morning?" he asked her when they stood outside the employees' door of Monique's again.

Julie nodded and then discovered the broken clasp of her bag and made a little sound of annoyance.

"I must have just done it," she said.

"Never mind. I'll buy you a new one," said Jeremy, and they stared at each other, he as much surprised as she by the suggestion. "That'd be all right, wouldn't it?" he added.

"No, I—I don't think it would, would it?" said Julie.

"I suppose not. Isn't it silly, all this repression and inhibition? Why shouldn't I give you a bag if I want to, and why shouldn't you take it, if you want to? You do want to, don't you?"

"Of course not," said Julie hurriedly, and ran indoors out of sight.

3

Julie stood back to survey the table critically.

Had she cut enough bread and butter? Did the scones look all right? She hoped she had put enough sugar in them. Jeremy had such a sweet tooth. The little cakes looked much smaller on the plate than they had done in the shop, but they would go round twice if only Dickie could be persuaded to fill the worst of his perpetual void with bread and butter.

She rather liked the look of the iced jam sponge, and it had been a brain wave of Mum's to put walnuts round the edge to hide the bit where Biddy had been "picking" at the icing. Biddy did not always remember to be refined!

Mrs. Cave came into the room behind her, and Julie's quick ears caught the rustle of silk. She spun round and eyed her mother lovingly.

"Oh, darling, you've put on the amethyst! How *dear* of you, and you look lovely!"

The amethyst dress had been new the last time long skirts and leg-of-mutton sleeves were in, and they were even going out again for the second time. The dress was a little tight across the front now and Mrs. Cave had to remember to keep her shoulders back to save the stitches from giving round the armholes, but she wore it with an air, and in her faded cheeks was a little flush of excitement which lent her something of a bygone charm. Julie realized how Biddy had come by her prettiness, and suddenly she gathered her mother into her arms in an overwhelming pity fo all those sorrows, the tears, the anxieties, the midnight hours of work, which had stolen her birthright of beauty.

"Oh, Mum—Mum darling," she whispered. "I'll make it up to you," and because Mrs. Cave had given to her younger daughter her face but to her elder her nature, she understood with no more need of words.

"I hope he'll like us, Julie," was all she said anxiously.

"He'll love you, anyway, Mum. In fact, I think it very probable that you'll cut me out with him! I only hope Biddy won't be too refined and Dickie keeps off the cakes. I wish he'd come home so that we can clean him up. What's Biddy doing? Dolling up, I suppose. What's she putting on?"

"She's made herself a dress out of that blue stuff you brought home, but I haven't seen it yet."

"Oh, Mum, I bought that specially for you!" said Julie reproachfully.

"Dear, what do I want with new clothes at my time of life?

It's you children who want things. You ought to have made up that blue for yourself, Julie. You've had that dress such a long time and you ought to have a change from brown"—eying rather disparagingly Julie's one "best"

25

dress, a plain little affair of dark brown silk with demure lace collar and cuffs.

Julia glanced down at herself and smoothed her skirt. Now that the magic hour was actually upon her and Jeremy was about to make his first appearance to the family, she did wish faintly that she had been able to make herself look a little more grand! Still, she reflected sagely, brown was her color and simplicity her style, and if a little brown mouse were suddenly to grow feathers it would only look ridiculous.

"It's serviceable," she said cheerfully. "Besides, with you and Biddy so grand, I'd be outclassed anyhow"—with a laugh.

"Your young man won't think so," said her mother fondly. "I wouldn't think much of his judgment if he did."

"You'd better not call him that, Mum. We're only—friends." But the color in her face and the light in her warm brown eyes were telltale, especially to a mother's vision. "Oh, Mum. I do hope you'll like Jeremy!"

Mrs. Cave had heard quite a lot about him by now, first just his name mentioned shyly, then what he did for a living, and gradually of the dreams and hopes and aspirations which he poured in Julie's willing ears day by day as they walked in the Park on fine days in the lunch hour.

Latterly they had not been able to do this, for summer had turned into winter with only the briefest of autumns, and it was Jeremy's complaint that he never saw her now except in the train that had led to this first diffident invitation to Streatham.

Jeremy had jumped at it.

"It's what I've been hoping you'd ask me for a long time," he said contentedly. "When shall I come? Next Sunday?"

Julie had gulped and nodded. She loved her shabby little home, her unpretentious surroundings, the small, faded mother, Biddy with her new, funny "naice" speech and manners, Dickie grubby cherub's face and hands with the nails always in mourning. But how would it all strike Jeremy, whom she always felt to be her social superior? True, he lived in cheap lodgings (he had told her all about that) and he had no money except his none too munificent salary and never spoke of parents or relations, and yet she knew instinctively that he could at any moment, if given the chance, walk out at his ease into a world such as she herself would never be able to enter without embarrassment and nervous qualms.

He had a father somewhere, he had once told her, but they didn't "get on", and his mother was dead and his brothers and sisters scattered and apparently careless of one another. So much he had told her, and she, in return, had told him all about her home, of her father's death and the struggle Mrs. Cave had had, left with the three of them quite unprovided for.

She had described more graphically than she knew the hours her mother had spent bent over the sewing machine. Julie could scarcely remember her mother apart from machine or needle; their life before her father's death had become a rather dim picture.

She still worked at her sewing, but Julie's job had relieved her of the necessity to work nights as well as days, and soon Biddy would, they hoped, be bringing in a little, though neither of them could picture that small bird of paradise gracing either office or work room.

She had told him, with tender laughter which held nothing unkind, of Biddy's "grand ways" and ambitions, which were highly colored if not spiritually lofty. She had told him too of Dickie and their hopes for him when he came out of the fog of ink fights in which so far he seemed determinedly enveloped.

Yet, waiting for him when the day and the hour were upon her at last, she wondered whether she had managed to convey the actual facts to him uncolored by her loving pride in her family.

There was a shout from the kitchen and Mrs. Cave and Julie, with one accord, swooped down on the returned Dickie, one hauling off his torn, bespattered blue jersey while the other filled the bowl at the sink with hot water and added a few knobs of soda. No need to look first to see if hot water were called for!

"How on earth did you get your jersey in this state?" asked Mrs. Cave. The sleeve was nearly ripped out, and part of the ribbed hem was torn off.

Dickie grinned reminiscently.

"Met Jimmy Elson," he said tersely.

"I can't see that that's any reason for your getting into this state," said Mrs. Cave.

Dickie's grinning and cheerful countenance emerged from the remains of the jersey, which Julie had stripped off.

"You should see Jimmy!" was all he said before she slapped a soapy flannel on the back of his neck and called forth a remonstrance.

"Aren't I going to put a collar on?" he asked.

"Not on top of that dirty neck," said Julie decidedly.

"Well it won't show," he grumbled.

Mrs. Cave had brought down a clean shirt and his best suit in readiness, and he eyed it sourly. Once encased in it, he was expected to keep clean.

"Say, Julie, who is this bloke that's coming?" he asked, allowing them to drag the shirt over his head.

"He's—just a friend of mine," said Julie self-consciously. "Dickie, do try and keep reasonably clean, won't you?"

Dickie snorted.

"Well, we don't get all dolled up like this when I bring Spot Jenkins home to tea. Not sweet on him by any chance, are you?"

"Of course I'm not," said Julie—sharply for her. "And I do wish, Dickie, you'd try to get out of that kind of talk you hear on the movies, cheap American slang words."

He whistled and stared at this new version of the long-suffering Julie.

"Gee, you sure got it bad, baby," he said.

"Oh, *Dickie!* You see, Mr. Denton's—well, he doesn't talk like that. He—he's a writer. He's going to write plays one day"—with a little lift of pride in her voice.

"Coo, I hope he'll do gangster plays! Are you going to act in them if he does, Ju? Bet you'd be the goods as a ganster's moll!"

"Oh, *Dickie!*" said his sister again, half laughing, half outraged, but his further comments were postponed by the sound of the door bell.

Julie threw down the hairbrush.

"Let me open it, Mum," she said in a quick whisper and ran into the hall, closing the kitchen door behind her.

And the next moment the wonderful thing had happened.

Jeremy was actually in the hall, in her own home, taking her hand in his big one, smiling at her.

"You—you found the way all right, then?" asked Julie, suddenly shy of him.

He gave her one of his eager, happy looks.

"The way to you? Of course I did, Julie," he said, and the world rocked for a moment and then stood quite still again.

The kitchen door opened and Mrs. Cave appeared, followed by Dickie, now miraculously complete, even to a tie, his hair plastered down, his face shining with soap and looking unnaturally seraphic.

"Mum, this is Jeremy," said Julie softly, and they looked at each other, sizing each other up.

"So you're the mother I've heard so much about, are you?" Jeremy's blue eyes were saying, and Mrs. Cave's, faded by almost forgotten tears, were replying: "So you're the boy who's put that look into my Julie's face. I wonder—I wonder . . ." and her thoughts trailed off and became, even in that instant of time, the long thoughts of mothers.

Jeremy shook hands with her and then grinned in the direction of Dickie, who responded with the reserve of his kind. Dickie was not giving anything away.

"Hang your hat and coat up here, Jeremy," Julie was saying, thinking with a little thrill how tremendously tall he looked in their little hall, and he even had to bend his head when he went down the two steps that led to the sitting-room. Julie's visitor could hardly be expected, on his first visit, to eat in the kitchen, though, as the work of cooking and washing up was done in the adjoining scullery, it made a comfortable family room and left the other room free for homework.

Jeremy glanced round the room approvingly.

"How homely it all looks, Julie," he began to say, when a little flurry of skirts and a clinking of high heels down the stairs made them all turn towards the door again and the Cave family, at least, gasped at what they saw.

They saw Biddy, but such a Biddy as their eyes had never before beheld, and Julie caught her breath quickly and drew her brows together in a little frown which her sister affected not to see.

In the blue dress, made rather shoddily in an ultra-fashionable style—one suited to the sophisticated thirties rather than a maidenly fifteen—with her pale-gold hair dressed high in little curls and puffs about her head and a flower on top. Biddy minced into the room on the high heels of Julie's one pair of evening shoes, her hand outstretched towards the visitor, her slim hips swaying in imitation of her favorite film star.

"How do you du-u, Mr. Denton?" she drawled, the outstretched hand offered to Jeremy while the other went in a studied pose to her back hair. It was the least of Mrs. Cave's shocks to recognize the bower as being the one from her best hat.

Jeremy, after the first electrified moment, rose to the occasion. Appearing in no way surprised at the vision thus presented to him, he took Biddy's hand (redolent of Julie's lavender water), bowed over it, foreign fashion, from the waist down with a perfectly flat back, and raised her wrist to his lips.

"I am enchanted to be presented to you, Miss Biddy," he said, so gravely that Biddy blinked, gulped, and then gave him a ravishing smile.

"Haow delaightful!" she said, and then flashed a look on Dickie that should have killed him, for he had burst into a loud guffaw and began to fan the air to suggest that he was overpowered by her presence.

Mrs. Cave, who had beaten a strategical retreat into the kitchen at sight of her younger daughter, now called her and Dickie in no uncertain voice.

"Come and help me carry in the tray, Biddy and Dick," she said, and Julie had the presence of mind to shut the door on them quickly before the storm broke over the kitchen.

Then she looked at Jeremy and they both laughed.

"Oh, Jeremy, what *does* Biddy look like? To think she's not sixteen yet!"

"She's got a future before her, that child," was his comment, and his look was pleasantly ruminative. "She should go far. In American parlance, she's got what it takes!"

Julie's face grew a little wistful.

"You think a lot of success, don't you, Jeremy?"

"You bet I do! What's the good of just sticking where you begin?" and to her sharpened fancy he looked disparagingly round the little room where Julie had begun and where she was still—stuck.

It was only her fancy that there was disparagement in his look, for actually he thought it all very homelike and pleasant and a charming setting for her, but when a girl is twenty and just falling in love for the first time she can imagine anything to her own disadvantage.

Tea arrived, and over it they all thawed, though to the very end Biddy remembered to keep her little finger crooked, both actually and metaphorically, Dickie providing a broad contrast to her excessive delicacy by slopping his tea in the saucer and picking out without dissembling the most exciting of the cakes, eating all round the edge and commenting audibly on the middle thus revealed.

"You just wait till he's gone, Dickie Cave, and see what you get!" said Biddy's sidelong glance at him, though her only spoken words were comments on the "weathah" in what Dickie called her "D.B.C." manner.

After tea they all sat round the fire and talked, and Mrs. Cave tried gently to plumb the depths of this young man who had appeared from nowhere to threaten the peace and unity of the nest.

Jeremy talked. How he talked! Biddy listened because she was firmly resolved to copy his accent and especially the way he had of saying "Oh, definitely—definitely!" Dickie listened because if he reminded them of his presence he might be hustled off to church. Julie listened because she loved him.

And Julie's mother listened so that she might find the man behind the words he spoke, know him and gauge his chances of making Julie happy, for in the mother's heart was no room for doubt as to what lay behind the soft brown eyes which watched this very talkative young man.

Later they went for a walk in the rain, he and Julie, for it had seemed the only way of disconnecting her from a family which, however nice they might be to him, had become distinctly *de trop*.

He opened his big umbrella, slipped his free hand under her elbow, and Julie's cup of happiness was filled to the brim.

"Your folks are topping," he said.

She gave his arm a little squeeze.

"Oh, Jeremy, I'm so glad. I did so want you to like them," she said happily.

"I think it was more to the point that they should like me—your mother, anyway," said Jeremy, but there was a little touch of arrogance behind the seeming humility of his words.

"But of course she'd like you," murmured Julie.

It was not a London street at all, with railings and tall houses on each side and rain pattering down on the paths, and buses spraying mud over them as they passed. It was paradise, and the streets were of gold and they were alone and about them was the scent of flowers and the song of birds and the peace of folded wings.

Julie looked up at him under the big umbrella.

"Do *you* like me, Julie?" asked Jeremy, and for once his young voice faltered and his arrogance was gone, and he was just a boy in love.

She nodded. Her eyes were starry.

"You know I do, Jeremy," she managed to whisper.

There were not many people about. Only lovers and people who have to be about are out of doors on wet Sunday evenings in November, so when Jeremy glanced hastily around, he saw no reason why they should not consider themselves alone in the world at that moment.

He stopped in front of the dripping railings which guarded an empty house and drew Julie more closely beneath the shelter of the umbrella. It made a sanctuary for them, and her face was like a rose, flushed and rain-wet.

He put an arm about her.

"Oh, Julie, you're so sweet!" he said unsteadily, looking down at her.

Her eyes were wide and fascinated, her mouth trembled a little and looked so soft and warm.

"You—you're sweet too, Jeremy," she said in a small shy whisper.

"May I kiss you, Julie?"

For answer she lifted her face and gave him her lips, closing her eyes as she felt his mouth come down on hers, nervously and uncertainly at first, but then so firm and compelling that unconsciously she began to struggle against him—and yet not against him, but against that strange, wildly sweet thing born of his kiss within her own self.

He set her free, and they stood there staring into each other's eyes, not smiling but just looking at each other, stilled by the wonder of their world made new.

"Julie, we—we love each other, don't we?" asked Jeremy, and the voice which had trembled a little and been uncertain grew sure and exultant.

"I've always loved you," said Julie softly, her voice very low and sweet.

"Do you think your mother guesses anything, Julie?" She smiled.

"I don't know. Mum's very wise, you know, and I've been terribly happy lately. You don't mind her knowing, Jeremy?"—on a sudden, surprised thought.

"Well—it's only that—well, you see, Julie dear, we may have to wait such a long time that I think it would be better, don't you, if we kept it to ourselves? Just our own secret?"

Julie looked thoughtful, a little worried. She had never kept a secret from her mother in all her twenty years. Was the new love already beginning to war with the old, tried, and faithful one?

"What is it, dear?" asked Jeremy.

"Well, I can just tell Mum, can't I? You see, we always tell each other everything, and she'll be so happy about it, Jeremy."

"Oh, yes, when there's anything really to tell," said Jeremy cautiously.

Julie had her pride, that frail weed so easily grown in even the loveliest of gardens, so quickly developing into a strong plant, so hard to uproot, so impossible utterly to kill where love is.

"I see," she said, after a pause, her voice small and clear. "You mean that—there isn't anything really to tell yet? That we're not . . ."

She could not bring herself to say the magic word "engaged," since he had not mentioned it.

He began to speak eagerly as they resumed their walk, his hand within her arm and grasping the umbrella which somehow seemed no longer a sanctuary.

"You see, darling, there's so much to consider, so much to do. Look at me. I haven't even got a decent job, or one with any prospects, and even if there were any chances of fat jobs at Butcher's, that isn't what I want. I'm not going to be all my life selling tours and sleeping berths to other people. I'm going to be one of the people who buy those some day. I want success, fame, money, the world at my feet. I want to get to the top, and I know I can. I know I've got it in me if only someone will give me the chance to prove it. And if they won't, I'm going to make my own chance, thrust myself forward so that people will have to see me. I'm going to do it some day, Julie. You watch me!"

She felt as if a cold hand had been laid over her heart. There was no reason for it, for she had heard most of this before, and many times before. Yet tonight it was somehow different. She was a romantic little person at heart, and she felt, without being able to analyze the feeling, that tonight should have belonged to her, to the present, to the sweetness of new-found love; not to that glorious and vague future.

For the first time she began to realize that she belonged to that future, whatever it was in actual fact, Jeremy's kiss had linked her with his life forever. When he built that palace above the stars, he was building for her too, and the idea made her feel dizzy. Suddenly and desperately she wanted to have their feet fixed firmly to earth, where it was familiar and safe. She was no adventurer, this Julie. She was of the sweet and tender and stable things of life, simple and humdrum things. The fires that warmed her heart were those built on the kitchen hearth, and the star by which her spirit steered its course was the lamp on the table.

She pressed her arm more closely against his.

"Oh, Jeremy, I'm afraid!" she said unexpectedly.

He paused for a moment to look down with some surprise into her face.

"Why, Julie? What is there to be afraid of?" he asked.

She gave a little shiver and crept closer to him.

"I don't know. Perhaps I'm just being silly, but—oh, *dear* Jeremy, don't let's miss our happiness for those things, for success and fame and—and the world at our feet. It's ours already because we're young and love each other."

He laughed at her, but there was tenderness in the laughter. So small and sweet she was, so terribly in earnest about life, so timid about going out to meet it! He thought of her mother, of the patient, defeated look in the faded eyes, the resignation she should not feel at her age—what was it? Fifty? Probably not so much, though she had the ways and look of a woman who had finished with life and was content to be allowed to linger in those of other people.

Not for him that defeated look at fifty! Not for him and not for Julie!

So he had both tenderness and laughter for her.

"At our feet, yes—but we're not going to kick it away from us. We're going to sit on top of it. You're getting me all mixed up in my metaphors, Julie darling; but what I mean is that we've got to wait, and then you'll see. Kiss me, Julie. I do love you so."

The song of birds was about them again in that London street, and there was the gold of the city dreams beneath their feet, and by the time they had reached Julie's home everything had ceased to matter save that they loved each other and that life stretched endlessly away before them. To the young, youth is going to last forever. They may conceive of others growing old, but themselves never. For them alone time will stand still.

"Will you come in again, Jeremy?" Julie asked him softly at the gate.

"No, darling." What a thrill it was to hear him call her that! "I can't face them again tonight. I'd rather go away and dream about you." And she laughed softly, her face radiant with happiness.

"I'll see you tomorrow?" she asked.

"Of course. On the 8:16?"

"Oh, Jeremy, I almost forgot. Sally—you know, I've spoken of her—Sally wants us to go somewhere or other with her and her boy tomorrow night. She's asked me so often and I've always said we couldn't, but—now . . .?"—hesitating over the delicious idea that he belonged to her, that she could make joint plans for their evenings.

He made a grimace.

"What sort of show is it? Dog-fight or something?"

She laughed.

"She's mad on dancing, so I expect it will be that. Can you dance?"

"No, can you?"

"No, but we can watch. Oh, Jeremy. I do hope you won't mind terribly!"

"I shan't mind anything so long as we're together," he told her satisfyingly, and held her against him for a long moment in that new and thrilling delight of contact with the beloved.

She broke away from him at last and went stumblingly over the few feet of pathway to the house, drunk with happiness.

The house was quiet. Dickie was in bed, Biddy absent on

some affairs of her own—probably practicing new poses and expressions before the mirror in the room she shared with Julie—and Mrs. Cave was sitting alone in the firelight, her hands for once idle in her lap.

Julie was glad of the darkness and stopped her mother when she would have moved to press the light-switch.

"Don't light up, Mum. I'd rather be like this." she said, and slipped down on the rug at her mother's feet and laid her head against her.

Mrs. Cave stroked her hair.

"Nice walk, dearie?"

"Lovely, Mum."

She longed to tell her mother—felt that the restriction was both unfair and unnecessary—but she had that night learned a new loyalty. The old ones go by the board at the imperious demands of nature, which have no truck with the old and must always be pressing on with the new, abandoning the born for the unborn.

But Mrs. Cave had no need to be told, though it caused her a pang that Julie did not give her the expected confidence.

When they rose to go to bed, they held each other in a long embrace which told of love and trust and understanding.

"Darling Mum," said Julie, a little tremulously.

"God bless you and give you—happiness, my Julie."

"Do you think one ever really gets happiness, Mum?" asked the girl, with a strange wistfulness.

"Yes, dear, if we try to understand what happiness really is—that it is being and not having. It isn't just pleasure, everything being fun, everything going right. It's much more often going without things and having them go wrong because it's then that you know the real worth of the things you *have* got, the things that never go wrong."

"You were happy with Dad, weren't you, Mum?"

"Very happy, dear."

"And you never had much, had you? Not—fame or success or the world at your feet?" And there was a quiver in Julie's laughter that betrayed her to the one who loved her best.

"No, I don't suppose anybody would have called what we had fame or success, but—if I hadn't the world at my feet, I held it in my arms when you were born, my Julie. Every mother does that."

Julie kissed her with a strange, hungry passion. Here was a love so familiar, so safe—a love that had been tried and never found wanting. Here was sure ground for her feet, air which she could breathe. What was this other love that both frightened and intoxicated her? That promised her heaven and yet made her want to cling to earth?"

"I wish I were a little girl again," she whispered. "I wish I were Biddy or Dickie."

Mrs. Cave smiled in the darkness, kissed Julie again, and let her go.

Dickie? Still an unknown quantity, a small, grubby boy whose heaven just now was a weedy pond.

Biddy? The mother's eyes were tender still, though a little amused and not anxious. Biddy would be all right, for her head would always rule her heart, and it is only when women's hearts run away with their heads that they know sorrow and disillusionment. Biddy would never be disillusioned, for even at fifteen she had no illusions.

But Julie?

Ah, Julie, her first-born, secretly her best-loved!

Julie was of the women who are born with a crown of roses and a crown of thorns, and they can no more miss the thorns of the one than the perfume of the other. Julie's head would never rule her heart, or surely she would at the very outset let this young man go, or take him lightly and lose him as lightly, as Biddy would.

Mrs. Cave did not know what she felt about Jeremy Denton, and she told herself that she would probably have felt just as bothered and unsafe about any other young man who came to take Julie from her.

Yet her last waking thought, hours after she had gone to bed, was, "O God, take care of my Julie and protect her from herself."

4

Sally arrived at the dance hall in pink satin frills and a lot of skin; Julie arrived in the brown silk.

Alfred wore a suit which consisted of striped trousers, dinner jacket, white waistcoat, and black ready-made tie; Jeremy had come straight from the office in his navy-blue suit.

Thus the evening did not have an altogether propitious opening, for neither pair thought the other looked "quite the thing," and yet each pair had a sneaking sensation of not being itself "quite the thing."

"You didn't tell me men wore evening kit at this thing," grumbled Jeremy to Julie, looking somewhat cynically at Alfred's broad short back encased in a coat cut for a long narrow back. Actually it had been purchased at a "Misfit" shop, and had misfitted even the long narrow back. Still, as one cannot see one's own back without performing gymnastics in front of the mirror, that did not worry Alfred.

"I didn't know," said Julie apologetically. "Still, I think you look very nice. You always do. It's I who feel like—like . . ."

"Like a sparrow strayed into an aviary?" asked Jeremy, lightening the situation for a moment with his love of the apt word. "Well, I like sparrows," he ended, tucking a hand within her arm; and Julie discovered that the evening was going to be lovely after all.

But it was soon clear that it was not going to be harmonious, for with the men vaguely scornful of each other, what hope had their womenfolk of being in accord?

"Togged up to the nines in his dress suit," ran Jeremy's thoughts, refusing to admit to himself that they were envious.

He had never owned a dress suit.

"But you wait a few years," he said to himself. "I'll show 'em! *And* the coat'll fit at the back. Jeremy Denton! A darn' sight better-sounding than Alfred Bates and a darn' sight better I'll look too."

'And Alfred's thoughts were: "Who is this fella-me-lad, anyway? Puttin' on airs and thinkin' 'imself mighty superior. Superior? I don't think! Tryin' to talk like a bally announcer and 'asn't even got a dress suit" drawing—his shoulders back before he remembered that by neglecting to maintain a nice balance between front and back he might come to a disaster at one or the other.

He was feeling a bit of a dog by this time, and began in a lordly style to order drinks, having conveyed his party to a table marked "Reserved."

"I know what yours is, Sal. A Guinness," he began.

Sally, the red flag flying in her cheeks, contradicted him with a sly wink at Julie.

"Well, you're wrong. Mine's a dry Martini," she said,

38

with a toss of her curl-mounted head.

Alfred's jaw dropped.

"What the blazes . . .? What's come over you? And how do you know anything about dry Martinis?"

"They always have them in the pictures," said Sally defiantly. "Remember the one we saw the other night with Cary Grant in it? They were always ordering dry Martinis, and what's good enough for Cary Grant's good enough for Sally Basset."

"Well, maybe it is—if they paid me as much for gasfitting as they do Cary Grant for making love to those stage birds," said Alfred, with a touch of sourness. "Anyway, what's yours—er—Julie?"

Jeremy interposed swiftly, glaring at Alfred:

"I'll get Miss Cave what she wants. What would you like, Julie?"

"Lemonade, please," decided Julie. She had never drunk anything intoxicating in her life, though she felt she was being hopelessly *ingenue* and wished she too had the courage to demand a dry Martini. Then she remembered that it would probably cost a lot more than lemonade, and was glad she had asked for the more modest drink.

She had already had an argument with Jeremy about the cost of their evening, trying to persuade him to let her pay her share. His refusal had been unequivocal.

"When I can't afford to take a girl out, I'll stay in," he had said, with that touch of grandiloquence which she loved because it was so essential a part of him.

Alfred gave Sally a baleful glance, reckoning up mentally the difference in cost between a Guinness and a cocktail; but Sally gave him an impish grin and showed no sign of changing her mind, so he gave the order with what grace he could to the waiter.

"Begin as you mean to go on," whispered Sally to Julie. "If you begin with lemonade, you'll never get any further. Look at the job I've got breaking out into cocktails after having started with a Guinness! You take it from me, the more you cost a man, the more he thinks of you. He's put money into you, see? So he isn't going to let you go in a hurry. If he hasn't spent anything on you, you're no more to him than all the rest of the girls he's never spent anything on, see?"

Julie imbibed this piece of worldly wisdom. It made her feel slightly sick. Hadn't Sally and Alfred ever walked in the rain and found paradise? And if they had, how could she be so hard and calculating? How could she want Alfred to spend money on her rather than save it for their home and their future together, or go to evening classes as Jeremy did?

Not that she could imagine Alfred having the urge to spend his free time studying history and English and French and all the other things that occupied Jeremy's leisure hours.

Sally sipped her cocktail and found it surprisingly potent, for she had suspected Alfred of meanness when she saw the lack of quantity. She began to laugh more loudly, and encouraged Alfred to buy her another Martini by letting him stroke her bare arms and plump shoulders. She even let him kiss her with loud, smacking kisses which made her roar with laughter and give him little playful slaps.

Julie, looking the timid little brown mouse she felt, was relieved when they got to their feet and danced. Sally pressed against her partner with an intimacy that amazed and revolted the unsophisticated girl, who felt embarrassed at even watching them.

When they returned to their seat, flushed and overbright of glance for each other, Julie unconsciously swallowed hard and moved an inch nearer to where Jeremy sat.

He got up suddenly.

"Like to dance, Julie?" he asked, in a queer hard voice.

She looked astonished.

"But—but we can't do it," she demurred.

"Nothing in it. I've been watching people. They don't dance at all. They only hang on to each other and shuffle about. Come on. All we've got to do is stop on one spot and shuffle our feet. It's really only an excuse for cuddling, as far as I can see."

Julie could not help laughing. She stood up, and Jeremy put an arm about her; and at the electric spark which was lit immediately between them, they caught each other's eyes and smiled. Was that all they had needed? An excuse for cuddling?

"Do you like it here?" asked Jeremy presently.

The whole dance tune had been played through and crooned over, but they had not succeeded in moving more than a few yards from their starting point.

As Jeremy had said, it was only a question of shuffling their feet more or less in time with the music, though even that seemed not to matter.

Julie was facing the corner where Sally and Alfred were sitting out. She was lolling against him, her hair a little dishevelled already, one shoulder strap of her revealing dress slipping down and making it even more revealing. There was something repulsive to Julie in such a gross display of human flesh. Even in the workroom she disliked the lovely gown that must leave so little to the imagination, and Sally had neither a lovely gown nor the *sveltesse* which was the only possible excuse for such a display.

"Not much—do you?" she replied to Jeremy's question.

His face, which had been clouded all the evening, cleared as if by magic, and he gave her a little squeeze.

Their dancing had not been very successful, for he could not bring himself to take her into the close and intimate embrace which seemed necessary for perfect dual rhythm—not in this public place, anyway.

"You darling!" he said. "I was afraid you were enjoying it tremendously. I suppose girls do like this sort of thing or they wouldn't come. Have you had enough of it? Would you like to clear out?"

Julie glanced back at their table. The pair sat interlaced, smoking one cigarette between them and sipping alternately from Sally's cocktail glass and Albert's tumbler of whisky and soda.

"Perhaps they wouldn't like it if we did," said Julie hesitantly, always mindful of the feelings of others.

Jeremy's face showed his disgust, and his voice was more than edged with it.

"Do you think they'll even know we've gone?" he asked. "Get your coat, darling. This place sickens me, and it's a vile environment for you."

After another hesitating and guilty glance, Julie let him carve a way for her through the shuffling, perspiring crowd, and as they went out into the vestibule off which the cloakrooms led, they were alone for a brief moment.

Jeremy caught her to him.

"Oh, Julie, let's kiss! We were losing each other in there. It isn't our sort of place and they're not our sort of people. They're cheap people with cheap emotions, cheap ideas of happiness."

Julie knew what he meant, but was drawn by a sense of loyalty to Sally to defend her. After all, Sally had devised this for their pleasure, and it wasn't her fault that they had not been pleased.

She tried to say so.

"It's only that they're different," she said, in the shy way she had when she presumed to set up an opinion against his. "That's their way of enjoying themselves, that's all."

His face expressed disgust and he let her go. People were coming and they were no longer alone.

"Are you making excuses for them or have you got a sneaking sympathy for that sort of thing?" he demanded, his voice curt.

Julie's sensitiveness shrank from that tone. He saw it and was quick to feel remorse. Taking her hand in his he gave it a little squeeze.

"Sorry, darling. You see what this sort of place does to me. Let's get out of here. I'll meet you here when you've got your coat."

But when they reached the outer door it was raining.

"Curse it, it would be!" said Jeremy. "What shall we do? Want to go home? It's only nine o'clock."

Julie had a swift vision of what it would be like to go home at this hour. She had rather flaunted in the face of her admiring family the fact that Jeremy was taking her to a dance, and now to come crawling home at nine o'clock would be something of an anti-climax!

Mum would understand, of course, and make Jeremy welcome, light a fire quickly for them in the little-used sitting room, and hustle the children out of the way if they were still up. Julie shrank from Biddy's inquiring eyes and mind, though. She would leap unhesitatingly at the truth, that the "dance" had not come up to expectations; and Julie was developing, with Jeremy's entrance into her life, a sensitiveness to even the gentlest ridicule. Everything connected with the wonderful Jeremy must be successful, and she was not going to admit that their very first evening's gaiety had been a failure!

"No, she did not want to go home yet; but what else was there to do?

Jeremy read some, at least, of her thoughts, and offered a compromise.

"Would you—what about coming with me?" he ventured. "We can't walk about in the rain, and there's nowhere else we can go at this time. Even at the pictures we shouldn't see the show through now. Will you come, Julie? Nobody will be about at this time of day. We could probably get the dining room to ourselves. Will you?"

"You mean—your digs?" asked Julie, wide-eyed. After all, she had started out on enjoyment bent, and if they had not found it—well, they must look somewhere else.

He nodded.

"Unless you can think of a better idea?"

She was beginning to think of the rain as her friend. Certainly it prefaced the most romantic episodes of her life at present!

"We'll get a bus to Victoria and then the train," said Jeremy, in his efficient way. He could always make up his mind so quickly. "It won't be far for you to go home afterwards, either. We'll be able to get a bus all the way."

She knew by now that he lived at a boardinghouse in Norwood. She knew by name and description all the people he shared the house with, and she felt she would recognize any of them. His power of description, of just hitting with one or two phrases on people's salient characteristics, had turned mere names into personalities for her.

She knew little Miss Teal, who had the flower shop at the corner; old Silas Munt and his overbearing wife, of whom he was but the pale shadow and echo; Mrs. Weaver, the "decayed gentlewoman" who lived in the past, wore clothes of a bygone elegance, and had a *penchant* for Jeremy, who teased her and used her for copy; George Cutting, who was out to sell anything to anybody, even his friends; the two Miss Spagetts, living on each other's nerves and yet unable to exist apart after nearly seventy years together; a few insignificant people whom Jeremy called "extras" and who came and went unobtrusively.

Julie knew them all, and if sometimes she felt guiltily that she ought not to be laughing at Jeremy's clever perception of them, too keen sometimes to be kind, she was too deeply in love to critize him or let it worry her tender heart too seriously.

"It's almost opposite the station," said Jeremy, and they made a last dash through the rain and arrived breathless in the porch of pseudo stone and marble, both of which were chipping off, to reveal the honest bricks beneath.

It was one of those tall old houses, typically Victorian, where nothing was what it seemed and everything had been

43

laboriously made up to deceive.

"It's a rotten hole," was Jeremy's comment, as he fitted his key into the lock of the front door, deal grained to look like oak.

Julie had thought it rather grand. It was palatial in size after 26 Hemming Road. Her eyes saw the stone and marble effect and took them for truth; Jeremy saw only the bricks and plaster beneath and preferred their honesty.

"Some day I'm going to have real marble outside my house," he said, with such certainty that Julie had an uncomfortable vision of herself amidst such splendour. What did one use for cleaning marble? She rather wished Jeremy had not such big ideas—but then, why shouldn't he have them? He had the power to make such dreams come true, she thought adoringly.

"Wait here a jiffy while I see where everybody is," said Jeremy in a stage whisper, and disappeared, leaving her alone in the hall with the hat stand (also deal grained to re-represent oak), two chairs (seats uphostered in cloth painted to look like leather), a near-Chinese vase and a drainpipe adorned with a design of bulrushes on a background of gold paint and standing on end. The latter held umbrellas and the former was filled with enormous tulips (paper).

To Julie it still looked rather palatial. At 26 Hemming Road there was not even room for a hat stand in the hall. They had to make do with a row of pegs fastened to the wall.

Jeremy came back, a finger at his lips.

"There's bridge going on in the dining room and the Spaghettis are quarrelling in the lounge. Mr. Munt and George Cutting are telling smoke-room stories in the writing room. Dare you come up to my room?"

She considered this, rather startled. Then loud voices came from the room on the left, and Jeremy caught her hand and ran with her to the front of the stairs and swiftly up the first flight, where they paused and listened.

"Allow *me* to know *something*, Bertha, *if* you please. As the elder . . ."

"No need to remind the whole house of that, dearest Maud. It is surely self-evident. Te, he, he!"

"Come on, Julie," whispered Jeremy, and she hesitated no longer.

He led her on up the next flight of stairs and into a small room at the back, littered, untidy, comfortless,

44

somehow forlorn and as if nobody really lived in it. She looked at the unlit oil lamp standing in the empty fireplace, a tin kettle beside it, and tenderness rushed to her heart as she compared his nightly homecomings with her own. Instead of that rather pitiful oil lamp was the cheerful kitchen fire, the friendly black kettle always steaming on the hob, and for his loneliness she had Mum's smile and her "How've you been getting on today, lovey?"

His landlady, Mrs. Beard, kept all her best "pieces" for the large front rooms which she could let at better prices than she could hope to get for the little back rooms, and into these last were dumped such miscellaneous bits of furniture as could not be used elsewhere.

Jeremy's furniture consisted of an iron camp-bed which sagged beneath its faded coverlet, a green-painted chest of drawers with a cracked mirror over it, a large deal wardrobe round which one had to walk to move anywhere within the room, and a substantial oak desk with a shelf filled with books above it.

He laid his hand affectionately on the ink-stained, scored oak.

"This is my own," he said. "I do my work here, though I'm afraid it's rather overflowed into the room." And he swept from a battered old basket chair its litter of books and papers, and pulled it closer to the little oil lamp, which he then proceeded to light.

"Let me do it," said Julie, noting the crusted, uneven wick which produced only a spiky flame and wisps of smoke when he tried to light it. "These things are terrible if they're not cut straight."

The little homely incident served to cover the first awkward moment, for to both of them had come a queer feeling of panic at being shut up in his room together. Neither of them had known where to look or what to say, but by the time the lamp was burning steadily and the kettle filled from a tap on the landing and set over it, they felt more at their ease.

Jeremy produced a tin of biscuits and another of *cafe au lait*.

"I don't go down to supper as a rule," he said. "It cuts up my evenings so much, so I just get myself a snack up here."

Julie felt very motherly and tender towards him, picturing him there alone every evening, making himself cups of coffee over the smoky, smelly little oil lamp and working on far into the night in pursuit of his star.

When the kettle had boiled and they had eaten a very different supper from what they had anticipated at the "Pally," Julie spoke again about his writing.

"Show me some of your work, Jeremy," she suggested, and he needed no second bidding, turning over his papers, choosing and discarding with that eager enthusiasm which made her feel so greatly his superior in age. He was like a small boy with a new toy, she thought lovingly.

"I'll read you the first act of the play I really think I'm going to be able to finish, shall I?" he asked. "Then I'll give you the rough draft of the rest of it. I'm going to make a model of a stage later on. That's what real playwrights do, I believe. You'll have to imagine it for now, though. This end of the room is the stage, see? Wings here—door here, and fireplace next to it—french windows into the garden there. That helps a lot. It does away with a change of scene, which is important in keeping the costs down, and it makes it more natural than having people bobbing in and out of an ordinary door into another room. Do you see? Can you make a mental picture of it? Now—Barlow is here by the door, Olive sitting at the desk—here's the desk . . ."

She watched him, hearing his voice rather than what it said, loving the quick way he moved, the dashing way he had of pushing aside even such small obstacles as a pen or a scrap of paper, just as if they were the brick walls she felt he could as easily brush aside with that eager enthusiasm.

His eyes glowed, he shook back a loose bit of hair as if it were in his impatient way; one hand held the sheaf of papers, but she noticed that he spoke with very little need even to glance at them.

He was in turns the various characters he had created, and he was inevitably an actor too, making each of them live for her through the medium of his words, whose beauty and clever choice she could not appreciate at their full worth, and his tone and gestures which gave them life.

"Well?" he asked at length, throwing down his script and coming in a stride to where she sat in the basket chair.

His face was pale and his eyes still wore that look of the dashing, self-opinionated Barlow whom his next act was utterly to confound.

"I think it's lovely," said Julie reverently.

Something flickered for an instant in Jeremy's eyes. It was as if a cloud had been drawn across the sun, or a curtain over a brilliant lamp. Julie realized that he was disappointed, but was at a loss to understand why. What had she said or not said? She had thought it lovely and had said so.

"No," he said shortly. "It isn't. It—well, it isn't meant to be lovely. I want it to be—well, definitely not *lovely*"—with a slightly derisive inflection on poor Julie's unfortunate choice of a word.

"I can't use the sort of words you do, Jeremy," she said timidly. "I only meant that—that it is terribly interesting . . ."

He was all eagerness again.

"That's better. That's what a first act must do—interest people. You see, nobody in the audience knows anybody in the play except by their names in the program, so the first act must interest them in all the main characters so that they form their own ideas as to what part they're going to play in subsequent acts. Tell me, how do you like them? How do they strike you? What about Olive? Will you want her to marry Barlow?"

Julie considered this with a little frown. In her heart of hearts she was a little afraid of the people Jeremy had created. They seemed unreal to her, seemed not to touch her own life in any way, and, realizing that they were the very fabric of herself—Jeremy—she felt that they took him away from her into a world of which she had no knowledge, in which she could have no part. She found these creatures of his hard, too clever.

"Is Olive the heroine?" she ventured doubtfully. "Is she—do you think she'd really ever want to marry anybody at all?"

"Of course she's the heroine. Don't you see that? She's in all their lives—Barlow's, Colter's, Barbara West's, young Beader's. She can link up with any of them. She holds them in her hands like strings. What will she choose to do? That's the problem I want everybody in the audience to feel faced with when the first curtain falls. What will she choose to do?"

"Well—I like Beader best," said Julie, and knew by his expression that again she had said the wrong thing.

"But he's so *simple*, my dear. He wouldn't do at all for a complex personality like Olive's," objected Jeremy almost

47

irritably. "He really suits a little nobody like Barbara—fireside and wireless and babies and so on, not life as Olive understands it."

Julie caught back a rather regretful little sigh. She saw herself as Barbara, knew that her own *milieu* was fireside and wireless and babies, and a little shiver went through her—for would not he, Jeremy, make a more fitting partner for Olive, with her ambitions and her open, grasping hands?

It gave her something of a shock to see the woman Jeremy had created for his heroine. To her simple and sincere mind the creation of such a heroine implied that she was of the type admired by the creator. Else why choose her for a heroine? And if that was the type Jeremy admired, what on earth was she, Julie Cave, doing in his life, presumably engaged to him?

Perhaps something of those unspoken thoughts found their way into his mind, for suddenly Jeremy threw down the papers he was fingering again, came to where she sat, and dropped down at her side on the floor. His hands closed over hers. All the ardor of the creator was gone from his face, and he was her familiar, beloved Jeremy again.

"You're cold and tired, my poor sweet," he said, "and here am I thrusting my puppets at you and asking you to live their lives instead of your own, which is so infinitely more worthwhile. Oh, Julie, let me hold you like this for ever! Never let me go!"

She sat with her world between her own two hands, and the menacing shape which had seemed to stand between them fled.

"I've so little to hold you by," she whispered unsteadily.

"So little? You've all that's worth having in the world or in heaven," he told her, between his kisses. "What's anything compared with this? I could lose my soul if I might keep yours instead of it, my Julie, my darling."

Even in his love for her he was either on the heights or in the depths. She was still a little afraid of him. She felt so truly that she had little with which to hold this ardent flame that burnt within him. She was a humble little person, and it seemed too wonderful for belief that Jeremy should love her, even for a little while.

He was kissing her hands, extravagant in his devotion to her as he was in anything else. Julie was dreamily content

48

when she could rid her mind of that fear that such happiness must be transient. She would enjoy it while she had it. At least, she would have been blessed.

"Julie, tell me something."

"Mm?"

"You seem so quietly contented, so utterly peaceful. Have you no ambitions? Nothing you want desperately that without it the world's gifts and glories are dust and ashes?"

She smiled at him.

"You'd laugh at me if I told you."

"I'd never laugh at you, Julie."

"Cross your heart, may you die?"

"Cross my heart, may I die!" repeated Jeremy.

"Then—a little home that I can love and work in, and—some day—a baby, Jeremy," she said very softly, and there were dreams in her eyes—dreams that made him feel strangely humble.

He laid his forehead on her clasped hands.

"And you thought I might laugh at you?" he asked, in a whisper. "Oh, Julie, I do love you so! When you look like that, say things like that—when I see how sweet and good you are, I feel so unworthy of you."

She smiled at that.

"Unworthy? You, Jerry? That's for me to feel," she said.

He shook his head.

"No. The things you want are worth getting. Deep down inside me I know that. I hanker after the destructible and you want the indestructible. Sometimes I think I'm reaching out after the shadows instead of the real things. It's like being in a place where you can't see the things as they are, but only their silhouettes on the blind, and the earthenware pot can cast just the same shadow as the golden vase. I know all that, and yet somehow it doesn't make any difference. I still want fame and power and everything else that money brings. I don't believe these things mean anything at all to you, do they, Julie?"

"Not much. You see, I've never had them, and yet we've been so happy without them. Perhaps having been so happy makes me a little—afraid of what might happen to us if we had them. You see, we shouldn't be us any more. We should become different people, strangers to ourselves and to one another."

He laughed, but there was love in his laughter. It did not hurt her.

"You'll have to get over being afraid because you're going to have all those things—place and power and money. You'll see. And now, my sweet, I'm going to take you home."

She rose a little regretfully. The regret, had she been able to analyze it, was rather because of something which in this intimate hour had been born to them—something alien to her, something vaguely disturbing. She did not want to end on that note. She longed to get back on her old familiar footing, and yet knew that there could be no stepping backwards. For good or ill, she must go forward now, and the way looked so much more strange and difficult than when she had so gaily entered upon it.

It was as if the Jeremy she had come to know and to love had turned to her another side which she had not dreamed was there, a side to which she would always remain a stranger. She felt that, turn which way she might, there was only one view of herself for Jeremy ever to see.

He gathered up his script carefully.

"If I get on with the other acts at the same rate as I've done the first, I ought to have the thing finished in a month or so," he told her.

"And then what?" asked Julie, rather wistfully.

"Then to find someone sufficiently interested to put up some money!" laughed Jeremy.

"I'll sit in the gallery on your first night and clap like mad," said Julie, as he tucked her into her coat and fastened the high collar closely about her neck in the proprietary way she loved.

"Gallery indeed! You'll be sitting in the stage-box and holding my hand to keep me from running away," he told her gaily.

She shook her head.

"I'd be much more comfortable in the gallery. Besides," she added sagely, "claps from the gallery will be much more valuable than claps from the stage-box that night!"

She was very quiet on the way home, quiet when he kissed her and left her on her doorstep, quiet while her mother, loving sometimes to turn her into a child again, helped her to undress in the room that sheltered the sleeping Biddy.

"Had a good time, my pet?" asked Mrs. Cave, brushing the silky brown hair.

"I didn't enjoy the dancing very much. I shall never turn into a grand society lady, I'm afraid"—with a little laugh that held a faintly strained note.

"You're something a lot better than that, my Julie."

"You're a doting and prejudiced old woman," said her daughter. Then, after a pause, "We left the dance early and I went to Jeremy's digs with him."

Mrs. Cave went on with the hair brushing, though for a moment her hand had trembled.

"He read the first part of his play to me," said Julie serenely. "It's clever—too clever for me, Mum. Somehow I—I don't think I like it very much, though that must be because I'm so stupid and ignorant. Only—it's a part of Jeremy I don't know, and it frightens me a bit. I know it's beastly of me, but in my heart of hearts I don't think I want him to be a playwright at all. I—I'm afraid I shall lose him."

"You love him, don't you, Julie?"

"Terribly," said Julie in a low, soft voice.

"It's a mistake to care for any man too much, darling," said her mother.

Julie smiled. Her eyes were misty—though perhaps that was only the effect of the candlelight.

"I don't think I should care for him too much," she said in the same soft voice. "Good night, Mum dearest. Go to bed now or you'll be dead tired in the morning."

Mrs. Cave sighed a little as she went softly away. Already, it seemed, this dear child was no longer altogether her own as she had been for twenty loving years. There was another, stronger claimant, and she, like all other mothers, must yield up the keys and just look on. There was so little now that she could do.

5

The front door bell rang.

"Postman," said Dickie between mouthfuls of porridge.

"I'll go, Mum," volunteered Biddy, sliding down from her chair.

"Expecting a letter from Clark Gable to ask you to do his next film with him, Greta Garbo?" inquired her brother affably.

Biddy "snuffed" him with the tea-cosy as she passed—an effective reply.

"Have you finished your history, Dickie?" asked Julie as he emerged.

"Almost," said Dickie, his voice thick with porridge, as he glanced down at the open book beside him. "The Peace of Utrecht 1713, the crowns of France and Spain shall never be united," he read. "What a lot of bilge! As if there wouldn't be the devil of a row in the world if anybody suggested uniting them!"

"Dickie, that's not your own observation," remarked Julie critically. "Don't hash up other people's remarks as if they were your own."

Mrs. Cave glanced at her in some surprise. Julie seldom had an edge to her tongue when she spoke to Dickie, but lately she had thought the boy was getting on his sister's nerves.

She sighed. It was all very well to say complacently that "the course of true love never did run smooth" when the true lover was not Julie, but Mrs. Cave felt that for Julie the way should be deep in rose leaves.

It was not that anything had actually happened between her and Jeremy. Rather was it that nothing had happened. It was now almost a year since that ecstatic walk in the rain. There had been the first weeks of radiant happiness, with Jeremy always in and out of the house, with Julie starry-eyed and dreamy, but after that the thing had drifted gradually into something Mrs. Cave did not understand.

There was no open talk of an engagement between them, and lately Julie seemed to shun any mention, however indirect, of the future. Her mother's heart ached for her, but she would not ask for a confidence that was not offered.

It did not occur to her that Julie understood the situation no better herself. She was ever ready with a dozen reasons why Jeremy did not come so often. Jerry was working all the free hours of the day and most of the night too, she said. Everything would be different when he got his play accepted, as of course he would in due course. The one or two people to whom he had shown even a part of it had said it was marvelous.

Her real thoughts about his neglect of her were hidden

deep in her heart lest she be even so little disloyal to Jeremy.

Although they had an occasional evening together, met frequently at lunch time, it all seemed so impersonal to her now. He filled the time with the constant recital of his hopes and fears, his railings against fate—fate which had seemed to Julie so beautifully kind in that it had brought them together—and in rehearsing to her speeches and scenes from his play, the play that was to lead them, or Jeremy at least, to the land of Heart's Desire.

Had they not already all that they really needed? Youth, love, jobs, each other? So thought Julie, but Jeremy thought far otherwise.

He seemed to despise these things, the quiet and durable things, because of the others that eluded his outstretched hands and of which Julie was so greatly afraid.

It had taken such a little time on that October morning to think all those thoughts, just long enough for Biddy to run to the door and open it—not to the postman, but to Jeremy himself, a Jeremy no longer disgruntled and discontented but radiantly glad.

"I've done it! I've done it!" he cried, rushed into the kitchen, snatched Julie up from her chair and whirled her round the room.

"Is this a private dance or can anybody join in?" demanded Dickie, while Biddy climbed on a chair and hammered Jeremy's head to make him aware of her excited questions.

He set Julie down at last, standing her on the breakfast table in spite of her breathless protests. Then he made her a sweeping bow.

"Madam, allow me to present to you Mr. Jeremy Denton, London's leading playwright, author of that astoundingly clever success, *The Bauble*, which . . ."

They shouted him down and gradually out of the pandemonium they elicited the information that the play had been accepted by Paston, a well-known London producer, and was to be financed by Roy Maitland, who had financed half the successful plays of the past few years and seemed to have an unfailing flair for potential winners.

Julie and Biddy and their mother plied him with eager questions, while Dickie got stolidly on with his breakfast, seizing an unprecedented opportunity, which might never come again, of eating Biddy's piece of toast as well as his own.

At last Julie and Jeremy were alone, walking down the road on their way to work.

"Julie, aren't you glad?"

She tucked a hand within his arm.

"Of course I am dear," she told him quietly—so quietly that he bent his tall head to look doubtfully at her.

"You don't sound very excited about it," he said dryly.

She smiled a little.

"Somebody's got to keep sane," she said, "and we'd better hurry or we shall lose the train."

"To blazes with the train! Think I'm going to the office today? Not so likely! I'm a playwright, not a clerk!"

He was laughing even while he boasted, and Julie's heart was tender as she listened to him. He was so like Dickie when he had shot a winning goal, she thought—only he wasn't really a little boy. He was the man she was going to marry some day. It gave her a strange little pain to say those words, even to herself. She found it hard to believe them. It was not the months of drifting apart, not his changes of mood which she could understand and forgive, not the failures and despondence which had given her at least the chance to comfort and uplift him.

No, it was his success which threatened to separate them, as she had always in her heart feared it would.

"Well, if you haven't got to get to work, I have!" she said, hurrying. "I'm still one of the world's workers."

There was his chance, she thought. Now surely he would speak, say something definite. She had given him such an opening!

Even though she had reached some measure of understanding of him and his reluctance to be openly engaged to her, she had had a secret longing, as all girls do, for the day when she could be his for all the world to see, would wear his ring on her finger so proudly. Yet not even to her mother had she ever spoken of Jeremy as her fiance. Rather had she locked away her thoughts from that understanding mind. She had suffered without rancour, if with a secret regret, the little darts and pinpricks of the other girls in the workroom, notably of Sally, still flaunting her diamond ring and amassing, in odd moments, a delectable trousseau.

She had given him this opening, now that there seemed no longer any reason to wait, now that the main reason for the secrecy no longer existed.

Her heart grew colder as the seconds passed and he

longed to hear, had waited so patiently for him to say all these months?

Instead she felt that he was hurrying a little.

"Perhaps I'd better go and tell them I'm leaving," he said.

She swallowed hard and summoned her courage. She had her pride.

"You'll have to go in, Jeremy," she said. "You can't just let them down without giving them proper notice, can you?"

"Do you think they'd hesitate to sack me if it suited them?" asked Jeremy pugnaciously.

"Not without notice," insisted Julie, and at last, half reluctant to surrender to her in the arrogance of first success, he allowed her to have her way and went to the office to give formal notice, though she felt that he was rather rushing his fences.

"Suppose the play isn't a success?" she ventured to ask him, though the question seemed almost presumptuous, in the face of his assured pride in his achievement. Surely Fame had marked him for her darling at the outset.

He scoffed at the suggestion.

"Do you think anyone as experienced as Maitland would put his money into it if he weren't certain? No, my sweet, I'm definitely leaving Butcher's at the end of the week, and if they've got any decency they'll let me off now, today. Why, Paston might want me any minute. I can't be bothered booking potty little tours all day."

She loved his little-boy cockiness even while she feared it. She was so little arrogant and self-sure herself, but when she ran up the stairs at Monique's and into the work room, unconsciously she held her head higher, catching a little of Jeremy's assurance.

She told Sally as she worked. Jeremy had not sworn them to secrecy, and it was more than flesh and blood could endure to keep it all to herself.

Sally was openly envious.

"Gee, don't I wish Alfred could do something like that! You can't make much of a stir in the world over gas-fitting, can you? Just fancy, Julie! He may make pots of money and you'll be wearing furs and jewelery and maybe we'll be making your frocks for you! He may even be a lord one day, or at least sir! Fancy you being a ladyship, Julie"—with a little giggle that was not all derision. There was envy and a new respect mixed with it.

Julie bent her head over her work without replying. How passionately she wished Jeremy were like Sally's Alfred, though still Jeremy, of course. But then he wouldn't be Jeremy if he were like Alfred Bates, stolid and stodgy, a nobody, just like herself. How complex it all was! She caught back the treacherous thought that the play might not, after all, be such a success.

The next few weeks went by in a whirl for the Cave family, who, through Julie, identified themselves with all that was happening to Jeremy.

Julie's secret and unacknowledged treachery seemed doomed to failure, for Maitland,, satisfied that he had again backed a winner, spared neither money nor effort to make a success of this play by the young unknown writer.

The Bauble went into rehearsal with a good London cast.

The girl first chosen to play the part of Olive was Mavis Becker, a queer, temperamental star who could be unrivalled in brillance or utterly dull according to the reactions of her public life to her private one.

Jeremy was delighted with the choice and raved to Julie about it.

"I've been with her this afternoon, talked the part over with her, and she's marvellous—simply stupendous, so exactly like my Olive that it gave me a queer feeling that I haven't invented her after all! Or else that I'd invented Mavis Becker. Would you like to meet her, Julie?"

"Heavens, no! I should be scared stiff," said Julie, aghast.

"The play's made now," rejoiced Jeremy, and though she had to go on fighting the spectre of losing him to fame, Julie tried to rejoice with him.

A few days later he came to her, savage and despairing.

"The play's ruined—absolutely ruined!" he told her.

"Why?" asked Julie patiently.

"Mavis has thrown up the part because there isn't anything suitable in the play for her latest lover," he said bitterly.

Julie was slightly shocked.

"Wants me to write in a special part, and after I'd seen the fellow, all beef and no brains, I told her it was hopeless, that it wasn't an American gangster play, and that finished it. Paston suggests Beta Ward. Beta Ward as

Olive!"—with profound disgust.

"But I think she's much prettier than Mavis Becker," said Julie, who had made it her business to study and become familiar with the photographs of the leading stage stars.

He frowned.

"That's just the objection. Olive's not supposed to be pretty. Pretty girls don't want brains and as a rule a reasonable Providence sees that they don't get any. That's my whole point. Olive isn't a beauty. She gets all she wants out of life by brains, ambition, ruthless riding over every obstacle. Beta Ward will insist on making herself look pretty-pretty and the audience will wonder why on earth she has to work so hard to get her man!"

He was obliged to put up with Beta, however, and as the play began to take shape he seemed reconciled to the fact.

He managed to smuggle Julie into a rehearsal, and she was greatly disappointed in what she saw and heard.

To begin with, it was not even a proper theatre, and she had not the necessary imagination to supply the lack of atmosphere. It was in a shabby, incredibly dingy room, and throughout the scenes, which were jumbled up anyhow and had no real sequence, people came and went, conversations were conducted, nondescript meals went on round about.

She was deeply dejected for Jeremy's sake because she felt how bitter was going to be his failure. Her one consolation was that he would turn back to her for the comfort which would give him back to her.

Afterwards, in a tea shop opposite the rehearsal rooms, he pressed her for the commendation he needed to bolster up his own failing hopes.

"Do you like the play, Julie?"

She hesitated, arranging the thick cups and saucers and the slabs of buttered toast on the marble-topped table.

She hated to hurt him, but she felt she must be honest.

"Well—I don't think I can really express an opinion," she said at last. "I think it's too clever for me, and then—it was so confused this afternoon, wasn't it? I couldn't keep my mind on the play for people barging about the room."

He fidgeted with his cup.

"I've got used to that now," he said. "Tell me why you think it's clever. Do you mean that it's obscure?"

She did not quite understand that, but she did her best.

"Well, it is clever, isn't it? The things people say, the

57

way they twist one another's words and make them sound like something quite different."

He frowned.

"I wish you didn't feel that way about it," he said.

"But what do I matter?" asked Julie cheerfully. "I'm such an idiot really."

"But you do matter. Not just you, but—well, don't you see? It's no good writing stuff just for the clever people. For one clever person there are a hundred more ordinary ones, and it's the hundred we want to attract, not the one. If it's too clever for you, it'll be too clever for hundreds of others."

She smiled and poured him out another cup of tea.

"Oh, no, not necessarily," she said. "I'm stupid about modern things. I like old-fashioned plays, stories about love and happiness and people like ourselves. That's why I can't understand your play. It isn't about people like you and me and Mum and Biddy—but that isn't to say there aren't such people, or that others won't like it, is it?" she ended hopefully.

His face was heavy and depressed. He felt in such moments of despair that success was beyond bounds of possibility, that Paston was not doing his best for the play, that Beta would ruin it by her pretty-pretty ways and baby-girl talk, that by cutting some of his lines and adding others the whole character of the thing was being most unwarrantably changed. Fancy anyone daring to chop Shaw about—or Coward! They'd tell Paston where he got off—and so would he, Jeremy Denton, one of these days!

In vain Julie tried to change the conversation, to wean his mind from his troubles even for a few minutes. He refused to leave the matter alone, arguing and deriding her well-meant assurances, shifting his ground, refusing to be cheered or comforted. In the end they came nearer to quarrelling than they had ever done before, for in the past their arguments had been friendly and Julie had always been able to shift the conversation in the end to more personal and easy channels.

Everything conspired to irritate him that day, however.

Outside, two days' fog had given place to a cold drizzle; the small sum of money which he had had when he left Butcher's had dwindled by now to almost nothing, and he was too proud to ask Paston for the advance which any other playwright would reasonably have demanded; he was unhappy and frightened about the play; Julie had a cold and a red nose and ought, he knew, to be in bed instead of listening to his woes.

And he hated the cheap place they were in, the marble-topped tables without cloths, the thick, chipped cups, the girls who gossiped with one another in the hearing of the customers, the shabbily dressed people about them with their clothes smelling of wet and grimy wool.

"Let's get out of this filthy hole," he said suddenly and savagely, ignoring the fact that Julie was still contentedly crunching toast.

She looked at him in surprise.

"What's the matter with it?" she asked, for it was the same sort of place as that in which they usually had tea when they were out.

"Oh, for Heaven's sake don't be so damned contended with everything," he flared out at her, pushing his chair back so violently that it fell over with a thud and drew the attention of all eyes to their corner of the restaurant. "How do you ever expect to get anywhere or be anything if you're always so smug and satisfied?"

Her face flamed and her eyes filled with tears. She blinked them away furiously. She was tired and cold and depressed and she had a bad cold in her head, but that, she told herself resentfully, was no reason for making an ass of herself by crying in a tea shop.

Jeremy stalked to the counter and paid the bill, held the door open for Julie to go out into the dismal street, and strode beside her in silence to the bus stop. She glanced at his face furtively, but its stoical indifference offered her no comfort.

"We're quarrelling, Jerry and I are quarrelling—and he doesn't even mind," she thought miserably as they waited at the curb.

And on the top of the bus, whither they always climbed in preference to the crowded inside, he settled her in the back seat and slid his arm about her shoulders. She cuddled against him and struggled to keep back the foolish tears of sickness and weariness, blowing her nose vigorously on her scrap of a handkerchief.

He looked down at her, his face changing at the forlorn sight.

"Sorry, Julie," he said in the constrained and difficult voice of one to whom apologies come hard.

"Oh, Jerry. I'm such an idiot," she whispered to him shakily.

"Darling, you're not. You're the sweetest and loveliest thing in the world and I'm a beast to make you cry."

"You didn't. I'm not crying. It's only my cold," said Julie with another blow.

"Forgive me, Julie. I could kick myself. I ought not to be let loose in the world when I'm in this filthy mood," said Jeremy, vehement in his self-immolation as in everything else.

She swallowed, blinked, and smiled.

"There's nothing to forgive," she said. "How can there be when two people love each other the way we do? Oh, Jerry darling, we mustn't ever quarrel. I couldn't bear it, could you?"

But he was looking straight ahead, a curious expression on his face, a sort of startled wonder.

"Do you know, Julie, I've just had such a queer thought. It was almost as if, for a wild moment, I could wish the play would fail so that I'd know there was no—no danger ahead for us, nothing we can't foresee, so that we'd just got to settle down to a humdrum life, me still at Butcher's and going up on the 8:16 and coming home every day on the 6:35 to find you there . . ."

His voice trailed off into a silence pregnant with Heaven knew what thoughts, and Julie closed her eyes against a vision so sweet as to be almost pain. If only life could be like that to them!

Then she crushed down the thought, realizing what such humdrum peace would cost him in failure and bitterness. No, Jeremy must succeed for his own happiness.

"I'll be happy anywhere—any way—with you," she said.

He held her closely in the dim emptiness of the bus stop.

"How sweet you are, Julie!" he said remorsefully.

She clung to him and they kissed. If only life could go on like this forever, this journey through the wet December night never end, Jeremy never be different from what he was now, his arm in its shabby coat sleeve about her, their faces close together, their hearts holding only each other.

They parted soberly at the door, Jeremy refusing to come in.

"I'm not fit company for anyone tonight, sweetheart," he told her, but there was a greater peace in her heart and on her calm little face than there had been for a long time.

What could go wrong with them if their love held? Tonight it was impossible to believe that it could ever break.

She did not see Jeremy the next day. He wanted to be all day at the rehearsal, preventing as far as was possible the inroads on his script which Paston made so unconcernedly and without reference to him, the author—"only the author" as he recognized himself to be. Incidentally he made a great nuisance of himself to those who knew so much better than he what was permissible and what was clumsy or merely dull. Paston sent him out on numerous fictitious errands, to look up details which nobody needed in records which were difficult to find, so that rehearsals could proceed in the orderly disorder which everybody but Jeremy understood and accepted.

But he spent the afternoon alone in his room, and that evening came a letter for Julie, dropped unstamped into the letter box of 26 Hemming Road by a Jeremy who did not even knock before he went away.

Julie slipped away from Biddy's inquisitive eyes and shut herself in the bathroom with her letter. It was the only place in the Cave establishment where any member of the family could find privacy. Biddy used it when she wanted to try out a new style of hairdressing or rehearse a new pose; Dickie took refuge in it when it seemed likely he would be impounded for washing up duty.

And Julie took her love letters there.

This was not a letter. As she read it, her eyes grew misty and very tender, and presently she knelt down beside the bath and rested her cheek against the typed sheets and closed her eyes.

"Oh, Jerry—my darling—my darling," she whispered.

This was what Jeremy in the fullness of his heart, in his love and understanding, in the knowledge of what was best in himself, had written for her:

AMBITION

The Child looked up with fearless eyes into the face of Life, who stood holding out to her an armful of delight— the toys of many lands, gay picture-books, multi-colored sweets, and fruits delectable. In the Child's arms was nothing but an old battered doll, its waxen cheeks pale from many kisses, its sawdust body shapeless from the close pressure of small arms. One fleeting glance of regret she gave it; then it slipped unheeded to the floor as she stretched out her hands towards the new, glittering delights.

The Girl gazed on Life with glowing eyes and parted lips, her hands clutching at first one and then another of the baubles he offered—but the silken stuffs fell to pieces as she caught at them, the jewels which had sparkled became strangely dull when she held them. She dropped them to snatch eagerly at some other thing that Life held out to her, only to let that fall in its turn where all the rest made an unlovely heap on the ground at her feet.

The Woman searched Life's face with restless eyes, her hands empty save for the torn threads of what had once been silk and the broken, tarnished metal that had looked like gold, its jewels now but bits of broken glass.

"And is this all?" she asked of Life; but he gazed at her with inscrutable eyes, and the tawdry scraps fell from her hands with a jingling clatter.

She groped amongst the rubbish for anything that might yet remain of all that had seemed so desirable and splendid, and as she groped, her hands found something which she lifted wonderingly, a strange warmth at her heart.

It was an old, battered doll.

Clasping it to her, she looked up again into the face of Life. He smiled with age-old wisdom and touched the thing she held to her breast. It stirred and uttered a cry.

The Woman looked—and at her breast lay a child.

The Mother looked with dream-filled eyes into the face of Life.

"See," she whispered, "at last I have laid aside all my ambitions."

Life smiled.

"All?" he asked.

The Mother looked at the child in her arms. Then she, too, smiled—and gathered it more closely.

6

Julie sat and watched a miracle.

She had refused all Jeremy's efforts to get her into the stage box which he, in all the glory of his first dress suit, occupied in company with Paston's wife and daughter and one or two theatrical folk who looked, to Julie's fascinated eyes, like denizens of an unknown world.

She sat tightly clasping her mother's hand on one side while on the other Biddy alternated between ecstatic enjoyment of the play and the need to appear sublimely at ease in a seat in the stalls and her very best dress.

Julie had survived the past two days solely by merit of her ability to remain calm in the storm center, for Jeremy had run the gamut of all human emotions and let her have the benefit of them. He had been in the depths of despair, torn with rage, with fear, with wild hopes, with jaunty pride, and again with utter despair after the final rehearsal, which seemed to prove beyond shadow of doubt that nothing short of a miracle could save the play from ghastly failure.

He had made such a nuisance of himself to everybody that Paston had threatened to throw the whole thing up and had put the entire cast into a fever of apprehension.

And yet, before their very eyes, this miracle had come to pass.

Julie watched with wide eyes and fast-beating heart and listened with ears which no longer cared whether they understood or not.

Jeremy's characters had come to life, were walking and talking and behaving as Jeremy had said they were to do. Beta Ward was no longer Beta Ward, the pretty and quite ordinary girl. She was Jeremy's Olive, hard, calculating, brilliant, her pretty face entirely subjugated by the intelliegence with which Jeremy had endowed her. Julie could not believe that these were the same people she had seen weeks ago, indolent, bored, mumbling their words and lounging through their parts in a way that had infuriated her for Jeremy's sake.

The first act—how poignant was her memory of the first time she had heard that!—left the audience interested, intrigued, unable to decide whether all this was very clever or merely silly.

Future audiences would have the advantage over this one. Basil Cargery of the *Meteor* and H. K. Liffer of the *Evening Sun* and Quest Malliter of the *Daily Wire* would have made up their minds for them, and told them what it would be fashionable to think about the new play and its writer, whether they were to be admired, laughed at, or

63

merely ignored. Tonight's audience, denied that inestimable advantage, had to make up its own mind.

As the play progressed, Julie's heart swelled with pride or shrank with pain for Jeremy according to whether or not their response showed them to be understanding the play as Jeremy meant it to be understood. He had talked to her so prolifically about it during these months that even Julie understood what each situation, each line almost, was intended to convey. Here people should laugh, here they should preserve a hushed and almost reverent silence, here they should seem excited and stimulated by a novel turn to the plot.

She watched for them all, scarcely daring to glance up at where Jeremy sat, white-faced and tense, suffering as she knew he must be suffering.

When the last curtain fell, the applause was reasonably satisfactory if a little restrained by uncertainty. The play had struck a new note, offered a strange flavor to the public palate, which of late had been given slightly insipid and over-sweet musicals.

The curtain rose to give them glimpses of Beta Ward, always a favorite with London audiences, again to enable her leading man to join her, and then the entire cast.

Finally it rose to reveal Jeremy himself, shepherded towards the footlights by a smiling, bowing Paston, who discreetly retired and left the author alone.

To Julie's loving eyes, into which the tears had started, he looked pitifully young and thin, unfamiliar in his new black-and-white splendor. Then he put up a hand and ruffled his hair in a well-known gesture, making one bit stick up straight above his head, and abruptly he became Jeremy again, though she could neither see him any more for the mist of her tears nor hear him for her heart beats.

People seemed to approve of what he said, of his unaffected, boyish demeanour now that extreme nervousness had robbed him of his arrogance. He made them laugh, which was always a good thing, and then the curtain fell for the last time and the home-going scurry began, decorously subdued for the few brief moments while the Almighty was petitioned to save the King.

With the thrill of the play over, with its success probably assured, with the curtain shutting away Jeremy in that unreal world of his puppets, Julie felt an unaccustomed loneliness and depression. She almost wished now that she

64

had yielded to his persuasions and gone with the people who would undoubtedly be sharing his happiness with him tonight.

"They only want to know him because he's important tonight," she thought rebelliously. "I belong to him. I'd want just as much to be with him if he had failed and was unhappy. It's I who ought to be there, not these people he's only known a few months. What an idiot I was not to go with him!"

She consoled herself with the thought of Jeremy's promise to have a word with her before she left, but though they hung about near the entrance for some time after everybody else had left, and the lights were being put out outside the theatre, they did not catch a glimpse of him.

Mrs. Cave spoke to one of the workmen who was covering up the plush seats in the foyer.

"Do you know whether Mr. Denton has left?" she asked. "The author of this play, you know"—with a little touch of pride.

"Couldn't say, madam," replied the man, obviously not impressed by the amethyst gown even though Julie had made a wrap of rabbit-edged velvet to go with it. "You won't be likely to get a sight of him at this door, though. Be leaving by the stage door. Got a party on, I expect. They generally do after the first night—that is, if the play's any good."

"Oh, do you think they will tonight? I mean—is the play good, do you think?" asked Julie uncontrollably.

The man nodded and went on with his work. He was tired and didn't want to stop, gassing to chatty females at this time of night. If they'd been to the play, they ought to know, anyway.

"It'll do," he said briefly. "About time we did put on something with a decent run 'ere. Proper Jonah, this place"—with which rather vague allusion he left them to go their way.

"Well, it's no good waiting any longer," said Julie at last, forcing herself to sound brisk and matter-of-fact. "I expect he has crowds of things to see to and people wanting to talk to him. Come on, Biddy."

Mrs. Cave found Julie's hand and gave it a little squeeze of understanding, but her private thoughts were not kind to Jeremy. He might have spared one moment from his triumph for the girl to whom he would have been just as dear—perhaps dearer—if it had been a failure instead of triumph. She had borne all the brunt of the past weeks uncomplainingly, and he would undoubtedly have fled to her if he had failed. When he had succeeded, it appeared that she no longer mattered.

Biddy was still in a haze of delight.

"Oh, Julie, weren't the dresses heavenly?" she breathed, as they waited for their bus. "Did you notice the silver-fox cape Beta Ward wore in the second act? How much do you think it cost?"

"About a hundred pounds, my chuck," said Julie.

Biddy sighed ecstatically.

"How gorgeous to be able to spend a hundred pounds on something you don't really need to cover you! When you're married to Jerry, Julie, you'll be able to have clothes like that, won't you? You'll be Somebody then."

Julie laughed a little sadly.

"I'm afraid I'll never be Somebody with a capital S," she said. "I guess I'll be the little brown sparrow at the end of the chapter. Besides, it wouldn't suit me to wear blue lame and silver fox. I'd fall over the train in the kitchen when I was making Welsh rarebit for Jerry's supper," she ended gaily.

"Pff! You won't have to be getting anybody's supper. You'll have butlers and things, and they'll call you moddom like they do in the big shops and bring round finger bowls with rose petals floating in the scented water."

Julie and Mrs. Cave laughed.

"What have you been reading—*Lady Gwendoline's Diary*?" asked Julie teasingly. "I certainly shouldn't know what to do with a butler if I had one."

"Well, *I* should," said Biddy with calm assurance. "I'm going to have ten servants at least when I get married. I simply couldn't do with less!"

They laughed at her again, but she never minded that. They were used to her aspirations and did not doubt her ability to achieve them or anything else on which she set her mind.

"First catch your millionaire," suggested Mrs. Cave. Then, with a little sigh, "If you weren't such an absurd child, I should be worried about your heartless greed."

Biddy grinned, twisting her face up to her mother's with one of those provocative looks which showed her already more wordly-wise than her older sister. It was the gesture of a born coquette, and Mrs. Cave recognized it with something between a laugh and a sigh. This seemed too queer a chick to have got into her nest. "The Cuckoo Child," Julie had once called her.

"Darling," said Biddy, "even millionaires are men, and there seems no reason why one shouldn't fall in love with a rich man just as well as a poor one. It's only a matter of care, and not being in too much of a hurry, and not falling for the first man that comes along. Look at Julie, now! It was a perfectly idiotic thing to fall for Jerry like that, though it seems it's going to turn out O.K. after all. I don't mind betting, though that if he'd shown signs of being a success when you first met him, you'd have kept out of his way, wouldn't you?"—turning her impish attention to Julie, who was unusually quiet.

"Would I?" she asked. "Well—perhaps. I'm not really cut out for a grand life with money and servants and things. I'd rather go on with the sort of life I'm used to."

"Oh, Julie, you do make me wild with you! You've always been silly about stray cats and dogs and filthy babies belonging to tramps and things. If it hadn't been for Mum and me being firm with you, you'd have turned the house long ago into a Home for the Lost and we'd have all had to go and sleep underneath the arches."

That turned into laughter a conversation threatening to become too big a discussion at a bus stop, and as the bus appeared at that moment, the subject was abandoned.

Long after Biddy had gone to sleep, probably to find in her dreams all the glories of her intended future, for she smiled angelically in her sleep, Julie lay awake.

She was struggling against the lost and abandoned feeling she had when the curtain dropped to shut Jeremy from her sight.

Until tonight he had been here. They had shared all that mattered to each other, intimately, exclusively. To no one else had he revealed his inmost self, his hopes, his dreams, his ambitions, his arrogant certainty of success, the rare moments of self-distrust. Only Julie had known him as he was. Only to Julie had he belonged.

And now, after tonight, after a success which, if not sensational, was still noteworthy, he was exclusively hers no longer. Tomorrow most of London would read his name and afterwards he would have his life planned for him by circumstances and other people. Into his play had gone so much of himself that until now only Julie had known. Now anybody who could pay for a seat would share her knowledge with her.

She thought of his life and could not picture it as her life too. Tonight he had become unreal to her. Between that slim, unfamiliar figure on the stage and herself had stretched a sea of people—people she did not know, would never know, who would have no place in her life. But all these people had had their faces turned to Jeremy. All of them had known who he was. They had smiled at him, clapped their hands, listened to him, laughed with him. They belonged to him and he to them. In none of it did she, Julie, have any part.

Had she known it, that moment had been as strange to Jeremy as to her, the sea of faces a formless mass which offered him neither comfort nor assurance. Then he had found himself speaking without knowing what he said. He was one of the actors in a play, speaking a rehearsed part. People had laughed a little and clapped; someone had drawn him back into the wings and he had shaken himself into reality again.

People were waiting for him, making much of him and congratulating him, the same people who had grown so tired of his persistence at rehearsals. Beta Ward was there, a pretty little nobody again now that she was robbed of the personality he had lent her; Clive Williams, her leading man, as suave and gentle off the stage as he had been ruthless and hard on it. Little Milly Erson, with her first real part, was excited and pleased, and hung on to his arm with a familiarity born of tonight's intoxication. He smiled at her absently.

Roy Maitland, cynically amused at himself for having again proved his perspicacity and further enriched his coffers, came to pat him on the back and make tentative inquiries as to his future plans.

Paston, revivified and beaming, came to hustle them all away to their dressing rooms and to invite them to supper later at the Mayflower, the latest and brightest night haunt for stage folk.

He turned back to Jeremy.

"We might as well get along, Denton," he said. "I've put in some useful work amongst the Press. Dannett of the *Daily Post* is coming along, and there's a new man, Joyce, from the *Evening Mail* who looks worth cultivating.

68

They'll all be glad of a word with you. Better tell me what you propose to say, and then say it. Don't blether, and for any sake don't get on that soapbox of yours about your ambitions and ideas and Lord knows what. Remember that anything you say will be taken down and used in evidence against you later on, when you've grown up and altered your ideas."

For Jeremy had let himself go once or twice, and shown them all how he proposed to remake the universe. Paston, worldly-wise and disillusioned years ago, had been faintly amused, but felt it would not do to let this youngster say things which later on, when success had matured him, his critics would make him eat.

"Remember, boy," he concluded, "you're in the hands of these men for good or ill."

Jeremy frowned. He resented the suggestion that anyone but Jeremy Denton could make or break Jeremy Denton. However, in the end Paston told him what to say and he found himself meekly saying it, though privately he reserved to himself the right both to think and to say what he liked in time to come.

When the Press representatives had left him, Roy Maitland was waiting for him, an inscrutable smile on his face. He had seen many stars rise and set, many of these "precocious youngsters" tried in the fire that proved them, as a rule, to be more dross than true metal.

"Coming now, Denton? I think you've handed out all the bouquets—and wreaths," he said.

Jeremy hesitated, looking round. He had half said he would see Julie before she left the theatre. A frown crossed his face. If she had done the sensible thing and gone into the stage box with him as he had wanted her to do, she would be here with him now, part of this queer, still incredible world he had invaded. Instead she had remained outside; and even while he resented her absence, he could not visualize her here.

"Come on, Denton," called Maitland from the doorway; and Jeremy fumbled a little self-consciously with the spring that turned a pancake into the glory of an opera hat and followed him.

After all, he had only half promised Julie, and he couldn't very well keep Maitland waiting any longer—and, anyway, it was her own fault.

At the restaurant, a gay place where the glory of

departed stars and the faint radiance of others not yet risen mingled with the splendors of those now in the ascendant, Jeremy was surrounded and made much of it. It was his day now. Stage folk, influential people, hangers-on of all sorts came to him, flattering, advising, making him drink more than he wanted or was good for him. His head whirled and grew a little too large and too light, for he was young and the world was a golden ball tossed carelessly at his feet. He could pick it up or kick it away, just as he liked.

So he drank and laughed and forgot Julie.

He remembered her again, overwhelmingly, when at last Paston left him, dazed and half asleep, in the tiny flat he had been persuaded to take in a little West End street. Everybody had told him he would find it more convenient than going out to Norwood, and he had not dared to think what he would do with it if *The Bauble* failed.

It was the flowers that reminded him of Julie. They were daffodils, a great sheaf of them in a blue jar standing on his table—not the old, ink-stained oak desk, but a new steel-topped affair.

She had brought him the flowers that morning, racing there in her lunch hour to give them to him, standing on tiptoe to kiss him, that inward, glowing look in her eyes which seemed to make them the very spirit and essence of her.

"They'll be the first thing you see when you come home tonight, Jerry," she had said in her soft voice. 'Whether it's been bad or good, whether you come home glad or sorry, you'll see the flowers here and they'll say to you, "Julie loves you just the same, whichever way it is.' "

He remembered, with a little touch of shame, that he had been inclined to sneer at her speech, had thought it foolishly sentimental. Girls simply didn't talk like that nowadays. Why, he'd be jeered at from the gallery if he made his heroine say things like that!

But tonight, with the inevitable reaction of the past exciting hours upon him, he was glad to remember what she had said. Somehow Julie was like that. She was such a quiet little thing, never obtrusive, always preferring the background to the limelight; and yet she had a way of stealing in upon you unawares, at times like this, and filling a need you didn't even realize you felt.

He bent down and smelt the daffodils, their cool petals
70

like the touch of Julie's fingers; and, raising his head again, caught sight of himself in a mirror and stopped, aghast. He looked away and then back again, fascinated with disgust. Was this really he, Jeremy Denton? This dishevelled, white-faced, red-eyed creature whose feet would not let him get as steady a view of himself as he wanted?

He reeled into the bathroom, plunged his head under the cold-water tap, scrubbed his wet hair vigorously with a towel, and went back, saner now, to look again at Julie's flowers. He seemed to draw from them something of Julie's own self—her freshness, her honesty, the sweetness that was the very essence of her.

He flung himself down at his desk and wrote her a wild, impassioned letter which would certainly have startled and upset her had she ever received it.

Perhaps she would have done had the telephone bell not rung as he was writing.

He glanced at his watch. Half past two! Who on earth could want to speak to him at such an hour?

Julie? His thoughts rushed to her in an agony of apprehension which sounded in his voice when he stretched out a hand and snatched up the receiver.

"Yes? Who is it? What is it?" he asked quickly.

A laugh answered him—a woman's laugh, low-toned, slightly husky, infinitely attractive—but certainly not Julie's.

Then she spoke.

"Is it you, Jeremy Denton?" she asked.

"Yes, but . . ."

She stopped his question by asking it herself.

"Who am I? You don't know. Perhaps you'll never know. And even if I told you my name, you'd be no wiser—tonight. Tomorrow, if you were sufficiently interested, you might be able to find out quite a lot about me, and then the romance would be over."

Jeremy was still not quite sober, and this woman with her alluring voice and her mystery had broken in on his impassioned love letter so that it seemed almost as if he had created her out of his thoughts—except that she did not sound in the very least like his Julie. She was just Woman—impersonal, mysterious.

He laughed a little unsteadily.

71

"Is this romance, then? he asked.

"Well, isn't it? What shall we call it? "Voice of the Night," by Jeremy Denton, the popular young playwright?"

Jeremy had learned quite a lot since his play had gone into rehearsal. For one thing, he had met a number of different types of women. Mavis Becker, in their one short interlude, had been an education to him. Tonight he had met more of them—lovely and clever women some of them, but each one with something to teach him. They had laughed with him, and he had found that his tongue had a light, gay twist to it when he so desired.

He was not tongue-tied with this unknown voice as once he would have been.

"Wouldn't it be more poetic to call it "Midnight Angel?" he asked.

She laughed.

"Except that it is long past midnight and angels fold their wings at night," she said. "Tell me, Jeremy: What does it feel like to be a successful playwright?"

"Am I that?" he asked.

She laughed again, softly and provocatively.

"Are you not? You'll be more successful in later plays, though."

"Why do you say that?"

"If I told you, you'd ring off."

"No."

"No? Is that a promise? Well—by the time you write another play, you'll have learnt more of life. You won't be so beautifully—young, Jeremy."

Her voice mocked him and he found himself flushing angrily. Only her taunt that he would ring off prevented him from doing so.

"Is that a crime?" he asked crisply. "How old do you imagine I am, by the way?"

"About sixteen, judging from the way you said that," she teased him. Then, as he made no reply: "Jeremy, are you still there?"

"Yes."

"Angry?"

"Why should I be? You so obviously don't know me, and I can't imagine why you rang me up," he said huffily.

"Can't you? Can't you, Jeremy?"

Her voice was soft and beguiling again, and he clenched his fist on the desk to remind himself that he was angry.

"Jeremy, are you still listening?"

"Yes."

"Then—shall I tell you why I rang you up, or shall I leave you guessing?"

"Why should you imagine that I have sufficient interest in you to trouble?" asked Jeremy.

"Because you're a man and young, and I'm a woman—and young too, Jeremy. Also because I'm mysterious to you and men love mystery in a woman, the lure of the unknown. You should know that, if you're going to write about men and women. In some men it works itself out in travel, exploring the wilds. But with you, Jeremy, it wouldn't work out that way. You'd rather explore the mystery of a woman."

"What makes you think you know so much about me?" demanded Jeremy.

Her voice and her laughter tantalized him. She seemed to offer so much and give nothing.

"I've been watching your play, listening to you and your ideas—and ideals—and you've given yourself away. In other plays you won't put in so much of yourself. You'll have learned discretion—and many other things!"

"Such as?" inquired Jeremy, not knowing whether to feel flattered or insulted.

"Oh—life in general. You've got so much to learn; and the lessons are going to be so fascinating to you—and to me, perhaps. Who knows?"

Through it all ran the strain of mockery which both attracted and enraged him.

"Who are you?" he demanded.

She laughed.

"Midnight Angel," she told him.

"Are we going to meet?"

"Interested, Jeremy?"

"Naturally. You'd have been disappointed if I answered that question differently, wouldn't you?"

"Perhaps. Some day, possibly. But, as I told you, we shall lose the romance once I clothe my voice with a body," she told him.

"Isn't it a nice body?"

"Oh, quite nice, I'm told," she laughed. "Anyway, good

night. Dream sweetly. You should do."

"Won't you give me any idea who you are? How am I to see you?"

The only answer was the click of the receiver; and after waiting for some moments in the hope that she might return, Jeremy hung up at his end and sat looking at nothing.

The room seemed strangely empty and cold now that her voice had ceased. He felt she had been there with him, intimately in his room, and had gone away again.

He tried to fit a personality to that voice, saw her only as a *femme fatale*, dark-haired to match the husky, rather deep voice, slightly indolent of body, luxuriously environed, a little spoiled by circumstances or she would not have over-stepped the bounds of convention by telephoning to a perfectly strange man at such an hour.

Here imagination failed him. He could not guess her age. She had told him she was young; but, as she seemed content to remain only a voice to him, that might have been a pose. She had sounded experienced, too sure of herself for extreme youth.

The thought of her tantalized him. He put out his hand to take up the telephone again with some vague idea of asking the operator who had been ringing him, but reflected that it would probably be impossible for them to trace a London call on the automatic dialling system.

His hand, in falling, touched the letter he had been writing to Julie. He read the words over. A few moments ago they had come from him, vital, warm with love and desire. Now they seemed oddly robbed of life. He could no longer associate them with the girl to whom they had been written. They would better fit some other woman, some more vivid personality. . . .

His thoughts paused. Had some mysterious agency been at work on his brain, a forewarning of that strange new contact he had made? He could conceive of these words—eager, passionately desirous—being devised for the woman with whom he had spoken; but they did not suit Julie. She would have been shocked at them, for he always felt that there was a little, just a little, of the prude about Julie—well, perhaps it was not so much prudishness as an old-fashioned primness.

Slowly he tore the written sheets across and across and dropped the pieces in the wastepaper basket.

Dear little Julie!

Loyally he tried to fill his thoughts with her when at last he was in bed, but she eluded him, and he dreamed of himself in an impenetrable forest, chasing an unseen himself in an impenetrable forest, chasing an unseen him, but never let itself be seen. The trees above him were making strange and unnatural noises, like the clapping of a million hands, and then a cold wind blew through them and the noise was more like jeering laughter, terrifying him so that he ran faster, but could not escape them. He knew that somewhere beyond the trees Julie waited for him, but she could no more get in than he could get out.

He woke in a heavy perspiration of fear to hear his telephone bell ringing from the next room. Cursing himself for his negligence in having forgotten to switch over to his bedroom receiver, he crawled out of bed and stumbled, still half asleep, into the sitting room.

It was Paston.

"Seen the papers, I suppose?" he was asking.

Jeremy's heart soared and sank. Until that moment he had actually forgotten!

"No. Any good?" he forced himself to ask.

"As good as one could hope, almost—certainly a lot better than one dared to expect," said Paston cheerfully. "Funny bloke, aren't you? What have you been doing? Sleeping?"

"I was late last night," Jeremy reminded him, wishing he would stop talking so that he could get at the newspapers.

"The devil you were—and a bit bottled too! Anyway, get hold of the papers. The porter will get you a batch; but for the love of Pete don't talk to anyone till I get there, you young idiot!" and he rang off.

The porter had obligingly anticipated his request, and a pile of newspapers came up at once in the service lift—which was a secret joy to Jeremy after the grudging and inefficient attention he had endured for so many years at the hands of Mrs. Beard and her satellites. All he had to do now was to press a button, speak into the tube, and his wants were at once supplied.

He snatched the pile of papers and glanced feverishly at the theatrical news in each to get the gist of the criticism on *The Bauble*. He could pore over them at his leisure once he knew the worst.

The worst, apparently, was that he was too young. He

grimaced at that, remembering the voice on the telephone, its mockery in the same accusation.

But the criticisms were favorable, even those which insisted on his youth. They praised his style, his contrasted characters, credited him with a certain crispness and clarity of dialogue which found favor particularly with the older reviewers, who were weary of ultra-modern fashions in dialogue, their slipshod English, and enigmatical allusions.

They praised Beta Ward, these older reviewers, for breaking away from the idiotic little-girl intonation and phrasing in which hitherto she had specialized; and Jeremy grinned at the thought that he, Jeremy Denton, was giving a leg-up to such an established actress as the Ward!

This play has most of the ingredients of success, wrote Dannett of the *Daily Post*. When Mr. Denton's experience of life and theatre craft is a few years older, I confidently look forward to his production of not merely a pleasant, amusing play like *The Bauble*, but a great play.

Jeremy glowed and set that one aside for further study.

It was all so much better than he had dared to hope. Even last night, with the actors bringing to vivid life his pen-and-ink people, he had felt that that huge audience would find him out, realize how ignorant, how inexperienced, how—yes, how *young* he was!

But they had clapped him, bless them! They had laughed with him and not at him. And now the newspapermen, whom he had dreaded, were telling other people to go and see his play.

"A great play," Dannett prophesied for him. Yes, he would write it! He would come to a day when he would look back on *The Bauble* with affectionate, pitying tolerence as a stepping-stone—his first.

He threw the papers aside at last and turned to the pile of letters which had come at the same time, business letters for the most part, for people could not have written to him yet about his play.

But yes—there was one from Julie.

He looked at the small neat writing with a feeling of warmth about his heart, a warmth quite different from the glow of pride the newspapers had given him. They praised him for what he had done. Julie loved him whether he achieved anything or not, and in that thrill of tenderness for her he pressed the paper against his lips before he read the letter, smiling at his own sentiment.

She had written and posted it before she went to the theatre on the previous evening so that, whatever happened to his play, he should have her letter the next morning.

It was like a bit of herself—simple and natural, a little inarticulate, yet breathing in every word her devotion to him.

He looked with a hot feeling of distaste at the torn scraps of paper in his basket, the letter he had been writing last night when the telephone rang. He was thankful that, whatever the cause, he had been prevented from sending it to Julie. She would have hated it.

"I want to speak to Miss Cave," he replied, to the "refined" voice from the showroom, and the "refainment" vanished at once.

"All right. Hang on a minute, will you?" And a few moments later came Julie's voice.

"I'll get in a row, Jerry." she said nervously. "We aren't supposed to use the telephone for private calls."

"That be blowed for a tale!" said Jerry cheerfully. "Lunch with me?"

"I'd love to."

"Right-ho! Top of the street at one?"

"O.K." And Julie sped away with wings to her feet.

"It hasn't altered him a bit, being famous," she told herself happily. He was just the same and wanted her still. Joy of joys, he wanted her still! She scorned herself for the wakeful hours of the night that had put shadows beneath her eyes.

But just before one, an apprentice came up the stairs.

"Telephone for you again, Miss Cave. Better look slippy. *She*'s down there."

It was Jeremy, very apologetic.

"Darling, I know it's a rotten trick, but I can't manage lunch today, after all. Maitland wants me to lunch with him at the Waldorf. I'm telephoning from his suite there now."

"Oh! Oh—well, all right, Jerry," said Julie, in a flat voice.

"I'm frightfully sorry. You know that. I hate to let you down, but this is so important. Fennimore's coming in after lunch—you know, Giles Fennimore, the actor-manager. It would be such a great stunt if he took my next

77

play, and Maitland thinks there's a chance. Oh, Julie, you do understand, dear, don't you?"

"Yes," said Julie.

She did understand. She knew that Jerry ought not to miss such a chance just to have lunch with her, yet it gave her a forlorn feeling of unimportance.

"Look, Julie darling. We'll have dinner somewhere tonight—oh no, I can't tonight. I've promised to go—well, you wouldn't know them, anyway. Tomorrow lunch, though? Cross my heart, may I die. Can you get an extra half hour?"

"I'll try."

"Oh, honeybunch, don't sound so—so flattened!"

"I feel rather flattened," said Julie. "I'll have to go now, though, or Madam will flatten me still more. You'd better not ring me up again here, Jerry. Good-bye"—and she put up the receiver before Madam completed her intention of sailing across the showroom with a reprimand to her.

"That's all Jerry and I seem to say nowadays—good-bye," thought Julie sadly. "Always good-bye. Oh, well . . ." And, like the philosophical little soul she was, she made the best of it and put in an extra half hour's work instead of going out during the lunch hour in order to be able to take longer the next day.

7

Jeremy's second play was produced nine months after *The Bauble*, and it was at once obvious to the observant that those had been crucial months in his life.

In the first interval on the opening night, the critics discussed him rather than the play, which he had called somewhat enigmatically, *Antimony*, and whose success was too much a foregone conclusion to be worth much discussion.

"He's grown up," grunted Dannett, of the *Daily Post*.

"Too quickly," said Pether, of the *Comet*. "I never could stand mushrooms, and they're often just toadstools."

"He's gained a lot in experience, though," argued Joyce, of the *Evening Mail*. "Edges are rubbed smooth. The dialogue flows. Nothing jagged about it as there was in *The Bauble*.

Bainbridge, their veteran, paused on the verge of a comment, and the others waited instinctively for him. They would never have admitted that they took their tone from him or anyone else, and yet they all knew they disliked being caught holding a completely different view from that of the grey-haired man who knew neither fear nor favor, and who had done much to keep up the standard of theatrical productions for a run of years.

"Isn't it usually the uneven edges which give a thing individuality?" he asked at last. "If all the ins and outs of our faces were rubbed down smooth, there wouldn't be much to distinguish any of us, would there?"

"You think Denton's become commonplace?" queried Dannett.

"No—not yet, anyway. He's still individual, and he has his own turn of wit—not always too kind in this play, I thought. He's gained a lot of knowledge of stage tricks, times his crises better; but he's lost quite a lot too. In his last play he wasn't so sure of himself. In this one he's a bit too sure. That's how it strikes me, anyway."

"He's more polished," demurred Joyce, who rather resented Bainbridge's supremacy.

"Yes. It's only when they cut and polish a diamond that they can get any real appreciation of its value," said the older man dryly.

"You don't suggest that Denton's no diamond?"

Bainbridge shrugged his shoulders and paid for his drink. He neither accepted nor paid for anyone else's on these occasions.

"Oh, no. He'll probably adorn the London stage for years and get more polished with each play," he said. "It all depends whether one's tastes are for real diamonds or just for something that sparkles."

"Are you going to damn it with faint praise?" asked Pether.

"No. I shall recommend it. After all, it's my job to give the public a fair idea of whether or not they are likely to enjoy a play. My personal opinion doesn't matter two hoots, because they'll like *Antimony*. It sparkles. Shall we go in now? That was the bell."

The play certainly did sparkle. It was lighter than *The Bauble*, and the audience, who had been uncertain about Jeremy Denton's first play but had been assured by the critics that it was clever, congratulated themselves now on their mental ability in being able to understand and appreciate cleverness.

Mavis Becker was the leading lady, for Beta Ward was still playing to reasonably full houses in *The Bauble* at the Vanity Theatre. Maitland had backed his own judgment by putting the new play on at the Duke's Theatre, which held another hundred or two in its more expensive seats.

Mavis scintillated in the part of Jeremy's new heroine, whose intrigues were redeemed from sordidness by sparkling dialogue and lavish display. Opposite her played Jack Lorrin, insolently assured of his place in the affections of London playgoers. They knew they were in for a long run, and they gave to the play all they had. The stuff was light as froth, spiced and perfumed with something which Jeremy himself had scarcely known he possessed until his lines, with their subtle innuendo, came trippingly from the lips of Mavis and her lover.

Paston rubbed his hands over the hard bargain he had driven with Jeremy, having no conscience about taking advantage of his youth and inexperience. These would not last for ever, and there would be time enough in the years ahead for Jeremy to make for himself the fortune which at present he was busy making for his backers.

Jeremy sat in a box with Maitland and Paston. The latter was an expert showman, and he had contrived to persuade fashionable London that it was the thing to be seen at a Denton first night, so the house was packed with an expensive audience. There was very little "paper" even in the stalls, for Paston believed in the power of *The Bauble* to make people pay for their seats at Jeremy's second venture.

Jeremy, assured very early in the play of its success, gave more of his attention to the audience than the players. He was still sufficiently *ingenue* to be secretly thrilled at the thought that all these people had come here, had dressed in lovely clothes, dined early many of them, in order to see his play and listen to the words he had written. He warmed to their interest and laughter. They gave him a swelling sense of power. He, Jeremy Denton, had this crowd of prosperous people in the hollow of his hand.

In the opposite box a woman sat alone, the darkness of the velvet behind her making a perfect background for her gown of dead white crepe, an extraordinary and arresting gown when most women wore intriguing color schemes or sophisiticated black. It was a gown which a young girl
80

might have chosen, and yet on this woman it lost its ingenuousness and served to enhance her complete sophistication.

She was beautiful. Her hair was as black as night, and her face was pale as a pearl in contrast, her eyes dark, her lips scarlet and provocative. They seemed seldom to smile but wore a half-mocking, slightly derisive look. There were diamonds at her throat, diamonds gleaming frostily in her hair, diamonds on the hand which now and then lifted her program, or lay for an instant on the velvet ledge of the box.

Jeremy had been aware of her all the time. Instinctively he glanced at her at every stage of the play, watching for her reaction to little snatches of dialogue which sent ripples of laughter over the house but which evoked from her, at most, a momentary deepening of that provocative half-smile.

At first her detached air irritated him. Then, as his mind became gradually released from his early fear for the success of the play, he found himself appreciating her attitude of calm consideration. He severed himself in thought from the sheep-like throng around and below him, people who laughed because others laughed and would cry for the same reason. He linked his mind with hers and silently awaited her calm, considered judgment.

He saw her smile—that speech, then, was better than he knew. His lips curled slightly—that was weak, cheap, must come out tomorrow.

What was her final judgment? The audience clapped almost hysterically at the end. Jeremy had shown them, with delicately pointing finger, so many little foibles and weaknesses of human nature which they recognized with delight—not their own, of course, but those of other people they knew. They loved him for it. They called for him so that they might tell him so.

Paston laid a hand on his arm, urging him forward, but Jeremy stood still in the shadow of the box, unconsciously waiting for her decision. It came unexpectedly, a slight lift of her body, her head turning towards him, and the faint, shadowed smile which he felt, oddly, was for him alone.

He went at once to the edge of the box as if she had bidden him to do so. He leaned over the velvet rail and bowed towards the uplifted, expectant eyes, and no one but him-

81

self and possibly the dark-haired woman in the opposite box knew that he bowed first to her and then to the rest of the audience.

"Ladies and gentlemen . . ."

Those nearest to the box heard his voice, saw him standing to speak to them, clapped him again, and then demanded silence for him.

How different was that considered, self-assured speech from his stumbling, awkward words at the Vanity nine months ago! These phrases were pointed, witty, his demeanor touched with a charming diffidence which appeared to be quite unstudied, and he ended on a note of hope that future audiences would be as kind and generous as this one, and that to this one he might be privileged to offer further amusement and interest in the years to come.

He remembered to include gracefully not only his leading lady and her man, but the humbler members of the cast; and when he sat down he might have felt reasonably proud of the way in which he had acquitted himself had he not let his eyes rest at that moment on the woman in the opposite box.

The expression of her scarlet mouth was slightly sardonic, and he wished he could see her eyes so that he might be sure whether she was laughing at him or with him.

He turned to Maitland. The others had gone, and he was to join them later at the Mayflower.

"Who is the woman in the box opposite, do you know?" he asked, as casually as he could.

Maitland went everywhere, knew everyone, his slightly cadaverous personality being accepted for the sake of his extremely vital bank balance.

"Stella Dale," said Maitland, with a curiously clipped inflection in his voice, as if a trap had opened with difficulty and closed quickly again.

"You know her?"

"Oh yes. Everybody knows her, I think."

Maitland's voice had regained its customary nonchalance.

"I don't," laughed Jeremy. "I'm rather out of her world, I fancy, to judge from her diamonds. Ought I to know who she is?"

"You will do eventually. She has the reputation of being

London's most complete heartbreaker. She knows all the tricks of the trade."

He was clipping his words again, and Jeremy glanced at him with some curiosity.

Roy Maitland was an enigma to most people. He went everywhere, met everyone, did everything at its appropriate time, and did it well. His wealth was reputed to be enormous, yet he never appeared to have any friends, or to enjoy any sort of emotion.

"You seem to know her pretty well, anyway," hazarded Jeremy, unable to let the subject drop.

"I am not an exception," said Maitland, without apparent interest. "Her husband was Brandy Dale, by the way."

Jeremy received the information with a distinct shock. Dale was a fairly common name, and even with Stella prefixed to it, it had conveyed nothing to him. But everyone had known of Brandy Dale, prominent racehorse-owner, yachtsman, racing motorist, and millionaire. The whole world had been startled and intrigued by his suicide, right in the midst of a phenomenal run of luck, with an almost certain winner of the Derby ready to run, and after he had just bought one of the most famous racing yachts in the world and had her overhauled preparatory to making a dash for a world victory.

To the general public, Brandy Dale had had everything to live for—and yet he had died by his own hand. That, at least, was the conclusion to which, after much consideration, discussion, and consultation with experts, the coroner had reluctantly come.

There had inevitably been a lot of talk, and Stella Dale's name had been bandied about with numerous unsavory stories attached to it, until at last she had brought an action for slander against half a dozen prominent Society women and won it. That had quietened the open discussion of her, and two years of unimpeachable conduct on Stella's part had brought her back, if not into the most exclusive houses, at least into a reputable social circle.

Some of this Jeremy knew. The rest he could only surmise. Certainly there had been no suggestion of embarrassment in the way in which she had occupied, alone, one of the most conspicuous positions in the theatre, dressed in that dead-white gown and her diamonds.

Maitland glanced at him speculatively during the silence which followed his revelation. They were still in the box they had occupied, though the theatre was now almost empty.

"Intrigued by the glamorous Stella?" he asked cynically.

Jeremy flushed and looked round for his hat and coat, which an attendant had brought into the box for him.

"Why should I be? I'm not in the least likely to make her acquaintance," he said.

"I should say there is every likelihood," said Maitland. "You're a success." And Jeremy told himself, not for the first time, that he definitely did not like Maitland. You could never tell if he were serious or jeering.

As he left the theatre, bound for a party which no longer thrilled him as a novelty, Jeremy thought of Julie. He was still feeling a little piqued by her refusal to come to the first night of *Antimony*, and yet—well, he had to respect the honesty of that refusal.

"I'm sorry, Jerry, but I don't like it," she said, after reading the script months ago; and she had stuck bravely to her opinion, even while her brown eyes sought his forgiveness.

He had argued with her, discussed his plot in so far as one could discuss with Julie anything as foreign to her experience and tastes, but she was not to be shaken from her assertion that she disliked the play and thought it unworthy of him.

So in the end he had stopped discussing it with her and trying to make her see his point of view, increasingly arrogant of his own powers as he inevitably became under the flattery and popularity which followed *The Bauble*. Tonight's reception of *Antimony* justified his belief in himself, but it widened more than ever the gulf that now yawned between him and Julie.

In the foyer he paused to speak to one of the attendants.

"Parker, do me a favor first thing in the morning, will you? Get some flowers, an armful of them, and have them sent to Miss Julie Cave, will you? Here's the address"—scribbling on one of his cards and giving it to the man with a pound note.

He could not rid himself of the irritation of her refusal to be present. Things were going wrong between him and Julie, but he did not see how he could have acted differently. After all, he must write as he felt, and he had

84

never pretended to her that he wrote for anything but to make a fortune—and a fortune for her to share, moreover. He did not feel that he was called upon to alter his own ideas merely because Julie could not accept them and would have preferred him to remain a nonentity, scratching along on a mere pittance at Butcher's.

So he sent her the flowers and tried to feel he had evened things up, realizing afresh how out of place she would have felt amongst the little crowd assembled to rejoice with him at the Mayflower. They were all there—Mavis Becker in a backless gown which was almost as frontless, Jack Lorrin, drinking heavily and making open love to one of the small-part actresses, to Mavis's open fury—Victoire Paston with her honied obscenities which only amused her husband—friends and influential acquaintances scraped together to use or be used by this new comet, Jeremy Denton, ere he faded.

He went home very late, sick of the atmosphere he had himself created, a little ashamed, a little panic-stricken at the feeling that he had started something he could no longer control. He seemed forever to have left the quiet ways he had walked with Julie.

He found himself longing for her, to feel her arms about him, her cool lips on his cheek, her voice in his ears.

He took up the photograph that always stood on his desk, a snapshot which he had taken of her that first summer, and which had been enlarged and framed in silver. She stood there in her cheap little cotton frock, smiling at him from under the brim of her old garden hat. The look of her was like a draught of clear water to a thirsty man.

He glanced at the clock. It was past one. She would be in bed and asleep long ago, but he felt that he must at least get somewhere near her, and he put on his overcoat, ran down the stairs, and signalled to a taxi.

The man demurred at being asked to go as far as Streatham at such an hour, but Jeremy promised him double fare and a return journey, so he consented after some more grumbling. He evidently took Jeremy for some bright young spark up to some mischief.

When they reached Hemming Road, No. 26 was shut and dark.

Julie's room was at the back; and, telling the man to wait, Jeremy slipped in at the gate which gave access to the little strip of garden at the rear.

Her window was as dark as the rest of the house, but he risked waking everyone else by throwing stones at it. In a few moments the sash was pushed cautiously up and Julie's head appeared. She was rubbing the sleep from her eyes, which widened at sight of the visitor.

"Jerry! What's the matter?" she called, in a whisper of fear.

"Nothing, sweetheart, except that I couldn't live another second without sight and sound of you. Julie—come down for a minute"—beguilingly.

She hesitated, torn between the longing to do what he suggested and her knowledge that it was a reprehensible thing to do. What on earth would Mum say?

"It's the middle of the night," she said, with a backward glance to assure herself that Biddy slept peacefully in the second bed.

"Does it matter? Just for a second—half a second—Julie, do!"

She drew in her head and listened, almost wishing she could hear her mother moving about in the next room and so have the knotty point settled. Clearly she would never be able to do such a thing with Mum's knowledge, and of late Mrs. Cave had begun to hint that the company Jerry was keeping was changing him. She would more than hint that it was changing Julie if she knew what Julie was proposing to do!

But the house was still as the grave—and below her, just down the stairs and on the other side of the door, love and Jeremy waited for her.

She closed the window, slipped on her dressing gown and slippers, and tiptoed down the stairs.

A few moments later Jeremy was in the kitchen and she in his arms, his lips seeking her mouth with an urge of passion that frightened her and made her struggle free. She was terribly conscious of her scant attire while he had held her so closely, and she could not resist the temptation to look down at herself to make sure that she really was clothed from neck to toe in her thick, old woolen dressing gown.

She laughed a little shakily and reached for the light switch, for Jeremy had given her no time to do anything but unlock the door.

He caught her hand.

"Don't put the light on. It's better like this—exciting, mysterious, in the dark, isn't it?"

Julie was not sure that she liked to feel mysterious and excited in the middle of the night. Except for the revelation of herself in her dressing gown, she would have preferred a light and the comfortable sight of the shabby kitchen. She did not like to tell Jeremy so, however. He had been different for a long time now, and though she loved him just as much, she did not feel quite at ease with this new, successful, prosperous Jeremy.

"How did the play go?" she asked him, to get on more familiar ground.

"Very well indeed—but don't let's talk of that now. Let's talk of us, Julie. Do you know how attractive you are?"—taking her in his arms again and holding her in that close, possessive way that frightened her. She told herself that it was Jerry—Jerry who had often held her in his arms and kissed her—but she could not rid herself of the feeling that he was a stranger. For one thing, he was still in his evening clothes, and his breath smelt faintly of spirits. It revolted her even while she chid herself for being old-fashioned and pernickity.

She laughed a little nervously and tried to hold herself away from so close pressure.

"I don't know how you can tell what I look like in the dark," she said. "Besides, my hair's a mess and I've got a spot on my chin and cold cream on my nose."

For answer he kissed her again—strange, terrifying kisses that did not stop at her lips but travelled to her throat, to her neck, to her shoulder where his lips had pushed aside the open collar to her dressing gown.

"Oh, Julie, I love you so," he was saying in an odd, thick voice between his kisses. "I love everything about you, the feel of your skin, the softness of you—oh, Julie!"—and he was suddenly on the floor at her feet, his face pressed against her, his breath coming pantingly. The air seemed hot and charged with some compelling yet sinister force that made her feel she was no longer Julie but some stranger, wild, uncontrolled.

"Juliet, let me stay with you—Julie . . ."

Something brought her back to herself suddenly, back with a jerk, which pulled her from his hold and sent her reeling against the kitchen door. She had raised her hand instinctively against she knew not what. Now that their eyes had become accustomed to the darkness, they could vaguely see each other, terribly serious, Julie's eyes

87

frightened, Jeremy's half triumphant, half ashamed.

"You'd better go, Jerry," Julie's trembling lips were saying.

She could not put into words, even in her thoughts, the thing that had menaced them a moment ago. She was aghast at the possibilities within herself.

"Yes," he said unsteadily. "I ought not to have come," and he rose to his feet and came awkwardly towards her. She moved from the door, but knew that she need no longer be afraid.

She managed to smile, but it was a rather pitiful thing.

"We—we oughtn't to have felt like that," she said shakily. "Why did we?"

He took her hand and held it against his cheek. It was an act of humility. It asked the pardon she had already given, for she loved him.

"Because we love each other," he told her gently. "I'm glad you're—good Julie."

She could not know the vision he had had suddenly of Mavis Becker in her shameless dress, her eyes and her speech venomous because her lover was fondling another girl. It seemed descration even to think of Mavis Becker in the presence of Julie.

They did not kiss again. When he had gone, Julie locked the door after him and slipped upstairs again with only tenderness in her thoughts for him, though she was still shaken and unnerved by her own bewildering response to that first touch of passion. Save that it had been for Jeremy that memory would have defiled her, she thought.

Jeremy had forgotten all about the waiting taxi, but when he met the man's accusing eyes, he apologized handsomely.

"Sorry, old man, awfully," he said. "I'll make it worth your while," and he did, for he was never lacking in generosity now that he had the wherewithal to give.

As he was unlocking the door of his flat, he heard his telephone bell ringing, and there was a faint frown of annoyance on his face as he went to answer it.

"Hullo," he answered rather brusquely, "who is it?"—although he had known from the first the voice which would answer him.

She had rung him up several times since the first night of *The Bauble*, always late like this, and he knew no more about her than he had done that first time. She would give him no clue to her identity, and he called her still his "Midnight Angel." He had come to know so well her warm and lovely voice. They had talked of many things with a strange intimacy which would not have been possible had they been face to face, an intimacy which was at the same time impersonal. She had ideas and opinions on most things and did not hesitate to express them. She looked at life from queer angles, had no reticences or reserves.

Generally, he welcomed these calls and picked up the receiver with a pleasurable sense of anticipation.

But tonight he did not welcome it. The thought of any other woman jarred on a mind still filled with thoughts of Julie. This unknown woman was a part of a new life which, since it held nothing which Julie might share, seemed tawdry and unsatisfying.

"What's the matter, Jeremy? Something gone wrong?" she asked him with that uncanny power she had on interpreting his mood at a word.

In spite of himself, he felt the lure of her voice. She never failed to affect him like that. She had shown him so many and varying viewpoints of her. That power to attract his interest, no matter what their moods, was the only constant thing about her.

His only answer to her question was a noncommital "No."

She laughed.

"I can't believe that," she said, "but at least I know it isn't your new play."

"You were there?" he asked her.

"Of course. Did you think it possible for me to stay away? I had to see how we came to life," for he had discussed his play with her while it was in the making, inviting her comments, which were often constructive and never merely destructive, on his characters and their natural reactions to the situations he had created. She had given him many a new angle when he had believed himself familiar with all the possibilities of certain actions. Through her eyes, he had come to a new knowledge of humanity, especially of women.

"Do you think we did come to life?" asked Jeremy, unable to suppress the eagerness in his voice.

"Delightfully, I thought. You've almost grown up, Jeremy," and there was a note that was half mockery, half regret in her expressive voice.

"Are you sorry? I thought that was what you wanted," he said.

"Yes, I did want it. Only—well, I'm a woman, and no woman is ever satisfied at the materialization of her desires."

"I think some women might be," said Jeremy, his thoughts still clinging to Julie even though the strange excitement which this woman's voice and mysterious personality infallibly stirred him.

"Never this one," she said with again that faint note of regret in her voice. "However, it would be inconceivable dullness to have all one's desires actually realized! Life is effort and desire, not achievement and satiety."

"What is your greatest desire?" he asked her suddenly.

She laughed, the sound trailing off in the fascinating way it had, as if there were always a "but" or an "if" in every thought that swayed her mind. That uncertainty, that hint of tempest all the time, was no small part of her charm for him. He felt sure she was lovely. He could not imagine so lovely a voice without a habitation fitting to it, nor could he conceive of anyone without supreme physical attraction having been able to garner such knowledge and experience of life. She was definitely not of the women whom life had passed by and ignored.

Yet she had always refused to reveal herself to him or to give him the slightest hint of where she might be found. She would give him no name by which he might call her and had told him that, if she attracted him, she needed no name whereby he might remember her.

"My greatest desire?" she asked him now in her trailing, exciting voice. "How can I tell you or anyone what I don't know myself? My desires are like the wind, always changing, veering this way and that, sweeping everything before them and then blowing off in some other direction when all resistance has been swept away."

"Isn't there, then, any charm for you in realization of desire?"

"I sometimes wonder that myself. I have had so many of my wishes gratified, and yet never seem to possess anything worth having. I think it is the finality of achievement, its—its *stillness*, that is unsatisfying. I'm restless. I love motion, the going and not arriving. Don't you feel that too? Don't you enjoy writing a play better than knowing it a success? Isn't there for you, too, a charm in uncertainty?"

"I suppose so. Is that why you enjoy this queer affair with me? Why don't you want to meet me or let me know who you are?"

"Perhaps. But—I do want to meet you, Jeremy."

His voice quickened in reply, came to her with urgent life.

"Do you mean that? Will you let me? When? Where?"

Her laugh trailed over space to him.

"You're laughing at me."

"Yes. Be glad that I am. When no one any longer wants to laugh at you, Jeremy Denton, you can put on your carpet slippers and pull up your lonely chair to the fire, because you'll know then that old age is upon you."

"But tell me when and where I may see you," he begged her, with that urgency in his voice which kindled her own.

"Oh, you child!" she said. "Listen. On Thursday I am going to Lady Melland's party, a terrible affair which begins at eleven and will be filled with solemn music and even more solemn listeners. I'll meet you there. Shall we be romantic and say at midnight?"

"But how on earth am I to get there?" asked Jeremy. "Lady Melland doesn't know me and is not at all likely to do so. I am not the sort of person to be bidden to her house as a guest."

"Still so humble?" she teased him. "Still mouse rather than roaring lion, Jeremy Denton?"

"Somewhat in between the two perhaps," he laughed.

"You'll have to learn to roar. Society will expect you to. I'll have an invitation sent to you. You'll come?"

"Naturally. How am I to know you, though?"

"Jeremy, how ungallant! Can't you trust your instinct to bring you to me?" she mocked him.

"If I am to trust you implicitly, I shall pick on the loveliest woman in the room and make for her," declared Jeremy.

"That was gallant, but not subtle enough," she said. "Anyway, I shall know you." Then, after a pause, "Jeremy!"

"Yes?"

"Jeremy, are you alone?"

"Of course."

"Are you always alone at this hour?"

"Certainly I am," said Jeremy, wondering.

"I'm glad," she said softly, and rang off without attempting to explain either her question or her comment on his answer.

8

The next day came an invitation for Jeremy to Lady Melland's "Reception, with Classical Music and Dancing." The card was all gold and twirls, infinitely vulgar, and Jeremy examined it with a thoughtful frown.

He rang up Maitland after some reflection.

"Who's Lady Melland?" he asked.

He could almost hear the shrug of the shoulders in Maitland's reply.

"All bosom, gold teeth, diamonds, and no aspirates. Why?"

"I've got an invitation for Thursday night to something she calls a Reception," said Jeremy.

"Yes, you would," agreed Maitland. "She loves lions."

"Are you going?"

"Oh, lord no. I should be infinitely bored, and I loathe classical music anyway. You'd better go, though."

Jeremy grinned.

"Why do you think I shouldn't be bored?" he asked.

"Because you can't afford to be bored, my boy, by ladies like Melland. Her store of gold doesn't stop at her teeth, and she's evidently taken a fancy to you to send you an invitation."

Jeremy had a horrid, revolting suspicion.

"Has she—by any chance a—a singularly attractive voice?" he asked.

"Voice? Good lord, what a question? Thinking of making her the heroine of your next play? She's got the sort of voice most fat women have. Devonshire cream and honey."

"You think I should go, then?" asked Jeremy, refusing to admit to himself that he had intended to go anyway.

"Decidedly—and be nice to her, do a bit of roaring, but don't show your teeth. She cackles a lot, but she also lays golden eggs," and Maitland rang off.

92

Jeremy put back the receiver and let his mind toy with that horrid suspicion which had been born in it so unexpectedly. Was it possible? Could that lovely voice conceivably be called Devonshire cream and honey? Could it belong to someone answering Maitland's description of Lady Melland? *Could* it?

The question tortured him during the intervening days so that he found himself thinking of little else but the coming reception and his Midnight Angel's promise to reveal herself. He almost began to wish the meeting could be postponed. Rather than face so disastrous a materialization of his fears he would have continued as they were, with the Midnight Angel no more than a voice to him. As the days went by, he had almost forced himself to the conclusion that Lady Melland was indeed his mysterious lady and that she had adopted this means of securing his interest because she knew that her voice was her sole physical attraction.

He did not see Julie during that week, and, though he wrote her a charming little letter, he scarcely thought of her. His mind was detached from her by its obsession with those other perplexities, intermingled with which was a certain excited anticipation of entering at least the outer fringe of a social existence so far unknown to him. Lady Melland might be all Maitland described, and her vulgar invitation-card suggested, but to Jeremy she represented an open-door, even if it were only the outermost one easily opened to all.

Julie wrote to thank him for his flowers.

How heavenly *of you*, Jerry (she had written, underlining her words so that they seemed to be spoken by her very voice with its little enthusiasms and her young eagerness of heart). *I've never seen so many flowers all at once, outside the shops, and to think they're for me! Mum and I spent more than an hour arranging them and they look* lovely. *We didn't have enough vases, so I went in to Mrs. Pringle's to borrow some, and I gave her some of the roses. We took some to the Hospital for Incurables, too, in the evening. I hope you didn't mind.*

But Jeremy's mind had become so much occupied with other things that that passionate interlude in the dark kitchen had no power to hold his mind. He had scribbled a

93

reply and almost forgotten her.

On Thursday night, he arrived at Lady Melland's huge London house in a state of horrible uncertainty, as nearly nervous as he could ever be. If the Midnight Angel had sought a means to make herself even more interesting, she had chosen the best way. He felt he could no longer live without knowing who she was.

Maitland had warned him not to be late, for Lady Melland, with all her vulgarity and lack of breeding, could have given a lesson to her betters (so-called) in the respect she forced her guests to show to the celebrated artistes whom she engaged, at fabulous fees, to entertain them.

It was only a little after eleven when he arrived and gave his name to the supercilious butler who, Jeremy felt, would have made a fortune on the films. He was almost too good to be true.

His hostess sailed toward him with plump, outstretched hand loaded with diamonds, with gleaming teeth and rows of pearls and a pile of incredibly golden hair.

"So charming of you to come, Mr. Denton. I was so delighted to hear that you would," she cooed, and Jeremy's heart gave a wild leap and then settled down steadily and quietly. Cream and honey her voice certainly was, but it could never have found the music, the changing tones, the ardor and the crystal coldness of the voice which rang so persistently in his brain.

He replied to her greeting with a warmth which she could not know was gratitude to her for being herself, and she made him known to several of the guests before returning to her place at the door. He found himself regretting the golden hair and the pearls and the teeth. She was so undoubtedly a great lady, and he wished he could set her down where she would still be honored and beloved, in some farmhouse kitchen, a big white apron about her comely person and a brood of children and grandchildren about her. In this great, satin-panelled room and amongst the well-dressed, artificial throng of parasites, she was merely ridiculous and a figure of fun.

However, he forgot his hostess in her guests, for he found himself to be indeed a lion in their eyes, even if as yet a young and modest one. He exerted himself to pay, with a little roaring, for the marvellous buffet supper at the finest cocktail bar he had ever seen.

He was restless, however, his eyes searching the room,

pausing first here, then there, watching some lovely girl, some perfectly poised woman, getting near her so that he might hear her voice and moving away again unsatisfied and yet oddly relieved. None of these woman fitted his conception of his Midnight Angel.

Presently, with the cocktail bar discreetly closed, chairs arranged facing the dais, lights lowered and voices hushed to a murmur, a world-famous trio of musicians played music which to Jeremy and to many other untrained and unappreciative hearers was merely a dreary dirge and a jangle of sound.

His attention wandered, and gradually he became aware of someone watching him from the other side of the room. Irresistibly he felt his eyes drawn from the players, caught and held by those of a woman who watched him. She was standing, every detail of her appearance picked out in the dimly lit room by a curtain of dull gold plush behind her. Her hair was dark as a raven's wing, so dark that there seemed to be almost bluish lights in it against the gold curtain, and she wore a dress of midnight blue in some dull, lustreless material which would have made most women look insignificant but which gave her a startling loveliness, clung to the classic lines of her figure in daring revelation and threw into relief the clear pallor of a face which might have been cut in marble save for those compelling eyes which gave it an instensity of life.

Jeremy recognized her at once. She was Stella Dale.

Then across the darkened room and the politely listening crowd, their eyes held each other's, and he knew who else she was.

She was his Midnight Angel.

The knowledge both shattered and rebuilt his impression of her. Of course she was Stella Dale. How had he not known before, and at once? Here was a body lovely enough to be possessed of that vibrant and seductive voice, here the mind that had known so great experience, that could reveal to him so much that was beyond his own conception and knowledge. The thought that it was she to whom he had talked, she to whom he had listened, she who had come here tonight to meet him, thrilled and awed him. Was it possible? Was there this link between himself and this lovely, inaccessible woman?

When the trio had finished and been rewarded by restrained applause and gone their ways, and Lady

Melland's guests were released for a time to their own devices, Jeremy made his way to where Mrs. Dale waited. She had not moved, and yet somehow as he came nearer to her he received an impression of terrific vitality, of eager, purposeful force against which little would be allowed to stand, able to stand.

As he came closer to her, she smiled. He remembered that smile. She had worn it once or twice in the theatre, watching his play, listening to some of the words which she herself had inspired. It touched her lips so faintly, scarcely reached the sombre darkness of her eyes—darkness of violet, he saw now, not darkness of brown. They were like hyacinths on a day of storm, he told himself absurdly, their deep blue untouched by sunshine, lovely, mysterious.

"Well, Jeremy Denton?"

It was she who spoke first, and he knew he had made no mistake. This was the voice which had come to him in the silent and solitary darkness of the night. To this woman had he revealed so much of himself, his hopes, his fears, his secret dreams. It was almost terrifying to realize, in that moment, how truly he knew her.

"So it's *you*," he said, his voice no more than a breath. "I ought to have known. It had to be you."

"Disappointed, Jeremy?"

He shook his head, gazed fascinated into her eyes. She was lovelier even than she seemed. Almost as tall as he, slenderly fashioned but beautifully proportioned, she seemed to him to make all other women insignificant and insipid. The artistry which had created her gown, given her the matt bloom on her skin, imbued her lips with vivid colour, set every hair in place, seemed but a perfection of nature. There was nothing that suggested artifice in her. She had already captured his mind. His young, untouched body went down before her beauty without a struggle.

"Must you stand and stare at me, Jeremy?" she asked him at last in that well-known voice, mocking and alluring at the same time, and he came back with a start. She was so breathtakingly lovely. He knew that she had gone to his head like wine.

"Forgive me. I didn't expect—this, you see," he said, and now her smile reached her eyes.

"They are going to dance," she said, for their hostess tried to leaven her hospitality with a little lightness in between the more serious items.

Jeremy, thankful that in the past six months he had taken Maitland's cynical advice and learned to dance, put an arm about her and led her slowly amongst the moving throng of dancers. They seemed curiously remote from all the others, shut into an intimacy of shared memories. His head felt light and his heart beat unevenly.

She moved her head to smile at him in approval as they danced.

"So many men are too short for me. You are perfect as a partner," she said.

To his fury, he blushed like a schoolboy, and she laughed softly.

"Oh, Jeremy, I've made you blush!"

"It's hot in this room," he murmured, conscious in every nerve of her nearness, of some subtle perfume he knew he would remember all his life, of that urgent vitality within her that filled him with a sense of excitement.

"Do you want to stay any longer?" she asked him quietly.

He flashed her a swift wordless question.

"Take me home, Jeremy," she said, answering it. "I'll get my wrap if you wait for me."

He found his hostess and escaped from her effusive good-byes to find Stella, wrapped in magnificent furs, waiting for him.

"I'm so sorry. I couldn't get away from Lady Melland," he explained apologetically.

"Oh, did you bother to find her? She never expects it. Scarcely anybody troubles about a hostess nowadays," she said calmly. "Have you a car here? If so, I'll send mine home."

Jeremy hesitated. He had a vision of what her car would probably be like.

"I shall have to go and get mine from the car park," he said doubtfully. "I drive myself. Do you mind waiting?"

"I'll come with you," she said, and paused to give a message to Lady Melland's incredible butler before going out with Jeremy into the cold night air.

"You won't be cold?" he asked her as they threaded their way through the mass of cars in the adjoining square towards the small, swift sports car which so far satisfied his needs and conformed with his finances. "It's an open car."

Stella laughed.

"My cloak is warm and I shall love it," she said. "Take me for a run first, to the country somewhere, or the sea perhaps."

"What, now?" he asked, startled, for it was one o'clock.

Her extraordinary eyes had mockery and laughter in their depths. He recognized in them the exciting mixture there had often been in her voice, and he responded at once to it.

"What are you afraid of, Jeremy?" she asked him softly. "Of me, or just of life?"

He held her eyes with his.

"Of nothing," he said, and got into the car beside her, operated the starter, and slid into the deserted London streets, heading south.

Stella laughed and nestled down into her furs. Above them, whenever he dared to glance at her, her face was like a pearl.

"This is a rum go," ran his thoughts as he drove on, mile after mile, through the darkness. All the familiar landmarks were blotted out and only the white kerb and the occasional gleam of the A.A. warning reflectors, picked out by his headlamps, marked their route from the commons and pasturelands through which they presently ran.

It was like a dream journey, nothing was real or had substance, Jeremy felt he would go on driving, driving, until his alarm clock woke him with a jolt to begin life again.

Stella spoke to him suddenly.

"Happy or unhappy, Jeremy?"

Her voice startled him, broke his dream, and sent him, inexperienced driver as he was, swerving across the road. He righted the car with more luck than skill and glanced down apprehensively at his companion. Most women would have screamed or clutched him. She just sat still and laughed.

"Sorry I startled the man at the wheel," she said.

"I was dreaming," said Jeremy. "Nothing of all this seems real."

"Didn't you want to wake up?" she asked him teasingly.

"I haven't wakened," he told her. "It's still all a dream."

He put his foot down on the accelerator and the car shot forward, but for once he did not mind. There was nothing on the road, which was like a long white ribbon beneath the wedge of light from the head lamps. His head might have been light and his thoughts confused, but the sixth sense which providence sometimes gives to drivers kept his hands and feet steady, and finally they came to the outskirts of a big town, its lights a crescent of diamonds set about a vast darkness which could only have been the sea.

Stella sat up and pushed from her face the blown strands of her hair.

"I wonder where we are," she said.

"I'm not sure, but I think it must be . . ." started Jeremy, but she put her hand over his lips before he could finish his sentence.

"No. Don't let's know. Or if you do know, don't tell me. That must be the sea. Let's go down to the edge of it and walk there a little while and then go back without ever knowing where we've been. It'll be mysterious—exciting—something I've never done before."

Her fingers were cold against his lips. The perfume she used, and of which all the time he had been subconsciously aware, came drifting up to his nostrils. It was sweet and heady. There was nothing of the simple cottage garden about it. It was like everything about her, subtle, complicated, exotic, exciting.

Unexpectedly came the thought of Julie and her lavender-water, Julie who was sweet and simple and always easy to understand, Julie who no longer seemed possessed of any power to excite. He thrust the thought of her away. He wanted to think only of Stella.

He could not answer her. He felt curiously tongue-tied with this woman to whom he had revealed his inmost thoughts.

He slid gently and almost soundlessly down the hill between the darkened houses, left the town behind him, and ran the car up a narrow side road which he judged would bring them out to the less built-up portion of the coast.

"I'd better go and investigate," he said, pulling up and getting out of the car.

"I'm coming too," said Stella, and he opened the door for her and helped her out. She seemed an incongruous figure in that setting in her sophisticated gown and the luxurious silver-fox furs of her cape.

He eyed her doubtfully from the blown wings of her hair to the blue brocade trifles she wore on her feet.

"You can't go on the beach in those shoes," he said.

"I can take them off," she said, "and walk in the water."

"What, in October?" asked Jeremy.

She laughed.

"Perhaps *because* it's October. I hate doing the things that other people do, when and where they do them."

She was walking beside him on her high-heeled shoes, picking her way between the hummocks of grass and the boulders that lay scattered about the cliff-top.

"You're a rebel, aren't you?" he asked her, a caressing note in his voice.

"So are you, Jeremy. We both hate life to be dull, and it's dull just as soon as one accepts the ruling of the herd and takes it for one's creed in life. There's so much that's exciting and stimulating that the herd never even suspects! It's the rebels like us who find it."

"Is that why you rang me up that first night?" asked Jeremy, making the first reference to their previous contact.

"Yes. I wanted a new adventure. Life threatened to bore me, and I never allow it to do that. I had enjoyed your play, though it lacked sophistication. I liked the look of you when you stood in front of the curtain."

"Even though I lacked sosphistication?" asked Jeremy with a smile.

"Yes, and looked so deliciously young," she said, giving him back his smile. "I didn't say that in derision, you know. It was—well, almost envy of your youth, Jeremy"—with a faint note of regret in her voice.

"You sound as if you were middle-aged," he said. "Careful here. You'd better let me go first and help you; for they had come to the shelving edge of the low cliff above the beach.

She gave him her hand, but at the end there was a drop of a few feet. Jeremy sprang down and turned back to her.

"You'll sprain your ankle if you jump in those shoes," he warned her.

"All right. I'll take them off," she said, and did so. "Catch me?"

He held out his arms and she jumped into them without hesitation. For a second he held her there, aware of her light body so lightly shielded from him, of the softness and warmth of the furs which swept his neck and face as if they held something of her own allure. For an instant her cheek had touched his own.

100

He set her down carefully on a patch of short grass which grew on the shingle above high-water mark. He was trembling a little though she looked serene and undisturbed.

There was a glow about her, however, the hint of hidden fire beneath the serenity, and his pulses quickened. Looking at her, the faint color whipped into her cheeks by the wind, the loosened strands of her hair, the changing lights in her eyes, he wondered that he could ever have thought her cold. There was a flame-like quality about her which could set a man on fire.

"How gloriously silent and solitary it is here!" she said, her voice soft and thrilling. "We might be miles from civilization. Jeremy, do you wish we were? How would you feel if we were alone on an island, miles and miles from anywhere or anyone, with no one able to get to us and no need to get to them unless we—desired them, should we desire them, Jeremy? Would you?"

He could not answer her. He was both hot and cold. His body ached for the touch of her. His lips burned with desire of her.

Her eyes told him that she knew what she was doing to him, and she lifted her arms above her head, stretching them upwards in a gesture of abandonment, a provocative and deliberately sensual gesture. The fur cape fell from her shoulders and made a dark pool about her feet. In the pale moonlight of the October night her arms and throat were white as milk.

He took a step forward, and at once she slid away from him, gathered the long skirts of her gown about her and ran over the sandy shingle towards the water. Jeremy saw, with a little shock that was oddly exciting, that her feet were bare. She had worn no stockings beneath the brocade sandals. He followed her, watching with fascinated eyes her white feet and ankles beneath the caught-up skirt, and suddenly, with a swift movement she stripped off her frock and flung it behind her and stood there in the path of the moonlight, naked save for the pale satin of fitted trunks and brassiere.

Jeremy stopped short and stared at her unbelievingly, inexpressibly shocked and, in the first moment of the shock, aware of no responsive excitement. He knew himself to be nauseated and oddly frightened. Every instinct within him was to turn and flee, to leave her there to save himself from all that she had aroused in him, to quench it for ever.

Then she began to dance, in and out of the breaking edges of the waves, back and forth in that pale wedge of silver light, now dark against it, now pale as pearl with a background of purple shadow. She shook her hair free. It was long and fell in a curtain about her arms and her breast and her white shoulders. The effect was indescribable on Jeremy, so inexperienced, so terribly young in passion. He had never seen a woman with long hair, and this black cloud flying in the moonlight and the wind seemed to catch him and entangle his senses and leave him without any thought of desire but to feel it in his hands, about his neck and throat.

He moved nearer to her, and she danced away from him, kept just out of his reach until at last, whether she had intended it or not, he caught her by the flying cloud of her hair, drew her into his arms, crushed her body against his own and her willing, passionate mouth to his.

She kissed him, and then twisted her head back from him to look into his face, her eyes dark with laughter, drowsy with desire.

"Are you getting a thrill out of this, Jeremy?" she asked him.

"You know what I'm getting out of it," he told her thickly, and held her again, possessively, fiercely, so that at last she laughed on an excited note and struggled free.

"I didn't bring you here to make love to me," she told him.

"Then why did you bring me here?" he demanded, an unfamiliar sense of inferiority, of being at a loss and out of his own sphere, coming to torment him.

Her eyes had grown suddenly cold.

"For the adventure of a drive through the night," she said.

"And this business of taking off your clothes and acting like this?" he asked her roughly.

"Adventure only," she said calmly. "I had a fancy to dance in that strip of moonlight. That was all."

She had reached the place where she had flung her dress, and now she picked it up, slipped it over her head with no least suggestion of embarrassment, and did not even glance at him as she adjusted the silver flower that

102

held it on one hip. She was sublimely sure of herself, and the knowledge drove him to the point of frenzy. By what right did she assume she was so safe? That it was so easy to sway him, to rouse him and then quench the flame she had kindled?

He covered the few feet between them in a stride and snatched her into his arms, held her imprisoned with her own at her sides, gave her quick, fierce, hungry kisses which had more savagery than love in them. Gradually, as if utter stillness had at last penetrated his mind, he released her and she stood motionless whilst, feeling somehow degraded and humiliated, he withdrew a few paces from her.

Her face was pale and cold. Her eyes were frosty.

"I suppose I merited that for forgetting how extremely young you are, my dear Jeremy," she said in a voice of deadly calm.

His eyes were still dangerous.

"You admit that you came here for adventure," he said. "Can you blame me if it is a different kind from what you had anticipated?"

"Not at all," said Stella crisply. "I blame myself for not having realized that you think of adventure in terms of Piccadilly Circus."

She maddened him. He had never felt like this before, never known the terrific power a woman could have over a man, the deadly force with which she could wield it, knowing her power.

"Well?" he asked harshly. "Supposing I do think in terms of Piccadilly Circus? How are my thoughts different from yours, when you invite a man to bring you here at this time of night and then act as you have done? Stripping yourself and not being in the least ashamed of it?"

He reached out again and caught her arms in a grip of iron, shaking her almost unconsciously as he went on speaking.

"You've played on my feelings for months, worked me up for just such a display as this, I suppose. Well, what are you going to do about it? You've made a mistake in your man. I'm not just a puppet on the end of a string, or a gigolo to do your bidding. The situation's gone beyond your control, so what are you going to do about it, Stella Dale?"

For years she had played with fire. Sometimes it had
103

burnt her, but still she had to go on playing with it. The fire was within herself, a flame for which always she sought fresh fuel. What would have terrified other women only amused and stimulated her. The one bad fright she had ever had was when Brandy, her husband, had taken their lives into his own hands and broken them.

Well, she had mended her own, and, as she prided herself on never making the same mistake twice, she would never be broken again.

Yet there was a faint, exciting fear that Jeremy spoke the truth when he told her that the situation had gone beyond her control. She had known from the first that there were secret fires burning within him. There had to be, or he could not have been the creative genius he was. What was it that actually she had desired of him, was seeking of him now? Passion? She had had a surfeit of it. Fame? She had had notoriety, at least. Money? Certainly not that, for Brandy (his name had been Brandwick, but everybody called him Brandy) had left her his vast fortune.

What, then? Romance? Something she had never yet known in her self-seeking, emotional existence?

Suddenly the anger died within her and she spoke to him softly.

"Well, so what, Jeremy? If I am in your power, if things are beyond my own control, what have I to fear?"

His hands still gripped her arms. His eyes looked into hers searchingly, with something of perplexity in their depths. What was she really? Angel or devil? Good or bad? The flame of the passion began to fade.

"Some day you'll take too many risks," he told her, his voice shaking oddly.

He could almost feel the relaxation of her relief and did not know whether to be glad or sorry that she had beaten him at the game.

"Well, when that day comes, it will be a new experience," she told him, the old, mocking note in her voice, and he let her go abruptly and turned away and walked across the shingle and up the slope and on to the waiting car without offering her any sort of help.

She smiled her small, secret smile and picked up her coat and her shoes and followed him. How beautifully young he was after all! Only a very young man would have been so self-revealing as to walk away and leave her like that!

When she reached the car to find him sitting in the driving-seat, the engine running and her own door standing open, she stood there and laughed into his grim, withheld face."

"You know, Jeremy, civilization does make it difficult to be dramatic, doesn't it? Here we are, bad friends with each other. All we want to do is to turn loftily on our heels and say "Good-bye forever," but you can't possibly leave me stranded here, in a strange place, in an evening dress, at dawn, and I can't possibly let you! I've simply got to get back into your car beside you and you've got to drive me back with such dignity as you can assume to town! Jeremy"—stepping into the car and laying a hand on his arm—"can't we be friends any more? It's been such fun."

He gave her a stubborn glance.

"How can we be friends, after—this?" he asked.

"How can we not be, after this?" she asked him softly. "I wish you could understand. There's the same streak in me that's in you, a longing to be free, untrammelled, not caught up and bound hand and foot by convention. I recognized it in you when I listened to your play and saw you alone there in front of the stage. Can't you recognize it in me when I fling off a senseless and unnecessary garment and dance in the moonlight?"

He lifted his other hand to lay it over hers on his arm.

"Stella, is that all it was? Just—wanting to feel free of conventions?" he asked, longing to believe her and yet with every instinct warring against belief.

"Just that," she told him lightly. "So—can't we still be friends?"

"I might want to make love to you again," he said grimly, removing his hand from hers and fiddling with the gear lever.

She laughed.

"Of course you might," she said. "Other men do, so why not you? Oh, I don't suggest that other men make love to me, but merely that they, like you, probably want to! Smile Jeremy."

"Why should you imagine I feel like smiling?" he asked without looking at her.

She made an impatient sound, sat down, and closed the door with a snap.

"Are you just eaten up with the herd instinct, after all?" she asked him. "I started out with you thinking you would enjoy something unusual and amusing, but you wanted to do the horribly boring and usual thing, after all. I'm disappointed in you."

He made no attempt to answer, but swung in the gear lever and started off, nor did they find anything to say to each other until they were so near to London that he had to know where to drive her.

"I haven't an idea where you live," he said distantly.

She told him.

"You see. I'm giving you my address," she added.

"What exactly does that mean?" he asked.

The long, silent drive had soothed them both, but he was very tired and there was still something of the small spoiled boy in his voice, a hint of sulkiness which she decided she had better ignore.

"That I should like you to remember it," she said softly. "My friends do, you know.

"Surely you don't bow to convention to the extent of having tea parties, do you?" he asked ironically.

"No. I have sherry," she told him, voice and smile mocking him gaily. He tried to steel himself against the familiar allurement of her, but she could play on his feelings like an artist on the strings of a violin.

He set her down at the door of a tiny, white-fronted house wedged in between two lordly dwellings in a fashionable street.

"I suppose I dare not suggest that this is a somewhat unconventional hour for a lady to be escorted home?" he asked.

It was nearly six o'clock in the morning, and London was stirring in the streets and behind lighted windows.

"My servants are discreet," she told him. "Good night my dear," and she slipped past him up the two or three steps, opened the narrow, blue-painted door and vanished without a backward glance.

9

Back in his own flat after that strange night, Jeremy drew the curtains to let in the morning and poured himself a long drink, sharp and pungent. He felt he needed both the clean cold morning and the long cold drink.

He was deadly tired and his mind was confused. Too

much had been crowded into twenty-four hours, and his nerves were playing him tricks after the hours of fast driving so that it was useless to think of going to bed. He decided that he would go and have a Turkish bath, and went into the bedroom to change. His whole being seemed set on the task of cleansing himself, body and mind.

He paused to reflect on that urge. Why should he feel unclean? There had actually been nothing unclean about this strange night, and yet the feeling of being soiled remained. Ugly emotions had left their mark on him. He felt oddly that he had touched pitch and had been defiled. He scorned himself, sneered at himself for the youth which Stella mocked, saw himself as puritanical and unmodern.

Yet, for all that, he went to his Turkish bath and slept for so long after the massage and the cold plunge that the attendant came to rouse him and ask if he were well.

He sat up and rubbed the sleep from his eyes, stretched his arms, felt the muscles flex responsively, knew that it was good to be alive and young.

"Why, what's the time?" he asked, for in a Turkish bath, time ceases to be, and there is neither day nor night.

"It's after six o'clock, sir, and I thought perhaps you'd want to go to the theatre," for Jeremy Denton was known to quite a lot of people by now.

"Six? In the evening, do you mean?" asked Jeremy, amazed. "Good lord, have I been here all day?"

He took an ice-cold plunge, had a shave, and dressed again, grinning now and then to himself over his lost day. What a change from the old grind!

He could think more sanely now over that wild night. He must had been mad to let such a thing happen to him. Stella was quite right to jeer at his youth. Only a very young and callow individual would have let a woman make such a fool of him, neither to take her nor be able to let her alone. Who was she, anyway? Stella Dale—notorious heroine of the most sensational drama of a decade, reputed mistress of half a dozen men. What was it Maitland had called her? The world's most accomplished heart breaker, or something like that. Well, she wasn't going to break his heart. He did not care whether he ever saw her again. The taste of her was still slightly unpleasant to his thoughts.

It was in this frame of mind, cheerfully emancipated, that he returned to his flat and a collection of letters, newspapers, and messages.

The house in which he lived was an old one turned into

107

service flats for bachelors. Fender, the porter, acted also as valet and personal attendant to the tenants. He knew all their affairs and was trusted by them to handle any emergency with discretion.

He was waiting rather anxiously for Jeremy, whose dress clothes had been brushed and pressed and laid out for him.

"A lady rang up, sir, several times," he said. "I told her you were out, and she wouldn't give her name. Not Miss Cave, sir."

"That didn't matter," said Jeremy curtly. "Anything else?"

"Yes, sir. Mrs. Hughes Belper rang up. Wants you to dine with her tomorrow night. I took the liberty of telling her that I fancied you were free. I should go if I were you, sir," the man added respectfully.

Fender took a personal and fatherly interest in all his "young gentlemen," and had more than once proved himself to be a reliable and well-informed guide to social circles. Jeremy had consulted him on several occasions as to the relative values of invitations which clashed.

"Important, is she?" asked Jeremy.

"Yes, sir. Knows all the best people."

Jeremy grinned.

"It won't be your fault if I don't do ditto within a few months, will it, Fender? By the way, how's your wife?"

"Not too great, sir. She's fretting a bit in the hospital, and wants to come home."

"Don't they think she's well enough?" asked Jeremy, with an interest not all simulated. He had a passionate interest in everyone who came his way.

"It isn't that, sir, so much as they think it's bad for her to be shut up here."

"Haven't you anywhere she could go, by the sea or in the country? Tell you what. I had lunch one day at a very decent little place near Brighton, nice, friendly people, sort of inn. If they'd let her leave the hospital, I'd run her down there in the car and fetch her back again in a week or two. It's on the bus route if I couldn't manage to take you down there often. It wouldn't cost you anything, you know"—feeling and looking a little uncomfortable. It was still so new to him to be able to help others, and actually he still felt far more at home with people like Fender than with Maitland and his crowd.

The man's face flushed and he stammered.

108

"Sir—well, sir—ir would be—well, Mr. Denton, sir, I don't rightly know what to say. It'd be the making of her, though. I know that."

Jeremy laid an awkward hand on his arm.

"That's all right, then. You fix it up, old man. I'll drop a line to these people and I can run down there with your missus any day."

He never forgot that he had been poor himself, that he had had to work every hour of the day and often the night as well, that there had been times when he would have been unutterably thankful for the helping hand which had never been held out to him, but which he himself could now hold out.

He dismissed Fender, glanced at the newspapers, slit open his letters, decided that there was nothing amongst them to prevent his accepting Mrs. Hugh Belpher's invitation, and sat down to accept it.

His letter stamped and put into the wire basket inside the service lift, he began leisurely to change into evening clothes, rather by habit now than from any definite intention of going out.

He liked to change at night, enjoyed the feeling of well-being and prosperity it gave him. He knew himself to be no longer young Denton, Butcher's clerk, but Jeremy Denton, the popular playwright, "somebody at last."

Inevitably he thought of Stella Dale, knew that the "lady" who had rung up must have been she. He was pleased to find that he had no wish to ring her up, and acting on impulse, took a taxi out to Streatham and to No. 26 Hemming Road.

Though at one time he would have been received with a warmth and an absence of ceremony in the comfortable, homely kitchen, now Mrs. Cave showed him into the seldom-used sitting-room, which the family called privately the "state apartment," and made some murmured explanation of why the fire had not yet been lit in there.

Jeremy tried to stop her as she stooped over the hearth, matches in hand.

"Don't light that, Mrs. Cave," he said. "What's the matter with the kitchen? I'm not a visitor. You don't have to open the state apartment for me."

Mrs. Cave glanced instinctively at his immaculate dress-clothes.

"You can't possibly sit in the kitchen in that suit," she

said. "Julie and I have been making jam this evening, and even the chairs are sticky. Dickie and Biddy couldn't keep their fingers out of it," and she insisted on coaxing the fire into a blaze, though the wind blew the smoke back and made them cough.

Julie, who had obviously made a hasty change of dress, came in to relieve her mother of the task of entertaining Jeremy, for task it appeared to him to be. It struck him that even Julie was a little reserved and aloof with him, and it made him uncomfortably inclined to shorten his unsatisfactory visit.

When he rose to go she made no effort to detain him, though once they had all hung on to him and refused to let him go.

He held her hand in his and looked down at her with a question in his eyes. There had been no love-making between them that evening. They had not even kissed, for Mrs. Cave had been there when Julie came into the room, and since then they had sat on two chairs and talked, mostly about his play and its success and the annual jam-making.

"What's wrong, Julie?" he asked her gently.

She did not meet his eyes, and he had a feeling that she did not want to answer the question.

"Nothing. Why should there be?" she asked quietly.

"I can't think of any reason," said Jeremy. "You seem—well, not so very glad that I came, and I've felt like a visitor instead of the member of the family I used to be."

She raised her eyes to his at that. There was a sort of pride in them that baffled him and held him at a distance.

"You've gone rather a long way from the family, haven't you, Jeremy? We can't entertain such grand people as Mr. Jeremy Denton in his evening clothes in our kitchen, can we?"

He could not decide whether she were mocking him or not. It was strange to be at a loss with Julie, who had always been so easy to read. He was reluctant to leave her. After the life he had been leading, the over-heated rooms filled with overdressed and insincere women, especially with the memory of Stella Dale still fresh in his mind, Julie's simplicity and honesty were refreshing. She was like clear water on a thirsty day. He looked into her eyes and was ashamed of memories she did not share, would have hated to share.

He took away with him thoughts of her which were oddly disturbing, though in the days that followed, each bringing its new amusement, each lionizing him a little more in his own and other people's estimation, the memory of her became less distinct.

Once or twice he met Stella Dale, for his circle of friends had begun to impinge on hers in its inevitable widening. Each time he was aware of a slight sense of shock at sight of her, as if an electric current ran from her to him. The cool touch of her hand burnt him. Her strange, faintly mocking eyes held his for a second, which all the evening, and until they met again, he found himself remembering.

Sometimes she telephoned him, very late. He did not answer, knowing it must be Stella, for no one else would ring him up at half past two and three in the morning. After a time he even left off his receiver when he went to bed, and presumed that she had ceased to ring his number. If they had to speak when they met, it was with conventional and uninteresting remarks which the world might hear.

Once he snatched a hasty lunch with Julie, ringing her up at Monique's and insisting on her meeting him at a smart and expensive restaurant where she knew she would both look and feel out of place.

She was gentle, but remote and uncommunicative, telling him when he questioned her that she ought not to have come here.

"Don't be silly, Julie. What's wrong with it?" he asked, half annoyed with her because he knew she was right.

"Everything's wrong, Jeremy, and you know it. I look what I am, just a workroom girl who has helped to make some of the very gowns other women are wearing. I'm not at home in places like this, and the people who know you and nod and smile at you are naturally wondering who I am and where you picked me up. We ought to have gone to the Corner House."

She had spoken with a quiet determination which could not fail to impress him, and, looking at her in her shabby brown suit and home-made hat, he had a sudden feeling that it was she who was worthwhile and all these other women, elegant, expensive, *soignee* as Julie could never be, not worth a button on her coat.

He leaned across the table so that only she could hear him.

"You're so sweet, Julie. I love you. I wish I could be with you all the time. With you I can be myself, the self only you know. Without you I'm a sham, and the shadow and echo of other people."

She did not reply. What was there to say? She let her eyes rest on his for a long moment and then looked away, suddenly afraid to let him read the deep sadness and yearning that must be in them.

It had been a little hard for her at home lately. She had avoided their eyes, Mum's anxious and filled with tenderness, Biddy's asking their shrewd, intolerable question.

She knew that they had both been expecting to hear that she and Jeremy were engaged, that she would have a ring to show them, would begin to talk of marriage and leaving Monique's. At the beginning, when she and Mum had talked of Jeremy, they had spoken as if eventual marriage were a foregone conclusion, its fulfilment only waiting for Jerry to be in a better position so that he could give her a home. But now, what was stopping that expected progress towards marriage? He was doing so well, had an assured future, was rich beyond their wildest dreams—beyond Julie's and her mother's dreams, anyway. There seemed nothing in their way, no interfering relations on either side, no problems to solve.

She had framed all sorts of excuses when she had to make any.

Jerry was busy. He had to work so hard, often well into the night, and had no time yet for anything but work. He might have to go to America to conclude negotiations for producing *The Bauble* over there. *Antimony* might be filmed, too, which meant extra work. Also he had to go to places, meet people.

The excuses sounded thin to Biddy and Mum, just as in her heart Julie knew they were thin. There was no real reason, as far as she could see, why they should not be engaged, why they should not quite soon be married. If he had to go to America, what difference did that make? She could go with him, or, if that were not possible, would quite happily stay in their home to wait for his return. She would not be an exacting or possessive wife. Jerry loved freedom, and she would leave him free. Of that she was so sure.

The family could get along quite well without her earnings now, too. Dickie had won his scholarship and was costing nothing beyond his keep and some of his clothes. Biddy was earning her fares and lunches and a trade at a beauty-parlor, and Mum had regular and less exacting work than she had had to do whilst the children were at school.

Nothing of all this showed in Julie's demeanor as she sat with Jeremy in that smart restaurant over her lunch, but she was afraid of what he would read in her eyes.

He took her in a taxi back to work, yielding to her wish not to let it set her down right at Monique's door.

"The other girls might see and then they would talk," she said, so they dismissed the taxi in Piccadilly and walked up Bond Street. Outside Monique's, they stood for a moment reluctant to say good-bye now that their meetings were not very frequent. Julie was thinking how handsome and prosperous he looked in his well-cut and very correct clothes, and Jeremy was wishing he could see her in some of the lovely clothes other women had worn at the place where they had lunched. It had hurt him oddly to see how shabby she was, though actually she was as neatly and suitably turned out as hundreds of other bright, jolly-looking girls dashing back to work at that time.

He glanced at Monique's discreet window, where only one dress was displayed against the subdued hanging of pearl-grey silk which framed it. It was a happy little frock of blue-green crepe, its belt and demure neck-line edged with tiny rolls of coloured silk, blue and grey and amethyst, and gay little buttons repeated the colors.

"You'd look sweet in that, Julie," he said suddenly.

She turned to look at it and laughed, but there was a faint edge to her laughter. Did he say that because he had realized how badly she compared with his new friends?

"Even if I had the money to buy it, I'd never have any occasion to wear it," she said.

"Why, how much would it cost? There's nothing much of it."

"It will be about twenty guineas," said Julie in her serene fashion.

"Twenty guineas for that!" gasped Jeremy.

"Yes. Madam only shows her cheaper models in the window. Anyway, I must go now, Jerry. Thank you so much for the lunch," and she had gone before he realized that they had made no plans for a future meeting.

He stood and stared at the frock, visualized Julie in it,

113

his newly acquired appreciation of the details of women's clothes adding to it grey shoes and stockings, ornaments of jade perhaps—or old-fashioned amethysts. He longed to buy it for her, but turned away at last, sure that she would never accept it from him, and what would he do with it then? Certainly it would in no way suit Stella Dale's classic proportions and sophisticated charms.

Stella Dale—why must he always revert to her in his thoughts especially when he wanted to think of Julie?

He went back to his rooms and set himself steadily to work on a new play, lost himself in his work, as he could always do, and did not let his thoughts wander for an instant, until, with a sigh that was half relief, half sheer tiredness, he threw down his pen, passed a hand over his rumpled hair, and realized that he had finished, in its rough state, the successor to *Antimony*.

Was it good or bad? He could not tell, and that worried him. He had believed that some extra sense would always tell him whether he had succeeded or not in his efforts. He had known *The Bauble* was good, had had no uncertainty about offering *Antimony* as a successor to it, but what of this play? Did his people really live? Would they have reacted like that to such a situation? Was the situation itself fantastic or, in the wider limits of fiction, conceivable?

He could not tell. The indecision made him restless and anxious.

In the end he stacked the loose pages of the manuscript together, threw them into a drawer, and locked it. Long ago an old man, author of several fairly successful novels, had advised him never to offer anything for publication until it had already stood to a small degree, the test of time.

"Throw it into a drawer and forget it for six months. Then read it through, and if it doesn't seem utter drivel to you it is probably worth trying out. The odds are that it will seem utter drivel, and if so, throw it into the fire and start again."

Well, he would give this the test of time, but he knew that he would never have the courage of that old spartan and throw into the fire a child of his brain.

He found that it was long past his usual dinner hour, rang down to Mrs. Fender to send him up a grill, and had a bath whilst he waited for it. He returned to the meal in dressing-gown and slippers, too drained mentally to want to go out and hoping he would be left in peace for the rest of the evening.

Later, sitting by his fire with one of the cigars he had only just begun to smoke, and which he preferred to take in small doses and privacy at present, his thoughts returned to Julie.

He knew that the time had come when he must face the position of himself with regard to Julie once and for all.

Did he, or did he not, love her enough to marry her?

A year ago, six months ago even, he would have found such a question impossible of conception. Julie had then been beyond and above everything else in his life save his chosen profession. She had figured in his dreams, been an essential part of all his future hopes, shared in his castles in Spain.

What had happened to them? Or, to be quite honest, what had happened to him? He had to confess that Julie was the same, still the sweetest and most sincere person he had ever known. She represented to him all that was best and noblest in woman, possibly in life itself.

Why then did he ask himself whether or not he wanted her to be his wife?

He rose from his chair and walked restlessly about the room, wandered to the wireless, found a Symphony Concert being given on the National wavelength, and switched over with a grunt to the Regional, where that maddening peal of church bells greeted his ears. Foreign stations provided him with unintelligible discourses in languages which made him realize his shortcomings, and at last he switched off the set again and returned to his customary seat at his desk.

Why had he, time after time, caught himself back when the very words were on his lips to make Julie for ever his?

Idly he pulled towards him his pad of paper, the pen which he had thrown down beside it. It had become natural for him to express in writing his thoughts, to marshal and sort his ideas in that way.

He began to write.

Reasons why it would be foolish to marry Julie Cave.

(1) *I have gone so far away from her in my way of life and my habits. I have met so many different women. Can I still be in sympathy with Julie's simplicity? Or will it bore me after a time?*

(2) *What would happen to our social life if I married her? She does not want to go into the sort of Society to which I am now accustomed. She would not be happy trying to accommodate herself to that life. Today she admitted that she would be happier at the Corner House than at the Typica where I took her. I prefer the Typica and all that it represents, and I don't want to go back to Corner House ways.*

(3) *I am getting a new appreciation of women's looks and like them to be smart and well dressed. Julie is sweet, but she is not even really pretty, and has no dress sense.*

(4) *She is definitely not intellectual. Would that worry me? Should I expect a wife to satisfy me in that way?*

(5) *She does not even approve of my plays or like them. Would that make perpetual discord between us?*

(6) *How about her family and background? Will she insist on living at their level and make me do so?*

(7) *Has Julie . . .*

Suddenly he flung down his pen. Swift and sure had come a revulsion of feeling, like a breath of sweet, cold air into the vitiated atmosphere of an unaired room. It swept away all thoughts of everything save Julie's sweetness, his longing for her. He knew shame and disgust at the way he had been weighing her up, and *dared* to weigh her up. He thought of the other women he knew, selfish, empty-headed, deliberately barren women not fit to clean the shoes of girls like Julie. Amongst them he thought, inevitably, of Stella Dale

Stella Dale—and Julie! The association of even their names seemed a sacrilege tonight.

He started to tear up what he had written. Then he paused and smiled and smoothed out the crumpled sheets again, folded them, and put them into an envelope. Some day, when they were both old and very wise, perhaps he would show it to her. They would read it together, their cheeks very close, his and Julie's and they would laugh to remember the presumptuous puppy he had been!

He took a fresh sheet of paper.

My sweet (he wrote, and now his pen flew fast),

Listen, tomorrow evening, even if you're going to do something frightfully important, scrap it because I want you, will you? Is that a good enough reason, whatever the

116

previous engagement? If it's another man, I'll kill him. There are such weighty things to discuss, my Julie, happy and lovely things. I'll call for you about seven and we'll go anywhere you like, do anything you like, ride on the moon and go a-fishing for stars.

Jerry.

He sealed it in an envelope and then the telephone-bell rang. He lifted the receiver automatically and frowned to hear Stella Dale's voice in ears that were filled with the memories of Julie's quiet, soft tones.

"Jeremy, you know who it is, of course?"

"Yes."

His monosyllable was curt and uninviting.

"Is it too late to talk?" asked Stella, her voice honey-sweet, and, in spite of himself, he felt a little of the old thrill in its tones.

"Well—it is rather late, isn't it?" he replied, not quite so curtly.

"Even for you and me?"

He did not reply to this, and her voice went on beguilingly:

"Jeremy, where has all the loveliness gone? Isn't there any romance for us any more? Did we leave it all—that night—by the sea?"

It was the first time they had referred, either of them, to that episode, and it made him feel hot and uncomfortable. Now that he had made up his mind what to do, he resented this thrusting of any other woman into his life given to Julie.

The resentment sounded in his voice when, after a long pause, he replied.

"You were right and I wrong," he said. "We should have been content to remain just voices to each other."

"How could we? You were never just a voice to me, you see. Did I so greatly disappoint you, Jeremy? Can't you make up your mind to forgive me, since it seems you can't understand?"

He felt the old weakness stealing over him. What was this uncanny power she had over him that he could not put down the receiver, could not deny that warm, seductive voice that seemed not to belong to the woman she really was?

"Is there any point in this discussion?" he asked at last.

117

She was silent for a moment. Then she spoke again, and there was a subtle change in her voice. If he could have analyzed it he would have known that the steel was shining faintly through the silken sheath of her words.

"Yes."

"My dear, what has happened to us? Are we not to be even friends because of that one—mistake?"

"Your mistake or mine?" he asked her.

"Oh—mine. I thought—well, never mind what I thought. It doesn't matter. I am saying to you *"mea culpa, Jeremy"*. Aren't you generous enough to accept that?"

"How can we be friends when, on your own admission, I can't understand you?" he equivocated, wishing he had the courage to finish with her now and for ever, and yet aware of the weakness which would not let her go.

"Then remedy that, Jeremy. Perhaps I didn't understand you, either. I hadn't realized how much you had grown up. I was a little—frightened that night. I had believed I was playing with a boy, and when I found a man I had to—defend myself."

He knew she was trying to flatter him, and could not entirely resist her.

"Perhaps we each of us found the other different from what we had believed," he said stiffly.

"I wonder," she said softly. Then, "Jeremy!"

"Yes. Are you in your bedroom?"

"No."

"Neither am I in mine. I'm much nearer to you than that."

He felt slightly startled. Her voice sounded so clearly in his ears that he could almost have believed her in the room, but he knew that was absurd. It was always beautifully clear on the telephone.

"Where are you?" he could not help asking, though he told himself with the next thought that he did not care where she was.

"I'm in a telephone-box immediately opposite your house, and if you put down the telephone for a moment and go to the window, you'll see me. I am watching for you to pull the curtain aside"—with the old, mocking, provocative note in her voice.

He was dumbfounded.

"But—good lord! Are you alone?"

"Naturally. There isn't much room for two in these boxes! Pull aside your curtain, Jeremy"—coaxingly.

It infuriated him to realize that he had to keep a tight hold on himself to refuse to do as she asked.

"I'd rather not," he said stiffly, and her laugh came clearly over the wires to him, maddening him the more.

"Then come down and let me in, Jeremy. I want to talk to you."

"Don't be absurd. This is a bachelor place. You couldn't come here in the middle of the night."

"My sweet, I don't suppose I'd be the first woman to cross those hallowed portals in the dark!" she mocked at him. "Come out and talk to me, then. I've got my car round the corner."

"I don't think so," said Jeremy.

"Afraid?"

"Of course not; but—look here. I want to tell you something," he said desperately, suddenly making up his mind to bring Julie to his aid. "I'm engaged—to be married, I mean."

There was a pause. It was so long that he almost thought she had gone away. Then she spoke again, very quietly.

"That does make a difference, of course. Well—what do we say now, Jeremy? *Au revoir? Bon voyage?* Happy landings? What is the phrase most suitable to the occasion?"

"I think—good-bye, Stella."

The name came as unexpectedly to him as to her. Its intimacy seemed to hang over the silence that followed, to bridge the space between them, to link them in some strange fashion.

"No, Jeremy—my dear. I think I'd rather say—*auf wiedersehen*—till we meet again." And she put up the receiver so softly that he scarcely knew she had done so.

He replaced his own and walked across to the window, drew the curtain aside and saw her leave the telephone-box on the opposite pavement. She was covered from neck to ankle in a dark cloak, but in the light of the street lamp he could see her face clearly. She was looking up, evidently expecting to see him there, and when their eyes met she smiled, lifted her hand slightly, and walked quickly away. He watched her turn the corner, but she did not look back again.

He drew a deep breath, squared his shoulders, and went

back to his desk, addressed the envelope to Julie in a firm hand, and went down into the street to post it. He wanted to make his decision irrevocable as soon as possible, and he had no least regret.

Back in the flat, he felt suddenly very tired. He turned off the lights in his sitting-room and went to bed and to sounder sleep than he had known for months.

10

Mrs. Cave glanced anxiously up at the clock.

Eight o'clock again and Julie not home. It was really too bad how that Madam worked her girls, and it was not as if she paid them anything for all this extra work they did. They were pouring money into Monique's coffers at this time of year, with all the winter fineries demanded for the seasonal gaieties.

Mrs. Cave herself was as busy as Julie would let her be, for the firm that employed her would have liked more of her careful, conscientious work which would not allow buttons to be hung on by a single thread or hems to be botched up anyhow. She had been glad to take the regular work that enabled her to be independent of Julie's earnings, that would leave Julie free to make her own plans.

She sighed again, and the worried frown came back to her face.

What was really happening with Jeremy? Why had nothing been settled between them—or, if it had, why was it not made public? The mother refused to harbor resentment at being kept as ignorant as everyone else. Julie was so ready with her excuses, and they all had a hollow sound to the woman who knew in Jeremy Denton's keeping was a pearl of great price.

Steps outside brought her to her feet, but it was only Dickie returning from a Scouts' meeting and bringing his scoutmaster with him.

Mrs. Cave held out her hand to the visitor, her smile the warm one reserved for her best-loved friends.

"Why, Ben, we haven't seen you for such a long time. Come in. There's coffee just made and a batch of parkin straight out of the oven, though I don't know that it's got hard enough to take off the tin yet."

120

Ben Elson smiled his slow, wide smile. It seemed to transform his plain face and redeem its homeliness.

"Well, it'll be queer parkin that Dick and I can't get off a tin after a meeting like tonight's, Mrs. Cave. What do you say, Dick?"

The fact that his sworn enemy, Jimmy Elson, was the brother of Ben did not in the least deter Dick from giving to his leader tremendous hero-worship, and he responded to the question with a smile of dog-like affection.

"Whatever you say goes with me always," he said, going with them into the warm, fragrant kitchen, where, on a side table, the tins of parkin had been set to cool and harden. "Help yourself, sir"—prising up a substantial slab for himself and biting into it with relish. "I say, Mum, can Ben help me finish tacking down the new carpet in Julie's room?"

"Well, that's hardly the thing to ask a visitor to do," demurred his mother with a smile, but Ben reassured her.

"Dick told me there was a job of work to be done," he said. "Julie not home yet?"—looking round with an elaborate air of indifference which did not deceive Julie's mother.

There was a subtle difference in his voice when he spoke of her, and Mrs. Cave stifled the quick feeling of regret she always felt when she thought of Ben and Julie.

She saw them in her mind's eye as so admirably mated, running between them just the sort of little home they would both love to possess. Of course Ben was no figure of romance. He was short and stockily built, a plodder apparently quite content with his job at a local garage. He would probably never get any further than he was now, but he would always be relied upon to give trustworthy, conscientious service. He never scamped a job, and men who entrusted him with a repair found that they could take their cars out on the road when Ben handed them back and could be reasonably sure they would not be let down a few miles off.

He was a good age for Julie too. He was thirty-two—ten years her senior; but she was more suited by temperament to a man of that age. Younger men nowadays seemed to look for so much superficial gaiety, so many outside attractions. They were unable to appreciate the solid worth that was in Julie.

Still, it was unlikely that she would ever look at Ben or

121

any other man whilst Jeremy Denton shone as the sun, moon, and stars in her heaven, thought Mrs. Cave sadly. Sun, moon, and stars? No, rather the lights above Piccadilly Circus, flashing and meretricious, and blotting out the sky with their garish announcements.

By which thoughts it may seem that Mrs. Cave was out of love with Jeremy, whatever Julie's own feelings might be.

She told Ben of the tale of Julie's late hours.

"Well, we've all got to go through the mill," replied Ben stolidly. "Hard work's for men, though, not for—for girls like Julie. Well, thanks very much for the coffee and the parkin, Mrs. Cave. They were first rate. I don't wonder Julie's such a topping little cook. Shall I just go up with Dick and fix the carpet?"

"Well, if you really don't mind, Ben. I've been paying into a club for the new carpet for her room, and I really wanted it to be a surprise, but it didn't come in time for us to finish it in Dickie's lunch-time this morning."

"I'd do a lot more than that for Julie if I had the chance," said Ben awkwardly.

"I know you would," said Mrs. Cave affectionately. "I do wish she'd come home, carpet or no carpet. She ought to be in by now. If she's not back by the time you've done, perhaps you'd go and meet her from the bus, Ben?"

He smiled but did not reply, and when he had followed Dickie upstairs Mrs. Cave took down from behind the clock on the mantelpiece Jeremy's letter. It had come earlier in the day, and she had already turned it over once or twice with a frown. Lately it seemed as if the only occasions on which Jeremy wrote to Julie were when he wanted to break one of the few arrangements he made to see her or take her out. She did not show these letters to her mother nor make much comment on them, but Mrs. Cave never failed to notice the slight droop in Julie's spirits, the wistful look in her eyes which revealed the hurt her mother, for all her love, was unable to heal.

She had come almost to hate Jeremy for the power he had to hurt Julie, and had half decided not to give her the letter tonight, tired as she would be already with her long day's work. Why couldn't he leave the girl alone entirely and let some better man have a chance to make her happy?

Soon the hammering ceased, and the two came down again.

"Dickie, you go off to bed," said his mother. "You haven't any homework tonight, have you?"

"Oh, Mum, just half an hour . . ." began Dickie, wheedling her.

"Off you go, Sonny Jim, when your mother tells you," said his scoutmaster good-humoredly, but with a tone in his voice that exacted obedience; and after the boy had gone up without a further question Mrs. Cave thought again what a good husband and father Ben Elson would make. If only that Jeremy Denton . . .

"Won't you wait for Julie, Ben? Or go to meet her? She'd be so pleased," she suggested, as Ben took down his hat.

He gave her a rather rueful smile.

"I'd be glad to think that, Mrs. Cave," he said.

Biddy was out at the pictures with a girl-friend, and for the moment they were alone.

Mrs. Cave opened her heart impulsively.

"Ben, have you any idea how things are between Julie and Jeremy Denton?" she asked.

"Well—you know, I haven't seen much of her lately," he hedged.

"She's not happy, Ben, and somehow I don't think anything is going to come of this affair now that he's making all this money. Julie was all right for him and this house a nice place to come to whilst he was poor and just a clerk," went on Mrs. Cave with unusual bitterness. "Now it seems we're none of us good enough for him, and when he does come, he's all dressed up to the nines and talking la-de-dah and making us all feel uncomfortable. It makes me so angry for Julie. She's worth a lot more than that."

"You don't have to tell me that, Mrs. Cave," said Ben slowly.

Mrs. Cave made a sudden resolve.

"Ben, do you love my Julie?" she asked.

He looked at her steadily and without showing any surprise. That was such a comforting thing about Ben. He took life so much as it came, was neither up in the clouds nor down in the depths. His feet just evenly trod the common earth.

"There'll never be anybody else for me, Mrs. Cave," he said. "I know there's no chance for me. She's never

123

thought of me at all, and she'd never look at me—now"—the last word filled with regret.

"She would have done, Ben, if it hadn't been for Jeremy Denton," said Mrs. Cave vehemently.

His steady grey eyes widened a little. There was a faint, incredulous hope in them.

"Oh—do you really think that?" he asked wonderingly.

"I do." Mrs. Cave, having once made the statement, proceeded to enlarge upon it, the wish being father to the thought. "She thinks a lot of you, Ben. She has said time and again what a splendid man you are and how much she admires your work with the scouts. You've made a man of Dickie. Ben—why don't you try to get her for yourself?"

The last words came out with a run. She was almost as much surprised as he when she had spoken them.

Ben's homely face was a study. He had adored Julie ever since they were children—she a tiny, shiny thing whom he had carried in his arms, who had ridden on his back and belabored his willing flanks with her small heels. Then suddenly, it seemed to him, she had been no longer a child but a girl ripe for love, and he realized that his feeling for her was no longer that protective tenderness with which he had regarded the child Julie. The tenderness was still there, and the desire to protect was almost a passion with him; but added to it was the deep and abiding love of a man for a woman.

Ever since that blinding moment of discovery he had dreamed of asking her to be his wife, had lived a secret life shared by her and the dream children she would bear to him, incredible and inspiring thought which had far more of the spiritual than the physical in its essence.

He had always been over-diffident, however, conscious of his own limitations, stressing in his mind an inferiority and unworthiness that existed largely in his own imagination. In his very anxiety to better his position he had been forced to the realization that already he had found his level, that at forty and fifty he would probably be the same poorly paid mechanic that he had been at twenty and thirty. Even if by some amazing stroke of luck, such as winning the Irish Sweep, he became possessed of his own garage, he felt that he would drag Julie down instead of settling on her the comfort and ease he felt to be her due.

So the months and the years had gone by, and whilst he dallied, seldom even venturing to ask her to spend an evening or a Saturday afternoon with him, another man had stepped in and, with no effort at all, had secured the prize that was Julie's heart. Julie herself had never even known of Ben's feeling for her! He had not made even that impression on her life. He would not figure in her memories even as one of the men she might have married!

It had been bitter knowledge to him, in those early days of Jeremy Denton's conquest, that the victor was in no better position to give Julie a comfortable home than was he, Ben, himself. Then the iron entered into his soul when Jeremy soared like a meteor in the sky and made for himself a position which would enable him to gratify Julie's wildest dreams.

With Jeremy an established factor in the home life of the Caves, Ben had withdrawn himself, rarely going to the house even when besought to do so by his devoted admirer, Dickie. He had broken his habit of refusal that evening only because of something Dickie had said to him. The carpet-laying had been only an excuse.

"How is your sister?" he had asked Dickie at the end of the Scout meeting. His hunger for news of Julie had got the better of him for once. He felt he would rather hear she was on the point of marriage than hear no news of her at all.

It was not the first time Dickie had been asked that same question since Biddy had shortened her hair, lengthened her skirts, painted her nails, and learned to flutter her eyelashes, and he greeted it with his usual grunt.

"Biddy? Hmph!" he remarked, or something to that effect, dismissing in that comprehensive sound hair, skirts, nails, eyelashes, and all the rest of the tricks that made up Biddy.

"No. I meant your sister Julie?" explained Ben.

"Oh, *Julie's* all right," said Dickie, absorbed in the intricacies of a new knot which Ben had been teaching them. It was a knot which Indians used to secure their victims to trees, and, thought Dickie, you never know!

"Does—er—is Mr. Benton still about?" ventured Ben.

Dickie looked up with a scowl.

"Him?" He returned to his knot. "He's a bit of a wash-out, if you ask me. Too grand for the likes of us now he's got two plays on in the West End theatres. Wears his soup and fish every night and talks like a bally announcer."

Somehow Dickie's words seemed to lighten considerably

the heavy load Ben had carried for all these months, and he summoned up courage to pursue the conversation.

"You mean—doesn't he come to your house so much? To see Julie?"

Dickie mastered the knot triumphantly and held it out at arm's length, one eye shut, to admire his handiwork.

"Naow!" he said, replying absent-mindedly to the question. "I don't think he and Julie hit it off very well now. I say, I've got that knot, haven't I? Golly, I'd better go! I told Mum I'd be home to finish nailing down Julie's carpet. Come along and help?"—looking hopefully at his hero, in whose hands tools and nails were miraculously obliging.

So that was how Ben, scarcely daring to hope for a sight of Julie, had come to the Caves' house that evening.

And now Mrs. Cave was saying to him, "Why don't you try to get her for yourself?"

Why didn't he? Could he? Was it possible? Was the way even open for him to try?

"But—there's—you see . . ." he floundered.

Mrs. Cave laid a hand on his arm.

"Oh, Ben, she'd be so safe with you," she said earnestly. "Jeremy's different from anyone we've ever known before. I suppose it's because he's so clever and brilliant—but that isn't what'll make my Julie happy. She wants the simpler kinds of happiness, a home which she can care for herself, babies she can love and tend, a man she can work for and be glad with and perhaps sad with. I can't somehow picture Jeremy with that sort of home around him. He's so restless, likes a nightclub more than an evening in the kitchen. Oh, Ben, I'm so *afraid* for Julie—Ssh! There she is"—and she let her hand drop from Ben's arm and hurried to open the door, to take Julie's dripping umbrella from her and exclaim at her wet shoes.

"I'd no idea it was raining, dearie," she said. "I've got your slippers warming, and there's liver hot-pot for supper, and I've made some parkin with nuts in it, the sort you like."

She fussed round Julie, mother-fashion, and brought her into the kitchen, where Ben waited awkwardly.

"Here's Ben, Julie—Ben Elson. He's been sampling the parkin too."

Ben's heart turned over at sight of her. In a shapeless old mackintosh, with damp wisps of hair straggling beneath her beret, with her face pale and her eyes deep-shadowed
126

with fatigue, she was still the loveliest thing in the world to him.

His mind was full of things he would like to be able to say to her, of thoughts that were poetry, that were fragrant and beautiful with his love of her—and yet he stood there, awkward, inarticulate, embarrassed, stumbling over a stool when he went to help her off with her mackintosh and pulling at it with such vigor that she nearly overbalanced and received a shower of drops in her face from a flapping sleeve.

"Nice to see you again, Ben," she said during the process, her voice soft and warm as ever. "It's lovely and cosy in here after the outside. The buses were crowded. I think all London must have been working late."

"Had a lot to do?" asked Ben superfluously.

What he really wanted to say was, "You're the loveliest thing on earth, and I adore you, sweet and beautiful Julie."

Yet all he actually said was, "Had a lot to do?"

"Heaps. Everybody seems to want a new dress or new undies on the same day. I can hardly believe Monique isn't the only modiste in London!"

Mrs. Cave's voice came from the scullery beyond.

"Just bringing your supper, duckie. There, I do hope it hasn't all gone to a slush, keeping it in the oven so long"—bringing in the dish and removing the cover, to set free an appetizing smell.

Julie looked into the pot and took up a spoon.

"It's gorgeous, darling," she said. "I've got good news, Mum. Guess what it is!"—and her eyes invited Ben to share her confidence. That was part of her instinctive kindliness.

Mrs. Cave only just restrained herself from looking up at the clock and the letter it barely concealed. What other good news could there be for Julie but something connected with Jeremy? In spite of her tiredness after her long day there was certainly a new joyousness about her tonight. Whatever she may have said to Ben, Mrs. Cave knew that nothing really counted to Julie for happiness but Jeremy.

"Tell us, Julie," she said uncomfortably, feeling that if she were going to announce her engagement to Jeremy it was unfortunate that Ben happened to be there.

"I'm coming out of the work room and going into the

show room," said Julie. "Isn't that news?"

Mrs. Cave caught her breath and glanced for a fraction of a second at Ben, whose relief was patent to any less casual observer than Julie, who continued to eat and talk by turns.

"Madam had me in this afternoon and asked me if I would like to as Miss Sadler's leaving to be married. It means another ten bob a week to start with, and of course I jumped at it. It won't mean these late nights, either. Only the work room girls have to stay late. After today I shall be able to leave when the shop's shut."

"Won't you miss the needlework, Julie?" asked Mrs. Cave, not quite sure what to make of this new development in Julie's affairs.

It certainly suggested that she had no thought of immediate, or even early marriage, for she would not have thought it worthwhile or fair to Madam to take on a new job for only a short time. What did her pleasure in the change signify? That she had broken with Jeremy, or given up hope of marriage with him?

"I am to get a chance of fitting, under Mrs. Tanner, and that may lead to a really good job in time," went on Julie serenely. "I'm glad I didn't leave Monique's when—when I had that chance to make a change," she finished rather hurriedly.

Her mother knew she was referring to the effort Jeremy had made, months previously, to get her to leave Monique's and take a job in a theatrical work room. It would have brought her into closer touch with the new world that had absorbed him, possibly into closer touch with him personally; but an unexpected streak of independence had made Julie cling to the job she had found for herself and the niche she had taught herself to fill in Madam's often expressed satisfaction.

"Things often work out for the best if we just go steadily on with our jobs and don't worry too much about the future," said Mrs. Cave quietly, and Julie gave her a quick look of affection and understanding. She knew what lay behind those gently spoken words. They found an echo in her own heart. She had had to go steadily on and try not to worry about the future, but it had been very hard of achievement when her heart ached with the inability to understand Jeremy, to see even a very little way into the future.

"Have some parkin, dear?" asked Mrs. Cave, rising to take away the emptied plate.

Julie put out a hand to restrain her.

"Sit still, Mum. I'll get it myself," she said, and, in rising, caught sight of the corner of Jeremy's enevelope tucked behind the clock.

She took it down and glanced at the writing on it with rising color and the light in her eyes which no number of disappointments seemed able to quench. She would rather hear from Jerry to put off a meeting than not hear from him at all—which goes to show how foolish a girl in love can be!

"Oh—that came this afternoon," said her mother rather guiltily.

"It's from Jerry," said Julie, and the soft voice, added to the rising color, the way her fingers closed over the envelope as if they touched the writer himself, told Ben more than any words could have done. Whatever Mrs. Cave might have said, or Dickie, or even Julie herself if she were cornered, there could be no real doubt in the world but that Jeremy Denton was the whole meaning and object of her existence.

He rose from his chair whilst Julie still fingered the envelope without making any attempt to open it.

"Well, I think I'll be getting along now," he said. "Thanks for the parkin, Mrs. Cave. Nice to have seen you again, Julie. Good night."

"I'll see you out," said Mrs. Cave, and they went out into the hall, leaving Julie alone with her letter.

"Do come again to see us, Ben," Mrs. Cave besought him.

His face hardened as much as it could ever do whilst he thought of Julie.

"What's the use?" he asked grimly. "Didn't you see her face when she found that letter from *him*?"

Mrs. Cave sighed.

"I know, Ben, but—I can't believe that things will go like that, not as Julie hopes, and not for long, anyway. That's why I feel I—I'd like you still to keep friends with Julie."

He gave a short laugh and shrugged his shoulders into his coat.

"Do you think she even knows I exist nowadays?" he

129

asked, and opened the front door.

Mrs. Cave went slowly back to the kitchen. Julie would have opened her letter by now. Would she be radiant with the prospect of another meeting with Jerry or downcast by another of those ingenious excuses for breaking an appointment? When Jerry did come to the house, he certainly seemed to be in love with her. He treated her like a queen and yet as her devoted lover, a combination against which few girls would have been proof—certainly not tender-hearted, loving Julie. If he were really so devoted, thought Mrs. Cave, why on earth did he not press her to marry him?

With these thoughts uppermost in her mind she returned to the kitchen.

Julie was standing by the fire, standing with her back to the door, quite still. She made no movement when she heard her mother come into the room—if, indeed, she heard her at all. Something frightening in that utter stillness made Mrs. Cave pause for an instant at the door and then sent her, on swift feet, to Julie's side. One hand gripped the edge of the high mantelpiece till the knuckles showed white, whilst in the other was crushed the sheets of Jeremy's letter. She could see the firm, masculine script, the straight, even lines.

But it was Julie's face which startled her mother after that first comprehensive glance. It was ash grey; her eyes were closed and her mouth set in a hard line. Save for the faint quivering of the nostrils it was a dead face, and Mrs. Cave cried out instinctively:

"Julie—oh, my darling, what is it?' What is it?"—her hands closing over the one that held the crumpled letter.

Julie opened her eyes. They were terrible to see. It was as if in one moment of time all the youth and the life and the hope had died.

Then she spoke, and her voice was not like Julie's voice at all. It was that of a stranger, and Mrs. Cave instinctively drew back, a hand at her breast.

"Jerry. He has sent me a letter. Reasons why I am not a fit person for him to marry—tabulated reasons . . ." And before her mother could speak or move she turned suddenly and ran out of the room and up the stairs. Mrs. Cave heard the key turn in her bedroom door.

For some moments she stood there motionless, too

stunned by the shock even to think. Then she went up to that locked door and knocked hesitatingly. She could not— *could not*—leave Julie suffering like that, and alone.

"Can I do anything, my darling, or would you rather be alone?" she asked.

She had always been too wise a mother to intrude on her children's individual lives, had accorded them their rights to privacy of thought and freedom of action in common with other people who were not her children. Perhaps that was why they trusted her so implicitly and gave her, unasked, their confidence. She valued their trust more than anything else in life, and only in Julie's desperate need did she offer the help which had not yet been sought.

Julie's voice came to her—muffled, Mrs. Cave hoped, by the tears that might bring some measure of relief.

"I'd rather be alone, Mum," she said.

"All right, darling. I'll keep Biddy in my room tonight—and—and I'll leave my door open all night, Julie."

There was no reply, and Mrs. Cave went slowly downstairs to wait for Biddy. She was filled with anguish for Julie, her heart's darling, and with a terrific anger against the man who had so grievously—so wantonly, she felt—stricken down the girl who worshipped him.

She called Julie's words to memory. What was it Jeremy had sent her? Tabulated reasons why she was not fit to marry him? Not *fit*? *Julie*? How dare he! Even if it were true, how dare he do such a thing to Julie!

Rather was it the other way round, thought Mrs. Cave wrathfully, and Jeremy not fit to marry Julie.

There were steps outside, voices, and the little flurry which always heralded Biddy's approach. Things had a way of happening to Biddy, and even the most ordinary incidents were invested with interest when her lively mind examined them.

The girl-friend departed and the kitchen door was flung wide, as it always was, by Biddy's eager hand.

"Lo, Mum, darling; we've seen the most gorgeous picture, with Ginger Rogers in the most glorious clothes. She's supposed to be quite poor, but her furs must have cost hundreds, though who cares about that? Gosh, wouldn't I love to dance with Fred Astaire! I've almost decided to go pic . . . Why, what's up, Mum? You look so queer. Anything happened?"—breaking off suddenly as the expression on her mother's face superceded her glowing recollections of the film.

"Close the door, darling. It's Julie. She's had a letter from Jerry"—and Mrs. Cave's lips pursed ominously.

Biddy threw down her bag dramatically.

"What, chucking her, the swine?" she demanded, in swift indignation.

"Yes."

For once Mrs. Cave did not remonstrate with her daughter over her choice of words. Possibly she envied her in her heart the ability to relieve her feelings in that way. Biddy varied between the ultra-refined and the frankly vulgar, her mother and Julie constantly endeavoring to make her steer a comfortable course between the two.

"Not only given her up, but done it so horribly, so cruelly," said her mother, her voice quivering with a passion of pity and resentment. "I can't tell you about it because Julie might not like it, but it's upset her dreadfully. Will you sleep with me tonight, Biddy, so that she can have her room to herself? You don't mind for once?"

"Of course not, Mum. I like sleeping with you, anyway"—with one of those swift, secret hugs which kept her mother always thankfully aware that Biddy's swift transition from childhood to womanhood had not, in its speed, crowded out the people who loved her, or lost her mother her place in the girl's strange, unknown heart.

Whilst Julie's life was an open book, Biddy's was secret and mysterious. She made her aspirations quite public, but to no one did she ever reveal the intimate and more serious thoughts which surely must lie beneath them. Mrs. Cave wondered about them, worried a little because so much was hidden from her, but knew that no one would ever succeed in getting from Biddy more than she chose to offer, either of confidence or of affection. She was a self-contained little person, abundantly sufficient unto herself.

"I suppose Julie wants to be alone?" asked Biddy.

"I think so. I went to the door and asked her. She never used to want to bear things alone, but—I suppose she's grown up now"—with a sigh.

Biddy nodded and blew into the fingers of her new gloves, an old-fashioned trick learned from her mother and never forgotten.

"Mm! I used to go alone to the dentist's, but you always had to go with Julie, remember? Gosh, I wish she'd never met Jerry Denton!" she added fiercely. "He was never good enough for her, not her sort at all. He wants someone like me, hard and able to give back as bad as I get. Why the devil couldn't she have fallen for Ben Elson?"

"You knew about Ben?" asked her mother, surprised, for she had thought it her own secret, evolved by her own perspicacity.

Biddy's eyes opened.

"But, darling, of course I did! So does Dickie"—after which Mrs. Cave felt she had flattered herself over her knowledge of her children—even Dickie.

"I shouldn't have thought *you* would have approved of poor Ben as a husband for anyone," she said.

Biddy gave her a funny little smile.

"Not for me, of course! but Julie's different," she said, moving where she could catch a glimpse of her lovely little face and the sophisticated rolls of golden hair above it in the kitchen looking-glass.

"You mean that it would be all right for your sister to be poor, though not for yourself?" asked her mother, a trifle sharply.

Biddy chuckled.

"Oh no, darling. I don't want anybody to be poor. It isn't just money I'm thinking of. What I mean is that if Julie had only fallen for Ben, she'd never get hurt, and that would mean a lot more to her than money. Now, nobody could hurt me, not the way Jerry's hurt Julie. I'm not built that way, but she is. She puts all her eggs into one basket and then, when the basket drops, they're all smashed and she's got nothing left but a few shells and a sticky mess. I've got a basket all right, but I shall be careful what I put in it, and they'll be unbreakable—stones, perhaps, or gold nuggets"—with an impish grin which made her seem both older and younger than her seventeen years. "If the basket does drop, no harm'll be done. I shall just pick up my nuggets and start off again. Julie's helpless because she's in love with Jerry. I shan't ever get fond enough of anyone to be hurt by them. That's why I know I shall be able to marry somebody rich"—with conviction in her tone.

Mrs. Cave smiled in spite of her anxiety. She had recognized in Biddy's cradle that inflexible determination to get what she wanted. She saw it now as a granite-like quality which would probably make her impervious to the shafts and spears of life, for Biddy's desires were concrete and physical. She could readily believe that no man would ever have the power to hurt this strange sister of Julie's.

The smile trailed off into a sigh, though—a sigh for Julie, whose heart was so unshielded, so cruelly open to those same shafts and spears. How had she and the husband, whom she had so devotedly loved, managed to divide so unequally the things they had given their children? How had they made Biddy so guarded and Julie so vulnerable?

"I could murder Jerry Denton!" said Biddy savagely.

"I'm afraid that wouldn't help poor Julie," said her mother. "Come along, dear. I think you ought to go to bed. Don't make a noise in case Julie's managed to get to sleep."

Biddy kissed her mother and crept upstairs, solacing herself for the lack of a nightdress of her own by rummaging in Mrs. Cave's drawer until she found a frothy affair of pink ninon and filmy lace, a garment which Julie had made for her mother's birthday but which the recipient had never ventured to wear.

Biddy tied the satin ribbons round her waist and turned herself in front of the long mirror of the wardrobe, taking a keen delight in her appearance. She had no feeling of shame, such as other girls during her last term at school had had, or the signs of too-early maturity in slender limbs and budding breasts. She rejoiced at the thought that her dreams could come true all the sooner, for she had the sense to realize that nothing of those dreams were possible to a little girl. Already men who came to the salon looked at her as she manicured their nails, smiled at her as they would not have smiled at a schoolgirl. She watched girls who were her customers, noted exactly what constituted their air of experience and self-assurance, and sedulously copied them. Standing before the mirror in the lovely but sophisticated garment Julie had fashioned for her mother, Biddy knew that if her day had not really come she was already at its drawing.

"Poor old Julie!" she thought at last, turning away reluctantly from the alluring vision of herself. "It's much better to be like me, to care for nice clothes and going out and having a good time than for a man like Jerry Denton. Catch me letting any man let me down!" And she climbed into the big bed, suddenly sleepy and hoping her mother would not be long.

It was nice to lie there in the silent darkness, to be in her mother's bed again, to forget for a little while that she was grown up, with all her aspirations and ambitions, and to be just a little girl again. Mum's arms were soft and warm. They were unfailing. They gave one a feeling of security which one did not even know one liked to have.

In the next room, Julie lay on her bed, still fully dressed, her eyes swollen with crying and staring hopelessly out beyond the dim square of the window, its curtains still undrawn.

She had heard Biddy creep up to bed and was grateful for the solitude her mother had secured for her.

On the half-landing below, Dickie's door opened surreptitiously, and she heard his bare feet on the linoleum outside.

"Julie!" came his voice at her door in a hoarse stage whisper that could have been heard all over the house. "Julie, if you run anything into your feet, it'll only be a rusty nail!"

11

It was both a relief and a nightmare to Julie to have to tackle her new work the next day. If the strangeness of it made her nervous, at least the need to give it all her attention served to distract her mind from its bitter sadness.

Yet, as she worked and listened to instructions with mechanical care, her mind asked its desperate, unanswerable question. How could he have hurt her so? Why could he not have just told her?

Madam watched her pale, unsmiling face with a little frown, wondering whether she had not, after all, made a mistake in taking Miss Cave into the show room. She had always seemed so bright and cheerful in the work room.

Once during the morning she spoke to her.

"Are you not well, Miss Cave?" she asked.

Julie flushed and blinked back at the weak, foolish tears. She was so terribly susceptible just now to outside influences, and Madam's tone had been hard and cold.

"Quite well thank you, Madam," she said in a small voice.

"Then please try to look a little brighter and be a little more pleasant," said Madam crisply. "Clients do not like to be waited on by girls who look as if it is too much trouble to please them."

Julie swallowed.

"I am sorry, Madam," she said, her eyes cast down so that they would not reveal their tears. "I did not intend to give that impression."

"Then please remember in future," said Madam, and sailed away, all gracious smiles, to greet two women—"clients" Madam called them rather than the bourgeois "customers" of the butcher, the baker, the candlestick-maker—who had come into the show room during this low-toned conversation.

"Good morning, mesdames. So glad to see you back again in England, Mrs. Milroy"—speaking to the other woman, but casting a speculative glance at the younger one.

She knew who she was. Everybody who studied the fashionable magazines as Madam did was obliged to do knew the features of the lovely Mrs. Dale, and it was very gratifying to see her in Monique's for the first time.

Mrs. Milroy, a woman quite frank about being in the late fifties, returned the greeting and the smile pleasantly.

"I'm glad to be back too, Monique. I'm very shabby, but I was so hungry for England that I didn't even stop in Paris for so much as a hat. When Mrs. Dale said she must get clothes, I suggested that she should come here with me. No doubt you can help us both?"

"But of course; I am enchanted," said Madam with an almost reverential smile at Stella Dale.

Mrs. Milroy's friendly glance had travelled round the luxurious grey-and-silver reception-room and come to rest on Julie. Her eyes warmed with interest. She loved young people.

"Someone new, Monique?" she asked.

Madam glanced round. The other assistants were busy, and for the moment Julie was the only one at liberty.

"This is her first day. I am afraid she is not trained yet," said Madam apologetically. "We should not give *you* anyone untrained, Mrs. Milroy"—with an arch look at this favorite customer. "Miss Cave, fetch Miss Moore, will you? Perhaps you can relieve her with Mrs. Austin. Would you like Mrs. Tanner, too, Mrs. Milroy?"

"Later, perhaps," said Mrs. Milroy with a friendly nod and smile at Julie. "Let Miss Cave attend to me at the moment. She'll want someone to practice on"—smilingly.

"Oh, there is Miss Moore. Let her give her attention to Mrs. Dale. Youth and beauty must be served, you know!"—with a bright, mischievous glance at the lovely, aloof Stella. "Oh, I know what's hovering on your lips, Monique. You want to remind me that youth and beauty can survive neglect where old age cannot. Never mind. This little girl and I will talk the sort of frocks I like, and you can amuse Mrs. Dale with the sort you and she like."

Julie, who had stood by uncertainly, smiled involuntarily as she met the friendly glance. Mrs. Milroy was one of those happy people in whose presence no trouble or grief can remain quite so heavy a load.

Madam intercepted the friendly exchange of smiles with a voice like honey thinly spread over sandpaper.

"Please attend to Madame in No. 4 dressing-room, Miss Cave. She will like to see the Viennese models, and also Henriot's gowns. What may I show you first, Mrs. Dale?"—turning back to the younger woman with that admirable blend of servility and friendliness which was one of her most successful assets.

"I like unusual clothes," said Stella smoothly. "I prefer them to be designed for me and if possible on me. I will see your designer first. Mrs. Milroy tells me she is quite wonderful."

Madam swept her away, gathering about her a little escort of attendant sycophants, whilst Mrs. Milroy, who evidently knew the place well, led the way to her favorite dressing-room, a place of neutral tints and graceful, old-fashioned furniture. Monique had a variety of dressing-rooms in different styles to suit the personality of her clients.

"I am easy to manage," said the older woman, with her warm smile which somehow reminded Julie of her mother and brought to her a mingled feeling of comfort and homesickness. She longed for nothing so much as to creep home and hide.

"I will do my best, madam," she said in her quiet way.

"I am sure you will, my dear. I dare say you know exactly what I shall like, one or two evening gowns, and something for afternoon bridge—flowing things which will suitably disguise my unfashionable silhouette. Not black, though I know it suits me best. My husband dislikes black on me, for some unimaginable reason, but it's reason enough for me."

137

Julie liked the way she said that. It was such a change from the way most women nowadays seemed either to ignore their husbands or mention them in the disparaging voice that conveyed the impression of "poor thing, but mine own." Mrs. Milroy spoke as if it really mattered to her whether her husband approved of her appearance.

Like a flash Julie remembered a model they had just made in the work rooms, a gown which her mind fitted at once to the gracious personality of her first customer. It was designed actually for a place in the coming fashion display, but Julie felt that did not matter if it could be sold before the need to display it.

She brought it to the dressing-room, a gown of soft, pale grey, a misty, trailing thing that would not be too revealing, but that would pick out the ash-grey of the hair and the deeper grey of the eyes.

"I think this would be lovely for you," she said shyly. Away from Madam's eagle eyes she was losing her nervousness and coming under the spell of Mrs. Milroy's easy grace.

"Yes, that's lovely, you clever child," said Mrs. Milroy, fingering the delicate chiffon approvingly.

"I think for you it wants very loose, wide sleeves with grey fox edging them," suggested Julie with temerity, for it was one of Mrs. Tanner's own designs she suggested altering.

"I agree. That would be exactly right. How about Miss Sadler modelling them for me as she usually does?"

Julie explained that Miss Sadler was being married.

"Well, it's not much use asking you wisps of girls to model my clothes for me, is it?" asked Mrs. Milroy with her jolly laugh. "Bring me some other frocks to see, and when I've chosen those I like best, they can be sent to my house and I can try them on. I can't spare the time now."

Julie worked with a will, ransacked the model-cupboards, visualized her client in exactly the right clothes and had the satisfaction of knowing that she was thoroughly pleased with her selection and likely to give a big order.

"Now, I'd like you to come yourself with these things," said Mrs. Milroy. "You seem to know just what I like, and you have made such sensible suggestions. I very seldom buy off the peg, even at Monique's, but we have been abroad so long, and I hate American clothes. Either I or the Americans are quite the wrong shape and style. I can't wait for things to be made."

Julie smiled, and Mrs. Milroy thought again what a nice little thing she was.

"I shall have to ask Madam," said Julie doubtfully. "I am so very new to the show room that she may think someone more experienced than I ought to do it."

Mrs. Milroy patted her arm.

"I'll see to that," she promised. "I like young things about me. I shall see that you always attend to me now. You seem to know just what I like—and what my husband will like, which, believe me, is much more to the point. Oh, here comes Monique. Monique, I want one or two of these things, and they'll simply have to be made right for me because I can't afford the time to have things made. This grey gown, for instance, is so exactly mine that I refuse to let it go."

Monique eyed the grey gown with disapproval. She considered it part of her job in life to make her ageing clients look younger, and she disapproved of allying grey clothes to grey hair.

"Is Madam very wise to wear grey?" she asked. "Miss Cave, bring Harriot's lavender cire."

Julie brought the gown, arranging its gleaming folds across the carpet, hoping earnestly that Mrs. Milroy would not have it. She felt it was too hard and bright for a woman meant by Nature and experience of life to be soft and charming.

Mrs. Milroy shook her head.

"Heavens, no, Monique! I'm not laid up in the lavender yet, I should feel armor-plated in that material. I much prefer the grey."

"Grey is not youth-giving," objected Monique.

"Rubbish! Why should I want my youth back? I'm fifty-eight, and don't want to lose one of my years, with their joys and sorrows and knowledge. The grey expresses me, and my husband has just given me the most marvellous emeralds. Emeralds—or do you think amethysts, Miss Cave?"—turning to Julie with a smile that flattered her.

"Emeralds, I think madam," said Julie shyly, and Monique had to nod her approval, though they could see she was slightly ruffled.

"I'd like Miss Cave to come herself with these things,"

said Mrs. Milroy, "About three o'clock. When I have made up my mind which of them to have, you can send your fitter. Shall we see how Mrs. Dale has been getting on?"

Stella was still leaning over a table of designs and a heap of material. Mrs. Tanner's clever pencil had been busy with amazing modifications of the human form divine as decreed by modern art.

Mrs. Milroy smiled. She had known Stella for years.

"I won't wait for you, Stella, my dear," she said. "A clever young person in there has found me just what I wanted and is going to bring the things out to me for my more leisurely inspection this afternoon. Will you come and advise and criticise? Your taste is so amazingly right."

Stella smiled absently.

"Perhaps I will," she said. "No. I don't really think that bunchy line is becoming to me, no matter what the fashion designers say. I prefer the straight, classic lines"; and she took up a pencil and ruthlessly drew lines all over a delicate water color which Mrs. Tanner had been showing her.

Mrs. Milroy gave an amused smile, nodded to Monique, gave Julie a friendly little glance and sailed out, perfectly at her ease, self-assured but unassuming, always a great lady, one felt.

Monique turned to Julie, her manner altering.

"In future, Miss Cave, you had better consult Miss Moore or Mrs. Tanner about what to show important clients. That grey is most unsuitable for Mrs. Milroy, and she pays much higher prices for her clothes than we can possibly charge for the things you have shown her. The grey is only nineteen guineas—ridiculous!"

In the last sentence lay Madam's real objection to having sold Mrs. Milroy the gown.

"You had better get Miss Moore to make a careful selection of gowns to take with you this afternoon, and I will see them before you pack them. There is a crushed velvet in the new mauve . . ."

"Mrs. Milroy does not like mauve," suggested Julie diffidently.

"Miss Cave, please remember that *I* control this business, not you," said Monique severely; and Julie was silent, though inwardly she resolved that Mrs. Milroy should not wear clothes unsuited to her and disliked by her merely to fill the coffers of Monique.

Punctually at three o'clock a taxi set her and her many boxes down at the door of Mrs. Milroy's town house, a large and dignified place which Julie felt reflected the restfulness of its chatelaine's personality.

A maid took her to a bedroom where Stella Dale, looking lovelier than ever, sat smoking a cigarette in a jade holder and talking to her hostess.

"Come in, Miss Cave. You are delightfully punctual," said that kindly woman. "I am indulging in the iniquity of tea at this time of the afternoon. I expect you would like a cup, wouldn't you? Bring another cup, Louise, for Miss Cave, and have the rest of the boxes brought up. I suppose there are some more to come?"—for Julie had not been able to carry more than one of them.

Her proposal to go down for them herself was waved aside, and whilst they waited for the extra tea cup, Julie unpacked the frocks and hung them up. Some of them were her own selection, but others had been chosen by Monique from the most expensive of her models, and Julie hoped devoutly that Mrs. Milroy would choose at least one of these.

The two older women watched the unpacking and compared views.

"Don't you really mind looking your age?" asked Stella curiously. "It isn't a pose? You really don't mind?"

"Not a bit," said Mrs. Milroy with a laugh. "Why should I? I've a vast store of amusing experiences to remember, and with sixty looming on the horizon I am still sought after and admired, and my husband still thinks me the most beautiful and desirable woman in the world, so what more can a woman ask? Of course I am aware that I have something material to give to my social circle, that my parties are agreeable, and that entertaining and important people are always to be met in my house. I am vain enough to believe, though, that there is still a certain attraction in me personally, though I am not foolish enough to think that at fifty-eight I can rely on sex appeal. It is the very fact that I am that age, that I have the store of experience which only years can give, that makes me still attractive. Oh no, my dear"—to Julie, who was unpacking the mauve velvet—"I could not possibly wear that shade. I should have to use a violet make-up, and it has taken me years to educate my husband into appreciating even powder and nail-polish! He would divorce me if I appeared in mauve rouge."

Julie finished hanging up the dresses, drank her tea from its priceless egg-shell china, and surreptitiously watched Stella Dale, her studied grace of movement which had become a natural asset, the changing expressions which gave her face mobility but never allowed it to be anything but lovely. She noticed the way she spoke and smiled, knew that much of her beauty was artificial, the pose studied, but appreciated the artistic effect of the whole. Every natural asset was made the most of, delicately brought to the observer's notice. Stella Dale was the finished product of an age newly awakened to the power of physical perfection.

She thought, as she must, of Jeremy. Nothing could yet cover that aching wound. Every word of that indictment still stabbed her. When he had been writing those cruel words, was this the sort of woman he had in mind? Was this the kind of wife he imagined as suitable to his present and his future?

Though she was in a world far removed from that of Julie, Stella Dale was conceivably of the world to which Jeremy had aspired.

Jeremy had told her, Julie, that she was not even pretty; sweet," he had called her. Her lips curled. Sweet, indeed! Sugar-candy for children. Mrs. Dale was beautiful.

Watching Stella, with no knowledge of her story and certainly no least inkling that Jeremy even knew her, Julie knew a terrible longing to have been made like her, possessing, as surely she did, all the things Jeremy looked for in a wife—beauty, intelligence, breeding, a social background—all the things impossible for Julie ever to achieve.

Suddenly the blood rushed to her cheeks and her heart stood still.

Mrs. Milroy, who, it seemed, had been absent from England for eighteen months with a husband who had the wanderlust and loved to explore the farthest places of the earth, was taking this opportunity of catching up with current affairs, and Stella was giving her information as to people they both knew and others whom Mrs. Milroy would have to know.

"There are so very few newly interesting people," the beautiful casual voice was saying. Then, with a little reminiscent smile, she spoke the words that had such a startling effect on Julie. "I ought to qualify that a little.

There's one notable exception—Jeremy Denton, the new playwright who is setting London by the ears."

"I like his name, though that's nothing to go by. His real name's probably George Bung, or something like that," said Mrs. Milroy with her whimsical smile. "Should I like him, or is he one of those sexless creatures, more than half female?"

Stella fitted another of her little green-tipped cigarettes into the jade holder.

"Oh no, my dear, I assure you he is quite entirely male," she said with a slow, indolent smile which had an amazing effect on Julie, for it made her feel angry without being in the least able to justify the feeling nor even to know with whom she was so angry.

"I take it from that that you know him?" asked Mrs. Milroy, prepared to be amused at another of the little scandalous stories of which she only amongst women was the recipient. She disapproved of Stella Dale in her heart and knew that Brian disliked her intensely, but there was a secret lawlessness in her which enjoyed the adventures of this beautiful rebel against society's accepted code.

"A little," admitted Stella smoothly. "He is an amusing animal at present, not quite sure whether to grow wings or a tail."

"And you're helping him to make up his mind, I take it?" asked Mrs. Milroy drily.

She had put on one of the new frocks, and Julie was kneeling on the floor pinning up the hem to let her see the shortened effect. She was thankful for the chance of hiding her flaming, unhappy face.

This time, Stella laughed outright, and the sound instinctively suggested to Julie's jealous ears a familiarity with Jeremy which she resented bitterly. And apart from that, what right had this woman to be amused at Jeremy, as that laugh suggested she was?

"He's an odd creature," said Mrs. Dale reflectively, the echo of her laughter still in her voice. "Do you know he actually has ideals?"

"Well, why not?" asked Mrs. Milroy, amused. "I've still got mine, even if they are a bit tattered and green at the seams, and I take it this man is still young?"

"Oh, quite amazingly—and amusingly so, though he is very angry when I remind him of it. But a playwright in these modern times with ideals! I ask you!"

"I shall certainly go to see his play," said Mrs. Milroy with determination. "What is it called?"

"There are two. Think of that for success. The first is called *The Bauble* and has been running for quite a time at the Vanity. The other, his second, is *Antimony*, at the Duke's."

"I take it they really are successful, or you would not be so much interested, my dear," said Mrs. Milroy, her smile robbing the word of real venom, though there was a spice of malice intentionally left in them. "Am I to understand his plays set forth these ideals at which you cavil?"

"His first one does to some extent, *The Bauble*. Fortunately he listened to reason before he produced his second."

"Whose reason? Yours?" asked Mrs. Milroy with that spice of malice still in her voice.

Stella smiled.

"Partly. I like you in that gown, Agnes. . . . But haven't you made it rather too short for Mrs. Milroy?"—the last words spoken in a patronizing tone to the kneeling Julie.

"Perhaps. Let it down an inch, Miss Cave, and see how it looks then. . . . I am quite intrigued about this Jeremy Denton. He is young, you say?"

"Quite extraordinarily so."

"And how old are you, Stella?" smilingly.

Mrs. Dale rose, crushed out the end of her cigarette, and went to the dressing-table to renew her make up.

"In years, thirty," she said. "In knowledge and disillusionment, seventy."

"In other words, you feel you are at the junction of— what is the quotation? If youth but knew and if age but could? By the way, what happened to young Addington, Stella? I thought you were engaged to him."

Stella shrugged her shoulders and continued her careful accentuation of the curve of her lips.

"He bored me," she said briefly.

"Won't you get bored once too often, my dear?" asked the older woman. "It is a habit which grows unbecomingly on the young."

"Oh, I suppose my final boredom will be another marriage," said Stella. "Meanwhile, I like meeting amusing people and doing amusing things. There are always cocktails and scandal to be had. Are you going to the Mattisons' tonight, by the way?"

"Yes. Brian wants to meet Miles Henway, the scientist, though the probable outcome will be a trip to the moon. It's almost the only place left for him," said Mrs. Milroy equably.

Though in public his wife pretended to be a slightly unwilling participator in Brian Milroy's travels in search of adventure, actually she loved as much as he this free roaming of the world, and was as much at home by the campfire or in a Lapp hut as she was in her own drawing-room.

Stella, adjusting a wrap of wonderful furs, gave her a smile that was faintly bitter.

"What a very devoted wife you are, Agnes!" she said.

"It pays me to be with a husband like mine," said Brian's wife in her peaceful fashion. "He's the sort who must have a woman to fuss over, so I might as well be the woman as—well, as you, dear"—with a smile which left Stella in no possible doubt but that Agnes Milroy had known of that one attempt she had made, nearly two years ago now and very soon after Brandy's suicide, on Brian Milroy's fidelity.

Stella prepared to take her leave.

"I shall see you at the Mattisons' then?" she asked.

"Yes. Am I going to meet your playwright there?"

Stella shrugged her shoulders.

"Possibly. One can never be quite sure of him, but if he is there tonight I'll see that you meet him."

Mrs. Milroy stepped out of the dress, whose hem now seemed satisfactory.

"Well, if I'm going to meet him, I'd rather it be whilst he is still a roaring lion than wait until you've toned his roaring down to the bleating of a nice tame sheep," she said. "Good-bye, my dear. Thank you for your help."

When they were alone, Julie took from its hanger another of the frocks yet untried. Her face was pale and there was such a look of dumb misery on it that Mrs. Milroy remarked on it in her kindly fashion.

"I've tried you out, my child," she said. "You look much too pale. Shall I ask them to send you up some more tea, my panacea for everything, or are you fashionable enough to prefer sherry?"

"Please don't trouble," said Julie shyly. "I'm not very tired. I never have much color. Will you try on this one next, or the ruby georgette?"

But Mrs. Milroy insisted, and made her drink the unac-

145

customed sherry, which brought color to her cheeks, before discussing the rest of the frocks.

Afterwards, whilst the girl was repacking some of the dresses to take back, and carefully hanging up those which Miss Moore would have to come to see the next day, Mrs. Milroy talked in her pleasant way, drawing Julie out and making her feel that she was a friend rather than Monique's little work-girl.

She touched on her home life, and here Julie was more at her ease, telling her with lessening shyness of the beloved "Mum," about Biddy and her funny little ways, about their hopes and fears for Dickie's future.

Agnes Milroy, whose heart knew its own bitterness of frustrated motherhood—her one child dying at birth and leaving her never able to have another—listened with a mind ever open for the many notes on life's great chorale. She could see so clearly, with such sympathy, that home and family which had given Julie life. This was a daughter from amongst her own dream-children, simple and sweet and sincere. The Stella Dales had no place there.

"And what of your own future, my dear?" she asked at last. "You've told me all about the others and your hopes for them, but what about yourself? Are there no hopes? Is there no young man in the case?"

Julie's face flushed and then grew pale again, and the kindly woman drew her own conclusions, hastening to repair what so unintentionally she had done.

"Life holds so many chances and changes for us all, my dear," she said gently. "I have not lived through more than half a century without realizing that each joy has its place and each sorrow no less a place and a definite value. There is no pleasure in sunshine which is there all the time. I know that, for I have spent months in a country so sunny that the first cloud in the sky, the first drop of rain, sent us all mad with joy. And you know yourself, in your own work, that a dark line, a little touch of black, brings out the beauty of a gown which might otherwise be too bright, adds strength and meaning to the whole. Isn't it so?"

Julie listened to the quiet, wise words, finding there some measure of peace if as yet there could be no comfort for her.

In her mind was still the insistent memory of Stella Dale. Although she knew now that there was the link of at least acquaintance between the two, she did not connect them with anything more intimate, but she could not help a feeling that some such woman must have been in Jeremy's mind when he had written that cruel document he had sent her. Unconsciously perhaps he had been thinking of this very woman.

Mrs. Milroy let her go almost regretfully. She sometimes referred to herself as "an interfering old woman," but it was hard to let this girl go without having been able to find and turn the key which she felt would unlock a sorrow which should not exist at that age. Sorrows were for the old, for the middle-aged in reason, but the young should be

12

happy. Even the longest day draws to its close, and Julie let herself into the house that evening with a feeling of thankfulness that it was over, even though she had yet to face the night.

Biddy was out on one of her mysterious errands, Dickie immured as usual in the other room with his books, and Mrs. Cave was in the kitchen with her pile of mending.

"Tired, darling?" she asked, pushing the socks aside to take Julie's favorite savory from the oven.

"A little. It's been an interesting day, though," and as she made a pretence of eating, knowing that the savory had taken a long time to prepare, she outlined her day, described her visit to Mrs. Milroy's beautiful house, but could not bring herself to mention Mrs. Dale or the coincidental discovery of her acquaintance with Jeremy.

Just as she had finished and was carrying the dishes out to the scullery preparatory to helping with the mending, the bell rang, two long rings and a short one, and she stood still, her face working queerly. Then she set down the dishes with trembling hands and went towards the door.

"That's Jerry. I can't see him, Mum," she said, and fled up the stairs and into her room.

Mrs. Cave, her mouth set in a grim line quite foreign to it, went to the door to admit the unwelcome visitor.

To her amazement, Jeremy showed no sign of embarrassment, but came jauntily into the hall, hung his hat on its accustomed peg, and gave Mr. Cave a boisterous kiss.

147

"Hello, darling," he said. "If my affections were not otherwise engaged, I'd be falling head over ears in love with you"—and he went into the kitchen, singing:

> "Lovely lady I'm falling madly
> In love with you!"

He looked round in surprise.

"Hello, where's my lovely lady?" he asked. "Not home yet? I telephoned to Monique's, but they told me she was out on a job, but she ought to be home now, oughtn't she?"

He laid down on the table the great sheaf of roses he had brought with him and looked inquiringly at the half-cleared state of the supper remains, which suggested that the last of the Caves to arrive had had a meal.

Mrs. Cave followed him into the kitchen and shut the door behind her. Her anger had risen to boiling point at seeing him so unperturbed. As if he could treat Julie like that and find all her family just as friendly as ever towards him!

"Julie's at home, Jeremy, but you surely can't imagine that she wants to see you," she said harshly.

Jeremy turned to look at her in bewilderment.

"But—didn't she get my letter?" he asked. "I wrote to her last night and posted it myself. She ought to have had it by now."

Mrs. Cave felt fiercely protective towards Julie. Even the gentlest of animals turns tiger when its young is threatened. Yet she could not help a feeling of rather helpless surprise at Jeremy's attitude. She might have thought Julie mistaken had she not seen with her very eyes the letter that had been written. Julie had pushed it into her hand without a word when she left the house that morning, and the sentences Jeremy had penned were burnt into her memory as if with a branding-iron.

"Yes, she did get your letter, Jeremy," she said in that same uncompromising tone. "That's why I wonder you have the nerve to come here tonight, to Julie's home and Julie's mother."

Jeremy's perplexity deepened.

"Look here, I don't know what this as all about, really. Did you see my letter, or has Julie told you what I put in it?" he asked.

"Yes. Julie gave it to me to read this morning. She had it

148

when she got in last night and was completely crushed by it. Jerry, how *could* you have done such a thing to Julie? Even if you had decided you couldn't marry her, why had you to do it so cruelly—so—so abominably?"

Jeremy caught at her arm, shook it a little.

"I haven't the remotest idea what you're talking about," he said. "Why, I'd made up my mind that I wanted, above everything, to . . . Good lord!" a horrible suspicion breaking in on his mind. "You say you saw what I wrote to Julie. Well, what did I write?"

"Jerry, you must remember what you wrote, putting down reasons why you couldn't marry her, telling her that . . ."

She stopped, for he had dropped her arm and was standing staring at her with his face dead white and his eyes filled with incredulous horror. His brain wase reeling under the shock of that realization. He tried to remember exactly what he had been fool enough to write, criminal enough to let her see, but the memory was only vague and confused. He knew, however, that it had been horrible. He had been disgusted at himself—and yet Julie had seen what he had written!

He pushed past Mrs. Cave unceremoniously and strode towards the door.

"Jerry! Where are you going?" she asked, following him.

"I'm going to Julie. Where is she? In her room? You can't possibly imagine that I *meant* to send her that?"—and he flung aside her restraining hand and dashed up the stairs two at a time, to the room he knew to be Julie's.

"Julie, let me come in! It's Jerry," he said, and then, as she did not answer, he rattled imperatively at the handle, finding the door locked.

"Julie, I must speak to you. Let me in," he said and then, as she did not answer. "Oh, Julie *darling*, open your door!"—in a desperate voice.

Inside the room. Julie stood motionless, her hands clenched at her sides, her face drained of color, her eyes stricken. Her throat was dry and she could not have uttered any words even if her mind had been able to conceive them.

Outside the door, Jeremy's voice besought her. To a heart wounded as hers had been, nothing he could say would make any difference.

"Julie darling, I must talk to you. You must let me explain. It was all a mistake, and I never meant you to see that—that beastly thing I wrote. Oh, Julie, do belive me. At least open the door and let me speak to you."

He heard Mrs. Cave on the stairs behind him and turned to her in desperation.

"Mrs. Cave, do get her to let me in. I simply must talk to her."

Mrs. Cave was shaken and distracted, not knowing what to make of all this nor what she or anyone could do to put matters right. It was all so inexplicable. If Jeremy had not intended her to see that, why had he written it? How had he come even to think things like that if he felt about her as it now appeared he did?

She pushed him aside and went nearer to the door.

"Darling, it's Mom. Will you let me come in? Jerry will give you his word not to follow me unleses you say you want him to."

"I won't see him," said Julie in a hard, tight voice, but at least she was persuaded to unlock her door.

She came out and stood on the landing between them, a tragic figure, a travesty of the girl they knew so well.

She looked straight at Jeremy.

"Please go away," she said in that same hard voice. "I don't want to see you again, ever."

He ached to take her in his arms, to break down that dreadful barrier he had, by his own crass stupidity, raised between them. He did not touch her, however. Somehow her still, tragic figure denied the possibility of physical contact.

"If you'd let me try to explain," he began in a shaken voice.

She stopped him with a look. Her eyes were dry and hard, not Julie's eyes at all.

"There cannot possibly be any explanation," she said.

"I never meant to send you that," he said desperately. "I wrote you quite a different letter after that . . ."

She lifted her hand as if to ward off a blow.

"Please, Jerry, don't," she said in that stricken voice. "What does anything else matter? You wrote those things. You thought them. What can possibly alter or explain that away? Please go. Mom, won't you get him to go?"—her hard voice shaking for a moment, her self-control threatening to break.

150

Mrs. Cave slipped an arm about her. She still could not understand. Perhaps an explanation was impossible. Perhaps simple people like her and Julie could never be made to understand a thing which a clever man like Jerry might do. But she knew how precious a thing is love, how terrifically strong and yet how pitifully fragile. No matter what Jerry had done, Julie loved him. Was that not enough to make it worth the greatest effort to mend this break before it became unmendable?

"Dearie, I think you ought at least to hear what Jeremy has to say," she said very gently. "Come downstairs and listen to him and then, if you still want him to go, he will—won't you, Jeremy?"

He gave his word, and they went back downstairs again, not into the familiar kitchen where Dickie or Biddy might burst in on them, but into the cold, and, to the Caves, comfortless sitting-room, that 'state apartment' at which they laughed. Just now they all three felt they would never laugh again.

Julie stood upright, her hand gripping the high back of a chair, tight-lipped. her whole attitude uncompromising, waiting for Jeremy to speak.

For once he could not find words. He felt wildly that if this had been a scene in one of his own plays, his hero would have found flaming words before which the heroine's coldness would have melted like snow in June. But then he would never make a hero of the sorry stuff of which, for almost the first time, he felt himself to be made. Nor could he have conjured from the workings of his own brain a heroine like Julie, bewildered, hurt to death, a tragic figure which would be proof against any words he could find.

"Julie, I'm sorry—most terribly," he said in a difficult, halting tone. Words were so inadequate in real life. "I can't think of anything but that to say. I am really too sick and sorry for words. I never meant you to see that vile thing. I must have addressed the wrong envelope to you. I—it helps me to think when I write things down. I—oh, Julie, what's the use? I know nothing I can say will ever atone for it, but I didn't mean it. What I really did mean was what I wrote afterwards, the letter I meant you to have and which must still be in my desk. It's a love-letter, Julie. I came here tonight to ask you to marry me, if you would—if you only *will*, Julie," with a humility quite foreign to him, but with no power to reach her.

Her fingers had tightened over the back of the chair, but she had made no other movement during his speech, nor had there been the least change in the frozen mask of her face.

"What, after weighting me up like that?" she asked in a cold voice utterly devoid of feeling.

"Darling, I knew I'd never be able to make you understand," said Jeremy desperately.

Behind them, unnoticed by either of them, Mrs. Cave slipped away. She realized that only one thing could help them now, and that one thing would be Jeremy's arms about the girl he loved, his lips forcing hers to forgive him even if she could never understand. Women were made like that, to forgive even without understanding.

"No, I don't think you will," said Julie steadily. "Do you really think it's worthwhile to try?"

"Yes. Yes, I do, Julie. Oh, my dear, can't you believe that I love you? Won't you accept that instead of having to try to understand what isn't really explainable, what I can't understand myself?"

She knew he was desperately in earnest, but she could not bring herself to look at him. She did not want to see in his face the anguish which she heard in his voice. She was cold and dead. She was sorry for him, but there was nothing she could do about it.

"How can you pretend to love me when you think of me as you do?" she asked without the slightest sign of relenting; and he ran his hands through his hair in the old familiar way, both angry and wretched at his lack of words when words were so vital to his happiness. Never had he loved her so much, never desired her so ardently. Had he known her, or other women, a little better, he might have taken her in his arms as Mrs. Cave had hoped he would, but he did not dare whilst she stood there so proudly aloof, with that untouchable air about her. The dignity which had come so newly to her was a very real thing, a fence which she had built up about herself.

"I know it must be hard for you to believe in my love if you judge from that—that criminal bit of work, Julie, but do try to forgive me, to believe me even if you'll never forgive. I do love you."

"Then why did you write down all that about me?" she demanded inexorably.

"I don't know. I'm trying to tell you how it happened.

I've got used to writing things down, to sort out my ideas . . ."

Suddenly she stopped him. She could not let this agony go on. He must go away and never come back again, and somehow she would live, would learn to live, until she had forgotten him.

"Jerry, please—don't. What does it matter why you wrote it? Whether I saw it or not? I realize that you never meant me to see it, but what difference does it really make whether I saw it or not? What matters is—that you could think of me in that way . . ."

The numbness was going now, and pain returning. It cried to him in her voice though she was still so aloof, so withheld from him.

"Darling, I don't think of you that way!"

"You must do—or you did then, and everything is still the same. I am still all those things—that aren't any use to you," and her voice broke uncontrollably on the last words so that he came to her in one quick stride and put out a hand to touch her.

She drew back, and his hand dropped again.

"No, Jerry. I think—I'd like you to go now," she said, feeling almost at the end of her tether.

"Please, Julie, not yet, not till I've tried to make you forgive me . . ."

She gave a sigh of weariness that was mental more than bodily, though she was physically tired as well. If only he would go so that this intolerable interview, this day, might end and the long years begin in which she would eventually learn not to care any more.

"It isn't a matter of forgiveness, Jerry. Don't you see that? I don't have to forgive you for realizing that—that I'm not the sort of person you want for your wife."

Her voice faltered over the sweetness of that last word, but she held her head high, kept her eyes steady.

"Julie, I *do* want you . . ."

She shook her head.

"No, not all over again, Jerry," she said wearily. "Part of you may want to marry me, the part that—likes me. But supposing I did marry you. What should I feel, remembering, as I must always remember, the things you recognize in me as falling short of your ideal wife? Do you think I could ever be happy? Ever really—believe in your love?"

"I do love you, Julie, with all that is best in me . . ."

"Perhaps you do, Jerry; but—a woman wants more than that. It isn't any use, my dear. We've gone too far from each other. At least, you've gone on, and I've stayed still, where and how you found me. We don't belong to the same world any more. That's the real meaning of all this, and nothing can alter it. I think—even if you hadn't written that—I should have come to the same conclusion. Nothing can bring us near to each other again. Perhaps it was—better that we should see ourselves and—each other quite clearly."

"Julie, don't you love me any more?"

For a second she closed her eyes against the immensity of that question and of the answer she must give him. She would not betray or belittle the greatest thing her life would ever hold.

When she opened her eyes they were deep and very sad.

"It's because I do love you that I won't marry you, Jerry," she said. "If I cared even a little less, I might persuade myself that I could forget what you—thought about me. Don't you see that all the time, whatever we did, wherever we went, whoever we met, I should be remembering? All the time I should be aware of my shortcomings in your eyes—that I am not beautiful, or clever, or well-born . . ."

"Julie!"

Her name, forced from his lips by the intolerable pain he knew she felt, a pain which had its echo in his own heart, made her stop. He came close to her, put his arms about her, held her as if by sheer physical power he would for ever possess her—but it was too late. She was so very sure of herself now.

She stood quite still within his arms, and if her ears heard his repetitions, his excuses, his explanations, his remorse, his avowals, she gave no sign. Inwardly she was afraid. She knew that her resistance was almost at an end, her courage nearly gone. In another moment she would yield to him, lull herself into a false belief that happiness was possible just because there wase such bliss in the touch of his arms and his lips, in his voice which told her things her brain would not accept.

Dumbly she listened to what he said, told herself with her subconscious mind that she must remember them all her life, because no man would ever speak them again to her, no arms would ever hold her again.

154

Chilled at last by her utter immobility, he set her free, stood looking at her, his pride coming to his aid in the end.

"Your love isn't worth very much after all, then, is it, Julie? Mine could forgive you anything," he said quietly, bitterness behind his words.

Blindly she turned, groped for the handle of the door, found her mother waiting anxiously in the hall.

"Mom—Jerry—I want him to go," she said, the words coming as if she made a tremendous effort.

Then she went past her and stumblingly up the stairs.

13

Jeremy was strolling moodily in the Park, his hands in his pockets, his eyes fixed on the wet asphalt, nothing in his appearance suggesting that he was, or very recently had been, one of London's pet lions.

It was the hour between tea and dinner, and at that time, on a winter evening, the London parks are not gay places. He had come there because the greyness, the dripping gaunt arms of the trees, and the general dank hopelessness of early February suited his mood.

It was three months since he had seen Julie, and he had made the worst possible use of that time. Like most creative artists, he lived either in the heights or in the depths. There was no comfortable medium for him. He had told himself that with the passing of Julie all life and hope had passed, and from that state he made no attempt to rouse himself.

Morose and depressed, and no longer popular with hostesses who expected him to be the gay dog he had appeared to be, he found invitations falling off and obstinately withdrew further into himself. Stella Dale rang him up more than once, but at the first sound of her voice, sometimes gay, latterly anxious, he had replaced the receiver and had finally given instructions to the telephone company not to put late calls through to him.

And when he had thus succeeded in cutting himself off from her, he sat at night, alone, moodily hunched up in a chair, or wandered about to dubious haunts, queer drinking-places, furtive little night-clubs, the Embankment even, telling himself that all his friends had left him.

Inevitably he dramatized himself, and now that he had been cast off by Julie, had separated himself from Stella, he was in the position of one who "enjoys bad health" but had nobody to whom to recount his ills.

He wrote to Julie, but she did not reply. He rang her up at Monique's, but was told "Miss Cave is very busy at the moment," and guessed that the message had been inspired by Julie herself.

He had returned to his desk and tried to write, but the moody depression showed in his work. His characters were without reality, their conversation boring, the situations which his brain evolved verged on the macabre. He could not recapture the brightness, the sparkle which had enchanted his audiences and made his critics careful. His two plays were still running, one touring the provinces with first-class companies, and *Antimony* still playing to good houses at the Duke's, but he had meant these to be only preliminary successes, and now he was terrified that he had already out-written himself.

Day after day he wrote wildly, and at night he filled his paper basket with the torn manuscript and wandered out in search of distraction, hoping to find copy where he had never found it, among the lost and hopeless and outcast of London, becoming himself the more hopeless.

It was in this black mood that he had thrown aside his work earlier than usual on that February evening and gone to walk aimlessly in the Park, and came face to face with Stella Dale.

She stopped right in front of him, and he could do no less than return in some measure her greeting.

"Jeremy—my dear," she said, and her voice was softer, kinder than he had yet heard it.

He held her hand for a moment, and then let it drop. In this blackest of moods he resented her intrusion into his life, but she would not be refused.

"Don't scowl," she told him. "The Park isn't yours, and I'm going to walk in it beside you, so I hope you won't be so ungallant as to run."

"I suppose it's no use telling you I'd rather be alone?" asked Jeremy morosely, though he was aware that something in him responded to the sound of her voice, to her smile.

She laughed and walked beside him, though she had been coming from the opposite direction.

"Not the least bit of use," she told him, and then, after a few moments of awkward silence, "Aren't you going to talk to me, Jeremy? To tell me what's wrong?"

"You wouldn't be interested," he told her doggedly; but she insisted, using all her charm and tact, and eventually he found himself telling her the story, or most of it, relieved to find that there was apparently no ridicule in her mind.

Rather did she discreetly sympathize with him, keeping to herself her inner thoughts, which were a strange mixture she would have revealed to no one, least of all to Jeremy Denton.

She found it difficult to explain, even to herself, what constituted his charm for her. She always admired success, and that was his early attraction for her, but there was some more personal quality which held her. She decided that for the first time in her life she was falling in love, and now that she was a free agent and possessed of all the money she could reasonably need, there was nothing to prevent her from doing so.

It had been a shock to her to hear, from Jeremy's own lips, that he was engaged, but it soon became clear to her that something had gone wrong, for the one or two glimpses she had had of him convinced her that he was no happily engaged man.

"Haven't you shut yourself away long enough from all your friends?" she asked him in that new, gentle voice of hers, deciding that the story of Julie must now be written off. "We're missing you, Jeremy."

It was a new idea to him. He had never considered himself but an outsider in the set to which Stella and her friends belonged, and he had certainly never thought that his disappearance would be regretted.

"You're only trying to be nice to me," he said with a grudging smile. "I don't belong where you do."

"Why not? Haven't you earned the key to the door?" she asked him gaily.

"Other people might not agree with you."

"Then come and find out for yourself. I'm giving a dinner party for the opera tonight. Join us. There'll be room in my box."

He hesitated. Now that he had been forced to talk to her, he found that it was a temptation to continue to do so. He felt vaguely surprised at himself, for he had decided that he would never rise from the depths into which his break with Julie had cast him. After all, why should he not accept Stella's invitation? He had never been inside her house, though he had been as far as the door. In many ways she was still a mystery to him, and there was a subtle attraction in his knowledge that she had run the whole gamut of human emotion and experience, though she was still only just out of her twenties.

Inevitably some of the many tales that were told about her had come to his ears. Apparently there had been many men in her life, and he had been sufficiently interested in her to obtain and read up the newspapers' accounts of the long-drawn-out inquest on her husband's body, with its sinister suggestions and inquiries. No definite link had been established between Brandy Dale's suicide and his lovely young widow, but there was no doubt about her having led a very gay life, to his distress and disapproval. There had even been attempts to overthrow the will, an early one made soon after their marriage and never altered; but Stella had come triumphantly through all the inquiries and investigations, possessed of both her reputation and her husband's fortune.

Since then there had been other men, affairs more discreetly managed, no open scandal of any sort, though her engagement had been reported more than once.

All these things Jeremy knew, and they excited and stimulated his imagination, invested her with an atmosphere of intrigue and romance. He had never thought of her in the way he had thought of Julie, and therefore he had no feelings about the men with whom her name had been associated.

She persuaded him with that new, disarming gentleness of hers, her hand laid lightly on his arm as they came to the Park gates.

"I want you to come, Jeremy. If that isn't good enough reason, come because you owe it to yourself to snap out of this depression. Why stay wallowing in the pit when there are so many attractive things to do outside it?"—with a smile.

"I may keep you waiting," he demurred.

"Get a taxi here, keep him while you dress, and come straight to me. You've three-quarters of an hour, and I've got to get home and dress in that time."

So he went to her house, sat beside her at Covent Garden to hear *Tristan and Isolda* for the first time, let the charm of her presence mingle with the voluptuous, tragic music.

She had deliberately made herself charming to him, changed at the last minute the gown she had told her maid she would wear, and wore lace instead of the silver brocade laid out for her. It gave her a softer, ultra-feminine appearance, and the maid, dressing her without expression or comment, wondered for whom this new effect was being created.

After the opera she contrived a moment alone with him, dropping behind the others when they left the box.

"You're not going to let yourself fall back into the Slough of Despond, Jeremy, are you?" she asked him.

He looked into her eyes with a perplexed, uncertain smile. Almost against his will the charm of her was stealing into his heart and offering peace. She was so lovely tonight. In this softened mood she was devastating to him. For hours he had forgotten Julie, and it was not Isolda who had made him forget.

"Will you care if I do?" he asked.

Her eyes held his.

"You know I shall always care what you do," she told him, her voice very soft and low, and they stood there so long looking at each other that another member of the party turned to call to them.

"Are you two rehearsing a Tristan and Isolda act on your own?" she asked.

They smiled at the speaker and walked on towards the foyer, but Jeremy could not let that speech of Stella's go unmarked. He felt oddly shaken by it.

"Did you mean that? Why should you care?" he asked.

She turned her head a little to smile at him.

"Does it matter greatly why I care—since I do care?" she asked him.

They had nearly caught up with the others. Soon she would be absorbed by them again.

"Stella, may I take you home?" he asked urgently.

She shook her head.

"I'm going on with the Masons somewhere," she said, and did not ask him to go too.

"When shall I see you again?"

It had suddenly become of vital importance that he should.

"Oh—we shall meet somewhere or other," she said, and joined the others, leaving him baffled by her inconsistencies, as she had intended.

He could not decide whether or not she had really meant that their friendship must continue, and he recalled, and tried in vain to interpret, the enigmatical smile she had flung at him as she entered the Masons' car and left him standing bareheaded on the pavement.

Eve Mason turned her empty blonde head and an amused smile in Stella's direction.

"I rather like your bear," she said. "Does he dance, too, or only growl? And is he safe off the chain?"

"Interested?" asked Stella coolly.

"Terribly. What are you going to do with him?"

Stella appeared to reflect on that. Then she spoke quite softly.

"Do you know, I rather think Jeremy Denton is not the sort of person one does things with," she said. "I should say he makes the choice."

Later, in her room and surrendered to the care of her maid, she thought over that speech of hers. It was only today that she had formed that opinion of Jeremy Denton. There had been a look in his eyes, a suggestion of domination, which had piqued her curiosity and aroused an even greater interest in him. It amused her to reflect that possibly she would not be able to set the pace with him, or decide on the goal or choose the stakes. There was an unsuspected force in him, something which she felt, with a stirring of her pulses, might sweep away the resistances which had hitherto given her command of any situation.

Before she was ready for bed, her telephone bell rang, and the maid moved across the room to answer it.

"I'll take it," said Stella. "Wait in the other room. I'll call you. I want the electric treatment tonight."

The maid obeyed rather sullenly. Stella was an exacting mistress and considered that because she paid her servants higher wages than they would get anywhere else she need show them no consideration. As a result, she kept her staff, but received from them secretly resentful and grudging service. Only the second-best can be bought with gold the world over.

Stella had known intuitively that it was Jeremy, though he had never rung her up before, but she kept carefully from her voice the triumph which her face revealed as she picked up the receiver.

"I want to talk to you, Stella. You're not too tired?"

It was the eager, alert voice again, and she smiled and let him talk. The words came tumbling over one another, and Stella, perched on the edge of the bed, listened with a sense of elation and excitement which no man had been able to give her for years. It was almost as if, finding again his eager quest for life, his zest in the living of it, he could impart vitality to her. Gone was the black depression which, a few hours ago, had buried his soul. He had climbed out of the pit, and it was she, Stella, whose hand had given him the impetus.

"I've got the idea I want for a new play, something different, sensational. Fennimore wants one with musical numbers, something spectacular. I've only just had it born in my brain, but it's like Aphrodite, fully armed, you know!"—with a little excited laugh. "Listen. I'll tell you," and out came the torrent of words, punctuated by Stella's, "Yes—yes—I see—go on," until he broke off with a quick: "that's it. What do you think about it?"

"I think it's got possibilities," she said calmly, and could almost feel the effervescence of his spirit subside.

"Only possibilities?" he asked.

"Well, it's got rough edges. That coincidence—it isn't very likely, is it?"

"But in a musical thing, Stella! We'll get gorgeous music. Nothing crooning, of course, but real tuneful stuff. That Viennese chap, what's his name?"

"Fennimore will want a good foundation, not just frills," she warned him.

She could feel his disappointment, but would not pander to it. She had still that odd, slightly uncomfortable feeling that she would not always possess herself as she did now, that if she gave way to Jeremy Denton even a little she would cease to be her own. Almost consciously she was fighting to retain her own individuality. She had never before felt that any man could rob her of it or become an obsession to her.

He offered her an alternative to the coincidence she had criticized, his mind quick to visualize one. It was as if he had found the magic touchstone which he had lost.

"That's better," she admitted. "It isn't good enough, though. It's commonplace, and you mustn't ever be that. You must intrigue your audience, shock them a little, make them sit up!"

"I'm trying to be subtle enough to make them believe they've thought of the solution themselves," laughed Jeremy, on the heights again.

They talked and talked, until Stella, laughing but inexorable, ended the conversation by telling him she could no longer hold the receiver.

"Tell me when I shall see you again, at least," he begged her; but she either did not or would not hear him, and the telephone went dead.

When the contact with her had ceased he felt the old depression returning, that strange, frightening distrust in himself. His thoughts returned to Julie.

He knew, with a secret sense of shame, that she would not approve of this plot which he had conceived in an abnormal, excited moment. He had offered up some of his ideals on the altar of success when he wrote his second play, *Antimony*, and Julie's criticism had been so final, although so gentle, that he had never been able to forget it.

"I don't like it. There may be thoughts and feelings like that in the worst of you, Jerry, but I feel you should always write up to the best of you," and she had never gone to see it because it represented to her something in Jeremy which she felt was unworthy of him.

How, then, would she have received the plot he had just discussed with Stella Dale? It was to be ultra-modern, cynical in its wit, pulling down old standards and flying instead of them paper streamers, making mock of the old moralities and the old virtues. The action on which the whole plot depended was not such as could have found any place in Julie's life or that of the simple, hard-working, decent-living men and girls amongst whom his lot had been cast when he was writing *The Bauble*, that play which seemed to him now fantastic and slightly absurd. Had he really believed that people lived their lives by such standards?

The people in this new play were to be modelled on some of those he had met in Stella Dale's circle, people with too much money and too much time on their hands, with their minds frittered away on superficialities. There was neither kindness nor virtue in this new conception of his.

He left his notes lying on his desk and went to bed, and all night long he seemed to be with Julie, for though he had not dreamed of her to his recollection, he woke with all the aching loneliness of a recent parting from her, though it was three months since he had seen her.

So strong was his impression of her that he went to the telephone and called up Monique's, careless of the rebuff he might meet.

Madam herself answered the telephone and was distant and formal.

"My employees are not allowed to take private calls," she said.

"I know, but if I might speak to Miss Cave, just this once?" begged Jeremy. "It's Jeremy Denton speaking, the—the writer, you know"—desperately.

Madam was unimpressed. Evidently she did not know.

"I am afraid that would not make any difference," she said, "but, as it happens, Miss Cave is away," and she put up the receiver and left Jeremy in a turmoil of anxious thoughts.

He dressed hurriedly and flung himself into a taxi. He could not wait to get his own car out of the garage. It gave him a queer feeling to be going out to Streatham again, ringing the bell at the familiar door.

Mrs. Cave opened it and looked both surprised and displeased to see him.

"Oh—it's you, Jeremy," she said slowly.

"I rang up Monique's. Is Julie ill?" he asked, without preamble.

"She has had influenza but she is better today," said Mrs. Cave. There was nothing inviting in her manner, and she made no attempt to admit him further than the doorway.

"Mrs. Cave, I want to see her. Do please let me," said Jeremy, and Stella, who had feared his domination of her, would have been surprised to see how all his self-assurance fled when Julie was concerned.

"I'm sorry, Jeremy, but I can't let you," said Mrs. Cave inflexibly. "Julie has made up her mind, and she made me give her a promise that I would not do anything to bring you two together again. I can't possibly take advantage of her illness to break my word to her—and believe me, it is really best for all concerned if things are left as they are."

"You can say that, Mrs. Cave, knowing that Julie and I love each other?" asked Jeremy.

Her face hardened. Though her heart had ached for

163

Julie's suffering when the break with Jeremy had come, she really did feel now that it was for the best. She had been overjoyed to find that Ben Elson had taken her hint and was quietly but persistently bringing himself into the foreground of Julie's life so that the girl, for almost the first time, was becoming aware of him.

Mrs. Cave realized that life with Ben would not be the exciting, glamorous thing Jerry could have made it, but she knew the value of safety and peace, and that they were likely to be more satisfying in the long run than romance.

So she hardened her heart against Jeremy's appeal. Julie should have her chance to forget him.

"I know she loved you, Jerry," she said steadily. "You never loved her well enough, though, or you could never have acted as you did or weighed up her worth to you. There are no scales on which she could have weighed her love for you, and you knew it. Well, that is over and done with now. Leave her alone. You can be no use to her, and she is getting over it."

That gave him a nasty jar. He had never really imagined Julie 'getting over it,' Last night's return to the gay world had assured him that he was a desirable and sought-after person and possibly it was that that had given him the courage to come to Julie's home. Whatever he had anticipated, it was not that Julie was 'getting over it.'

"I don't want her to forget me," he burst out. "I want to keep her love, to marry her."

She would never know real happiness with anyone like you, Jerry," said Mrs. Cave sternly. "You are not the right type of man for my Julie, and that is why I hope you'll have the decency to acknowledge it and let her alone so that she can find real happiness with a man who will value her as you are not capable of doing."

"Do you mean she has already found another man?" asked Jeremy incredulously.

Mrs. Cave's head went high at that suggestion.

"I hope and believe that she has, Jeremy," she said, and fortified her conscience with the memory of Julie as she had been last night, sitting up in bed and looking really pretty, with a little color in her cheeks, playing chess with Ben. They were not very good players, but they were enjoying their battle of wits with a comradeship and a suggestion of happy intimacy which had sent Mrs. Cave away with a little prayer of thankfulness in her heart.

She made herself remember that when she saw how Jeremy seemed to sink into himself at that information.

"I must have been quite mad," he said dejectedly.

She laid a hand on his arm.

"My dear boy, try to forget us," she said. "Make your life afresh as Julie is doing, and—God bless you, Jerry."

He laid his hand over hers for a moment and then turned without another word and left her, and she went back to her work with a rather heavy heart and some pricking of her conscience. Jerry was such a dear. They had all loved him, and the house had never seemed the same since he had gone from it. He had always been able to impart to them some of his eager enthusiasm, his love of life, his certainty that the world was his oyster.

She felt she would not be able to forget for a long time that sight of him with all his pride and hope and eagerness gone, but she was sure she had done the right thing for Julie. The girl's inflexible determination not to marry him was built on a foundation which nothing could undermine. Neither remorse nor apology nor promise could alter her humiliated knowledge that he had considered her beneath the standard he set for his wife. Nothing could condone that or wipe it from Julie's mind so long as any memory of Jeremy Denton remained, so it was her mother's one hope that that memory would be short-lived.

Yes, definitely she was doing the best thing for Julie.

Jeremy went back to his flat with aching heart and angry mind, that strange combination which is the prerogatiove of human love, but in the days that followed he deliberately encouraged the anger to have its way. He forced on his thoughts a bravado which acted as an anaesthetic for the pain he resented.

He worked with feverish activity on his new play, rewrote the script and found that his mind was acquiring a rapier-like edge to its wit, that there was a cutting quality in the bitter gibes which came, startling and unbidden, into the words of his puppets. His anger with Julie made him derive satisfaction out of creating siutations he knew she would hate, personalities from which she would recoil, and when at last he talked again with Stella Dale, took the manuscript to her house, he had deluded himself into the belief that he had applied to his wound not a corrosive plaster but a healing salve.

He looked into Stella's eyes and laughed. He was cured,

he was free. He had his fate within his hands. He could twist and wring it as he would. He had for ever cast out the thing which had limited his powers and enchanted his imagination.

Stella approved of the altered script. Its daring amused and excited her, fed her growing infatuation for Jeremy.

She used a half-forgotten acquaintance to inveigle Giles Fennimore to her house, a little chagrined to find that he and Jeremy had already met, for it pleased her to play the god-in-the-car. She furthered the actor-manager's interest in the playwright, however, and persuaded the one to bring his manuscript and the other to read it in her house and presence.

Jeremy read the first act through, outlined the rest of the plot, quoted one or two extracts, infusing the whole with an ardor which was edged with that new bitterness of his.

Fennimore listened, motionless and silent, and then, when Jeremy waited for his opinion, gave a wry smile.

"Caustic in parts, isn't it," he asked.

Jeremy shrugged his shoulders with a nonchalance he did not feel. It mattered intensely to him whether Fennimore took the play or not. It would be an experiment if he did so, for the introduction of musical numbers and dancing into the action of the play made it a lighter affair than Fennimore had ever yet undertaken, and was a rather daring half-way house between drama and light comedy.

"Does it matter?" he asked, parrying the other's question by another.

Fennimore smiled again.

"No, I don't know that it does," he said reflectively. "I rather think it will tickle the palate of a public that is getting sick of sugar-plums and yet has no fancy for plain roast beef and Yorkshire. The censor will have a cut at it here and there, though"—with an appreciative chuckle, holding out his hand for the manuscript. "Yes—yes, I like that," he commented, running an experienced eye down the script, pausing here and there, tapping his teeth with the pencil with which now and then he made marginal notes.

"I'd like to have it, Denton," he said at last, and in Stella's drawing-room, over her excellent sherry, they completed their deal.

"The thing now is: have we got any money?" asked Fennimore. "Is Maitland coming in on this again?"

"Well, I think he would, but . . ."

Jeremy paused. For some inexplicable reason he did not want Maitland to finance him again. When they had met lately there had been an expression on his face that seemed vaguely condemnatory, and there was that in Jeremy which made him reluctant to take help where he found at the same time disapproval and that vague feeling that he was being watched with a faint contempt.

Stella spoke swiftly, laying a hand on Jeremy's shoulder.

"Why need we go outside for help?" she asked. "Aren't we the perfect triumvirate? The brains to create, the ability to act, the—mere money to make both operative?"

The two men looked at her. She was a little flushed, and her dark eyes were glowing. Fennimore recognized her as the most supremely attractive woman he had ever met, though she left him physically cold. He glanced speculatively from her to Denton. Well, something amusing and sensational was bound to happen between these two, and during its happening there was no reason why he himself should not make his own harvest.

He waited for Jeremy to speak.

"Do you mean that, Stella?"

Up to this she had been "Mrs. Dale," but now it seemed he had almost forgotten the presence of a third person.

She smiled into his eyes.

"Why not? It's a business proposition. I'm going to make money out of you, Jeremy."

He drew a deep breath, knowing that that was not why she had made the suggestion.

"Supposing I failed you?" he asked.

She shook her head.

"You won't. You'll see to that, Mr. Fennimore, won't you?"—deliberately including him again.

They discussed the financial aspect of it, agreed that they would get Paston if they could, and the two men left together. Fennimore with the manuscript under his arm, discussing the plot from the point of the censor.

"I think I'd better take the thing myself to Ladsley. I know him well enough. No need to start pulling the thing to bits until we've satisfied ourselves how much will be necessary. Gad. I wish we could put the thing on as it stands!"—and Fennimore chuckled at the remembrance of

167

some of the sentiments, expressed and implied, which he knew no British arbiter of public morals would allow at a public performance.

Denton was clever, damned clever. Oddly caustic, though, for so young a man. What was between him and Stella Dale? Surely he wasn't going to burn his fingers at that fire?

14

Jeremy sat in the empty theatre, leaning back in his stall, his hands thrust deep into his pockets, his face an expressionless mask.

A dress rehearsal was in progress on the stage, the final one. Tomorrow the play would be launched.

He had learned much since the production of *The Bauble*, chief amongst his knowledge being the wisdom of letting things take their course, of not interfering with people who knew a great deal more about producing a play than he did and whose business it was to give life to the dummies he had created. Hence he had seen nothing of the production of *Midnight Angel* from the final signing of the contracts with Fennimore, Paston, and Stella Dale until this afternoon.

There was a slight sound near him, and he glanced up to see Stella slipping quietly into the next seat. They exchanged brief, impersonal smiles and gave all their attention to the stage again. The rehearsal dragged on, depressing, infuriating, as all the final rehearsals are. Stella was restless, but Jeremy sat on stolidly, his face betraying nothing of his feelings.

It was an elaborate, spectacular affair, but the settings, the musical score of the beautiful ballet which formed part of the theme, the breathtaking scenery and costumes had been allowed in no way to detract from the action of the play itself. Jeremy's conception, his characters and the situations, his daring and sparkling dialogue, had been given paramount importance, and the combination of witty play and spectacle was a novelty which was to make London enraptured with Jeremy Denton.

When the last act was finished, everything spoken save

that final, superstition-forbidden word, Paston humped wearily down in the corner of the set at which he had been standing, an incongruous figure, shirt-sleeved and collarless, as he always worked, and Jeremy and Stella turned with one accord towards each other.

"Well?" she asked.

"Rotten," was Jeremy's comment, but she laughed, reading beneath the gloomy tone and sensing, as if an electric current ran from her to him, the excitement that he strove to hide.

She rose to her feet, looked down at him and she laughed.

"Come out and eat, bear," she said. "I'll let you growl today because I shall have to listen to your roaring tomorrow."

They had become comfortably intimate, though always as an undercurrent to their intimacy was that sense of adventure, of still being in process of journeying—whither?

He followed her out of the theatre and into the quiet little restaurant to which, without consulting him, she had told her chauffeur to drive, with a careless, "You can send someone to pick up your car later, Jeremy."

He sat silent while she ordered dinner for them, early though it still was, for she guessed rightly that he had not even lunched, that his air of complete detachment during the rehearsal had been only a cover.

When he spoke it was of the play, without preamble or apology.

"You think it isn't altogether putrid, Stella?"

"It's going to be marvelous," she told him.

"You don't think the ballet scene spoils the sequence?"

"No. It's too cleverly interlaced with the action of the play."

"Do you think Fennimore really appreciates the significance of that conversation with Garret in the second act? The one about the latch-key? I thought he hurried it rather."

She smiled, stretched out a hand and laid it, white and cool, on the one that had been fidgeting with a fold on the tablecloth.

"Darling, you're worrying it as if you were a dog with a bone. Forget it for a little while and let's go somewhere to distract our thoughts—the pictures, I suggest."

He gave her a look of mingled relief and worry.

"Stella, if I failed, I couldn't bear it. It would send me stark, staring mad."

She smiled into his eyes.

"You and Failure are for ever strangers, my dear," she said softly.

He gave her a quick, half-startled look, drawing his brows together at a sudden, disquieting thought.

"Stella, how would you feel if I did fail? Would you—care so much?"

Her eyes were always enigmatical, never more so than now, when she answered his question with another.

"Do you really doubt which it is that attracts me, you or your achievements?" she asked, and when he thought about that reply of hers afterwards he was no nearer satisfying himself as to its meaning.

The next night *Midnight Angel* declared itself beyond shadow of doubt as a success. The critics went home from it to write their assurances that Jeremy Denton had again scored a hit and that his play would amuse London for many months.

Only Bainbridge went to write of it regretfully. He suggested that Jeremy Denton had started on his gallant way with *The Bauble*, had arrived at the cross-roads with *Antimony*, but had definitely chosen his path with *Midnight Angel*. Bainbridge saw that as an artificial garden-path, pretty to look at, easy to tread, limited in its power to arrive anywhere, when Jeremy Denton had been free to choose the high cliff road whose top lay in the clouds of heaven.

But what matter what an ageing, slightly disillusioned dreamer thought when all London laughed and clapped, when tomorrow even today's queues would be doubled and trebled for the cheap seats, when the box-office and the agencies would be besieged and dates quoted for months ahead? The first-night audience who had already taken Jeremy Denton to their hearts hugged him there ecstatically. The sheer audacity of the play made them gasp, the exotic settings, the exquisite conception of the ballet, enthralled their eyes and ears, and the place was in a tumult when the final curtain fell.

Stella, wonderful in a gown which looked like spun gold, waited for him to come to her. Her cheeks were faintly flushed, there was a deep glow in her eyes.

There were other people in her box, but Jeremy passed them unseeing and went straight to her for the crowning tribute of all this acclamation of voices.

"Well?" he asked her, fever in his eyes and his voice. She had never seen him look more vitally alive. She kindled to his fire.

"What do you want me to add to all that?" she asked him, her voice for him alone.

"I want to hear you say your bit," he said, with a laugh that shook his voice.

"Take me home, Jeremy—or must you stay with the crowd?" she asked him, in a low tone, for Paston had come into the box behind them.

"Who else will be with you, Stella?"

There was a fresh undercurrent of excitement in his manner.

"No one at all," she said softly.

Their eyes held each other's, and the excitement, the sense of adventure, grew. The brilliance of the setting, the whole atmosphere of the place, was a perfect background for Stella Dale. Jeremy, intoxicated already by success and the plaudits of all these people, knew that he was losing his head, but did not care. All he wanted was to take her away from the crowds, to be alone with her.

Deep in his heart at that moment of his power came the thought of Julie, of her coolness and her sweet sanity, but it seemed to him that all that had belonged to another life, not to his at all. Where in all this had Julie a place?

He shook off the trammelling thought of her, resenting its appearance. She had cast him off, refused to believe that he loved her. Well, then, why waste any more thoughts on her? This was where he belonged, to this gay, successful life and to this beautiful, subtle woman.

So when their eyes lit that spark between them, he let it burn for her to see.

"Let's go," he said to her.

"Can you, Jeremy?"

"Why not?"

There was arrogance in his tone, in the lift of his head, in his conquering eyes, and she laughed and laid a hand on his sleeve with the least hint of possessiveness as they turned to face Paston.

He eyed Jeremy almost sourly. There was within him something of that sane resentment against his success

171

which had actuated Maitland. He was clever and it seemed he had an uncanny way of being able to put his finger straight on the pulse of theatrical London. Far more worthy plays had failed simply because their authors lacked that power, that subtle appreciation of public taste.

"Ready, Denton?" he asked.

"I'm not coming," said Jeremy calmly.

Paston's eyebrows went up.

"Not coming? Damn it, you'll have to," he said shortly. "They're expecting you. Got an ovation ready for you—old Spanish custom, you know."

"Sorry. They'll have to ovate without me because I'm not coming," said Jeremy again, and swung past him with Stella, serenely cool and confident, on his arm.

Paston stared after them, bitterly resentful. Even if one could forgive him for that silly young fool who knew no better than to believe that the world was made for him and would remain his exclusive property, he had no right to flout and hurt his friends and colleagues, all these people who had helped him make his success and were waiting to celebrate it with him.

He went slowly away and revolved in his mind the speech which he would have to make on Jeremy's behalf and in his apology.

Meantime Jeremy took Stella through the passages that led from the box to the foyer, choosing those rather than the quicker route through the stage door because of the meed of praise that would be his in the more public places. Stella, recognizing the motive, smiled at it but did not regret it. Rather, holding her lovely head high, did she court the glances which came their way. This was his hour. It might well be hers as well.

But he was not to go unchallenged, for in the crush round the main door he found himself pressed against Maitland and could scarcely avoid an exchange of civilities.

"Oh—that you, Maitland?" he asked guardedly. "Terrific crush, isn't there? Sorry if I barged into you."

The tall, grave man smiled with his lips. His eyes just touched Stella's and then left them again, coldly inscrutable as ever.

"An immensely gratifying crush to Jeremy Denton, surely," he said, and then, as Stella gave him a belated and slightly nervous smile, he contrived to bow to her. "How do you do, Mrs. Dale?"

She drew back into the crowd a little, and Jeremy moved with her. He heard his name passed on before him, following Maitland's recognition of him.

"Jeremy Denton's coming out. The author, you know. Wrote this play," and many heads were turned curiously and admiringly towards him.

His name reached the ears of a very young, cheaply elegant young person who had come out of the gallery exit and was standing watching with envious eyes and calculating mind the gorgeously dressed women coming from the main door.

She turned to her companion, a girl of her own age.

"Hear that? They say Jerry's coming. I'm going to stop and see him," she said, her eyes bright with a slightly guilty anticipation.

Her friend sniffed.

"Well, I'm not going to miss the last through bus for him," she said. "Come on, Biddy."

Biddy stood her ground. Over the heads of the departing crowd she had glimpsed Jeremy's tall one, and the equally tall Stella beside him. She caught the gleam of her golden gown and was determined to get nearer to it. Jerry might even introduce her!

"Oh, all right. You go on. See you tomorrow," said Biddy, and her friend slipped away contemptuously. Catch her making up to Jerry Denton if he'd treated her sister like he'd treated Julie Cave!

Meantime Stella and Jeremy, with Maitland still perforce close to them, had arrived at the pavement.

Stella pressed her hand on his arm to call his attention.

"There's Firth," she said, indicating her car a few yards down the street, and they paused to look uncertainly at Maitland. It seemed churlish not even to ask him if he had his car there, but, in turning, Jeremy caught sighty of Biddy's lovely, eager little face.

The color rushed to his own, and he looked instinctively behind the girl to see if she were alone, and at that moment the little group of people separating her from them melted away and left them face to face.

Impulsively he spoke.

"Biddy! Is—Julie with you?"

Biddy shook her head.

"No, I'm alone, Jerry," she said, shy now that she was

173

actually talking to him.

He saw the longing in her eyes, knew what it meant, hesitated for the fraction of a second, and then turned to Stella and Maitland.

"This is Miss Biddy Cave," he said to them. "Mrs. Dale and Mr. Maitland, Biddy."

Her face flushed and her eyes took fright, but she looked charming as she stood there, so young and diffident and eager.

Stella's eyes took her in at a glance, and she gave a small, guarded smile before turning her attention back to Jeremy, an amused question in her look. She ignored, if she saw, Biddy's uncertain, quickly withdrawn offer of a handshake at the introduction, but Maitland, with a consideration which Jeremy remembered with surprise afterwards, instantly held out his hand and engulfed with it Biddy's nervous little paw.

"Charming to meet you, Miss Cave," he said, in his grave, unsmiling fashion, and her giddy little heart gave a whirl of joy. He looked so distinguished, so very much the gentlemen, she told herself exultantly. And he was standing outside the theatre, amidst all those wonderful, wealthy-looking people, shaking hands with her!

Her blue eyes, innocent as bluebells in a wood, gave him a look compounded of all these thoughts, and he found himself smiling down into them.

Stella's voice interrupted that look.

"Firth has managed to get nearer. I think we'd better walk down to the car now, and he can turn down the next street," she said. "What about you, Royal?—turning to Maitland carelessly. "Have you your car, or shall we give you a lift?"

It gave Jeremy a little shock to hear her call him by that name. He had scarcely realized what Maitland's Christian name was, though he had seen it on those first agreements they had made. Plenty of people referred to him familiarly as "Roy Maitland," but no one had ever addressed him by his real name in Jeremy's presence.

He glanced swiftly from one to the other; but Maitland's face expressed nothing. Rather did he turn away calmly from Stella to look again at where Biddy Cave stood, uncertainly hopping from one foot to the other like a little bird.

"Thanks. I have a car somewhere about," he said. "How
174

about you, Miss Cave? Have you far to go? May I take you anywhere?"

In spite of himself Jeremy could not forbear a grin. How Biddy's family would revel in the tale she would presently tell them, embroidered a little perhaps, but with enough truth behind it to make it credible! The thought stabbed him, showing him how strong was that link that held him to Julie, stretch and strain upon it as he might.

He frowned and turned to follow Stella, who was making her way towards her gleaming grey-and-silver car. He just took time to smile a farewell to Biddy and nod one to Maitland, though neither of them took much notice of it.

Biddy lifted her guileless blue eyes again. She had command of herself now, and was determined to make the very most of this amazing stroke of luck. If only he would take her out to supper somewhere, to some risky nightclub, or one of those cabaret shows! Then she looked at him more closely and decided, rather regretfully, that he was "not that sort."

The regret was short-lived, however, for when, apologizing to her for having to ask her to walk along the street and up the next one to a parking square, he finally opened for her the door of quite the most superb car there, her cup of happiness was full. Nobody with a car like that could possibly be "that sort," and, lying back in a dream of bliss against the blue upholstery and watching his fine, strong-fingered hands on the wheel, she wondered for a moment whether it would not be better to give him the address of one of those big new houses round by Talford Avenue and then slip off to Hemming Road when he had gone. Wiser and better counsels prevailed, however, and when he had maneuvered the car skillfully away from the park and asked her where she lived, she told him quite truthfully, adding:

"You probably won't be able to find it straight away. It's quite a little road. If you get to Streatham Hill Station, though, I'll guide you. Sure you don't mind going all that way? It would be quite all right if you put me down on the bus route, you know"—anxiously.

His smile reassured her, though he did not take his eyes off the road to look at her.

"I shouldn't dream of leaving you anywhere but on your doorstep," he said. "How did you come to be alone at this hour of the night, a little girl like you?"

"I'm eighteen," said Biddy.

175

He gave her another of those smiles which she was beginning to look for and like.

"So old?" he teased her, and realized with a feeling of surprise that it was a very long time since he had wanted to tease a girl, and this was such a very young and callow one!

"I come up to town every day on my own," said Biddy, chatting away happily now that the first feeling of awed unfamiliarity was passing. Somehow it was easy to talk to him, grand gentleman though he was! "I'm in a beauty parlor, manicuring mostly, though now and then they let me help with a perm and watch the setting. We've got a model to practice on. Flora we call it, and I tried a new style on it the other day, and Ruperto—that's Corelli, the boss—copied it on some woman's head, and I heard him tell her it was the latest thing from Paris!"

She chuckled at the memory.

Maitland, never talkative, was content to drive the car in silence and listen to her steady stream of chatter. It was a new experience to him. His affections had for so many years been centred on a woman of ultra-sophistication and experience that he would never have believed he could see an attraction in anything as young and untried as this child. Questioned, he would have said he would be profoundly bored, and it was intriguing to find that it was not so. He was feeling almost fatherly towards her—*almost*. Queerly tender, anyway.

"Mom won't be waiting up for me—at least I hope she won't," said Biddy, as they neared Streatham and she began to give him directions for reaching Hemming Road. "I don't think she was really very keen on my going to see Jerry's play, but so long as I don't say anything about it to Julie, she won't really mind."

"You call him Jerry? Known him long?" asked Maitland. "And who's Julie?"

"She's my sister, and we've known Jerry—oh, years and years," said Biddy, and there was a touch of scorn in her voice which interested Maitland.

"And Julie's known him years and years too, I take it?" he asked.

Biddy sighed.

"Yes. She met him first. They used to work near each other and she was really engaged to Jerry. That was before he got so potty, though!"—with the scorn very definite now.

"I see. They—got over it, I suppose, with Denton's altered circumstances?"

"Well, he got over it, but Julie—oh, I dunno. I never did know the rights of it. Mom knows, but she won't tell, and somehow you can't ask Julie things like that. Still, she was terribly in love with Jerry, and Julie isn't the sort that changes," said Biddy soberly. "There's Ben, of course, but—oh, well, she may take him as a sort of makeshift, but I should think when you've been in love with a person like Jerry, everybody else is only second choice. Not but what, to my way of thinking, second choices don't sometimes turn out better than first. You sort of go potty on a thing when you see it first, and disappointed if you can't have it. When you've got to make do with something else, often you realize in the end that it wears better."

This time he took his eyes off the road for a moment to give her a curious, interested glance.

"That's a strange piece of wisdom to have grown up in eighteen years," he said.

She laughed.

"It isn't really mine at all. It's Mom's," she confessed. "This is the road. The house is the one by the lamp-post, on the left."

He drew up quietly at the curb, but Biddy had hopped out and was standing on the pavement before he could get there to open the door for her. Perceiving that that had been his intention, Biddy scolded herself for being so quick. Next time she must remember that evidently the thing to do was to sit tight until he had got there to help her out.

Next time! Idiot, how could there be a next time?

The faint regret showed in her little flower-like face as she gave him her hand.

"Oh, I *have* enjoyed that so," she said fervently, and that strange impulse which had made him offer her a lift made him now suggest something further.

"Is your mother sitting up for you?" he asked. "If she is, perhaps I ought to come in to explain myself."

Biddy stared at him, the color rising in her cheeks, her eyes incredulous. Did he mean it? That he would actually come in?

"Wait here. I'll pop round the back and see. If there's a

177

light she'll be up, and I'll let you in at the front," she said, and slipped away up the garden path and round to the back door.

Mrs. Cave rose at the sound of her hurried steps, putting down her knitting.

"Mom, somebody brought me home in his car. That Mr. Maitland Jerry talked about. You know. The one that helped him with his first play. He's outside now and he wants to come in."

Biddy's words had come in a breathless torrent.

"Wants to come in? Here? Mr. Maitland?" asked her mother, startled, drawing back a little.

"Yes. It's quite all right. He's ever so nice. You go into the other room. I'll let him in the front door; and Biddy gave her a little push, opened the door of the next room and gave a brisk look round and then ran to the front door, while Mrs. Cave automatically took off her apron that she had put on to see to Biddy's supper and straightened her soft grey hair.

"It's all right," called Biddy cautiously from the open front door. "You can come in. Mom's still up; and Maitland, smiling involuntarily at the cautious, slightly breathless whisper, found himself being ushered into the stuffy little hall and the sitting room with it's unmistakable air of being the "state apartment."

Then he forgot the strangeness of it all in the need to put the rather fluttering, disconcerted little "Mom" at her ease.

"Miss Biddy let me bring her home as she was alone and I had an empty car," he explained in his grave fashion, aware, with an amusement that was yet oddly tender, of the pride and delight with which Biddy was regarding him.

"That was very kind of you," said Biddy's mother shyly. "Can I offer you anything? I'm afraid we don't go in for fashionable drinks, or even whisky and soda, but tea, or coffee?

Not yet knowing Mrs. Cave well enough to trust her coffee, but feeling it would be unkind to refuse everything, he agreed that a cup of tea, if she were making one, would be more than acceptable, and she slipped away to make it while Biddy took off her hat and coat and stood on tiptoe before the mirror in the overmantel to push the waves of her bright hair into place.

With her hands still raised, she paused to look sideways

178

at the visitor, flushing to find him already looking at her.

"It really was awfully nice of you to bring me home in your car," she said. "I've never ridden in a car like that before, though I've often imagined myself doing it"—dreamily.

He laughed. It was quite a loud sound in the small house, and it reached the wondering, half-awake ears of Dickie on the floor above and took him, still half asleep, out of bed to look out of the window. The sound had apparently come from outside, and yet it had sounded quite near, as if there were a man in the front garden.

He blinked uncertainly and wiped the sleep from his eyes at the sight of Maitland's great car, its black cellulose gleaming under the light of the street lamp.

"Golly!" he said. "It's at our house!" And then came the masculine laugh again, and he realized that it was in the house itself.

Tying his pajama-cord more tightly about his slim little middle for safety's sake, he tiptoed down the stairs, paused in the hall, and then hid himself behind the coats hanging from the pegs as his mother came out of the kitchen with a tray and opened the door of the sitting room to reveal to those unsuspected eyes the sight of Royal Maitland sitting at ease on a chair in his immaculate dress suit, while Biddy sat on the edge of the table swinging her legs and laughing.

"Golly!" gasped her brother again before he scuttled back to bed. "Blowed if she hasn't caught her millionaire after all."

15

Jeremy sat in the warm darkness of Stella Dale's car, his mind in a whirl, knowing that he was in complete possession of himself but caring nothing for that, if the feelings he had included this terrific consciousness of adventure.

The silence was more pregnant with emotion than any words could be. Their minds reached out to each other's and met without even the touch of their fingers.

Presently Jeremy leaned towards her and caught her hands in his, drew them towards him, drew her nearer. She could see the shining look in his eyes, and her excitement rose even while she withdrew her hands from his.

"Not now. Later," she said, and the whisper made his
179

senses reel with their promise.

"Hadn't Firth better go and fetch your car?" she reminded him as they stepped out of hers. "Or did you leave it in a garage?"

"It'll be all right," he said, not at all clear where he had left it. "I can get a taxi presently."

She smiled and led the way into the house, opening the door with her key.

"I told the servants they need not wait up for me," she said evenly.

The house was still and warm. Lights burned discreetly from hidden sconces in Stella's own sitting room, a room to which, so far, he had never been admitted. There was a soft, diffused radiance when she pressed the light switches. It seemed to have no definite source and was infinitely restful, both hiding and revealing.

She threw her cloak down on a chair and crossed the room, her golden gown making a sweeping sound as it moved over the thick, creamy carpet. Jeremy's fingers touched her cloak as he moved. Its soft warm fur seemed vital from her own glowing source of life, and he took his hand away, thrilled and yet afraid. He could not resist the force with which she drew him to her.

"Drink?" she asked. "Long or short?"—opening the cocktail cabinet and speaking as if unaware of the tension in the atmosphere.

He went swiftly to where she stood, took into his the hands which had moved amongst the glasses and bottles, turned her so that she had to face him.

"Neither," he said. "I want nothing but you, Stella."

His eyes were hot. Even now he would have resisted her with one part of his mind, but that part was powerless against the urge of the rest of him.

She let her hands lie in his. Utterly motionless as she was, she yet conveyed to him that sense of a terrific force within her.

"I know," she said. "I've known for quite a long time," and her voice was honey-sweet.

"What are we going to do about it? I can't go on without you. You—you're like the wine of the gods to me, Stella. I've sipped at it, and now I can't any longer live without it. I've got to have you—everything. You're life to me."

His voice was hoarse and unfamiliar. He would have

drawn her closer, but she laughed softly and withheld herself.

It was just such a situation as she loved, and she intended to make it yield every scrap of its power to thrill and excite her. She was no young, foolishly ardent girl snatching with hands so eager that things slipped from their grasp from sheer inability to hold so much at once. Every moment was to be prolonged, savored to the full.

She revelled in that look in Jeremy's eyes, in the nervous quiver in the hands that held hers. She was an artist in the ways of passion. She knew to perfection just the touch, the depth of feeling, to produce the required reaction. This was meat and drink, this the wine of heaven to her. For this ecstasy of emotion she had played so many times, delicately, artistically, with complete mastery of herself and the situation.

There was a piquant newness, however, in not being quite sure of Jeremy. There was something she did not understand in him, some inhibition perhaps.

So she laughed and withheld herself from him.

"I wonder what effect it would have on an audience if you put things like that into a play, Jeremy," she teased him, her eyes half closed, her lips provocative.

Swiftly, so swiftly that she had no time to guess or to frustrate his intention, he caught her in his arms, crushed her against him till the perfume she used seemed to enfold them in a sweet, heady mist. He closed her protests with his lips, his mouth hard and firm over her own, and at last she fought against herself no more but drifted with him out on to that sea of enchantment.

When at last he set her free she was flushed and breathless. There were both triumph and surrender in the look she gave him.

"Brute force," she told him.

"You liked it," said Jeremy.

She nodded.

"From you," she said.

His hands caught her arms again. There was a look in his eyes that compelled her own.

"How many other men have made love to you?" he demanded.

She laughed.

"That is a question no gentleman should ask," she said lightly.

181

"I'm not a gentleman," said Jeremy brusquely. "Eighteen months ago I was a clerk in an office. Now I'm earning thousands writing plays, but that doesn't make me a gentleman. That fact gives me an advantage presumably. I can ask those questions.

"It doesn't make me answer them, though," retorted Stella, her eyes narrowing.

"You mean you're afraid to answer?" he demanded, gripping her arms so tightly that she felt they would show bruises tomorrow. He was so strong. There would be pleasure in resisting—pleasure in ultimate surrender. Each had power to quell the other.

She eyed him steadily. There was an insolent defiance in her look.

"I'm not afraid to answer," she said. "I rather think you're afraid to hear, though."

He flushed under her taunt, knowing it to be true. He hated the thought of those other men in her life, would never be able to forget that they had existed.

"Well, tell me," he insisted stubbornly. Perhaps that ghost would be laid by such means.

She laughed. Her tone and look held that exciting quality which both lured and revolted him. It was so largely animal.

"Other men, my dear Jeremy? Well, since you must have it—lots of other men. How else do you imagine I have arrived at a state of such utter sophistication?"

He drew a sharp breath, but his hands on her arms did not relax.

"Why can't I hate you?" he asked.

She relaxed consciously. That had been a bad moment. She had had a wild thought that she had tried him too far, had for once misread her man.

Her face and her voice grew softer.

"Because you love me, Jeremy," she said.

He dropped her arms abruptly and strode to the window, stood there looking out, trying to recover his sanity, to beat back the waves of her fascination for him. She was not worthy of love, and yet he craved what, in his sane moments, he knew to be destruction.

She came to him, linked her hands about his neck from behind him, bent her head so that her cheek lay against his neck, her dusky, scented hair brushing his skin.

"Because—you love me, Jeremy," she repeated very

182

softly, and he swung round and caught her fully in his arms, kissed her mouth, held her against him as if by sheer physical force he would conquer that resistance that was within himself rather than in her.

"Yes. Yes, I do love you," he said thickly. "I've never known anything like this, never thought it possible. I love everything about you, your hair and your eyes, the way you look, the way you walk, your smile, your mouth—your mouth, Stella" and he took it again, hungrily, greedily, trying to slake a thirst which could never be slaked at that fountain.

In his mind was no longer any thought of Julie, any thought in the world save of the glorious woman come to his arms, giving him back his kisses with an abandonment which maddened him, her body, lovely and sensuous, so closely held to his that he could feel the leap of her heart through her golden gown.

"Stella—my star—I can feel the beat of your heart," he whispered.

She took his hand and laid it against her breast.

"For you," she told him, her voice soft and sweet and yet with an undercurrent which swept him away.

Her skin beneath his fingers was cool and tormenting.

"I want you, Stella," he told her thickly.

She nodded, her eyes brilliant.

"I know. I'm not carved out of ice myself, Jeremy," she said.

"Stella . . ."

Sure of him, she resisted him, played with him until he was in a frenzy of desire.

"What about these other men who have loved me?" she asked him, smiling.

"They don't matter—nothing matters. I will make you forget them. In my arms, you will never remember other men's kisses—Stella . . ."

"I shan't, but you will," she said, still resisting him, leaning away from him, holding her lips from his seeking mouth.

For a moment a cold hand clutched his heart, for he knew it was true. Later, when sanity was restored, when the world had ceased to rock and time went on its rushing way again, he knew he would remember.

But not now—not at this moment—not while his arms were about her.

"You'll make me forget," he told her thickly.

She gave him her enigmatic smile, yielded to the urge of his arms, sighed in the exquisite relief of that surrender to herself.

"Yes, I'll make you forget everything in the world but that I am yours and you are mine, my beloved," she whispered.

Somewhere in the room a clock struck. Its silver chimes came vaguely to their consciousness.

"Midnight," said Jeremy. "Midnight angel in my arms at last."

She laughed.

"I have folded my wings—or tucked in my horns, Jeremy. Which?"

"Some day I'm going to hate you," he said.

"Well, what matter, so long as you love me first?" she asked him, still laughing. "*Tout passe*, even first love. Am I your first love, Jeremy?"

The ghost of Julie passed, so close to him that he shivered at the touch of that floating, intangible presence. Then he flung himself free of its tender, undemanding hands.

"My first, Stella," he said, and the little ghost shrank away and vanished in the shadows.

Stella laughed and threaded her fingers through his hair. It would be fun teaching him, watching him as he absorbed the lessons, playing on the sensitive strings of this imaginative, creative mind.

But the ghost of Julie had done its work. Some of the fever was gone. There was a restlessness, an awareness of time and place. The completeness of his subjection to their desires was marred.

He took his arms from Stella, half unconsciously switched on more light, shook his mind free of the clinging tentacles that had bound it.

"It's very late," he said. "I shall have to go."

Her eyes narrowed again. It seemed she did not know him, after all. How was it that he had evaded her? By what unknown and inexplicable force had he resisted her? She had not intended that he should leave her. She had brought him here, to her own sitting room, because through that door, partially open, lay her bedroom. The scene was set, desire kindled, herself lovely and willing—why then must he talk of leaving her?

184

But she was too experienced to make the fatal mistake of trying to rush her fences. She had made a miscalculation. This man was not so easily to be wooed and overcome. Well, it was only a matter of time, and the realization would in no way be lessened by further anticipation.

"May I telephone you after I get home?" he was asking, looking for the coat which he had laid down on a chair.

"If I am not asleep," she said, schooling her voice so that it appeared merely friendly and casual.

She knew it would be hours before she slept. She was keyed up, consumed with her own frustrated desires; but these things were not for his knowledge. Some men prefer to be the hunted, but not this one. He must always be the hunter, the woman his quarry. If her ardor could not ensnare him her coolness would.

"Can you sleep so easily?" he asked her, knowing his own turmoil.

She shrugged her shoulders and gave him her Mona Lisa smile.

"We should. We have blameless consciences!" she told him, and let him go. They did not even kiss. To both of them a farewell kiss just then would have been bathos.

Jeremy walked to the place where he had left his car. The night air was like a draught of cold water to a thirsty man. It calmed the tumult of his mind and body, restored to him the power of thought.

What did he want of Stella? He was perfectly clear about the thing from which he had consciously run away. He was no vicious *roue*, but neither was he the *preux chevalier*. He had had the casual adventures in sex of most men nearing thirty, none of them of any importance or lasting memory. Girls nowadays were ever ready to offer, and most men ready to accept, and passion had been lightly given and as slightly taken.

He could not think of Stella Dale as he had done of these frivolous, adventurous girls. She was certainly no young girl bent on experience first hand, nor could he take her and forget her. What then did this desire for her mean?

Love? Was he in love with Stella Dale?

The ghost of Julie touched him again with its pale, cool fingers, and he shivered and then thrust away the clinging hands in revolt. Why must he think of Julie when he thought of love? How could he compare what he had felt

185

for her with this terrific urge he had towards Stella?

Did he want to marry Stella? Or, probably more potent question, did she want to marry him? She had left him in no doubt as to the outcome she had expected of this night's adventure. He had not missed the suggestion of the open door, a shaded lamp burning in the room beyond, its circle of light over the satin-spread bed with its turned-down sheets. Had it not been for that queer feeling of Julie's presence he would undoubtedly have yielded to Stella's intention, gone with her into that lamp-lit room—and after that, what?

He could not conceive of Stella carrying on the sort of vulgar intrigue whose only alternative then would be marriage, so it appeared that she had wanted to marry him. He knew that her name had been linked with those of several men, but they had been men of her own social class, popular philanderers, or men who could give her something—power, wealth, a new interest or amusement. His recognition of that was unpalatable but honest.

Then—marriage?

He was brought up short by the sight of a policeman standing by his car, note-book and pencil in hand, peering by the light of his torch at the details on the license disc.

"Spot of bother for me, Officer?" he asked.

"Well, sir, two hours is the parking limit here, you know," he said reproachfully. "Matter of fact, I thought somebody must've forgotten their car."

"I almost did," admitted Jeremy with his cheerful grin, which never quite forsook him. "Went home with a lovely lady and—well, you probably know that story by heart."

The officer grinned. He was just coming off duty, and he was not one of the many who consider their whole duty to be running down motorists for every conceivable offence.

"Taking it away now, sir?" he asked.

Jeremy nodded and opened the door.

"Yes, if it's O.K.," he said.

"Better not forget it another time, sir," said the man, and Jeremy offered him a cigarette, not daring to offer him anything else, and drove away.

The incident, irrelevant as it was, had served to separate him from the too impressive memory of that hour with Stella, and when he had reached his flat he felt no temptation to speak to her again that night.

Anyway, she would be asleep, or so she had suggested.

It was she who made the next approach, ringing him up in the morning as he lay in bed with the pile of congratulatory papers.

Her voice was gay and friendly.

"How about lunching with me and celebrating our success?" she asked him.

Remembering that he owed much of the success to both her brain and her money, he could not well refuse her, even if he had wished it.

"One o'clock at the Berkeley? Or may I call for you?" he asked.

"No, I'll be there. But make it half past, will you?"

She kept him waiting twenty minutes, and then brought another woman with her. He was faintly chagrined, but also realized that it eased an uncomfortable moment.

"Jeremy, I want you to know Mrs. Milroy. You have been so near to meeting her many times, but it has never actually materialized."

He thought the delightful, mature woman a strange companion for Stella, but then part of her intriguing charm was her unexpectedness. He had come to the conclusion that the only thing to expect of Stella Dale was the unexpected.

"I was so much disappointed at not being able to attend your *premiere* last night, Mr. Denton," said Mrs. Milroy, "but if I hadn't stayed at home to entertain some tiresome friends of my husband's, I knew I should be faced today with the information that we were off to the North Pole or Darkest Africa in a canoe this afternoon. They are all crazy, and it is only my austere common sense that gives us any comfort at all."

"I believe I have heard your husband lecture," said Jeremy. "I was tremendously entertained. He's a great adventurer."

"Oh, he is, he is!" agreed his wife ruefully. "I can never imagine how he remained in one country and in civilization long enough to discover me and marry me!"

"He probably forgets that he ever did so, and picks up wives of various colors and dimensions as he goes about the world," suggested Stella.

Mrs. Milroy gave her lively, infectious laugh.

"I see to that!" she said. "Mr. Denton, you behold in me a woman of no home, with no rest to the soles of my feet,

187

with almost no country. My only comfort is that when my husband has been eaten by a crocodile or fallen off the North Pole or been drowned trying to discover a new country at the bottom of the Pacific, I shall be the world's complete tourist agency. I shall know so exactly where no one should ever go!"

"You know you love these adventures every bit as much as he does," said Stella, and her friend laughed.

There was about her an aura of happiness such as Jeremy felt one rarely met nowadays. Her personal happiness had not made her, as it made the majority of women, indifferent to the woes and joys of others. There was a largeness of outlook, a breadth of sympathy, a welling spring of humanity, which was as enduring as it was surprising.

The three of them talked cheerfully and well, and when he suggested that they look in at the matinee of his play, Jeremy felt that the uncomfortable question of last night had been shelved for the moment, if not yet answered.

"Stella tells me that the ballet is worth seeing just for itself," said Mrs. Milroy. "It isn't fair to either author or players to see a thing in unfinished bits, but we might have a look at the ballet, and I'll make an early opportunity of seeing it as a whole."

There was an amusing incident as they made their way out through the now sparsely peopled room.

"Look, Jeremy, there's Roy Maitland," said Stella, drawing his attention to a table by which they were soon to pass, "and he's got with him that queer little person we saw when we came out of the theater last night."

Jeremy's amazed eyes lit on Maitland, grave and remote as ever, and Biddy, wearing her cheap little coat and jaunty beret with an air that was exclusively and disarmingly her own.

She caught sight of him as he looked, and her face wore an expression of mingled dismay and triumph which brought an involuntary smile to his own. Absurd, amazing child! How on earth had she secured the escort of Roy Maitland? And by what extraordinary feat had she inveigled him into bringing her to the Berkeley? Surely a Lyons Corner House would have been more suitable and pleasant to them if they had to "make a date?"

Maitland had seen them and risen. His face wore its usual imperturbable expression. There was no least hint in his voice or look or manner to suggest that the situation, and his companion, were in any way remarkable. He greeted the two women, nodded amiably to Jeremy, and presented Biddy to Mrs. Milroy.

"Cave? Biddy Cave?" cogitated that lady aloud, returning a friendly smile for the little exaggerated bow which the girl, swift to learn, had substituted for the handshake of the inglorious past. "Why is that name familiar to me? Oh, I know. Of course, I believe I know your sister. Is Julie your sister?"

Biddy flushed, but held her head high. She had arrived, by tortuous and torturous ways, to an exact decision. Inflexibly determined that Royal Maitland should be the answer to her maiden's prayer, her very sensible little mind had brought her to the conclusion that she would have nothing to gain with him, and everything to lose, by pretending to be any other than she was. He had been to her home. He had sat and talked to Mom and drank tea with them in the state apartment. He knew she worked at Corelli's. She would make no pretence to him, and told herself valiantly and loyally that she had no need to be ashamed of any of them, Mum or Julie or Dickie.

She gave back a straight and honest look for Mrs. Milroy's friendly smile.

"Yes. She's at Monique's in Bond Street. I expect that's where you've seen her, and I suppose she must have mentioned me," she said. "She's in the showroom," she added, for she might as well give Julie all the importance and credit she deserved.

"Yes, that's where I've met her," agreed Mrs. Milroy. "She's a very charming girl, and a clever one, as I take care to let Monique know. Good-bye, my dear. Good-bye, Mr. Maitland. We're just going to see Mr. Denton's ballet." And she left them with that unfailing impression of her charm and dignity.

"That's what I'd like to be like when I'm old," said Biddy almost reverentially.

Maitland nodded.

"You've got good sense—and good taste," he said.

She gave him her wide, innocent, fascinating look.

"Oh, do you really think I have?" she asked fervently.

He laughed. It was surprising to him how many times he had laughed since he had yielded to that queer, unexpected impulse to call at Corelli's, to insist on waiting until Miss

Cave was free to manicure him, and then to invite her to lunch with him.

"It is at least one thing we have in common," he said in answer to her wide-eyed question, and she laughed, flushed adorably with an innocent betrayal of the youth she deplored, and gave herself up to the intriguing delights of the *peche de soie* he had ordered for her.

He could not explain his interest in her. Young girls had never attracted him, even in his extreme and almost forgotten youth. Was it a sign of approaching senility? He asked himself the question as he watched her undisguised enjoyment of her ice, asked it again when, depositing her at a discreet distance from Corelli's Oxford Street shop, he found himself suggesting that he take her out on the following Saturday.

She gave him a shining look.

"Oh, d'you really mean that?" she asked, in an awe-struck voice.

"Why not?"

"Oh, but I'd just *love* to!" she breathed.

"Good. What time shall we say?" he asked, debating whether she would choose dinner and a late show or the theater and possibly supper.

Her answer was so unexpected that it took his breath away.

"Well I could be ready quite by three," she said. "We close at one, and I should just have to pop home for lunch and to change."

His expression gave no inkling of the lightning change of plan her answer necessitated. He was courteous pleasure personified, and Biddy, seeing his look of absorbed attention in her, hoped somebody from the shop might be passing while they stood there beside his marvellous car, complete today with chauffeur. Not that any of the girls would believe anything but the worst!

"Shall we make no plans until we see what kind of day it is?" he suggested. "If it is as fine and warm as today, we might to down to the sea. Would you enjoy that?"

"Love it," sighed Biddy ecstatically. She almost wished he would let her go now so that she could go on with the marvellous dream, a sort of serial story, which for years she had been inventing and telling herself, a story which was surely reaching its crisis now!

"I wonder if you would be able to telephone me during

the morning on Saturday?" he suggested. "Or could I telephone you at the shop?"

"Oh, no, don't do that!" said Biddy quickly. She wasn't going to let those grinning, gossiping, catty-minded girls in on this, even if she had wished for a moment they could see her with Maitland. "I could telephone you."

He found a card and gave it to her.

"If you can ring me up about ten o'clock, we should know by then what the day is like and can decide what to do. Good-bye, and thank you so much for your company."

Biddy's feverishly acquired rudiments of correct behavior in all circumstances failed her at this juncture, and she could only blush and stammer out an incoherent "Thanks ever so much for lunch" before she took to her little high heels and sped along the street and disappeared into Corelli's.

16

Jeremy consciously avoided any chance of intimate talk with Stella Dale for some time after that *premiere* of his play, but he knew that it could not be avoided for ever, and when, some weeks later, an offer for the American rights in the play was cabled to him, he decided to accept the inevitable and reach finality with her.

Her voice over the telephone was slightly mocking.

"You aren't suggesting we should talk this over alone, Jeremy, are you?" she asked. "Are you sure you can risk it?"

"Can you?" he parried, and in spite of himself the prospect thrilled sim. She, no more than he, had forgotten that night and its potentialities.

"I love taking risks," she said with a laugh.

"All right. When may I come? This afternoon?" he asked recklessly.

"Is daylight any safer than midnight?" she asked him.

"Perhaps I am no more in love with safety than you," he suggested.

"Then—this evening? Will you dine with me?"

"Why not?" asked Jeremy with that new reckless note in his voice.

And a few hours later he stood with her in that same

room, pregnant with memories, and took her in his arms without preamble.

"You're the most exciting woman I've ever met," he told her, his pulses leaping at her touch.

"And possibly just now—the most excited?" she ventured, withdrawing herself from his arms and giving her parlor-maid permission to enter.

It was a delightful and intimate meal, served to them by a perfectly trained staff, and Stella was at her most attractive best, exerting herself without any obvious exertion to entertain and amuse him, and when at last they were left to their cigarettes and coffee, she knew she had him at her feet again, if not in her arms.

He came to the point at once, as soon as they were safely alone.

"Stella, where is all this leading?"

She smiled.

"Darling, what a restless person you are! Where do you want it to lead?"

"You know, Stella."

"To the voice that breathed o'er Eden?" she asked him, half exasperated, half charmed by the knowledge.

"Naturally. You never really imagined I meant it to lead to—to . . ."

"To a discreet little apartment with one bed and two keys?" she supplied.

He frowned. The evening had turned suddenly cold, and she had lit the electric fire. He stood apart from her, looking down at the simulated flames leaping amongst the fake logs. The true artist in him disliked any sort of fake. He would have preferred honest-to-goodness red-hot wires.

"I wish you wouldn't say things like that, Stella. They're—cheap," he said.

She laughed. Dear, respectable Jeremy!

"Darling, have I shocked you?" she asked.

"Oh, I dare say it's funny to you that anyone who can write a play like *Midnight Angel* is not shock-proof, but—you know as well as I do that I write with my brain, to make money, not with—well, with the part of me that's in love with you."

"Are you in love with me, Jeremy?" she asked him softly.

"You know I am. Why else should I want you to marry me?"

She gave a little sigh and traced with the point of one satin slipper the pattern of a footstool. She felt it was a thousand pities he should have this marriage obsession. Would it last? Did she want it to last? Would she be happier as his wife or his mistress? There was nothing in her make-up to match his dislike of intrigue and furtive love affairs. Rather did it whet her appetite and increase her enjoyment if there was a spice of danger, and what danger would there be if she were respectably married to him? Chiefly the danger of boredom, and that was not a risk but a certainty.

"Are you sure you do want to marry me?" she asked.

"Of course I am. You should know that."

She gave a thoughtful little frown.

"Marriage is such a horrible final thing in this country," she said.

He stood looking down at her, both loving and hating her, desiring her with every nerve in his body, repelling her with a mind that, without reason, distrusted her.

"I'm not interested in anything less final," he told her and wondered if that were true or if he were just making himself out to be the hell of a fine fellow.

She rose with her sinuous grace of movement and locked her arms about his neck.

"Darling, we could have such fun. We might bore each other so profoundly by marrying. We should enjoy each other so much more if we were not always together. I'm not really a great success as a wife, I've tried it, and I know. Poor Brandy—well, let's forget that, but he knew. I'd make a really successful and adorable mistress though, Jeremy."

"Stella, you don't mean that!" said Jeremy.

"But, dear heart, I do! If I were your wife you'd soon see my faults, see me in all sorts of unpleasant moods and get an exact and truthful estimate of me. I'm not really a nice person at all, and I should know, for I've lived with myself for so many years. If I had the right to choose your times of access to me, you'd never see anything but the side of me that you're in love with, and so—love would last much longer, my dear."

Though she spoke lightly, smiled as she spoke, kept her arms twined round his neck and now and then touched with soft lips his cheeks, he could sense the undercurrent of earnestness in her voice. He believed that she really did fear that thief of love, too great knowledge of the beloved. It only increased his tenderness towards her and confirmed him in his intention to marry her.

"You think of yourself unfairly, my sweet," he told her. "I believe I know you better than you do yourself."

Her eyes held a slight exasperation with him for his stubborn blindness.

"Jeremy darling, you're hopelessly bourgeois!" she said.

He laughed.

"Probably. I've told you I'm of the people. Perhaps that's why I've got a few decencies and ideals left. Stella, when will you marry me?"

She let her hands fall to her sides in an impatient gesture.

"Oh, Jeremy!" she exclaimed.

"When will you?" he persisted doggedly, and suddenly, at sight of his face on which youth and experience sat, mingling oddly, her resistence melted. After all, they could have such fun together, and she had come to sufficient knowledge of him to know that he would never be light-hearted while his inconvenient and prim moral code warred against his enjoyment. And even in England marriage need not be a life sentence.

So, giving in with laughter which was silenced by the passionate demand of his lips, she told him she would marry him "in the winter."

"In the winter! But, darling, it's only July now. When does winter begin? August?" he asked.

"You'd be such a disappointment to me if you were not impatient," she told him. "Well—October, then"; and from that she would not be moved.

"I've got to get used to the idea of being engaged to you first," she said. "Then I've got to get clothes, oceans of them."

"You won't need them," he said, and at his look she melted into his arms again.

"Oh, Jeremy, let's go to Italy. It's marvellous there in October. Think of it—you and I . . ."

"Can you wait till October, Stella?"

She laughed and kissed him again.

"If you can," she said.

He returned to his flat in a mood of hard determination. While the memory of Stella, compliant in his arms, remained with him it was easy to retain that mood. He felt exalted, his head in the clouds and his heart accommodating itself to its desires.

In the long, wakeful hours towards morning, however, one is apt to become deadly honest with oneself, and it was of Julie he thought rather than of Stella, picturing her asleep in the room she shared with Biddy, a room which he imagined had texts pinned on the walls and a marble-topped washstand with pink china arrayed on it.

He tried to shake from his mind that picture of Julie, to set in its place a vision of Stella in the room he had once glimpsed, a room of mauve and silver, a wide, low bed in silvered wood with satin eiderdown and delicately tinted pillows, shaded iridescent lights, a grey carpet and walls, mauve-flowered silk at the long windows. He tried to picture himself sharing Stella's life with her, sharing rooms like that, intimately and as a right. His mind rebelled. How much easier to imagine himself in the Hemming Road life, the shabby, homely kitchen, the place where he could be always and entirely himself!

He remembered the time he had gone there, impelled by his need of Julie, thrown stones at her window and brought her down, trembling and self-conscious, to open the door to him. In the dark kitchen, in her comfortable, shabby old dressing gown, she had trembled in his arms like a captive bird, had been frightened, his dear little love, by the fierceness of his kisses. She must have known that he would not hurt a hair of her head, that it was only because he needed her so, loved her so that he held her so closely, kissed her . . . .

He broke off and forced the thoughts from him, refused the memory so suddenly poignant. That was finished forever. For each of then there was now someone else. Her mother had told him Julie had put someone in his place, and he—he had Stella, though not in Julie's place. No one would ever be there. When she had left the room in his heart empty, he had locked and sealed it. He would be a good and true husband to Stella, but that one locked door would be inviolate forever.

In the morning he went to the Goldsmiths' Company in Regent Street and bought a ring for Stella, giving more than he had intended or could really afford for it as a sort of penance for the thoughts of the night. Coming away, he ran into Bainbridge, remembering that that old warrior had given him the one bad notice his latest play had received, and resolved to tackle him over it.

"Come and have a drink and a row," he invited him.

Bainbridge smiled.

"Don't mind if I do," he said, for in spite of his outspoken criticisms, he found something unmistakably likable about this young Denton.

"Now, what's the matter with my play?" Jeremy demanded, when they sat over the beer they both preferred to what Bainbridge termed the "more aristocratic drinks."

"I rather think I made that clear," said his companion.

"I know what you *said* about it, but what do you really *think*?" asked Jeremy.

"If you really want a row, here's the truth. It's cheap," said Bainbridge in his direct fashion.

Jeremy flushed. Though probably he would not admit it even to himself, he would rather have this one man's approval than that of all his other critics put together. And in his heart he knew that accusation was true.

"The audience liked it the night you didn't," said Jeremy.

"Quite. And if you'll excuse me for saying it, it was a cheap audience too. That's why."

"Cheap? There was no paper in the house," objected Jeremy quickly.

"Granted. I didn't mean there was an absence of money, but of intelligence."

Jeremy stared, inclined to resent the affront. Then his sense of humor triumphed, and he laughed.

"They're the sort of people who bring success to a play," he said.

"Oh yes, if that's all you're after," grunted Bainbridge.

"Does it occur to you that I may be cheap myself?" asked Jeremy. "*Midnight Angel's* the best I can do—so what?"

"Well, if it is, you've lost something, boy, something I was ready to swear you'd got when you started, something so hopelessly out of date that I'm almost afraid to mention it, something called—idealism."

Jeremy could find nothing to say to that. Julie had said something very much like that once. It was when, filled with the eager optimism of youth, its belief that it can bring the millennium to a lost and hopeless world, he had been writing his first play.

"You've got power, Jerry," Julie had told him with shining eyes when he had read her one passage which, in retrospect, seemed pitiably grandiose. "When your plays are being acted, thousands of people listening every night to your words, they'll think all sorts of thoughts that have never occurred to them before—great and inspiring thoughts."

He had cut that passage out of *The Bauble* now. In fact, he had altered it quite a lot, and the version still going round the remoter parts of the country had something far more approaching the modern Jeremy than London audiences had had.

Julie again!

Bainbridge, his glass empty, was inviting him, but Jeremy shook his head.

"Thanks, I won't. I'm lunching with a woman. That'll mean rather sticky wines."

Bainbridge regarded him with speculation and at length voiced something he felt he might have been wiser to keep to himself. He seldom interfered with people's private lives, regarding them as private lives. In young Denton's case, however, he felt that his inward conviction justified it.

Laying his hand on Jeremy's arm, he spoke with unaccustomed gravity.

"If you want to be popular, write more stuff like this last; but if you want to be great, get back to yourself, work till you sweat blood if you must, but get back. And—get out of the set you're in. If you want a backer still, Maitland will back another thing like *The Bauble*."

Jeremy flushed, realizing the implied knowledge of his affairs.

"I don't need to ask him," he said stiffly. "Seeing that he has lost faith in me, it would hardly be palatable either."

"He hasn't lost faith in you, only in the piffle you're producing and the sort of people who're helping you to do it. Get rid of the lot of them, Jeremy, and wash your hands clean. With your experience, you can produce a successor to that first play of yours which I should be proud to boost to high heaven—that is, if you choose to produce it."

Jeremy started to move towards the door. His face was expressionless, his jaw set.

"Sorry, Bainbridge," he said. "You've got a wrong estimate of me. Fortunately you are in the minority. Which way are you going?"

"Not your way," said the older man—said it with a rather grim twist to his lips which gave point to his words, and on that note they parted.

17

"Here's Ben, Julie."

Julie glanced up from the fashion paper from which she had been painstakingly copying figures and draperies. She had neither skill nor technical knowledge, but something which she dare not admit, even to herself, was spurring her to learn something, do something, be something more than a mere showroom assistant.

Mrs. Tanner had good-naturedly given her some hints on the rudiments of designing and suggested that, as a preliminary and to test her ability, she should make copies of printed models, giving them little finishing touches of her own.

It was July, a cold, wet month which had sent people shivering back to their winter clothes and their fires.

Julie felt indifferent to the weather. Since November, when she had parted from Jeremy, something had happened to her. She was perfectly well, was as gentle and considerate as ever with those with whom she came in contact, but there were two people at least who knew she was different, who watched the dimming of her radiance as if by a dark curtain, knew that she did not smile as often, that she lived a life indefinably remote from them. One of these two people was her mother.

The other was Ben, who was waiting in the hall for her.

He never walked straight into the room where she was. Even though they had become so much closer friends during these months, he never presumed on their friendship or attempted to take more than the little Julie offered him.

So he stood outside until she answered her mother's call with a "Come along in, Ben. I'm doing one of these awful drawings."

His eyes, as he entered the room, rested on her like those

of a faithful dog, a dog who knew himself not to be first favorite of the beloved but was content just to be allowed to adore. If Julie were a little more worldly, a little less sweet, she would have been irritated by an adoration which she could not use.

"Why bother about it and strain your eyes over it?" he asked.

"Oh, I d'know," said Julie, with a little sigh, her head tilted on one side to get the effect of one preposterously long limb which she had just added to an abbreviated torso. "I suppose it's because I know I shall soon be a back number if I don't do something to better my position."

"But you like it in the showroom, don't you, Julie?" he asked cautiously, his spirits rising at this first suggestion that she was not happy in her job.

"Better than the workroom, in some ways, though some of the customers are cats. Others are dears—people like Mrs. Milroy, for instance."

Conversation flagged while Julie put in a few more half-hearted strokes. Then Ben offered a diffident suggestion.

"I wondered if you'd like to go to the pictures, Julie. There's a good one on at the Astoria."

"Who's in it?" asked Julie, without much interest.

"I—I've forgotten. I did look, but it's gone clean out of my head," confessed Ben apologetically.

Poor old Ben, she thought indulgently. He admitted that all the people on the screen looked alike to him, so how could he be expected to remember their names? The only ones he really recognized on sight were Mickey Mouse and Donald Duck.

Biddy came into the room.

"'Lo, Ben. Like my hair," she asked, revolving so as to give him the full benefit of a new coiffure, a bunch of little golden curls set on the crown of a head which was difficult to realize had been in existence only eighteen years.

Ben regarded it gravely and critically, bringing to it the weight of mind with which every problem was considered by him.

"No, I don't," he said at last. "I like something simple, like—like Julie's'—his voice taking on a different inflection as he shifted his gaze reverently to Julie's soft brown head, which made no pretences to fashion but always looked the same.

"There's no style at all about that sort of hairdressing,"

said Biddy scornfully, looking at herself with complacent satisfaction in the mirror.

Julie laughed.

"Leave off admiring yourself for once and tell us what's on at the Astoria," she suggested.

"Myrna Loy and Herbert Marshall in *Queen's Knight*," said Biddy at once. "There's a funny one, too, and a Mickey Mouse, and Tim Moran's band on the stage."

Ben stared at her.

"How ever did you know all that straight off?" he asked.

"By using my eyes, ears, and intelligence, Mr. Elson," said Biddy pertly.

"That's very rude, Biddy," objected Julie, beginning to clear up her drawing materials.

Biddy laughed, came behind the chair in which Ben was sitting, and dropped a kiss on the top of his head.

"Ben and I are buddies, aren't we, my pet?" she asked. "And don't think that because I've kissed you I've fallen for you, will you? I've got to get some practice in with someone, haven't I?"

"Before you start on your millionaire?" chipped Dickie's voice from the doorway.

Biddy swung round and made a face at him, but before she could start on the never-finished wrangle their mother had interposed.

"Dickie, do get on with your homework, and, Biddy, if you're going out, you'll need a mackintosh. It's simply pouring."

"Don't worry about that, Mom," put in the incorrigible Dickie before he fled with his books. "The royal duke will bring the car up the front steps for her."

He dodged Biddy's well-aimed cushion as he fled.

"Are you going out with Mr. Maitland again, dearie?" asked Mrs. Cave, a little anxiously.

"Mps," said Biddy, with a satisfied smile. "Only pictures, worse luck."

"What else do you expect?" asked Julie. "Dinner and a cabaret?"

"Some day. He's promised," said Biddy serenely. "That's the car now. Do you want him to come in, Mom?"

"Not tonight, dear. We're all in a muddle," said her mother. "You can bring him back afterwards for coffee, if you like."

"Right ho. Bye-bye, sweetest."

She kissed her mother, flung her gay smile like a mantle over Julie and Ben, and a few moments later they heard the car purr gently away again.

Mrs. Cave sighed, and at the rather worried little sound Julie slipped an arm about her and gave her a squeeze.

"Biddy can look after herself, Mom," she said, "and you've said yourself that you like Mr. Maitland."

"But she's so young, Julie, and he's—well, we aren't his sort, after all, however nice he may be to us. I wish you'd meet him, Julie, and see what you think."

But Julie only smiled and shook her head. She had her own reasons for not wishing to meet Roy Maitland, and Mrs. Cave knew what they were. Not even remotely did she want to be brought into contact with Jeremy Denton again.

"Biddy won't lose her head," she said. "There's more in it than the golden fluff that grows on it! Ready, Ben?"—for she had put on her hat and mackintosh while they had been talking, and taken the family umbrella from the stand. "We'd better go now so that we can get in before it's too crowded."

He knew that what she was really thinking was "before we have to pay more than a shilling," and though he appreciated her thoughtfulness for his pocket, he felt enraged that it should be necessary. It seemed all wrong to him that little, flighty, calculating Biddy should be whirled away in a luxurious car and into the best seats while Julie, for whom the world's best was not good enough, should have to trudge through the rain and crowd into the cheap seats.

He had tried so hard and for so long to get a better job for himself, but it seemed he must tax himself to the limit even to remain where he was, earning a wage which he felt to be totally inadequate to his dreams for Julie.

They enjoyed the show, and afterwards he took her to a shop for coffee and sandwiches in spite of her protests.

"Let me, Julie," he begged. "I'd like to take you," and rather than hurt him, she consented.

Actually she had no wish to be left to her own company and thoughts, with a feeling that sleep was unlikely for hours yet, and though Ben's companionship was not exactly exciting, it was at least preferable to her own.

For days she had felt depressed and miserable, knowing it to be foolish to yield to such feelings. She had seen in one of the Society magazines to which Monique subscribed for the benefit of waiting clients a photograph in which Jeremy had appeared with "the beautiful Mrs. Dale." She had gazed at it until she could no longer see for a mist of tears. There he was, so good-looking, so debonair, so much at home in the smart restaurant where the flashlight photograph had been taken, and she remembered quite clearly "the beautiful Mrs. Dale," whom, then and ignorantly, she had decided bitterly was the type whom he would consider fit to marry him.

Was he, indeed, going to marry her?

She had read the letterpress that accompanied the photographs, snobbish gossip whose chief concern seemed to be to introduce the names, frequently the Christian names, of titled people. Jeremy was spoken of as "that popular and brilliant young playwright, whose *Midnight Angel* has taken London by storm," and there followed a "rumor" that a link of more than professional interest bound him to "the lively young Society widow who made no secret of her backing of his play."

Poor Julie.

She had hidden the paper beneath a pile of old ones, but its memory was not so easily buried. Jerry had been lost to her from the moment when she had opened that bitter letter he had not meant for her eyes, but she did not realize to the full the irrevocable nature of that loss until she saw his pictured face there, smiling across a table and a champagne bottle at Stella Dale.

So she had been glad to be taken out of her thoughts for a few hours by Ben, glad when he followed her into the house and saved her from being too soon alone.

Biddy had not returned, Dick was in bed, and their mother was busy with her hospitable preparations in the kitchen, making the coffee and the little snow cakes to which Royal Maitland was especially addicted.

"Can I stop a few minutes, Julie?" asked Ben diffidently.

"Yes, please do, Ben," she said in her kind way. "You can probably manage another cup of Mom's coffee."

He was so obviously ill at ease that afterwards Julie wondered she had not guessed what was in his mind. Her own was so preoccupied, however, that when he managed to get out what had been weighing him down for months past she was totally taken by surprise.

"Julie, I—I've got something I want to—at least—Julie, you must know how awfully fond of you I am."

He had blurted it out at last, red-faced and awkward, and Julie had to struggle to take in the import of what he was saying.

She stared at him wonderingly, frowning a little.

"Why, Ben, you—you don't mean . . ."

"I do, Julie, I do. I've meant it for years. It's always been you, never anyone else." Now that he had started, nothing was going to stop him till the pent-up spate of words had run their course. "I know it's awful cheek on my part to hope you would, and I know you're a thousand times too good for me, but—oh, Julie, I'd be awfully good to you if only you would!"

Her face was filled with surprise and dismay, but her voice was gentle.

"You mean—do you mean that you want to—marry me, Ben?" she asked, struggling to assimilate the idea which had never occurred to her.

"It sounds the most colossal nerve, Julie, but—Julie, won't you? I know you don't care for me like—like—well, you know," floundered the luckless Ben.

"You mean Jeremy, don't you,, Ben?" she asked quietly, the very serenity of her voice giving him greater ease of mind.

Julie was like that, cool and sweet and serene in the midst of any chaos, a fountain in the desert.

He nodded.

"Couldn't you forget him, Julie—now?" he asked.

The last words smote her like a blow. Before she could fend it off with words he spoke again, taking her hand in his with clumsy tenderness.

"He isn't worthy of you, dear. He never was. Forget him. Leave him to his Society dame and . . ."

Her caught breath checked him.

"You—you know about her, Ben?" she asked.

"Biddy told me," he admitted regretfully. Why had he been such a clumsy idiot as to hurt her?

Biddy, thought Julie. She had known, then, about this Stella Dale. How? Probably Maitland had told her. If that was so, there must be a lot of truth in it, not just the idle gossip of a Society paper. How long had Biddy known?

Her thoughts went back to some days ago, when, without apparent reason, Biddy had offered to brush her hair, to dress it in a new style, to manicure her nails, to do anything and everything within her power to do. It had been her practical way of showing her sympathy. Dear little Biddy.

Julie's eyes were wet with sudden tears, and Ben saw and was deceived by them.

He pressed the hand he held.

"Don't cry, Julie. I couldn't bear it if you did. Perhaps I oughtn't to have spoken of it. That's just like me, though, hurting you when I'd—I'd lie down on broken glass and let you walk over me!"

She smiled and blinked away the tears.

"It's all right, Ben," she said.

"Julie, I'd be good to you. I'd worship you all my life and never let anything hurt you if I could help it," he said humbly.

Poor Julie. It was not worship she wanted. It was something warmer, more human. It was simply Jerry's love, with all its faults and weaknesses.

"I'd be thankful for just anything you could give me, Julie, even if it's only liking and—well, the sort of friendship we've been having these last months. You do like me, don't you, Julie?"—anxiously.

Her smile was the gentle one she gave to Dickie.

"Of course I do, Ben. I like you very much, more than—almost anyone. Marriage is different, though. It's such a big thing. It—isn't easy to think of it, not just now."

"I know, Julie dear. It isn't as if I didn't understand. I'm not going to worry you, though. I just want you to know that I'm right here on the spot and that you've only got to say the word. If—if ever you can say it, Julie, it would be almost too much happiness for me."

"You're such a dear, Ben," she said shakily.

There was comfort in the touch of his big, rough hand, comfort and a sense of protection. Why, why could she not feel for Ben what she felt for Jerry?

But no man or woman can love to order, and in the weeks that followed Julie realized how futile it was for her to try to care for Ben or for any other man as she had done—still did—for Jeremy Denton.

Ben's stolid, unshakable devotion had its effect, however, and she realized how much she was beginning to

204

depend on him, to look for his coming, to feel rested and calmed by his undemanding presence. Her pride, so sorely wounded by Jeremy, inevitably revived in Ben's reverence, in his simple acceptance of her as above and beyond all other women. To him she was perfection, and she would not have been human and a woman had this enthronement meant nothing to her.

There was, too, the strong pull of the knowledge that she could grant to Ben his heart's desire, and it was not in her nature to ignore the possibility of giving so great happiness if it lay within her power.

And then one morning her heart leaped wildly in her breast and then seemed to die, for, returning to the showroom from a visit of inquiry to the workroom, she found Monique in obsequious attendance on Stella Dale, and heard her say, "It was not a white bridal gown of which you were thinking, Mrs. Dale?"

"No, one could scarcely do that," laughed Stella. "I think gold or silver lame might be made to serve, though, don't you? I tried to persuade Mr. Denton to come with me, but it seems he has an inhibition against dress shops! I warned him that the penalty would be forgoing my company for hours and hours. Now, Monique, let's be really clever over my gown, shall we?"

Oh, she looked a queen, a conqueror! Julie's hands trembled and her feet faltered and she would have fled with her grief had not Monique's eagle eye perceived her, the only person in the showroom at the moment save themselves, and sent her hot foot to find Mrs. Tanner.

"And better come back with her yourself, Miss Cave. The pearl room."

Julie knew that it was suggested with kindly intent, Madame thinking that it would be good experience for the budding designer, and she had no alternative but to go with Mrs. Tanner to the pearl room, to listen to the discussion on materials and styles, to watch Stella Dale's dark, glowing beauty triumphantly displayed against the pastel walls and the pale inlaid furniture which gave the room its name.

"It's rather hard that, because I made a tragic mistake when I was so young, I can't appear as a regulation bride now that I am marrying the man I love," said Stella, throwing aside for once her cloak of proud reserve and appearing to them as the young and radiant beloved. "I'm determined to be as bridal as I can, however, and I refuse even to think of an afternoon gown and a hat."

They suggested at length a gown of silver and orange, and Mrs. Tanner was to fly to Paris forthwith to see if she could obtain the material which had been used in an exclusive dress show there.

"I will send you some Russian mink furs I have," said Mrs. Dale. "If they can be used, get a really first-class furrier to cut them. I believe they are valued at something over a thousand pounds."

The discussion went on interminably to the pale, crucified Julie, who stood contributing nothing to it, not even thought. All she could think of was that this woman was to be Jeremy's bride, that for her were the kisses whose memory stabbed her, for her the tender words, the laughter, the passion she had refused.

That was a curious thought. She, Julie Cave, standing there as an insignificant part of the background, had been held in Jeremy's arms, known his kisses, shared his hopes and joys and despair, before he had given even a thought or a handshake to this radiant, conquering woman. This woman would be his wife, but she, Julie, had been his love.

But the day ended, as all days must eventually end, even though there has been an age between the rising and the setting of the sun, and Julie left the shop, white and exhausted, with a set face, to find Ben waiting for her in Bond Street.

He was like a lifebuoy flung to a drowning man. Never had she imagined herself so glad to see him.

"The guv'nor offered me the afternoon off, as we're slack," he explained. "I thought I'd come up and hang about till you came out and perhaps we'd—go out to tea, or the pictures or something."

The day had been hot and airless, panting for the thunderstorm which would eventually relieve it, and Julie thought, as much as she could think of anything, of the freshness and quiet of the countryside.

"Let's get on a bus and go out of London," she suggested feverishly. "It doesn't matter where. We can go along to Marble Arch and take the first Green Line coach that comes along."

Though the hours of that evening the drive out, the homely meal at a cottage, the walk through fields of stacked corn, with a lark singing overhead, the journey back to town, Julie let her mind lean against the constancy of Ben's love just as, in the last half hour, she let her tired body rest against the arm which he dared to put behind her shoulders.

What was there left for her? The second-best. Only that ever. And if she could get that and at the same time give to faithful, worthy Ben what he considered the best, wasn't it better to do it than give herself selfishly up to grief and old maid loneliness?

So when, last of all, they stood for a few moments along in the kitchen at 26 Hemming Road, and she saw the look of a faithful spaniel in his eyes, she took his hand and held it closely.

"Ben, do you still think about me like that? Want me like that?" she asked, her voice shaking a little.

The light of incredulous joy that shone in his eyes, like a brilliant lamp suddenly switched on in the darkness, made her afraid. He would give her too much for the little she had to offer.

"Julie, do you mean that you possibly *could*?" he asked her fervently.

"Oh, Ben, if only you didn't feel like that," she said in a troubled voice. "You care too much."

"No one could care too much for you, Julie," he said, and there was dignity in his utter simplicity. "I'll give my life to making you happy if you'll let me."

"Then—shall we see what we can make of it, Ben—dear Ben?" she asked, and in that moment died a little death. How could she, how dare she, give away that which was forever Jeremy's?

But Ben, taking her carefully into his arms, kissing her cheek and then, with shy and unaccustomed and awkward lips, her mouth, knew only that the heavens had opened and poured all their glory into a world that held only Julie and love.

18

There was quietness again in Mrs. Cave's eyes when Julie wore on her finger Ben's ring, a cheap, pretty little trifle of diamond chips of which he tried not to show inordinate pride.

There had been just one moment when mother and daughter had looked into each other's eyes and spoken with no words.

"I can't talk about it, but you understand, don't you?" Julie's had said, and her mother's "I understand and want only your happiness, my heart's darling."

After that there had been new laughter in the house, more bustle of coming and going, little plans for this and that pleasure, a bubbling of happiness from Ben which was somewhat of an elephantine nature and revealed itself in cumbersome jokes and heavy horseplay with Dickie, who still gave him hero-worship, if of a more restrained and less blatant type.

Julie had a great thankfulness for his happiness, and if her own heart still ached and felt forlorn, she could not remain insensible to the joy that was in Ben. She had secret cause for thankfulness in that he did not press for an early marriage. He seemed for the moment quite content with her promise and the sight of his ring on her finger.

So Mrs. Cave was quietly happy about Julie and could turn her rather bewildered attention to Biddy, that strange chick she had hatched.

Biddy was in process of being glorified. There was no doubt about that. She had a natural aptitude for making the best of her physical charms, and she spent every penny she earned on buying materials which she plagued Julie into helping her to make into clothes more to her taste than the cheap, ready-made garments she despised. The result was that she had blossomed suddenly into what her mother privately called "a young madam," waved and manicured and perfumed, and appearing far more expensively clad than she actually was.

It was not this that gave her mother food for anxious

thought however. It was a look in her blue eyes, a new restlessness, a watchful, expectant air which belied her assumption of the old, childish satisfaction with herself.

Royal Maitland had put that look there, of course. That needed no second thought, and the sight of his long, sleek car at the door, the sound of his quiet, well-bred voice in the hall, was becoming a nightmare to Mrs. Cave. She had a troubled idea that she ought to be "asking him his intentions," but knew that that was quite impossible to her. Biddy had always seemed so eminently capable of managing her own life that it was bewildering to see her apparently bent now on running her head against a brick wall.

Dickie tormented her unmercifully, as is the way of brothers, and Biddy was getting curiously touchy about it.

Worrying over her, she did not notice her younger girl come in until Dickie, looking up from the newspaper, observed conversationally:

"I see there's a fifth suit of cards out now."

There was that tremendous geniality in his tone which made his mother suspect at once that he was baiting Biddy, but it seemed an innocent enough remark.

"Well, as we don't play cards, I don't see what interest that is to us," she observed placidly.

"Not to you and me, Mom, but it is to Biddy—isn't it, Bids?"

Biddy tossed her golden head and there was a gleam in her eye.

"It's called Royals," said Dickie with a chuckle. "Fancy calling a suit of cards *Royals*, with a King of Royals and a Queen of Royals!"

And suddenly Biddy turned on him, her face white, her eyes ablaze with anger, her hands clenched as if to strike him, though she kept them at her sides.

"You're beastly, and I hate you, Dickie—I hate you!" she cried, and rushed from the room, leaving the boy and his mother to look at each other in amazement.

"Golly!" gasped Dickie.

"Oh, Dickie, you shouldn't tease her so," said Mrs. Cave, and after a moment's hesitation went up to Biddy's room, to find her, as she expected, flung across the bed in a tempest of tears.

She gathered her into her arms like the baby she had suddenly become to her mother, and presently the storm abated and Biddy lifted a woebegone face streaked with mascara and lipstick.

Mrs. Cave poured water into the basin, sponged off the havoc, and found Biddy's powder compact for her.

"Here, darling, dust yourself up," she said, knowing her Biddy; and, with a final gulp, the girl complied.

"Now, what's it all about, chicken?" asked Mrs. Cave gently. "I suppose it's—Mr. Maitland?"

Biddy nodded and fixed her eyes on space. They were still, thank God, the eyes of a child.

"Biddy, is it really worth your seeing him so much? I thought at first it was only fun. You know you've always talked about catching a millionaire, and you didn't mind us teasing you about it, but—well, that was only idle talk, wasn't it?"

"Perhaps it was—then," admitted Biddy reluctantly.

"But, darling, you're older and more sensible now. You don't really still hope to marry a wealthy man?"

Suddenly Biddy turned to her, desperation in her eyes.

"It isn't because he's rich, though it was at first. Mum—I love him, terribly."

Mrs. Cave was dismayed. It had never occurred to her that Biddy's avowedly calm and callous little heart could be engaged. She had seen the trouble over Royal Maitland as no more than a disappointment of her ambitions.

"But—does he know, Biddy?" she asked doubtfully.

"No, and you're not to tell him. Nobody's to tell him," said Biddy imperatively. "Promise, Mum—promise!"

"But of course I shouldn't dream of telling him, child. Only—oh, Biddy, how could you have been so foolish as to let this happen? You're only a child to him, and not even a child of his own social world. I never have approved of it because I couldn't see any sense in it, and I felt he would make you discontented with our way of life. I have been trying to summon up courage to ask him to let you alone . . ."

"Don't do that, Mum! I should *die* if he went away now," said Biddy, her tragic child's world in ruins about her at the first trouble.

"But, my dear, what will be the end of it? He'd never think of marrying you. For one thing, he must be at least twenty years older than you are, and we don't belong to his class . . ."

"I know. Of course, I know. Do you think I haven't told

myself that all the time? It doesn't do any good, though"—miserably. "I still love him just as much —more."

Mrs. Cave rose.

"Well, child, it's got to stop. I'm not going to have you making yourself miserable like this over a man when it can't possibly come to anything. "Biddy"—on a sudden thought—"he hasn't made love to you, has he?"

Biddy's face flamed, but her eyes met her mother's with relieving honesty.

"No, never. He's never even kissed me. But—oh, I do wish he had, just once!" she wailed.

Though she was acutely conscious of the tragedy this was to Biddy, Mrs. Cave could not repress a faint feeling of something approaching amusement at the depths of misery which this hard-boiled child of hers had reached after all her assurances of being immune to such suffering. Poor, funny little Biddy!

"Well, someone's got to see Mr. Maitland, so I suppose it'll have to be me," she said reluctantly. It seemed she was never to have peace now that her children were growing up—first Julie, now Biddy, and presently it would be Dickie, though his world did not yet contain the other sex.

Biddy's face grew mutinous.

"Please Mum, leave it to me," she said. "I don't want anybody to interfere, even you. I know it's been silly of me to care like this, and that it's got to end some time—somehow"—her voice faltering again. "I've got to see him again, just once, for the last time. Mum, don't stop me! He'd hate that so, and he'd have to be nice to you. He's like that"—her voice trailing off again as she reflected on what else he was "like."

Mrs. Cave gave way reluctantly.

"You're giving yourself a very hard task," she said.

"I'd rather do it myself," said Biddy, with that stubbornness of hers which her mother knew so well; and presently, when Maitland's car came sliding to the door, she heard the girl come swiftly down the stairs before anyone else could open it.

It was a Saturday afternoon, hot and breathless, and Biddy had put on a new frock which she and Julie had made, a flowered organdy in which she looked fresh and cool. Instead of a hat she had tied a scarf of the material over her head, for she knew that Maitland would have the car open on such a day.

She was at the door before he could ring, and his eyes kindled at sight of her. She was a constant delight to him, and he was aware of the flowering of her beauty on these days of summer. Into the future he had not troubled to look. It had been an empty vista for so many years that he had become accustomed to ignoring it as non-existent.

"You'd better bring a coat," he said. "Unless you particularly want to be back early, I thought we'd run down to that place we found beyond Bognor and have dinner on the way back. It may be chilly by then. That be all right with you?"

She gave him her wild-rose look, paused to take from its peg her everyday coat, and run out to the car. She had not risked going upstairs to get her best coat in case her mother, in spite of her reluctant promise, could not resist the opportunity to "tackle" him. She had this one day, and nobody was going to take it from her.

He tucked her into the car in the way she liked best, treating her as something to be cherished. Defiantly she determined that she would let nothing mar this day, no thought of the future nor of the promise to her mother, which somehow, at the close of it, she would have to fulfil.

There was all that hidden in the smile she gave him, and he thought again what an adorably lovely child she was and how proud of her some man was going to be some day.

"Do you think you'd like to bathe when we get there?" he asked presently. "If so, we could stop in Bognor and buy you a costume."

That gave her a little thrill, for it was the first time he had ever suggested buying her anything but meals and sweets, but she shook her head.

"I shan't want to bathe," she told him.

He gave her a speculative glance.

"Why not? Doesn't every girl swim nowadays?" he asked.

Privately she thought it very foolish of him to ask such a question, because he must know that a girl would not always want to explain why she would not bathe, but she decided to tell him the truth.

"Yes, I can swim, but I don't want to bathe today because I'd be messy and untidy afterwards," she said.

He laughed and steered expertly through a jumbled mass of vehicles.

"You always take care of your looks, don't you?" he asked, amused.

"I have to. They're all I've got," Biddy informed him frankly, and he laughed again.

She had had the extraordinary effect of renewing his youth for him—no, not even renewing it, because he had never had any that he remembered. She had created youth in him by her own vitality.

"You're being rather inconsistently modest," he told her.

"No, I'm not. I'm being quite truthful for once. I know I'm not clever. I never was any good at school, though I used to scrape through somehow, generally by getting one of the boys to help me. I was at a mixed school before I went to the High School," she explained.

"And I suppose it was the co-educational system which gave you such an ability to handle my sex? One of the things you graduated in?" chickled Maitland.

"You're laughing at me," said Biddy serenely. "I don't mind, though. I don't mind anything today—not yet"—adding the last words almost beneath her breath.

For a second he took his hand off the steering-wheel to touch her own as it lay in her flowered lap.

"Nice child, aren't you?" he said approvingly.

Biddy sat silent. That fleeting touch had done strange things to her, had sent the blood hammering through her veins, had made her heart beat until she thought he might have heard it but for the sound of the engine.

Nice child—yes, that was all she was to him, all she had ever been, all she would be in his memory. Yet she knew that she was no child; that, for all her brevity of years, she had a woman's body and a woman's heart, both of them set on the loving of this man who did not know she had even grown up.

She gave him a furtive little glance, and her heart turned over in her breast at sight of his lean, haggard face, the eyes deep-set in their sockets, the hair already thinning and grown grey about the temples. For all his wealth, he was a man who lived hard, bestowed on himself few luxuries other than his car and a superlatively efficient man-servant, who was valet, butler, secretary, and friend. Almost his only pleasure lay in the making of money, but, once made, it turned to ashes for want of the desires which it could have satisfied.

Biddy watched his hands on the wheel—lean, strong hands which once she had manicured, just once, and then only because, as he had admitted afterwards, it was the only way in which he could make her further acquaintance. She wished she could do them again. She wished she dare suggest it just so that she might touch his hands, hold them for that little while and so impersonally in her own.

She was faint with the longing for him, only half recognized and half acknowledged by a mind which had no experience. If only he would look at her again, smile at her, make her feel that, if only for the moment, she belonged in his life!

The intensity of her gaze brought about the thing she desired, for he turned to smile at her for an instant before giving his whole attention to his job again. On Saturday afternoon the roads to the coast were crowded with cars and bicycles, and it needed all his skill and judgment to make use of the mighty power that lay beneath the bonnet of his car.

"Thoughts?" he asked her.

She shook her head and smiled. How could she tell him she had been dreaming of herself in his arms, giving back his kisses? He would probably stare at her in bewildered discomfort and turn round and take her straight back home to her mother!

He found again the secluded little spot they had visited once before, actually a part of the foreshore which belonged to one of the big private houses. The owners were away, but Maitland knew them, and, as on that other occasion, called at the house and left his card with the caretakers and an assurance that his presence would not be objectionable to the owners. They did not doubt his word. There was that about him which forbade that, so today, as before, he and Biddy had the tiny, tree-guarded beach to themselves.

He spread out a rug for her, and she lay under the shade of a tree with the sea lapping gently against the stones only a few yards away, for at high tide the water almost reached the grassy back at this time of year.

"Sure you won't bathe?" Maitland asked her. "I'd go back to Bognor for the necessary."

She shook her head, but presently took off her shoes and
214

stockings and walked along the edge of the water on the fine, shady shingle. She was dreaming happily, forcing herself to live in the moment only. Tonight was still a thousand years away.

Maitland lay on his back and watched her. What a sweet kid she was! How strangely happy he felt when he was with her! He did not try to analyze it. He only knew that it was so. The radiance of her happiness touched his own rather gloomy mind, and he did not ask himself whence came that happiness. It seemed innate in her.

He called her back to him and she stood on the edge of the rug, her feet wet and pink. He noticed, with some amusement, that the nails were colored to match her fingernails, an orangey pink to tone with the slight sunburn her face and hands had acquired during the summer.

"How about finding a cup of tea somewhere?" he asked.

"If you like," she said, but scarcely knew that her lips had uttered the words, for he was idly tracing with his finger the outline of her bare toes. All feeling rushed to meet his touch.

"How are you going to dry these, you baby?" he asked.

"On my hanky," said Biddy.

"Or mine. It's bigger. Sit down on the rug and I'll do them for you. You know, you've got charming little feet, Biddy. In fact, you're a very charming little person altogether, aren't you? Not that you need me, or anyone else, to tell you that!"—ending on a teasing note, for he had long ago plumbed the depths of her vanity.

She sat there blissfully, her back against the tree-trunk, while he dried her toes, found her stockings and absurd little shoes, and proceeded to put them on her in a businesslike and quite unloverlike manner.

He held up a shoe and regarded it scornfully.

"Fancy coming on to the beach in things like that!" he said, for it was pale fawn suede with high Spanish heels.

She took it from him and put it on.

"The wages *and* tips of a manicurist won't rise to a pair of shoes for every occasion," she said. "These are my best, and, of course, I wore them today."

His wish to tease her died. For all her little vanities and her appreciation of her looks there was in her a quality of sterling honesty which never failed to win his appreciation. Never at any time had she striven to show herself as other than she was, and he felt that she had quite unconsciously rebuked him for his criticism of her shoes.

"Your best, in my honor, Biddy? he asked her, a new and softer note in his voice.

She nodded, busy with the fastening of the shoe.

"The world's a very unfair place," he said, so suddenly that she stopped in her task to look up at him.

"Why did you say that all at once?" she asked.

"Well, here am I with more money than I could possibly spend, with really very little on which I want to spend it, and yet a girl like you, who should have everything in the world as the right of your loveliness, can't afford an extra pair of shoes."

She flushed and returned to the matter of that crazy little fastener. "Your loveliness," he had said, and had meant that he really did think her lovely.

"And the ridiculous conventions are such," he went on, "that I couldn't possibly whisk you off into Bognor and buy you a dozen pairs of shoes, and you couldn't possibly accept them!"

"I should say not," said Biddy. "What on earth would Mum say if I arrived home after an afternoon with you and brought with me a dozen pairs of new shoes."

He laughed.

"I don't know what she'd say, but there's no possible doubt what she'd think," he said. "Here, let me do that up; you're making a day's work of it; and she leaned back and closed her eyes as his fingers clasped her ankle and the job was quickly done—far too quickly.

She was all child again over tea, and consumed huge quantities of scones and jam and cream buns, though he warned her that she would not be able to eat her dinner.

"Oh yes, I shall!" she assured him. "You've no idea what I can eat, and, by mercy of Allah, I never put on weight with it."

"Let's hope you won't marry a poor man, then," said Maitland. "Do you think you could fight off starvation long enough to pour me out another cup of tea, no sugar this time?"

The task he gave her served to cover up her reaction to that first sentence, the flight of the laughter from her face and the light from her eyes for that unguarded moment.

"I may not marry anyone," she said, when it had passed. He smiled and took the filled cup from her.

"You're much too sweet to be wasted," he told her.

"There will be a good many men ready to attend to that!"

Oh, if he knew! But he mustn't know, ever.

"What shall we do now," he asked, when they had finished and he had paid his bill—paid it in the lordly way he had, without troubling to reckon it up. She hated to be out with a man who studied the items of the bill before paying it, and once a boy who had taken her out to tea made her wait while he argued with the girl about the number of pieces of toast she had eaten. She never went out with *him* again!

"Anything you like," she said, though as a rule she was full of bright ideas on that subject.

"Well, how about going along the coast to Fareham, where I rather want to look at a boat I might buy, and then going back through Surrey? There's a good little hotel near Guildford where we can have dinner—if you can last so long!"

She smiled, but not with her heart. That was saying to her back through Surrey—back to London—back home to be lonely forever.

She refused to let the shadow linger, though, and wa; her most companionable self while they drove to Fareham and Maitland found the man and the boat he had come to see.

He referred to the boat as "a neat little tub," but to Biddy's eyes it was a princely yacht, for she had never been in a private seagoing craft before, and she poked about happily while the two men talked technicalities and terms, finding fascinating little cupboards and lockers in unexpected places, trying the camouflaged beds in the main saloon, and enchanted with the properly equipped sleeping-cabins with their shining white paint and gay chintzes.

"Have you really bought it?" she asked, awed, when at length they were back in the car.

"Well, I've paid him a deposit, and agreed that it is to be repaid, or the balance handed over, when I've had a trial trip in her," said Maitland. "Did you like her?"

"Oh yes!" sighed Biddy ecstatically.

"Like to come out in her if I buy her?"

"Adore to," said Biddy, and then remembered, with a sudden descent of the curtain, that that could never be.

For a moment she rebelled against her mother's dictum and the promise she had extracted from her that she would make a break with Maitland tonight. What right had anybody, even her mother, to control and direct her life? It was her own, nobody else's. Then stern common sense, of which she had her full share, prevailed, and she knew that her mother was wise, that some day the break must come and that the longer it was delayed the worse it was going to be.

She was very quiet on the homeward journey, and during dinner he teased her about having no appetite.

"I told you the cream buns would do it," he said, as she refused the inevitable roast lamb and went on to the sweet, at which she pecked without enthusiasm.

"Perhaps I'm taking to heart what you said about not marrying a poor man," she said, with a momentary revival of her spirits. "I may be thinking of your pocket."

"Not at all, because I've got to pay for the dinner you don't eat as well as the bits you're eating," he told her laughingly; but presently, when they were in the car again and driving too swiftly back through the darkening country roads, he became aware that something lay beneath her quietness and unusual silence.

"Anything the matter, Biddy?" he asked. "Tired?"

The gentleness of his tone, the sense of intimacy and faint melancholy in the tree-arced lane he had chosen rather than the busy main artery, made it impossible for her to answer him, and, after driving on for a few moments in rather perplexed silence, he drew in at the side of the road and stopped the car.

"What is it, my dear?" he asked her, a little anxiously, for in the dusk her face looked white.

"I—I . . ."

She could not find the words, and now, really alarmed, he leaned towards her and slipped an arm behind her as she sat forward in her seat, looking at him with those wide, half-frightened eyes.

"Why—Biddy—little girl!"—for at the contact she had flung herself against him, into his arms, crumpled up with her head on his breast, her hair brushing his lips. It was extraordinarily warm and soft against them. In the midst of his turmoil of feelings that one contrived to register itself on his mind.

Only for a second were those strands of warm gold against his lips. Then she raised her head, and it was her own mouth that lay there, passionate and compelling.

"Kiss me—kiss me— I shall die if you don't," came her

218

wildly abandoned whisper, and his mouth closed over hers in a sudden unexpected and bewildering surge of passion.

"I love you. I adore you—adore you," she whispered in between those kisses which, passionate though they were, he knew instinctively were the first kisses of her womanhood. It made him feel strangely humble to hold her in his arms, to realize the ardor she was pouring out to him, her utter defenselessness.

Presently, oddly shaken himself by that storm, he freed her gently, set her back against the cushions, leaned over her, and looked down into her eyes.

"You know you shouldn't do that to a man, little girl," he said, half in earnest, half smiling, wholly tender.

"Why not?" asked Biddy in a whisper, her eyes still lost in fascination, fixed on his exultation in them.

He had kissed her! She had made him!

"Because it might well make him think things that—well, that mustn't be thought," he said.

"What mustn't be thought?" she asked, and longed to use his name, but dare not, even after those kisses.

He looked at her more gravely.

"What are you, Biddy? Child or woman?" he asked.

"Didn't you know when you kissed me—Royal?"

She had used it. It sounded unfamiliar to both of them. Only one woman had ever called him that. Biddy's use of it seemed suddenly to bridge the years between them, and, after the way she had spoken it, he could not laugh lightly away an episode which his reason told him must be forgotten.

"I haven't played the game with you, Biddy, have I?" he asked her gravely.

"Why do you say that? Because you've made me love you?"

"You mustn't love me, Biddy."

"I can't help it. It's just happened," and he could have thought her child again with those words, so ingenuously spoken, until she stirred beneath his speculative gaze and slid her arms behind his head and drew his lips down to hers again. Then he could not doubt her womanhood, and it made him afraid.

"Biddy, Biddy, what am I to do about you?" he asked her, releasing himself before his own passion could surge through him again.

She gave a little breathless laugh, thrilled with the

219

delicious knowledge of her power over him, knowing he had been weak in her arms.

"What do you want to do about me?" she asked beguilingly.

He gave an exasperated sound between a laugh and a sigh.

"What I ought to do is to take you back to your mother and tell her to give you a whipping and put you to bed," he said.

"I wouldn't mind you doing that," she said, and he gave her a little shake and sat back in his own seat, looking at her with such perplexity that she laughed and snuggled down under the rug he had tucked about her.

"Well, if you go on looking like that I might," he said, and determinedly pressed the self-starter and sent the car on its way again.

Neither of them spoke again until he pulled up at her door, and then she gave him a smile compounded of mischief and fear. Was he going away now? Must she send him away?

"Aren't you coming in?" she asked.

"I'd be wiser not to," he said uncertainly.

She traded on the uncertainty.

"Not even—to put me to bed?"—in a mischievous whisper, leaning towards him.

"You little devil, you know how much I'd like to, don't you? I think I'd better get your mother to give you that whipping."

"Well, you'll have to come in to do that," said Biddy, and got out of the car and stood on the pavement until, knowing very well that he would be wiser to go, he joined her and went up the steps with her.

"I've got the key," she whispered. "Don't make a noise."

"Your mother is sure to be up," he reminded her, but she tiptoed into the house and took him into the dark and empty sitting room.

Inevitably, a moment later she was in his arms. Neither of them knew which had first gravitated towards the other, but the result was the same. She was in his arms, and as her eyelids closed beneath his kisses she felt that the solid earth was gone from beneath her feet, that she stood on air, upheld by a new element, both safe and deliriously insecure.

"Oh, Biddy, what am I to do with you?" he asked her

220

again. "What are we going to do with each other?"

She still stood within the circle of his arms, her bright head, the pale oval of her face, her starry eyes vivid in the darkness.

"Mom told me I was to send you away," she said.

"She was wise. Why didn't you?"

"I couldn't until—until you'd kissed me," whispered Biddy. "I had to know what it would be like in your arms."

"And now that you're there and I have kissed you?"

"Now I can't because you *have* kissed me," she said. "Darling, kiss me again—it sends shivers all down my back when you do."

"That sounds like a cold in the head," he told her.

"It isn't. It's a fever in the heart," said Biddy. "Kiss me—Royal."

"No, not again."

"Kiss me—darling—darling," and the flame forked between them again, lit them until they were fused, body and spirit, into that fire which burns and does not consume.

When he released her he was as pale as she, and his eyes were very grave.

"Biddy, do you realize what's happened to us?" he asked her, his voice as grave as his eyes.

It sobered her.

"To us? To us, Royal? You mean—to you too? You're in love with me?" she asked in a hushed whisper.

"It looks like that, doesn't it? And I'm old enough to be your father."

She laughed softly.

"But you're not my father, are you?"

He would not be won from his gravity. He had not the light-hearted exuberance of youth, to which all things are possible.

"Biddy, do you really want to marry me?" he asked, his brows drawn into a frown.

Had he any right to take her, to use her freshness for his own revival, to take the unminted gold of her and be able to give nothing in return but a bit of worn metal and the things that mere money can buy?

"More than anything else in the world," said Biddy, with an ecstatic sigh.

And at that moment Mrs. Cave, standing outside in some perturbation of spirit, decided to open the door.

There could be no doubt as to what had happened, for his arms were still about Biddy and her flower-face wore an enchanted, newly kissed look.

They both turned at the opening of the door, and Maitland's arms dropped. His face was pale and grave, Biddy's flushed like a rose and filled with laughter.

Mrs. Cave looked from one face to the other.

"Biddy—Mr. Maitland . . ."

He spoke quickly, knowing at once what must be said.

"Mrs. Cave, I've just asked Biddy to marry me," he said. "Of course we can't decide anything like that without your consent, as she is so young, but . . ."

He paused and Mrs. Cave answered him slowly.

"Yes, that's it, isn't it? Biddy is so young," she said, and turned a rather troubled look on this daughter who had always been something of a problem to her. Was this the solution of the problem?

Her eyes turned back to Royal Maitland's face, and into her troubled heart came peace and a certainty, without reason or foundation, that to this man she might safely leave Biddy. He would know, far better than she, how to solve the problem, because Biddy loved him.

She spoke to him directly and ignored the girl.

"Do you truly love her?" she asked in that direct fashion that was also Julie's.

"I honestly believe so," he answered her very gravely, and in the words he chose she found added comfort. She would far less have believed an extravagant declaration.

She laid one of her work-worn hands, with their pricked fingers, on his.

"And I know my Biddy loves you," she said. "You'll be good to her, won't you? And remember that she *is* very young, and also sometimes, I am afraid, very foolish?"

The look that passed between mother and daughter was a dear and intimate one.

"I will remember both of those things," said Maitland with a smile.

Mrs. Cave took her hand from his and looked at the clock.

"It's very late," she said.

"Five minutes?" he asked, with a look at Biddy.

The mother nodded.

"Well—no more than five," she said. "Good night. Will you come to see me on Monday, Mr. Maitland?"

"If I may. Early in the afternoon?"

"That will be best," said Mrs. Cave sedately.

"But I shan't be here. I shall be at the shop!" objected Biddy.

He turned to her with a smile.

"That's exactly why we have arranged that hour," he said.

"Well, don't forget that it's me you're going to marry and not Mum," said Biddy.

They laughed.

"I'm not sure that wouldn't be a better idea," really," said Royal, and then Mrs. Cave slipped away and left them to their five minutes.

19

Of course Julie had now to meet Royal Maitland, and of course he had to find out about the broken romance in which Jeremy Denton had figured.

Biddy told him as much as she knew about it, sitting curled up on his knee in the state apartment, which was now almost exclusively devoted to such purposes.

"Well, Julie and Ben don't cuddle, so it doesn't matter to them that the easy chair in the kitchen won't hold two," Biddy had said airily, when her mother suggested that there were other members of the family. "Besides, *Royal* can't be asked to sit in the kitchen"—tossing her golden head.

"Are you going to become too grand for us, my Biddy?" asked Mrs. Cave rather sadly, but Biddy had hugged her and assured her that the Empire's throne was not too grand for the loveliest mother in the world.

"Still," she added in self-defense, "the fact remains, people like Royal don't sit in kitchens."

"Well, what I'd like to know is, where am I going to do my homework?" grumbled Dickie.

Mrs. Cave settled that by giving him a table and a book-shelf in his little slip of a bedroom, and peace reigned again, though sometimes she felt she would be almost glad when her conscience would allow her to lift the ban on the early wedding Biddy urged.

"Not until you're twenty," was the fiat, though she had

to yield so far as to allow a notice to be put in the London papers.

Biddy worded it in triumph and showed it to Maitland before it went to the printers.

He read it out with some amusement.

"A marriage has been arranged and will shortly take place . . ." But, darling, people don't say that nowadays, really. It's regarded as slightly old-fashioned."

"I don't care," said Biddy stubbornly. "That's how it's always worded in the books I've read about Society engagements, and that's how I've always dreamed of having mine worded."

He laughed and put the slip of paper into his pocket.

"All right. Have it your own way," he said. "It doesn't matter a puff of wind to me how you put it, so long as you wear this"—turning on her finger the wonderful emerald marquise he had given her.

Her blue eyes grew misty.

"Oh, Royal, I do love you," she said, "but it isn't human nature not to be glad you're so rich."

"You're a mercenary little baggage," he said, for Dickie had not failed to acquaint him with the family tradition of Biddy's wealthy marriage.

She grinned.

"You know, shouldn't I have been in a mess if I'd met you and you were poor?" she asked. "Well, no. If you'd been poor, I shouldn't have cultivated your acquaintance."

Julie had her doubts; Dickie laughed disbelievingly at her open devotion to Royal; her friends and fellow workers made no pretence about their certainty that she was marrying for money—but Maitland knew and was satisfied. Only he had seen that look in her eyes, heard the quiver in her voice, felt the swift beating of her heart at his touch.

Biddy was in love with love, in love with life, in love with all its fun and glamor and luxury, but more than all she was in love with Royal Maitland.

Stella Dale, glancing idly through the paper that had been brought in with her breakfast tray, came upon the stilted announcement, and sat so long with the printed sheet in her hand that her coffee grew cold, and she roused herself at last to ring for some fresh.

"Mr. Denton is here, Madam," the maid told her when she brought it.

Stella glanced at the clock. Half past ten. Hell, she must get a few early nights or she'd be a hag.

"Tell him he can come in," she said, and did not trouble to draw more closely about her the little coat of lace and swansdown which ostensibly added warmth to the gossamer pink ninon of her pajamas.

She had time, however, before Jeremy's knock, to glance at herself in the mirror, pass a powder-puff over her face, and remove the confining net from her hair.

"Come in, darling," she called, and Jeremy complied with a hesitation he could not overcome.

He kissed her, and she patted the bed in invitation.

"Sit down and tell me the news," she said gaily.

He removed the papers first, glancing at them.

"You've forestalled me, haven't you?" he asked. "I haven't looked at the paper this morning. Anything interesting?"

"Nothing much. I've only read the agony columns. There's one announcement which should interest you. Roy Maitland's engaged."

"Oh, is he?" asked Jeremy without much interest. "Anyone we know?"

"I don't think so. The name's quite unfamiliar," and she turned over the newspapers to find the ones he wanted and quoted from it—" 'Miss Bridget Mary Cave.' "

He frowned, a wild idea shooting through his mind. Bridget? Biddy? No, absurd, of course—but he took the paper Stella held out to him and read the rest of it for himself.

There it was. There could be no reasonable doubt. "Miss Bridget Mary Cave, younger daughter of the late Lewis Cave and of Mrs. E. J. Cave of Streatham."

Biddy.

The thought was almost too fantastic to credit, yet there it was—Biddy and her millionaire, though Maitland was probably not quite that. Still, he was a wealthy man, and Biddy had played her game and won it swiftly.

In spite of the dragging of his thoughts in Julie's direction, he could not forbear a smile. The little minx! Maitland, of all men, too! He wondered what her family thought about it, whether they were proud or worried, her mother and—Julie.

Stella's voice trailed across his thoughts.

"Poor Royal!" she said with a little reminiscent laugh.

"Why do you say that? Biddy's a lovely and delightful child," he said, quick in his defense of her before he had had time to wonder why he wanted to defend her.

She stared at him.

"Biddy? Why, do you know her?" she asked, astonished.

He flushed.

"Yes. You've met her. That day at the Berkeley. Don't you remember. A very pretty little blonde."

Her face was a study of incredulity, chagrin, dismay, a curious anger.

"Jeremy, you can't possibly mean *that* girl! You must be mistaken!" she cried when she could speak.

"Oh yes, that's the girl," he said. "I—used to know the family"—averting his eyes.

Stella's laughter was a little shrill and forced.

"But, Jeremy—*that* girl! I mean—well, men don't *marry* girls of that class, not men like Royal Maitland!"

He felt a wild surge of anger rising, but forced himself to hold it in check.

"Why not, if he's in love with her? And presumably he is," he said.

She gave that odd little laugh again.

"Darling, how divinely blind you are!" she said. "Of course he's not in love with her. Why, he's been in love with me for years—poor dear!"—reminiscently, her mind savoring the titillating pleasure of that thought.

Jeremy stared at her.

"With *you*, Stella? But . . ."

"My sweet, your stupefaction is not very flattering," she said. "Men do fall in love with me, you know! Or you should know."

He smiled a little absently, his mind assimilating the rather startling new idea and remembering now the impression he had received that first time he had seen Stella and had asked Maitland who she was. Poor Maitland—or should it not rather be poor Biddy?

Then, remembering that she would consider the capture of Maitland's bank balance all-sufficient return for the surrender of her attractive young person, he decided he need waste no pity on her. So it came back to poor Maitland.

"Well, we must send them a marvellous wedding present," Stella decided. "What does it say?" "Shortly take place." How Victorian! I wonder who thought of that? I don't expect it means before our wedding, though, darling," and she lifted her arms to draw his head down to her in one of those passionate, experienced kisses which both entranced and repelled him. He could have wished that she, and not he, were the pupil in the science and art of love.

"Not long now, dear," he said, coming up from that warm, perfumed embrace when he had been overconscious of the thin silk and revealing lace she wore.

"Will you be glad?" she asked sensuously.

"You know I shall," he told her, and spoke truthfully, for since their engagement he had neither worked nor had the urge to do so.

For one thing, Stella seemed determined to uproot him from the old ground and transplant him, root and branch, to the soil in which she herself flowered.

"You must go about," she insisted. "You must get to know people, all sorts of people, important men and women. There's this Swedish producer coming over, Fahlkrantz. We must meet him. He's got half a dozen theaters in his pocket, and it's an open secret that he has come over here to buy plays. He's got to buy Jeremy Denton's."

"Do you know him?"—doubtfully.

"Not yet, but I will." And only two days later Fahlkrantz was lunching with them in Stella's circular, blue-and-gold dining room, and, though he did not actually commit himself to taking *The Bauble*, the only play of Jeremy's in which he seemed interested, he left them with the impression that he would make an offer.

"And he won't dare to make it less than his highest figure after that lunch, darling!" laughed Stella gaily.

Hither and thither she had rushed him, making him feel that she was a showman and he her *chef-d'oeuvre*, suggesting to him that the sort of impression he ought to make on this person and that, until he felt that he was no longer himself, Jeremy Denton, but a mixture of all the impressions he had to make on other people. Resenting it, feeling he was in danger of losing his own personality, there was at the same time a curious lethargy about his mind which made him bear, with no more than an inward rebellion, even her suggestion that he owed both the theme and the success of *Midnight Angel* to her.

He had no time for reflection, however. In between the

227

social functions, at which he was expected always to be witty and spectacular, there was Stella herself and the feverish pace at which she set their love-making. Restless and changeful herself, she demanded ever something new of him, drained him of his vitality, and yet seemed able ever to find new springs of life within him, so that he felt she was vital to his existence.

Sometimes he paused, breathless, to ask himself what were his actual feelings towards her. Did he love her? He supposed he did, for what other name could he give, with any self-respect, to this consuming desire for her, this restless feeling of incompletion when he was away from her? Life had ceased to have any meaning apart from her. He was intoxicated with her. She swayed his thoughts, kept his mind captive to her own. Life had become a feverish dream from which he had lost the will to awake.

In his saner moments he worried over the fact that he was doing no work, and when he had conquered his nerves sufficiently to sit at his desk, his door locked and the telephone receiver off, he was frightened by the discovery that his mind seemed incapable of clear thought and was little more than a rag-bag of useless oddments.

He told Stella, a worried frown on his face.

"It's because I go out too much, get overtired, use myself up with all these stupid dinners and receptions and even more stupid cocktail parties. I talk such rot for most of the day that my mind won't think anything intelligent any more."

"Oh, most gracious and gallant gentleman!" she mocked coming to sit on the arm of his chair and ruffling his hair and smoothing with cool fingers the new furrows on his brow.

They were alone for a snatched half hour in her sitting room.

"It'll come back, my sweet," she said. "You vegetated too long. You would in the end have become just a cabbage if I hadn't rescued you—a cabbage, when life intended you for, what shall we say?—a tiger lily?"—teasing him with butterfly kisses.

He rose from the chair, deliberately shaking off the touch of her fingers and the cloying sweetness with which, in this mood of hers, she sought to seduce his mind.

"Dear, don't you realize I've *got* to work? I've got nothing in the world but what I earn, and the royalties on my plays won't last forever unless I keep producing others, and how am I going to produce them out of a brain stuffed with cottonwool and gin?"

She laughed, though behind the laughter and at the back of her eyes was that hint of triumphant possessiveness which always made him faintly resentful. It was as if she regarded his personality and his genius as mere expressions of her own dominating power. Loving possessions, she treated him as if she had acquired him as she had acquired her furniture and her carpets, evidences of her taste and ability to obtain the best on the market.

He moved across the room restlessly, refusing to look at her because he knew how weak he was when she chose to exert the power of her beauty.

"If I don't produce another play for the autumn I really can't see how we can be married," he burst out at last, voicing the thought, a strange mixture of fear and relief that had been troubling his mind for weeks. "We're spending money all the time and . . ."

She caught his hand and held him near her.

"Well, what of it? We're having fun, aren't we?" she asked, smiling into his worried face.

"Yes, I know we are, but—I've got to work if we're going to afford fun at that rate," he said. "All this entertaining may be amusing if one can afford it, but soon I shan't be able to, and then what?"

They had never discussed actual ways and means, or a future budget. Jeremy was determined that he would never live on Stella, and until lately it had not occurred to him that he might have to consider it. The phenomenal success of his plays had given him the feeling that money would now flow in to him like water, and like water he had spent it. The affair at the Duchess Galleries the other night, for instance. . . .

He spoke of it to Stella.

"That thing on Tuesday night cost a small fortune. The bills are beginning to come in, and the one for champagne alone appalled me. I simply can't entertain on that scale unless I get out another play."

"Bear up, my angel," she said lightly, going to the cocktail cabinet and considering its contents with a mind already becoming negligent of him. "That was a really useful function, as I told you. The people there formed the nucleus of your best-paying first-nighters, and their opinion is worth a few dozen champagne and an oyster or so."

"If the stuff I write is worth seeing they'll come to see it whether I feed them or not," he said.

"Cocktail, my sweet?"

"No, thank you. I loathe the things," he said ungraciously.

She poured one out for herself.

"You're a bear today, Jeremy. Perhaps you'd better go and immure yourself in your pit. If it is really work that appeals to you and keeps you amusing, then for any sake go and work!"

He went to her, took the cocktail glass from her hand and set it down, held her by the shoulders, and looked into her eyes with a sort of desperation.

"Stella, is anything happening to us?" he asked. "Am I disappointing you, or what?"

She gave him her enigmatical smile, reminding him of the aloof, mysterious woman she had seemed at that first sight he had had of her.

"Disappointing me? No, not that. It is just that—when you are not amusing, you become a little heavy and boring, my sweet," she said lightly.

He dropped his hands and turned away, irritated and baffled. Amusing? Was that what one had to be to the woman one loved and was about to marry? Was that his only claim on her interest and affection?

The question could not, must not, be answered. With or without reason, he had come to assess Stella as the credit side of a balance sheet to whose debit stood so much that had made up his old life—the hard, exacting life of strenuous work to earn a bare living, the friends who had liked him for himself and not because he was a popular success, the set hours for work and play.

To its debit stood also Julie.

Thrusting that last thought aside, he knew a sick longing to be back on the old life, with its hardships, its repressions, its joys, which were not merely the hectic, expensive pleasures which stood for them nowadays. Where all life is a round of enjoyment there can be no real joy. He had already found that out.

Stella's cool voice broke across his thoughts.

"I've been thinking, darling, that perhaps we shouldn't like Italy, after all, in October."

He gave her half attention. He did not mind a great deal

230

where they went for their honeymoon. He was so un-travelled that most places would be new and exciting to him.

"Where do you suggest then?" he asked idly.

"Oh—still Italy, but not perhaps in October," she said slowly, and with a deliberateness which showed him this was a well-considered thought.

He gave her all his attention.

"You mean you want to postpone our marriage?" he asked abruptly.

She was not looking at him, but at the lights in the cock-tail glass, which she was holding up reflectively.

"For a little while, perhaps," she said smoothly, "There are one or two things going on in October which I don't want to miss, and the McLeods have an amusing party at their place in Scotland about that time. After all, there is no wild hurry about getting married, is there?"

Jeremy felt chilled, and yet, deep down and aware of disloyalty, he was aware of faint relief. The longer this engagement lasted the more difficult was it to visualize their marriage. That in itself was food for the thoughts which his mind strenuously resisted.

"Well, that is for you to decide, my dear," he said, after a pause, and at the hint of complacency in his voice she set down her glass abruptly, and with a little gesture of an-noyance. She resented his taking it so calmly, and had been prepared for argument and the rather exciting stimulant it would afford their mutual passion.

"What an impatient lover you are!" she said, with faintly curling lip.

He made a gesture that exasperated. What did she want other than complete compliance with her wishes?

"I told you already that I have a great deal of work to do before we ought to be married," he said. "I think the best thing for me to do is to get on with it as quickly as I can".

"And—meantime?" asked Stella.

"Well, you seem to have everything mapped out, includ-ing Scotland," he said.

She threw him a speculative look. Was it possible that he was getting tired of her? Such a thing had no place in her experience or her scheme of things. She tired of men, not they of her. The thought piqued her.

"You should ask if you'll be almost glad that my

schemes will include you," she said.

He smiled at that.

"Dearest, you're rather a disturbing element in the life of a working man," he said. "Doesn't that explain it?"

And with that she had to be satisfied, though she retained that queer, humiliating impression that he was relieved at both the postponement of their marriage and her proposed departure from London, for there seemed now no point in her refusing another invitation she had had to join some friends at Harrogate.

There was a special beauty treatment she had there, for one thing, and, for another, London in the heat was insufferable and, as far as she was concerned, almost empty.

When, a week later, Jeremy stood on the platform to see Stella off, he hoped that the relief he felt had at least the decency to hide itself. Without any open rupture, there had been that little friction between them which was irritating to their nerves, and he felt that this separation was best for them both.

Stella was newly contented. Sufficient of her friends had preceded her to the famous spa to ensure the right sort of companionship for her, and safely in the luggage van were the several large trunks which would provide her with adequate covering for any and every occasion. What more could the heart of woman desire?

Jeremy thought, but forbore to say, that to his mind the essence of holiday was a complete change and not simply the removal from one place to another of one's whole environment. As far as he could see, the holiday in Harrogate was going to be exactly the same round of visits, bridge, and amusements with exactly the same people.

"I shall miss you, darling," said Stella when she had assured herself that she had every necessity for the journey in her first-class Pullman—magazines, newspapers, cigarettes, flowers, her elaborately fitted dressing case.

"Naturally I hope you will," replied Jeremy cheerfully.

On the ground at Stella's feet was her small dog, a hairless atrocity on four legs which had to be wrapped in a tailored coat in all but the hottest weather in England, and which Jeremy, dog-lover though he was, disliked intensely.

At his own side was Bill, a massive bulldog which he had bought in a moment of self-assertion and which had grown into his life and his heart, as is the way of dogs. Stella called him an ugly brute, and avoided contact with him, but to Jeremy Bill represented the stand of his manhood against the dallying lotus-life he was leading with his fiancee.

Just now, while their owners made the best use they could of those embarrassing and intolerable last minutes before departure, the two dogs exchanged a few withering remarks of their own.

"You're an ugly brute. Your hair's like wire, your mouth is fifteen sizes too large, you snuffle, and I don't like you," said Chrissie, her sharp little nose in the air.

"Well, come to that, you're not a dog at all," retorted Bill, "and if we're speaking of hair, it's something to have any at all!"

"I'm an aristocrat," simpered Chrissie, and it must be admitted that she turned sideways a little to give Bill the benefit of her slender little middle. "*She* says so, and she ought to know because she bought me at the most exclusive kennels in England, and I have to be taken great care of"—with a coy turn of the head.

"Hh!" said Bill. "Well, he bought me off a rag-and-bone-man who was going to throw me in the river with a stone tied to my tail, and I don't have to be taken care of, I can live any old how, and I'd die for him."

"*She* says I'm a beauty," remarked Chrissie wheedlingly.

"What *he* says about you won't bear repeating," said Bill.

"You're a nasty, ill-mannered brute," said Chrissie, sidling up to him as he stood with his massive head rising above the level of the floor of the compartment.

"I'd scorn to say what you are," replied Bill, sitting down with a force that almost shook the platform.

"Better take your seat, madam," warned a porter, and Bill smiled as the door was abruptly shut on Chrissie's self-satisfied little face.

When the train had gone he rose with a contented snuffle and lounged along beside his master, aware that there was a lightness in the step of his god which had been absent from it.

"Bill, old son, we're marooned," Jeremy told him as they made their way to the gleaming cream-and-silver car which was one of his latest acquisitions, made necessary bu Stella's deslike of his open sports car, which spoiled her coiffure. "How're you going to like it when we do a job of work for a change? There'll be time for a tramp at night, though, to make up for your being stuck in all day. Hop in, pal—any seat you like now.

Bill chose the front seat, and in his mighty heart was a vast and abiding peace. He was too perfect a gentleman to show any lady that he disliked her, but he was thankful to be rid of both Chrissie and her mistress.

He sat upright beside the driving seat and the world was his.

"Happy, old son?" asked Jeremy, offering him a hand for a second.

Bill swiped it with an enormous tongue and was understood to say that life had nothing more to offer.

In a traffic block they espied on the pavement Mrs. Milroy, and Jeremy attracted her attention.

"Can I take you anywhere?" he asked her.

"Can you feed me, or are you meeting Stella?" she asked.

"I've just seen her off to Harrogate, and my time is my own, or, rather, entirely yours," said Jeremy, opening the door for her and hustling Bill into the back seat.

She humped in quickly, oblivious of the hoots of other cars and the swerving of buses. As she remarked, she had not braved the dangers of the world to be defeated by Piccadilly Circus.

"I didn't know Stella was leaving town," she said. "I've been away. Brian's thinking of buying an island off the Cornish coast, and I thought if I didn't go with him he'd forget he wanted to stop there and go on to Mexico or Hawaii."

Jeremy liked Mrs. Milroy. With her he felt at ease and was at his best. He smiled at her affectionately and took her to find the best lunch in town.

"Now entertain me." she commanded, when they had ordered a lunch which gave him a new respect for her knowledge and judgment, and made him wonder for the hundredth time how this attractive and beautifully finished woman could be happy in the forgotten places of the world for months at a time, living in a tent and always within reach of a gun.

"That's a rather alarming beginning," smiled Jeremy. "I know nothing that reduces one to imbecility more quickly than an invitation to be intelligent."

"Well, I release you from the need to be that if you will be merely human. Who is left in London besides ourselves? You couldn't possibly be engaged to Stella Dale without knowing everybody in London, so tell me who is in town, and all the latest scandals. Who is that nice little thing in blue over there, and what does she hope to get out of the lump of a man with her? And why does the grey-haired man opposite glare at them?"

"Oh, don't you know?" asked Jeremy. "She's the grey-haired man's mistress, and he's wondering why she is taking so long to put the poison in her husband's wine, and whether she managed to persuade him to take out a life policy in her favor before the fish."

"Oh, Jeremy, it's so nice to be idiotic again. Brian's gone highbrow and I've got a little dizzy. Shall we amuse each other for the rest of the day? If you make love to me a little, I shan't mind, and if people think you are my gigolo, it will be a new experience for you. Tell me how work is going, and when you are going to put on another play."

It was a vast relief to Jeremy to talk to this woman, whom age and experience had mellowed, whose humor was never malicious, and whose interest was sincere and not assumed.

During the day, most of the hours of which they spent as she had suggested, amusing each other, he found himself forgetting the artificiality of his new life and going back to old days, amusing her with reminiscenses of life behind the counter in the tourist agency and showing her the essential simplicity which lay beneath the cloak he had been taught by Stella to wear.

Mrs. Milroy, for her part, found herself liking him more than she had ever imagined she would do, for until now she had talked with him only in the company of others and she had regarded him as belonging to Stella's artificial world, another of her conquests and neither more nor less interesting than his forerunners.

She wondered how and why he had become engaged to Stella, and gradually came to the conviction that he was no more contented with that state of affairs than, in due course, she felt Stella herself would be. They were in essence too dissimilar, their personalities too distinct and divergent.

"As you appear to be a sort of Robinson Crusoe in London, Jeremy, let me be your Man Friday," she said, when at last, after the midnight cabaret show and supper which had followed the theater, they took leave of each other.

235

"You won't be working every hour there is?"

"I shall have to eat and sleep," he told her.

"Well, I can do the one with you, and, after the marvellous day you've given me, wish I were still young enough to do the other! She laughed. "Do you know, I rather enjoy London when it's empty of most of the people I know. Isn't it comforting to give voice to anything as frank and disagreeable as that for once? What I mean is that when I am freed from obligations towards society I can renew old friendships with museums and picture galleries, wear old clothes, and let myself generally run to seed."

"I don't know whether to feel flattered or not, then, at your interest in me," laughed Jeremy. "Am I classed with the museums or the picture galleries? And if you are going to run to seed, what sort of fruit may I expect?"

"Heavens, but I wish I were young again for you, Jeremy Denton! You'd better go before I get sentimental, but don't forget I'm in town, will you?"

Why did she make him think of Mrs. Cave? The two women were so utterly different, and yet about them was something which linked them.

Or perhaps it was that his mind was always fastened by a spring to Julie, so that when it was no longer held taut by Stella it flew back instantly and arrow-like.

Julie—why could he not forget her?

20

Jeremy had been looking forward to a return to his work, had, during the last few days before Stella left, managed to find time to order a new stock of paper and furbish up the little model theater with which he worked.

He told himself he could not expect to start writing at once. He would need time to work out a plot, to get to know his characters, to get a general idea of his theme. The first thing obviously was to get the paper and fix up the model stage.

As the days went by, however, he found that was both the beginning and the end of his achievements. He gave himself every chance, made a variety of excuses for himself—he was out of practice, tired, his nerves were on edge, he had had too much excitement and too little sleep. He would run about the countryside in his car, have odd days at the sea, just lazing and waiting for the ideas that would come, must come.

But they did not come. Nothing on which he could even remotely base a plot occurred to him, though, beginning to feel frantic, he veered his thoughts from the modern, spectacular stuff of *Midnight Angel*, with its somewhat meretricious brillance, to the almost forgotten idealism of his earlier writing. He had been like this before, unable to think or work, and Stella had saved him, inspired him, helped him. Was it possible that he could not work apart from her?

But he had not been able to work when she was with him. She had consumed him with her demands on him, drugged his mind with the urgent desires of his senses and the partial satisfaction she gave him. Did this mean that they must marry before he could work again? But how could he afford such an expensive wife as Stella until he had produced another play?

The vicious circle ran on, and it seemed that ill luck dogged his footsteps, for the American contract for his *Midnight Angel* brought disappointing results, and the film company who had been nibbling at an offer withdrew all interest when the play had, to all intents and purposes, failed in New York.

Then at the back of his mind was the question of what he was going to do for money to produce the new play if and when he could complete it. He ought to be in a position to stand the initial costs of production himself, but in Stella's company, and for her suitable entertainment, he had spent far too much, and half-empty London would not justify for very much longer the expense incurred with every performance of *Midnight Angel*. Paston was already suggesting that it might be politic to take it off shortly and put it on again, when London began to fill up once more, at a bigger theater. It would have a good run before the pantomimes wanted the theaters.

"Why not have a shot at a super panto?" Paston asked him, more in joke than anything, but the words stung a little, for there had been something remotely suggestive of the modern pantomime in his last play, and he knew it.

237

Pantomime—the principal boy and the dame, the fairy godmother and the transformation scene and all the rest of the thing—was that his real metier. It was a humiliating thought, and he rushed from his interview with Paston to try to exorcise the demon of fear which had come with it.

He went from his desk, exhausted and worried, to seek a respite in Mrs. Milroy's cool, shaded drawing room. It was always an amazement to him to see how she could, in a few weeks, a few days even, transmit something of her own personality, its graciousness and ease of spirit, to these hired houses which had to stand to her for home because the restless soul of her husband could never stay long enough in one place for her to acquire permanent roots. Some day she would probably refuse to go with him to the ends of the earth, but that was a queer fatalistic streak in her which made her utterly sure that, when that day came, it would end a happiness which had few parallels in modern-day life. Brian would not return to her. Either in life or in death some remote, uncivilized part of the earth would claim him from her, and while it was possible for her to go with him, just so long would she continue to uproot herself from the shallow soil where, for such time as she could, she made a home for his wandering, restless feet.

She heard Jeremy's oft-repeated tale, gave him tea in the cosy, fragile china which was so often stored, plied him with thick slabs of anchovy toast when she discoved that he had forgotten or omitted to have any lunch, made him relax in one of the deep chintz-covered chairs in that dim, cool room.

"You're flogging what would probably be a willing enough steed if you let it make its own pace," she said when she had heard once more his story of failure and despair. "Why not take tomorrow off? Don't think of work. Get into your car and drive to the edge of the country somewhere, anywhere. Go to sleep under a tree, lie on your back on a raft all day—anything that isn't trying to write a play."

"Come with me, then," said Jeremy.

"I can't, though I'd like it. I've got some ghastly relations of Brian's to entertain. Go alone. Better for you, you know. If you've got company, you'll only worry and grouse."

"Well—thank you," said Jeremy, and prepared to go.

"For advice you won't take?" she asked rather sadly. "Tell me something, Jeremy."

"Anything in the world, past or present," he said.

"I don't really know which of those it is, or whether it is even future, but—are you missing Stella too much?"

He flushed a little but would not avoid her eyes.

"Not in the way I think you mean," he said. "In fact—well, it sounds disloyal to her, though I don't mean it that way—I think we're better apart for a bit. Together we live a life rather too hectic for a working man."

She sighed a little and patted his arm.

"Well, that's as it may be. Anyway, you take my advice and have a real mike alone, or, if you must have company take one of your own chorus girls. It'll give you something different to think about!"—dismissing him with laughter.

The laughter died as soon as he had gone, however, and she went about her small household tasks with a thoughtful frown. What was he doing, linked up with Stella Dale? How had he come to let her possess him, for she could find no other word to describe it. Deep down in him was something fine which a woman like Stella could neither find nor possess, and which, finding it or leaving it to die, she would eventually and inevitably destroy. She had seen it happen before, only Stella's other men had never interested her sufficiently for her to mind personally what she did to them.

Only Roy Maitland—and Mrs. Milroy's frown relaxed into a little smile. Roy had worshipped Stella, but had never let her possess him. Recognizing his feeling for her for exactly what it was, a sensual admiration for and a desire for her beautiful body, he had refused to be dragged captive at her chariot-wheels. When she had indolently and capriciously declined his first offer of marriage, he had never asked her again, although, piqued by his indifferent acceptance of her decision, she had begun to regret it. Stella, who for some obscure reason chose this older and very safe woman for her confidante, had admitted all this with some chagrin.

And Royal, far from languishing, had consoled himself with that lovely chit whom everybody would believe had married him for his money—everybody, that is, except the few who knew Maitland well enough to be quite sure that he would allow nobody to do that. He was no infatuated boy, no sensualist, and if he had decided that Biddy Cave was worth marrying, he would make the marriage itself worthwhile. Mrs. Milroy liked Maitland very much.

Well, he had escaped the snare of Stella Dale, but Jeremy had not. She felt worried and unhappy about it, but could think of nothing that even an interfering old woman could do about it. She could only hope devoutly that Stella would stay away long enough to get used to doing without Jeremy for good, or else would become enamored of another man, which would amount to the same thing.

Meanwhile, Jeremy, ignoring the wiser counsels he had sought, began to work with grim determination on the thread of an idea which had come to him. It was a slightly worn thread and had been used in countless pieces of work already, but he must make it serve him. Once he had got to work, playing with words again, taking up the familiar medium and twisting it with a brain which had once fashioned masterpieces with it, surely his cunning would return and he might even be able to throw aside this cheap, rather trite work and evolve something worthwhile.

So he worked doggedly on through the hot days with which a wet, dull summer was belatedly trying to vindicate itself, keeping to a strict schedule, trying to make up in method and careful stagecraft what he lacked in inspiration and fire. The result, as he knew to his bitterness, was a painstaking protrayal of ordinary people in ordinary situations, and, try as he would, he could infuse no new life into them or make them less wooden. Very occasionally his brain would produce one of its old witty epigrams and he would work it in feverishly, turning and twisting the action to make its insertion less obvious, and as the play neared completion he began to hope that it was only his self-distrust that found it unsatisfactory. When he showed it to Fennimore, who had asked for an option on *Midnight Angel's* successor, he would find his fears as groundless as he tried to make them.

The thing was finished at last. He had worked at it, ground and polished it as he had never done to a play before, and when he could do no more to it he threw it into a drawer and slept like the dead for fifteen hours. Waking to the soft melancholy of an autumn evening, he found himself thinking of Stella and the stimulation of her mind and her lovely, desirable body. Why had he not insisted on their keeping to their plans for an October wedding and a honeymoon in Italy? On the thought, he looked up a train, threw some things into a bag, and, pausing only to pack up and dispatch the finished manuscript to Fennimore, dashed off to King's Cross. Relieved of the stress of his work, he felt light-hearted and glad to be on his way to Stella. She would be surprised, and, he hoped, pleased at his hot-foot dash to her.

She was surprised, certainly, when, slightly dishevelled after his night in the train, he came upon her by accident as he entered the hotel. He had not the knack of appearing still fresh and clean after long hours in the train, and he had hoped to get a wash and shave before seeing her.

Looking exquisite, she was walking across the flagged loggia as he came up the steps and saw her. A young Air Force officer was with her, and they both stopped short at Jeremy's rather flustered greeting.

"Why—Jeremy of all people!" said Stella, her voice revealing to his experienced ears the irritation which belied her smile. "Has London collapsed, or driven you out or anything? Oh, Gerald, this is Mr. Jeremy Denton—Captain Emworth."

"I shall have to see if they've got a room," muttered Jeremy, nodding in the direction of the dapper little officer, beside whom he felt even more disreputable and unwashed.

"I certainly agree that this is the chief requirement at the moment," laughed Stella, with that edge to her voice. "I expect there are one or two vacant. I shall see you at dinner, I suppose?"

"Dinner?" asked Jeremy, with a surprised frown. Dinner was some hours away yet, and he had reckoned on spending most of them with her, once he had bathed and shaved.

"About eight? Captain Emworth is trying out a new 'plane this afternoon and is motoring me to the flying-ground. We haven't too much time, have we?"—turning to her escort.

He shot out a cuff to glance at his watch, and agreed.

"Well, round about eight, Jeremy," said Stella, and turned her back on him, leaving his feelings extremely flat.

In the vestibule he caught a glimpse of himself in a mirror and took heart of grace. He certainly did look a sketch, and no wonder she had been ashamed of him and preferred not to mention the fact of his being her fiance!

He wandered about the reception rooms when he had dressed for the evening, hoping against hope that she would return early, but when, by half past eight, she had still not made an appearance, he became anxious. What if she had gone up with that young fool (so in his jealousy he termed him) and there had been an accident?

He asked at the desk for the number of her room, found it, and knocked at the door. After a pause her voice, to his vast relief, answered him.

"Yes? Who is it?"

"Stella, it's I, Jeremy," said. "May I come in?"

"Why not?" she asked, and entering hurriedly, he stopped short at sight of Captain Emworth sprawled over a chair, while Stella at the dressing table was putting earrings into her ears.

"Oh—oh, I was getting a bit anxious," he said, feeling both awkward and humiliated.

She turned to smile at him, and he caught his breath as her loveliness smote him afresh after the weeks apart. She was peerless, and his heart beat quickly at the realization of it.

"Why? Did you think Gerald had crashed with us?" she asked, flashing her smile on Emworth in a way that made Jeremy very sure that the two were good, if not old, friends.

His jealousy rose, and, hot-headed, he strode across the room, took her into his arms, and kissed her. Her lips tightened and her eyes dilated at the unexpected embrace, and she freed herself from it with a deliberation which could not be mistaken.

"Really, Jeremy!" she expostulated, and he saw that her eyes were angry. The sight further incensed him.

"Don't you expect your fiance to kiss you after a month of separation?" he asked.

Emworth, aware of the tension, rose to his feet and sauntered towards the door, which Jeremy had closed behind him.

"Well, two's company," he said. "Dancing after dinner, Stella, or am I too much supplanted?"—with a cheerful grin at the unsmiling pair.

"Certainly I will dance with you," said Stella. "Shall we go down?" and she swept between the two men and was the first to leave the room.

They exchanged embarrassed glances.

"Sorry, old man. I had no idea," muttered Emworth.

"That's all right," said Jeremy stiffly, and followed Stella
242

to the lift. Emworth had the good sense to choose the stairs.

Stella and Jeremy dined alone, for most of the guests had left the dining room and the others were ready to follow them.

He made an effort to entertain her, aghast at the discovery that it was an effort and that the effort was needed, but she was cool and uncommunicative, politely interested in what he said, but offering him none of the warmth and friendliness he had come to seek.

He spoke of his play.

"It's worried me a bit," he admitted.

"Why?" asked Stella.

"Oh—out of practice," he said, with a forced laugh.

He had come overcharged with the pent-up emotions of that month, its frustration, its fear of failure, its loneliness. He had been ready to pour them all out to her and receive healing and new strength. Instead he could not begin to tell her of any of them. He feared the look of scorn which might come into eyes which were unfriendly in their regard of him; shrank from an ungentle touch of the rawness of his wounds. How could he tell her of that fear of failure, knowing how little use she had for failure? Once Fennimore had taken his play and the demon of fear was killed—then he could tell her and laugh with her at the bare idea of failure.

So they talked of generalities, talked with their tongues and not with their hearts, and he grew afraid to meet her cool, oddly speculative eyes.

Later, when they danced and he felt her mood changing to the excited beat of the music, he held her very closely.

"Feeling better pleased with me now?" he asked her, his cheek against the dusky softness of her hair, the remembered perfume she used in his nostrils, trapping his senses.

"Have I said I was not pleased?" she asked.

"Not in so many words, but in your eyes and your—resistance. I believe I'd almost forgotten how beautiful you are."

That pleased her better, and she smiled.

"What a boy you are still!" she said.

"I haven't felt very young these last few weeks," he said, making another bed for her sympathy. "I've had the devil of a time, with my work, you know. It simply wouldn't go right . . ."

"Jeremy, *dear!*" she expostulated. "Haven't we had enough of your play for one evening? You've talked of hardly anything else all through dinner, and you can't expect me to go on being thrilled about a play I haven't seen, can you?"

He was chilled. What a fool he had been to take her relaxed body as an indication of a relaxed mind!

They finished the dance in silence and afterwards came Emworth, slightly diffidently, to claim her.

"You don't mind, Denton?" he asked as Stella rose.

She gave a little amused laugh.

"Gerald darling, he doesn't *own* me, you know! I still do what I like with my own arms and legs!"

She seemed indefatigable, and Jeremy, tired out after the previous sleepless night, waited for her with dogged patience, determined to have just a last five minutes of privacy with her. He had not come all this way just to talk platitudes with her and watch her dancing with another man.

When at last she declared herself ready to go up she invited Emworth to join them.

"I've got drinks in my room," she said. "I know what yours is, Gerald— fire-water. What will you have, Jeremy?" and she linked a hand beneath the arm of each and led them towards the lift.

Jeremy's jaw stiffened.

"Sorry to be rather boorish, Emworth," he said, "but I'm tired, and it's natural I should want just five minutes alone with Mrs. Dale before we call it a day. Do you mind?"

"Of course not. Perfectly natural," he said, with excellent grace, though Stella's eyes narrowed and her hand slipped from Jeremy's arm. "Riding in the morning as usual?"

"If I'm not kept up too late tonight," said Stella, with steel in the smoothness of her voice.

In the corridor Jeremy turned the handle of her door and stood aside for her, following her in.

"I suppose as Emworth is allowed in here, I may share the privilege?" he said curtly.

"If you're feeling too tired to be pleasant, Jeremy, isn't your own room the better place?" asked Stella evenly.

He made an effort.

"Sorry, darling. I didn't mean to be unpleasant,

only—well, I hoped you'd be a bit more glad to see me. Aren't you glad, dear?"

"Well, naturally I am. You rather burst in on me, though, didn't you? And you really did look pretty awful when you arrived, you know."

"Forget about that. I'm quite respectable now, aren't I? And—kissable?"—invitingly.

She came to his arms half reluctantly, but he stirred the quick passion to life beneath his lips, so that, breathless and laughing now, she pushed him away and stood with a steadying hand on the bedrail.

"What a demanding lover you are!" she said.

"Too demanding?" he asked, exulting in the knowledge that she was all his in this moment, resentment forgotten, Emworth forgotten. It did not occur to him to be actually jealous of Emworth, but he was glad to see Stella utterly forgetful of him.

She melted into his embrace again.

"Could you be too demanding?" she asked him in a whisper, and what he read in her eyes took his breath away, made him shiver involuntarily with rising excitement.

"What does that mean?"

She held his eyes in that intoxicating, maddening look. The coldness which was part of her personality, the part that the world saw, had melted beneath the warmth of their passion, and he knew her to be ardent, desirious, surrendering.

He took his arms from her and stepped back.

"Darling, don't look at me like that," he said, in a shaken voice. "I—I can't stand it."

She laughed. It was a thrilling little sound. He shivered again to hear it, closed his eyes against the seduction of her, a determined and intentional seduction, as he knew. It both fascinated and revolted him to be aware of it.

"What makes you think you ought to—resist your own desires, Jeremy?" she asked softly.

"You know you don't really mean what you're saying," he told her almost harshly.

"Oh, but I do? Darling, I'm no ignorant young girl. I'm a widow, after all, and thoroughly experienced! Why shouldn't we take what life offers us and damn the rest? You know what I want—you, my love!"—with that light

245

laugh laced with her passion.

"If I stayed, you'd loathe me in the morning," said Jeremy.

She laughed again.

"Haven't you grown up any more than that, even now?" she asked. "That was the right attitude of mind when our mothers' lovers had to hop out of the wrong bed in the morning, but we have finished with those inhibitions, and I assure you, far from loathing you in the morning, I should be much more in love with you if you stayed! We should have shared such fun."

The fascination fled and the revulsion grew. His up-bringing by two old aunts, now dead, his years of idealism, his instinctive fastidiousness, revolted from what she so calmly suggested. Her very beauty and the appeal it made to him seemed to increase that feeling of revolt. It was as if he were watching a maggot at the heart of a perfect rose.

"You know quite well that there would be no pleasure—no fun, as you call it—in—in forestalling the delights of marriage," he said stiffly.

"Darling Jeremy, you're really a Victorian survival after all," she mocked him. Then, with the smile fading and anger creeping into her eyes, the anger of a frustrated woman: "Don't you realize that, if you don't accept the invitation, someone else might do so?"

He stared at her.

"What do you mean?" he asked.

"Beloved idiot, Gerald Emworth is only waiting for his opportunity, and I dare say he is quite exciting to sleep with!"

"Stella, you wouldn't do that? You wouldn't!" he said, unutterably shocked.

"Oh, I might, some day," she said calmly.

"What, sleep with another man while you are engaged to me?" he asked incredulously.

She shrugged her shoulders.

"Oh—that? Well, perhaps not *while* I am engaged to you, my dear Jeremy," she said, and moved to the dressing table and began to take off her rings and drop them one by one, with a little tinkling sound, on the glass tray. His own had been the first.

"Stella, do you want to break our engagement?" he asked abruptly.

Her hands were still for a moment.

"Do I want that? I—don't—quite—know," she said very slowly, and suddenly came to him the thought of how many happy hours they had spent together, of all the fun they had had, of all their plans and hopes. It could not end like that, all in a moment, with her kisses still warm on his lips, the fragrance of her all about him.

"No, Stella—not like this," he said, following his own thoughts. "We're both overwrought, and I, at least, am very tired. We're not ourselves. Don't let's say any more tonight. We might speak now and regret it for the rest of our lives. Good night, my sweet," and he turned on his heel and went swiftly from her.

Stella stood where he had left her, idly making patterns on the dressing table with her rings.

Did she really want to break her engagement to Jeremy? Actually, it had not occurred to her before. She had not realized that she had recovered from her infatuation for him until today, but the scene they had just enacted had shown her that he no longer held her captive to him.

Well—she was tired, anyway.

But in the morning, and during the few following days, they had no intimate moments. Stella, surrounded and absorbed by her friends, Gerald Emworth her devoted attendant, was all but inaccessible, and Jeremy realized with increasing bitterness that, though she still wore his ring, it meant so little to her now that their relations would have been no different had she just ceased to wear it.

And at the end of the week, with Stella talking of joining a party about to tour the Dalmatian coast in a privately chartered yacht, he suggested to her that he might as well return to town.

"Why not come with us?" she asked indifferently, and for answer he held her eyes for a moment and then, to her relief, released them. She did not want his company, and knew that he was aware of it.

"Well, anyway, I shall be back in town in a few weeks," she said. "We must go places then and do things to make up. Perhaps the new play will be in production by then. Let me know, won't you? I'd like to be there your first night."

21

"Where to, Sir?"

Jeremy came partially out of his brown study at the bus conductor's question.

"Oh—I don't know. Anywhere," he said vaguely, and tendered a sixpence.

The conductor glanced at him curiously, and then, used to queer customers, gave him a sixpenny ticket and left him.

And it was just at that moment that he saw Julie.

She was standing on the pavement in the rain. Queer how the rain had followed his course with Julie. It had been pouring with rain when he had first kissed her, and there was her face outlined against the dripping back of her umbrella, just as it had been then.

He did not think of all that, of course. In the same second that he saw her he sprang from his seat, rushed to the platform of the bus, and called to her.

"Julie! Julie!"

She tilted back the umbrella to look in the direction of his voice, and, at peril of his life, Jeremy swung outwards and backwards, and, followed by the curse of a following busdriver, spun down into the road and staggered forward to keep his balance.

Julie came hurrying forward, reaching him just as he managed to reel on to the pavement.

"Jerry! Whatever did you do that for?" she asked breathlessly, assured by now that he was unhurt.

He gripped her hands, umbrella and all.

"I saw you, Julie. If I hadn't jumped, I should have lost you again. Julie—Julie . . ."

"Oh, Jeremy," she said, very quietly and sadly now, though he had not missed the look in her eyes when he had first called to her.

"Where can we go, Julie? To talk. We can't stand here in the rain. Where were you going?"

"It's so wet that I was just going home," she said, looking up into the sky as if she could scarcely believe that the sun was not shining while she stood there with Jerry's hands holding hers.

"Aren't you going to work today?" he asked.

"No, this is the last day of my summer holiday," she said, with a little laugh that, in spite of knowing it to be all wrong, would turn itself into a trill, infinitely joyous.

It found a friend in the heart of Jeremy, and he turned to walk beside her, his arm thrust through hers, one hand still closed over the one that held the umbrella.

"You can't just go home now," he said. "Have you had lunch? Tea? Where can I take you?"

"I've had lunch, and I don't take tea at this time of the afternoon," she said.

"Then come out with me somewhere. Curse it, why have I put the car in for repairs on his particular day? Just my infernal luck! Let's get on a bus . . ."

"If you promise not to leap off like that again!"

"What, with you in it? There's a Green Line coach stopping. Let's get on that."

They ran madly, hand in hand, jumped just as the coach was leaving the curb, flung themselves down on a seat, laughing and breathless.

"Where are we going, do you suppose?" asked Julie.

"To heaven," said Jeremy, and somehow their smiles fled and they looked into each other's eyes, suddenly very serious, until the conductor interrupted them to collect the fares.

"We don't know where we want to go," explained Jeremy cheerfully. "We'll have a shilling's-worth each, and perhaps the rain will have stopped by then."

Julie sat with shining eyes that held a curiously still look in them. She sat motionless, just as if she knew this was only a dream from which, if she moved, she would wake.

Jeremy felt suddenly shy with her now that they were sitting there together, the first moment over and so much to say that he could say none of it. Glancing sideways at her, he thought she was thinner, that she looked a little pale and tired, but how infinitely dear!

She felt his glance and turned her head to smile.

"I can't believe that it's really you and I," she said softly.

"Are you glad, Julie?"

"She nodded, and looked out of the window again.

"Any news?" he asked her.

"Not very much. Oh—news about Biddy, though you

probably know it already," she said.

"About her millionaire?" he asked with a smile. "Clever child. She brought it off just as she said she would."

"The queer part about it is that I believe she's really fond of him," said Julie, glad to have found something to talk about, something that was not really important to them, her and Jerry. "You know Royal, don't you?"

"I ought to. I believe I introduced him to Biddy," smiled Jeremy reminiscently. "I hope she is fond of him. He's such a good sort. When are they going to be married?"

"Not till she's twenty, Mom says, though it won't make Biddy change her mind, however long she waits. She's quite determined to marry him, and he's given her the most marvelous engagement ring, which she flaunts to the world"—laughing that tender laugh with which she had always colored her thoughts of her sister. The sound of it gave Jeremy a thrill that was almost a stab of pain. They might have been parted only a day rather than for all these months.

He found her hand and held it. She struggled for a moment to free it, and then left it there, aware in every pulse of her body of that close contact.

Softly his fingers caressed her own, traced their outlines and came to a sudden, startled rest at the little bulge made by her engagement ring in the cheap little glove. He felt her hand grow taut at his discovery, and then he deliberately peeled off the glove and sat looking down at the little diamond trifle, pledge of all that was dear in life to the donor, but meaning—she realized it the more fully now—so pitifully little to the girl who wore it.

Her eyes and Jeremy's met above it.

"Is it on the right finger, Julie?" he asked.

She nodded.

"Who put it there?"

"Ben Elson. We—we're engaged, Jerry," she said, with the least of defiance to her voice.

Why should he come back into her life like that and expect to find her just the same? Expect her to have waited—for what?

She found herself justifying those feelings, though he had not uttered a word.

"You're engaged to Mrs. Dale, aren't you, Jerry?" she asked, still with that defiant note in her voice.

"Yes," he said shortly, and dropped her hand and sat

250

looking across her and out of the window with a look on his face, an expression in his eyes that baffled even her knowledge of him. She knew only that he was not happy, that in some way he had missed all those things that surely, surely were his due.

"Don't let's think of—that now," she whispered, moved to offer him comfort for that which she could not begin to understand, and the smile he flashed on her told her how unerringly she had found the right thing to say.

"No. Let's think only of ourselves—of each other, Julie."

He spoke her name with a lingering tenderness that lay on her heart like a flower.

"Tell me about yourself, Jerry. You're such a famous person now, aren't you?"

Actuated by a strange pride, he boasted a little, told her nothing of his fears for his waning power, of the play which Fennimore was taking so long to consider—far, far too long. Jeremy had even rung him up one day and had not been solaced by the evasive and noncommittal answer Fennimore had given him. He was obsessed by the fear, almost the certainty now, that Fennimore was going to decline to take up his option.

So, partly to bolster up his failing hopes, partly because to Julie he must come in brave array, with flags flying and trumpets blaring, he said nothing of all this, and she rejoiced so sincerely and sweetly in his success that he felt ashamed but could not take back his idle boasting.

"Look, the rain's stopped," she said presently; then, as they passed through a village, "Oh, Jerry, a fair, I love them."

"Shall we get out? We can catch a bus back later," suggested Jeremy, and quick as the thought they were on their feet and out of the bus and it was moving off again and leaving them with a strange, exciting feeling of being cut off from the rest of the world.

He caught her hand and they ran like children back to the village green on which the fair had been set, a tawdry enough affair with the rain running down the canvas roofs and dripping from swings and roundabouts on to the sodden, squelchy mud that had once been grass.

The sun was shining again, however, and Jeremy tucked the family umbrella under his arm and they wandered round the wretched little booths, trying everything with little success but much enjoyment.

"Let's go on the roundabouts," suggested Julie, and he perched her on the back of some fabulous monster and rode, swaying and dipping, beside her until they both felt slightly sick.

"Here's one we haven't had a shot at," said Julie, chose a number at random and, a few moments later, was handed the prize: a hideous fur monkey.

"I shall call it Jeremy," she said, looking down at its hairy, repulsive features.

"You little toad. If you do, I'll . . ."

"Yes?" she prompted him, lifting to him eyes that dazzled him with their happiness.

"Kiss you," he finished, on a low, tense note, from which the laughter had fled and she lowered her eyes quickly and began to walk away, careless of direction, until they found themselves climbing some rickety steps that led to a pay box.

"What is it?" asked Julie.

"Haunted House, miss," somebody told her, "price threepence."

She hesitated as if she would turn back, but Jeremy put down his sixpence.

"It'll be fun," he said. "Come on."

Once inside, a door slammed and they were in total, inky darkness. At the first step the floor began to rock, and as they put their hands to steady themselves the walls receded and then seemed to rush back at them again.

They struggled and laughed, Jeremy's arm coming about her in the darkness to hold her, while from other parts of the place shrieks and cries told they they were not alone.

"Is that your arm, Jerry?" asked Julie, hysterical with laughter.

"Don't you remember what my arms feel like, Julie?" came his answering question, and she caught her breath quickly.

The next moment she felt his other arm come about her, lifting her, holding her.

"I'm going to find a place that doesn't rock," he told her, and, in some dusty corner, found what he sought, but made no attempt to put her down.

"Julie—darling little Julie," he said in a choking voice, "I've wanted you so terribly all this time," and she felt his lips upon her cheek.

With a wild joy surging inside her she turned her head so that his mouth found her own.

"Oh, Julie—Julie . . ."

It was as if he could not say her name often enough, tenderly enough, now that she was in his arms again, her mouth soft and warm, her body surrendered.

"To have you again—to hold you and kiss you, Julie . . ."

"I love you so," she whispered against his lips, knowing that they were doing a mad thing they might afterwards regret, but just now having neither the will nor the strength to resist.

"How have I lived without you, Julie? Or you without me? We belong, my little heart. We must never lose each other again."

Bathos came with a flood of light and a raucous voice saying: "Time's up, guv'nor. We're all going 'ome to tea. Open again at six, and they laughed and made their way over the crazy, jolting boards and into the daylight again.

They looked at each other, Jeremy exultant, Julie flushed and adorably shy. Then he tucked his hand beneath her elbow.

"Tea's quite a good idea. Let's go and find some," he said.

They found it in the crowded little parlor of a cottage, a mountainous tea which they could not eat because of the turmoil in their hearts, because of the wonder of this thing that had come so suddenly to them to turn their world, so laboriously made, upside down in a moment.

Jeremy pushed his cup away and came to stand by Julie's side, an arm about her, her face pressed against him.

"What are we going to do about it now, Julie?" he asked, half triumphant, half ashamed.

"What can we do?" she asked him, in a low voice that told him she was not prepared so easily to accept what Fate had laid in their laps.

"What we ought to have done ages ago. Get married, my little love," he told her.

"She freed herself with some dignity, her face grave.

"We've both got—other obligations now, Jerry," she said soberly. "There's Ben, and there's—Mrs. Dale."

"She need not count, Julie. It was a mistake. She's tired of the engagement and wants to break it. I've just come back from where she's staying, and we talked of ending it. It's only to be made final, and no hearts to break. It was a mad sort of engagement, anyway."

"It was the sort you thought you wanted, Jeremy," she reminded him with some spirit.

He flushed.

"Darling, have we got to remember that all our lives? Haven't I suffered enough for the crass stupidity and conceit? I love you, Julie. You love me. Doesn't that outweigh everything else in the world?"

"You forget—Ben," she said quietly.

"You don't love the fellow. You can't, if you love me"—with the old arrogance creeping into his voice.

Julie faced him steadily.

"I am not really sure that I do," she said, to his infinite surprise and discomfort.

"Julie, you can't possibly mean that? Why—just now—when we kissed each other . . ."

Her face was pale and serious. In her mind was a strange turmoil of thought. Did she love him? Could she, disapproving of so much that seemed essential to his nature?

"Jerry, we're old enough and—experienced enough to be able to recognize things for what they really are," she said at last. "I suppose in that way we do love each other, if it can be called love, but the love that is real and lasting can't be based on just that physical attraction when—our minds are not in love with each other's."

He could see the effort it cost her to speak like that, for she was a reticent and self-contained little person, and words did not come easily from her. His recognition of that fact gave added weight to what she said, and he knew that this feeling went very deeply with her. He felt oddly shaken. The ground which he had thought so solid beneath his feet was trembling.

He spoke with a desperate note in his voice.

"Julie, what's happened to you? Why are you so different? You don't really believe that what we feel for each other is only sex attraction?"

"Well, what else can it be when you so quickly and easily transferred your affections to someone else and became engaged to her?" retorted Julie with spirit.

He swallowed hard. This was a version of her he had never even suspected. In the old days she had been so gentle and malleable.

"I have never loved Stella," he said, realizing for the first time the entire truth of that. "That certainly was mere sex attraction. She is a supremely beautiful woman, and she took an interest in me that turned my head. And, come to that, you got engaged to Elson."

"Not in love, Jerry," she said softly and regretfully. The regret was for Ben, whom she would have loved if she could. "Ben knows that—that . . ."

She paused. How could she finish that sentence?

Jeremy finished it for her, in quick triumph.

"That you're still in love with me?"

"No. No, Jerry, I'm not," she said, too vehemently, too swiftly. "How can I be when I don't even respect you? And when you don't respect me?"

"Are you going to hold that up against me all our lives?" he demanded, exasperated at the futility of all this argument, when all he wanted was to take Julie in his arms and kiss her into forgetfulness.

"No, I'm not holding it up against you, Jerry. Time heals everything, and I suppose I've outgrown the hurt, because it doesn't really matter any more to me. We've made our lives over again, and that's all that matters."

"I haven't made mine over again, Julie, and if you are no longer hurt by memory, why won't you marry me?"

"Because we shouldn't be happy," said Julie steadily. "We have different standards of living. Besides, I intend to keep faith with Ben. I'm not going to empty his life."

"But mine's empty without you, Julie."

She smiled at that. It was a grave, wise smile, as of a mother to her child. That was how, just now, she was thinking of Jeremy.

"You only think that at the moment because you see something you want, or think you want, and can't have," she said. "Your life isn't empty. It's filled to the brim with all the things you used to long for: fame and success and money, the means to go wherever you like, to make interesting friends. You have everything but me. Ben has nothing but me. I know that sounds as if I thought a lot of myself, but it isn't that. You know Ben. He's such a dear, but he's not the sort to achieve anything. He can only plod on in a rut, but it's very straight and faithful rut, and . . ."

"And mine's neither straight nor faithful, I suppose?" burst in Jeremy.

She smiled.

"Oh, Jerry dear, yours isn't a rut at all. It's a broad and glorious highway! You'll find so many friends and lovers to jaunt along it with you, and in the end you'll be so glad you didn't take me along. I'm better just plodding along with Ben."

"Julie, I . . ."

"Please, Jerry, not any more. Let's go now, shall we? The bus will be along any minute, and we don't want to miss it."

They made the homeward journey in silence, and Julie would not even let him get out with her at the Streatham stop.

"I'd rather you didn't," she said, with that new dignity and assurance which had rather stupefied him. "The bus will take you on up to Piccadilly, or wherever you want to go. Good-bye, Jerry."

"Good-bye—darling Julie."

She walked with tears blinding her now that there was no need to keep up that composure. Why had she let Jerry say good-bye to her? Why had she been so beastly to him? Why had she tried to pretend that her love was dead? Why, with every part of her craving for him, had she sent him away again?

One of the answers to those tormenting questions came down the road to meet her.

"You don't mind my coming to find you, dear? We were getting anxious because there's going to be another storm," said Ben.

She slipped a hand under his arm, held it closely as if it were a lifebuoy flung to a drowning man. That was how she felt towards Ben, as if he were her only refuge in a stormy sea.

"I'm glad you came," she said, and he heard the quiver in her voice and saw that her cheeks were wet.

"What's happened, Julie?" he asked gently.

"Nothing that's going to make any difference," she told him almost fiercely.

The latent fear in him rose to the surface.

"Julie, have you seen Denton?" he asked.

"Yes, but it doesn't make any difference," she repeated.

They walked in silence for a few minutes. Then Ben spoke again, though he felt the words he uttered might well be his own death sentence.

"Julie, if it ever does make any difference, if you ever feel that—that you can't go on with me—well, you know I'd let you go, don't you?" he said humbly—much too humbly.

"Oh," thought Julie wildly, "if only he wouldn't be so kind to me! If only he'd have said he'd kill Jerry and beat the life out of me if I so much as thought of anyone but him! If only he weren't so stiflingly generous!"

But, unkind or ungenerous, he would no longer have been Ben, and she choked down the feelings that had arisen in her.

"I don't want you to let me go, Ben," she said. "Jerry's nothing to me—*nothing!*" and again she was too vehement, though Ben's ears were not keen enough to realize it.

"I'm glad, Julie. You know that," said Ben soberly. "Only I want you to know that—that your happiness is the thing that matters most, and if ever you felt you could find it better with someone else, even with Denton, I'd—I'd not want to keep you from it."

"You're much too good and generous to me, Ben," said Julie, fighting down that maddening revolt against him.

"Nobody could be that," said Ben. "Here we are. Shall I come in for a little while?"

"Not tonight, dear. I—I'm rather tired. I think I'll have a hot drink and go to bed, if you don't mind."

"All right, darling. See you tomorrow?"—and they kissed in their unexciting fashion as they parted.

But as she lay sleepless it was not Ben's kiss that stung her lips in memory, but Jeremy's demanding, possessive, drawing out her very heart and giving it to him with every breath.

22

Julie sat with Mrs. Milroy's letter in her hand.

"Don't let your breakfast get cold, lovie," her mother said, and the girl came back to earth with a start.

"What do you think I'd better do about this, Mom?" she asked, passing the letter across the table. They were alone, for Dickie had gone to school and Biddy had not yet put in

257

an appearance. "It's from Mrs. Milroy, and she's enclosed two theater tickets."

"Well, isn't that nice of her! What are they for?" asked her mother, putting on her glasses.

"That's the point, Mom," said Julie slowly. "They're for—for Jerry's new play, for the first night. We were talking about the theater the other day, and she said then that she would send me some tickets. I didn't know she meant for this."

Mrs. Cave looked worried. She had realized a long time ago that Julie's affair with Jeremy Denton could not be settled quite as easily as they had all hoped. Though she wore Ben's ring, and had been affectionate and loyal to him, appearing quietly content, she had never found her lost gaiety, never again been the joyous girl whom Jeremy had discovered.

There were times when Mrs. Cave had felt desperately she must do something to prevent this marriage with Ben, cherished project though it had been. She knew, however, that Julie would emphatically resent any such interference with her affairs, and so her mother had had to play the hardest part in her life: that of the helpless onlooker at the wreckage of her child's life.

"Oh, well, Jeremy's plays are something of an event, and I expect she thought you would like to see a first night performance," she said cheerfully. "Will you go?"

"Wouldn't you like to go, Mom? You and—Biddy?" suggested Julie.

"Biddy will probably be going with Royal, anyway," said Mrs. Cave. "You go, dear. Take Ben. It would be a treat for him"; for she knew that eventually Julie would not be able to resist the temptation to go, and the best off-set to any remaining attraction towards Jeremy would be the presence of the faithful Ben.

Julie felt a shrinking at the thought of listening to Jerry's play with Ben beside her. Her body would be with the one, but her spirit and her heart with the other.

She gathered up the tickets and put them carefully into her bag.

"Well, I shall have to dash off," she said. "Don't say anything to Ben. I'll think about it. Heavens, Biddy, do you know what the time is? You'll get the sack"—as that young lady strolled negligently into the room, yawning.

"Not me," said Biddy. "Too many people come in for a

manicure just to see what I look like. It makes Royal a bit wild, but it's all good for trade, and it tickles them to give six penny tips to the future Mrs. Maitland."

"I don't think you ought to take tips now, Biddy, even if you feel you must stay on there," said her mother. "It isn't very nice for Royal."

Biddy kissed the top of her mother's head.

"Darling, Royal's got to marry me as I am, and he knew from the beginning that I'm thoroughly mercenary. Besides, who's going to pay for my trousseau if I give up my regular sources of income? Pass the milk, beloved."

That evening, with Julie and her mother alone as usual, though Ben would be popping in later, Mrs. Cave referred to the theater tickets again.

"I'd go if I were you, dear," she said, for her day's anxious thought had resolved itself into the feeling that it was time Julie's affairs came to a head, and if, as was likely, she were to see Jeremy Denton again at the theater it might crystallize her thoughts and desires.

"I don't know whether I want to—see Jerry again," said Julie at last, slowly.

"Have you seen him again at all since—since that time?" asked her mother.

"Yes. I met him one evening two or three months ago," said Julie, flushing a little at that memory. "We went for a ride on the bus somewhere into the country. I don't even know where we went, but there was a fair, and we went on the roundabouts and things and—well, that was all. I haven't seen him again."

Mrs. Cave was staggered. Mingled with her surprise was a stab of pain because Julie had hidden this thing from her, but she had always allowed her children their separate entities, never made them mere satellites of her own.

"Didn't that make things difficult for you, dear?" asked the quiet voice.

"Yes, it did," admitted Julie frankly, glad at last that she was relieving her mind of that hidden memory. "We didn't plan it. It just happened. It was at the end of my holidays, and he was in a bus and saw me on the pavement and jumped off to speak to me. Then—well, I don't quite know how it happened, but we went off together for the afternoon and evening. We had a lovely time"—her voice soft with memory, her eyes wearing the look they had worn for no one in the world but Jeremy Denton. Her mother, recognizing that look, was stabbed with pity for Ben.

"And—how did it end, dearie?" she asked, perplexed at the way young people acted nowadays. It seemed incredible that they could meet like that and part again, leaving no effect on their tangled lives.

"Jerry asked me to marry him," Julie told her in a low, careful voice which betrayed so little to the listening ears. "I told him it wasn't possible. Then we—well, we just said good-bye."

"Did you want to marry him, Julie?"

"Terribly. In some ways, at least. Then I thought of Ben, and the sort of life Jerry likes, and I knew that in the end it would be better for me to stick to Ben. You see, I'm all he's got, and he really does love me in a way that isn't possible to Jerry, who has so much in his life and so many things to divide his affection. I'd rather be all the world to Ben than—just one of the things that make up Jerry's universe."

It was bravely spoken. There was thought and common sense in the words. Mrs. Cave's intelligence approved—but she knew that Julie's heart was no more following her head now than it had ever done.

"Do you think Ben knows how you feel about Jerry?" she asked, when they had sat silently stitching their thoughts into Biddy's trousseau.

"I don't know. I told him I'd been with Jerry, and he—offered to give me up if I wanted Jerry back. Ben being like that makes it impossible to—oh, well, to think of ever giving him up," said Julie, which made her mother the more sure that Julie had such thoughts.

"Jerry's got his success, Ben's got you, but what have you got out of it all, my Julie?" she asked tenderly.

Julie's face was pale, but she managed to smile.

"I've got Ben and all of you," she said. Then, with a sudden change and a cry from her heart: "Oh, Mom, don't make it harder! I've got the feeling that I'm doing the best for all of us, myself included, but—do you think I don't *want* Jerry?"—and she rose precipitately from her chair and fled to her room.

Soon her mother knew she would come down again, their familiar, serene Julie. She could do nothing but look on at her girl's battle with aching heart.

Ben, consulted later by a now calm-eyed Julie, thought it

kind of Mrs. Milroy to send the tickets, though he could have wished they were for another play than Jeremy's. Still, it was months now since that day when Julie's eyes had been wet because of him, and she had steadfastly and resolutely chosen to remain engaged to him, so Jeremy Denton could not mean anything to her now.

So on the Thursday night he and Julie went to the Regency Theater to see the new play from seats in the stalls, not so near the front that they need feel awkward about not being in evening dress.

They had arrived early, and Julie was able to point out to Ben a number of well-known Society women who came to Monique's for their clothes. She watched in vain for Stella Dale, however.

Stella was not there.

She had returned to London in December, opening her town house and giving several expensive parties there. Jeremy, still ostensibly engaged to her, since she still wore his ring, had a feeling that he had been included in the invitations rather as a matter of course than because she really desired his company.

Gerald Emworth, now attached to the new Government flying school, and making spectacular tests with new machines seemed an accepted habitue of the house, and wherever Jeremy went he found the young airman fetching and carrying for Stella, hail-fellow-well-met with all her friends and curiously indisposed to resent Jeremy Denton. This last fact gave Stella's fiance food for thought, but she offered him no chance of intimate talk with her, and he shrank from any resumption of that bitter and sordid quarrel they had had at Harrogate.

When, however, he had had the expected refusal of his play by Fennimore, he felt bound to tell her. For one thing, it altered his financial position, for he would have found plenty of backers had Fennimore been taking up the play. Now he would be in a quandary unless Stella offered to find the money. Of course, it would only be a temporary accommodation for the receipts would very soon enable him to repay her advance, but the fact remained that the money would, in the first instance, have to be borrowed. He wished it need not be from Stella, in the circumstances, but even less did he feel he could approach Maitland, who had openly told him of his dislike of *Midnight Angel*, which he called "cheap rubbish."

"Fennimore says it isn't quite the style of thing he's looking for at the moment," he told Stella, with a nonchalance he did not feel. At heart he was sick and sore and badly needed both sympathy and encouragement, but neither was forthcoming from Stella, who had no use for anything but success.

Her eyes narrowed.

"He liked the style of *Midnight Angel* all right, and had a big success with it," she said in an odd, cold voice.

"This one's the same sort, but—well, he says he wants a change; doesn't like to run two of the same style in succession. I've offered it to Ardern."

Stella frowned.

"My dear Jeremy, Ardern's not in the same street as Giles Fennimore. He puts on cheap stuff at popular prices, Regency stuff."

"I know, but there's a slump in the theaters now, as you know, and Ardern's better than nothing," said Jeremy, and wished he could have bitten the suggestive words back when it was too late.

She shrugged her shoulders.

"Well, it's your own affair, of course, though I should have thought it was rather *lese-majeste* for Jeremy Denton to put on a play at the Regency with seven-and-sixpenny stalls."

He swallowed, hating the conversation, feeling utterly humiliated because of his dependence on her with their personal relationship what it was.

"Ardern's things always pay," he said, "and this isn't as expensive to put on as the last one. Still, it needs financing at the beginning, of course."

Stella laughed a little cruelly.

"You're not inviting me to finance a play at the Regency, are you, my dear?" she asked.

"I had hoped you would. It will be only temporary, of course, and could be repaid out of the six months' takings with a good return."

"Six months? Ardern never keeps a thing on so long. You've said so yourself. I'm sorry, Jeremy. I would have backed you with Fennimore again, but I'm not a philanthropist, and I can't afford to throw money down the drain."

He felt desperate.

"It wouldn't be thrown away, Stella, I can assure you," he said. "You sound as if you don't believe in me any more."

"Well, do you really believe in yourself, Jeremy? Perhaps we mistook for genius a mere fleeting trick of Fate, and you were really safer in your tourist office, after all."

He winced. That cut him more than anything else she said. Was it true? Was he nothing more than a balloon filled with gas which needed only the prick of a pin to reduce it to a scrap of wrinkled rubber?

"That wasn't necessary, Stella," he said.

"My dear, why not be honest with yourself? Do you believe in this play which Fennimore's turned down?" she asked, with scarcely veiled contempt in her voice.

"Yes, I do," he said stoutly; and when she shrugged her shoulders and smiled: "What does all this mean, Stella? That we're finished? I think that's what you want, actually."

But the essential feline in her nature could not let him go while there was any life or feeling in him at all, and she stretched out a hand, its claw sheathed, to keep him within reach.

"Darling, have I said so? Come back to me when the play's running, and you'll see."

"Meaning that you'll want me only if it's a success?" he asked harshly, wishing he could break with her, hating the spell she could still cast over him, his body aching for her while his mind revolted from contact.

"How crude!" she laughed. "Yes, come in, Gerald. We are having a little domestic trouble, and it's high time someone broke it up. Cocktail, Jeremy?"

"No, thanks," and he turned on his heel and left them.

That had been three months ago, and now, waiting nervously for the curtain to go up, Jeremy felt he had lived through three months of nightmare. Though Ardern had said he would take the play, he could make no suggestions as to where the money was to be found, though he had obviously imagined the play would have Stella Dale's financial and social backing.

In the end Mrs. Milroy had unexpectedly come to his rescue, and to his personal anxieties for the play was added the additional one lest she should lose the very considerable sum she had lent him with no security other than

263

her faith in him and her affection for him.

That, of course, accounted for her choice of play when sending Julie the tickets, and in the stalls and in her box were gathered numbers of her own friends.

"What about Stella?" she had asked when Jeremy invited himself into her box.

"She won't be here," he said curtly. "I suppose actually we've finished with our—romance"—the last word on a bitter note, and Mrs. Milroy did not pursue the subject. She had long felt that that unsuitable engagement could not end in marriage. She had also come to the conclusion, without any real foundation for the belief, that in the background of Jeremy Denton's life was some other woman, some girl from his earlier existence presumably, for she knew most of his present circle of friends, which was more or less her own, and she could fit none of those into the place she wanted to fill.

Leaning forward over the rail of her box, she caught sight of Julie in the stalls, and as the girl looked up at the same moment they nodded and smiled.

"Sweet girl," commented Mrs. Milroy affectionately.

"Who is?" asked Jeremy without interest.

"A little girl who helps me with my clothes," she said. "I sent her tickets for tonight, and I see she's down there in the stalls in a green frock. Such a pretty name, too—Julie. You ought to use it in a play, Jeremy."

"Julie? *Julie*?" asked Jeremy, roused to interest by that name. "Where is she?"—looking down into the house.

"Towards the back of the stalls, about the fifth row from the back, next to the gangway, in green. See her? By the way, her sister is Roy Maitland's fiancee. You know, that quaint affair. Charmingly pretty girl, but personally I prefer Julie's type."

But Jeremy was not listening. He was staring down at the girl in green, devouring with his eyes that beloved brown head, longing and yet dreading to look into her eyes if she glanced up again, keeping in the shadows of the box in case she did so.

Mrs. Milroy became aware of tension, and turned to look up at him as he stood behind her, saw the expression on his face, the hungry love in his eyes, heard him whisper Julie's name, though he did not even know that he spoke it aloud.

"Julie," he whispered. "Julie."

264

"Why, Jeremy, you look as if you had seen a ghost," she said. "Do you by any chance know Julie Cave?"

He brought his attention back to her with a conscious effort.

"Know her? Why—yes. Yes, I know her," he said, and a sudden and bewilderingly bright light broke in on the astonished lady.

Here was the girl she had tried for so long to fit into his life. She knew it beyond shadow of doubt, and began to remember other things that at the time had meant nothing to her. She had talked about the play to Julie Cave when she was at Monique's the other day looking at the new styles from their Paris workrooms. The girl had displayed considerable interest in the success of Jeremy Denton, had lengthened out the conversation beyond its expected limits, had—now she came to think of it—seemed almost hungry for news of him.

There had been—why, yes, certainly there had been—the same look in her eyes as was in Jeremy's at this moment.

Then the curtain rose on the first of the many scenes which the program promised them, and she gave all her attention to the play. There was plenty of time to think about Jeremy Denton and Julie Cave afterwards.

Jeremy had communicated to her some of his fears for the success of his play.

"I may lose your money for you," he had said only last night, fresh come from the depressing spectacle of the final rehearsal.

"Well, if you do, why worry?" she had replied. "I've got all I want in this world, and I can't take the money with me into the next. Even if I could, Brian would never let me buy one of the celestial mansions with it and settle down with my harp. He'd want to charter a yacht and have a look at hell before we'd been there a week."

But it was apparent almost from the first that Jeremy's fears were to be realized. People had come with the anticipation, engendered by his previous plays, of being amused and a little shocked, but their hopes, as they watched the unfolding scene after scene, gradually gave way to surprise and disappointment. They were on edge, waiting for something to happen, and nothing seemed going to happen.

The story was thin, and though the players did their best

with it, and the scenic effects were elaborate, it was soon obvious that boredom had settled down like a blight over the house. Jeremy's stories always had been a little thin, but nobody minded that, for the plot had been merely the flimsy structure on which to hang his wit, his genius for happy epigram, his artful fun-poking at established codes. Now it seemed he had lost the lightness of his touch, the point of his rapier wit, and the bare bones of the play showed through in all their unattractive nakedness. He seemed hoplessly to have underrated the intelligence of his audience, that unforgivable crime in a playwright. The situations were artificial, the dialogue labored, and old friend Coincidence was worked to death.

The applause, which at first had been of a hopeful nature, gradually died down to a half-hearted politeness. People laughed, but at the wrong places, and after the second act none of the newspaper men even troubled to return. As far as they were concerned, the play was finished.

Jeremy sat through it silently, white-lipped, his hands gripping the edge of the box, making no movement, uttering no word even in the long intervals occasioned by too-elaborate settings for the old-fashioned theater.

Mrs. Milroy watched him with aching heart, and did not even remember the money she was going to lose when she heard those misplaced ripples of laughter and saw him wince as if the sound had touched an exposed and tortured nerve.

Once she ventured to speak to him, touching his arm.

"A first night is so often wrong, Jeremy," she said gently.

He did not even turn his head.

"This one isn't," he said grimly, and she could find no comfort to offer him.

Then she looked down at Julie again, and for a moment levelled her opera glasses at her so that she could see her face more clearly. It was an interval, and the lights were up.

Julie was sitting staring straight in front of her, her face white, her eyes filled with tears which, as Mrs. Milroy looked, brimmed over and ran unchecked down her cheeks.

She hesitated no longer. It was nearly the end of the last
266

act and people were getting restless. Many had already left, and others were gathering up their belongings to do so. There was just one of those short, ineffective scenes left, and the end had been obvious from the beginning.

Mrs. Milroy scribbled a few words on her program, tore off the page, and folded it. Jeremy did not even notice that she had left the box, not that the others who had shared it had already gone rather than be forced to talk to him afterwards.

"I want you to take this to a young lady in the stalls," said Mrs. Milroy to an attendant. "Row M, next to the gangway on the right, a young lady in a green afternoon dress."

The attendant took the paper and Mrs. Milroy's half-crown and sped away.

Alone in the box, Jeremy sat staring at the stage and his last scene, the look of despair frozen on his face.

Possibly the only person in the theater, other than the players, whose attention was fixed wholly on the play was Julie. Her face wore a look that matched Jeremy's, save that with her horror was mingled an unbearable compassion for the man at whom she no longer dared to look, but who she knew was in Mrs. Milroy's box.

At first, in the amazing suspicion that things were going wrong, she had looked at him, but now she could not bear to look. Her heart was wrung with pity for him. She forgot everything in the world save him, forgot the patient Ben sitting by her side, aware of her emotions and their cause, and working out his own tragedy alone.

Delicate in every contact with her as he was clumsy in every other thing, he had left her during those frequent, mistaken intervals. He had sensed her need to be alone, known that there were no words which might be said.

Then, just before the final curtain, an attendant bent down to speak to her. She had had to touch her arm to attract her attention, and Julie took the folded paper from her in some bewilderment.

She read, by the light of the girl's torch, the words scribbled on it:

Julie dear, there is a private lobby behind this box.—Agnes Milroy

For a second the words conveyed nothing to her. Then, not even pausing to wonder how Mrs. Milroy knew, she rose to her feet.

"Will you show me the way?" she asked the girl.

Ben watched her go. She had forgotten even that he was there.

Slowly he crushed in his hand the program of Jeremy's play as he rose to leave the theater. He knew that Julie would not return. He knew that, as far as he was concerned, she would never return.

Well, at least he had had her sweetness all these months, months that would live in his memory all his life, months of such blessed happiness as no other man in the world would ever know, save Jeremy Denton.

He did not want to think of Jeremy Denton just then.

Through the open door of the box, across the tiny lobby, Julie saw Jeremy sitting there motionless, though the curtain had fallen and everybody else was standing to the National Anthem.

She put up a hand as if to check the sob that rose in her throat at sight of him, alone and defeated. Then she moved and spoke his name, her voice a thread of sound so thin that she wondered that he heard it.

But he did hear it.

Julie's voice pierced the darkness of his soul when no other sound had power to reach it.

He turned, stared at her unbelievingly, and then rose to come stumblingly towards her.

"Julie—Julie."

Straight to her arms he came, his head bowed on her breast, clinging to her as if he clung to life itself.

Her cheek lay against his hair, and her arms were about him.

"Jerry," she whispered. "My darling."

"Stay with me, Julie."

"I'll never leave you," said Julie.

And somewhere a star was born.

are you
missing out on
some great
Pyramid books?

You can have any title in print at
Pyramid delivered right to your door!
To receive your Pyramid Paperback
Catalog, fill in the label below (use a
ball point pen please) and mail to
Pyramid . . .